'The reader is instantly emotiona
story, at the heart of which
unreliable narrator. Mahmood
combination of beautiful prose and a bloody great story.
I will read anything he writes'
Ayisha Malik

'Imran is probably the most exciting crime fiction author in the UK right now and *All I Said Was True* is further proof of that. The dual narrative is exhilarating, the plot complex and layered, the writing is perfect and the narrator's voice is somehow both unreliable and trustworthy. Superb stuff'
M. W. Craven

'A twisting path to the moment of murder via a police interview where the truth meets its match. A relentless, absorbing thriller of the darkest paranoid noir'
Janice Hallett

'Imran Mahmood expertly balances a complex narrative in *All I Said Was True* … as his beleaguered protagonist Layla tries to convince the police that a murder she is accused of was committed by a man who does not seem to exist'
Financial Times

'Offering powerful insight into Layla's tortured mind, while also revealing parts of the mystery like a set of Russian dolls, each one concealing another, it underlines barrister Mahmood's considerable talents as a crime writer'
Daily Mail

'I loved every single page!'
Gillian McAllister

'Original and ingenious. There's an authenticity to Imran Mahmood's books that is so rare and rewarding. *All I Said Was True* is the very definition of a compulsive page-turner'
Chris Whitaker

'Wonderfully twisty and kept me guessing all the way to a really satisfying denouement'
Ajay Chowdhury

'Imran Mahmood's *ALL I SAID WAS TRUE* is beautifully complex and arresting. I was swept away in Layla's story, though not quite knowing who I should be trusting and when which – for me – is absolutely key in great storytelling. The way that Imran continues to challenge society, and all our many preconceptions within his books is so powerful'
L. V. Matthews

IMRAN MAHMOOD is a practicing barrister with over thirty years' experience fighting cases in courtrooms across the country. His previous novels have been highly critically acclaimed: *You Don't Know Me* was a BBC Radio 2 Book Club choice, Goldsboro Book of the Month and was shortlisted for the Glass Bell Award; both this and *I Know What I Saw* were longlisted for Theakston Crime Novel of the Year and the CWA Gold Dagger. *You Don't Know Me* was also made into a hugely successful BBC1 adaptation in association with Netflix. When not in court or writing novels or screenplays he can sometimes be found on the Red Hot Chilli Writers' podcast as one of the regular contributors. He hails from Liverpool but now lives in London with his wife and daughters.

@imranmahmood777

BY THE SAME AUTHOR

You Don't Know Me
I Know What I Saw

ALL I SAID WAS TRUE

IMRAN MAHMOOD

RAVEN BOOKS
LONDON • OXFORD • NEW YORK • NEW DELHI • SYDNEY

RAVEN BOOKS
Bloomsbury Publishing Plc
50 Bedford Square, London, WC1B 3DP, UK
29 Earlsfort Terrace, Dublin 2, Ireland

BLOOMSBURY, RAVEN BOOKS and the Raven Books logo are
trademarks of Bloomsbury Publishing Plc

First published in Great Britain 2022
This edition published 2023

A catalogue record for this book is available from the British Library

ISBN: HB: 978-1-5266-4755-9; TPB: 978-1-5266-4753-5; PB: 978-1-5266-4750-4;
EBOOK: 978-1-5266-4751-1; EPDF: 978-1-5266-4754-2

2 4 6 8 10 9 7 5 3 1

Typeset by Integra Software Services Pvt. Ltd.
Printed and bound in Great Britain by CPI Group (UK) Ltd, Croydon CR0 4YY

For Sadia

The wonder that's keeping the stars apart

To Shahida who gave me life
To Sadia who changed my life
To Zoha who made my life
To Shifa who completed my life

Man can do what he wills
But he cannot will what he wills

Arthur Schopenhauer

Life is a game of cards. The hand dealt to you represents determinism.
The way you play it is free will

Jawaharlal Nehru

I didn't choose to have free will

Anon

None are more hopelessly enslaved than those who falsely believe they are free

Johann Wolfgang Von Goethe

1

Now

'You do not have to say anything but it may harm your defence if you fail to mention when questioned something you later rely on in court. Anything you do say may be given in evidence. Do you understand the words of the caution?'

'Yes. I'm a lawyer,' I say. A chemical smell radiates from my skin.

'And you are declining your right to free legal advice?'

'Yes. As I said, I am a lawyer.'

They swabbed me. I was made to stand on a paper sheet as they bagged my clothes and took every swab they wanted. They poked cotton-tipped sticks into my cheek. Cut my nails. Wordlessly for the most part, as if I wasn't there.

'But not a criminal lawyer. You're a personal injury lawyer, aren't you?'

'Can we get on with this? I'm sure there are more pressing questions than my career trajectory. I've been sitting down there in the cells for ten hours now.'

The detective runs the tips of his fingers over his knuckles like an old-timey villain ready to punch someone. 'You've been arrested on suspicion of the murder of Amy Blahn. What can you tell me about that?'

I sigh. I am tired and I need someone better to be asking these questions or nothing is going to happen. 'It's not a great question, is it, Officer? Do you want to be a bit more precise?'

'Did you murder her?'

'No.'

'How do you know her?' he says then, picking up the pace.

'I don't know her. I've never met her.'

'So you have no connection to her at all?'

I hesitate. What is a connection after all? Did I know her? No. But was I *connected* to her? Of course I was. Everything that has happened in the past weeks has confirmed nothing if not that. 'No.'

He takes a breath now and looks down in his hands as if he is reloading. 'Then what were you doing with her on that rooftop? And how did she end up with a hunting knife in her chest?'

It seems so simple when you see it on the TV. Just tell the truth because life deals in and values truth. Life is there to help you find ways to achieve some perfect resolution. Just tell the truth. What could be easier?

I touch the scar on the back of my hand. It's the thing that makes me doubt, more than anything else, that it took place in the way I think it did. I remember this injury and how it happened differently from how he does. In his mind it was one way, but in mine I'm certain about a different version, and so I'm confronted now by this problem of more than one truth. The scar hasn't healed properly; it flares sometimes in the night. Throbbing, burning. It might not ever fully heal, but isn't that the point of a scar? To mark the slings and arrows?

As I trace the jagged line I meter out in my head what I need to say and what I can't. And which parts of it might have to be recast. I see the detective looking and immediately hide the mark under my hand.

'Fishing knife,' I say firmly, but it's not enough to distract him.

A chill enters the room from somewhere under the metal-framed door. It makes me shiver. The detective folds his hands and waits, the picture of patience.

'Take your time,' he says and as if to prove he means it, he leans back in his chair. Dogs bark in a distant street far below. I had always assumed these places were soundproofed but the sound is all around, leaking in, like poison gas.

'Take your time,' he says again. The permission he implies – it annoys me.

'Officer –?'

'Metcalf. Detective.'

'Detective Metcalf,' I say. The dogs are barking like crazy now. I wait till they quieten. 'Do you think I killed her?' I ask.

'That's what I am trying to find out, Miss Mahoney.'

'Ms.'

'Ms Mahoney. If you didn't do it –'

'Or Layla is fine.'

His face softens. There are lines around his eyes that give him an avuncular look. I wonder whether he knows that and presses it into service whenever he can. 'If you didn't do it, Layla, now's the time to say.'

What he wants to say is *before it gets worse*. I think about the stones and bottles that were being pelted at the van when they brought me in. Being shown such hatred by strangers is bewildering and intoxicating at the same time. I haven't been called *Paki* in decades and that more than the other things – more than *bitch* and *murderer* – is what stings the most.

'Does it matter? You think I did it. They,' I say, vaguely indicating the outside world, 'think I did it.'

'I'm keeping an open mind, Layla. Yes,' he says and unclasps his hands. 'Right now, they think you did it.' He breathes deeply as if wrestling with what to say next. 'But they want someone to blame. She was beautiful. Had young children.'

My throat goes dry. 'Did she? Have children?' I had never thought about that. Not for a second. *Young* children, he said. How young, I wonder? And how long will their motherless futures be?

'Why were you on the rooftop, Layla?' He leans forward and stares at me. There isn't more than a foot between us and I can see the green flecks in his eyes. He waits, holding my gaze, and I wonder how long it will be before he blinks me away.

I take a breath. I have to tell him something. From law school I remember they can only hold suspects for so long before they have to charge them or release them. But I think that's at least twenty-four hours. It's going to be tough to string this out for that long without telling him anything.

And then there's this one immovable fact – I can't face a murder charge. I didn't do it. But there's a danger in saying too much, which could be worse for me than a murder trial. Which is greater: the risk of being killed or the risk of a conviction? He looks at me, as if it is him and not me on the precipice of a huge drop, expectant.

'It was Michael,' I say at last. 'Find Michael and you'll find out everything you need to know.'

He looks up at the camera to make sure the red light is on and that we are recording. There is surprise drawn into his face but he does well to keep it from his voice. 'Who is Michael?'

'I thought he was an angel or something, once.' I did. I thought he was there to save me. 'But he's not, you know. He's a thing with a hundred faces.'

2

Then

It was hot and the light was rich, the day it began. Five weeks ago, when the sun was still near enough to paint the pavement the colour of desert sand. Summer in London isn't like summer anywhere else. There's no romance in it at all.

I passed the first bus stop by and pressed on as usual towards Waterloo Bridge. The extra walk helped force the day behind me so by the time I got home, it would be as if I'd been washed clean. I thought of Russell now, making things from chorizo and peppers, the kitchen alive with chaos. He'd be pouring olive oil over salad leaves and adding fistfuls of salt. Russell came alive when he cooked even the simplest things, and whatever he touched became infused with his joy. The food always felt like love no matter how it tasted.

On the pavement it was cloying, even at 5 p.m. Buses and trucks radiated a hot and greasy air that clung to everything. Moisture trickled down my back as I tugged my bag further up my shoulder. Thankfully there was a shop on the corner, before the bridge proper got underway, where I could buy a drink. I shifted my path towards it.

Inside, the shopkeeper wilted extravagantly at the counter. I smiled at him – *look at us in this heat* – I was saying, but he didn't take up the motif. *I'm stuck here, you're not*, he seemed to say in reply. I didn't have an answer for that.

I took the coldest can from the fridge and placed it onto the counter. But when I rummaged in my bag for my wallet, I couldn't find it. The shopkeeper was looking at me with drooping eyes, waiting. I fumbled with the can and shrugged an apology at him, but didn't have the energy to explain more than that. The shop was too suffocating. Behind me the clang of a bell chased in a customer. I picked up the can to return it to the cooler but as I turned, the swollen air moved and the new customer pulled in alongside me. Too close.

'It's okay, I've got this,' he said, touching my arm. I flinched. He smiled at me, shark-like.

'It's fine, thank you.'

'Do I know you?' he said, and then, answering his own question, he added, 'yes, I do.'

I stared at him as he continued to smile at me. There was something familiar about him – but not in a good way.

'No,' I said, 'you don't,' and I darted away, leaving the can to sweat on the counter. Though I didn't look back, I sensed him watching me.

On the burning pavement again, I remembered that I could have paid with my phone. If he hadn't barged in like that, I would have. So now as well as being thirsty and hot, I was irritated. Had he done it deliberately to unsettle me? There were men who did that. They bodied their way into your spaces, crowded you and made you anxious so they could gain control of things.

I brushed away the thought and refocused on leaving the day behind me, shucking as I walked. Russell would be at home already. I pictured him smiling at me and handing me a beer. Two fingers would be raised. 'Take two sips. Then we can talk.' And then two sips later the heat would have dissipated enough. And I wouldn't care as much any more about whatever it was that I was burning with.

On the curve where the bridge began, I met the tang of Thames salt and stew coming off the water. A breeze blew across the surface; there was nothing cool in it. The exhausted crowd gathering at the lights stood, steaming in the weather, just waiting to cross the bridge. The seconds dragged until there was a shift in the mass and people began slowly to wade across the road.

The standing traffic rumbled low. A bus wheel screamed. I started to jostle forward, when I felt a presence by my side. It was more than just another person in a crowd. At the feather-ends of my nervous system, I knew something wasn't right.

I tensed at the solid presence of a man, too close, beside me, breath and bone, out of my eyeline but looming. I shifted minutely away from him, just enough to take the weight of his arm off mine. My heart beat in my throat. He was just a fraction behind me now. The seconds pulsed on. I waited in the huddle, hoping to merge with it into the flow until we were lost to one another. Finally, the crowd ebbed slowly forward, and I waited impatiently for some space to move into. When the front-runners crossed to the halfway point, making room for the rest of us, I stepped onto the road but as soon as I did, I was wrenched rudely back, as if my bag or sleeve had caught on something. My pulse rabbited. A hand was on my arm, gripping hard, pulling me just as a silver BMW careened off the tarmac and ploughed into a lake of people on the pavement.

In the pocket of silence between the firework's light and its bang, airbags thumped inside the windscreen one after the other. A second later, the sky was filled with smoke, with screams and the hum of pandemonium. Time stopped and then fast-forwarded.

Some people swarmed the car, while others shouted in agony, calling for help. I stood, rooted. The man beside me dropped my arm and leaned in to whisper into my ear.

'Keep breathing. You're okay,' he said softly.

I was too stunned to reply.

'Just take a breath. That's why I'm here,' he said. When I tipped my head for his meaning, he added, 'To save you.'

I couldn't speak so simply stood watching the chaos whirl around me. Seconds later an ambulance came and scattered the onlookers. Then the police arrived and with them more screaming as the shock that had silenced some, dissipated. Somebody bellowed something about the driver bleeding or being close to death. A man in shorts and a basketball vest was warning a teenager not to move a woman who was lying in a puddle of blood. But amongst all this activity, was I, frozen, staring at the point of impact. I had been standing at that precise spot. If the stranger hadn't pulled me back exactly when he had, I would have been dead.

'Thank you,' I said and turned to look at him, but he'd gone. I scanned the crowds behind and in front, but the man had melted away as if he'd never been there at all.

3

Now

'I'd like to start by asking you a bit more about how you found yourself there on that rooftop. How did you know her?' He is reading from a page of notes decorated with scribbles. When he finishes the question he looks up, pen poised.

'I told you. I'd never seen her before.'

'Just take a moment and have a look at her,' he says and slides a photograph across the table.

Her face smiles at me. The picture's been taken on a sunny day in the park. The light squeezes her eyes nearly shut. And then with a metal thud I remember she is dead. 'She *is* beautiful,' I say. 'But no.'

He flares his nostrils. 'Her beauty isn't going to be much help to her orphaned children.'

'I didn't kill her,' I say, quicker than I expect.

'How did you end up there? On the roof?' he says, looping around again.

The questions are too quick. I need to answer some, slow him down before I get myself into trouble so deep I can't climb out. But that question isn't straightforward; there are so many threads in the answer. The tapestry they weave, grotesque or charming, is the important thing. The picture that resolves behind the coloured yarn. But I can't get there without drawing the threads together, and I don't want to do that yet, do I?

'Russell. It's Russell, my husband, his building. Well, he works there.'

'So, you were there with him, your husband?'

'No. He wasn't there. I thought he was. I went up there expecting him to be there, but he'd gone by the time I'd arrived.'

Metcalf sniffs deeply. The impression he'd given earlier, of friendliness, is beginning to ebb away. 'Sorry, I don't think I'm following this. You'd arranged to meet him there?'

'No. Not arranged.' I take a breath to order my thoughts. 'What you have to understand is that we weren't getting on. Our marriage, it was breaking. I thought he was having an affair.'

The detective shares a look of sympathy with me but it doesn't feel real. It seems just like a way to slice in a question. 'Did you suspect him to be having an affair with the deceased?'

'I didn't know.'

He pauses, pen to his mouth. 'You said your husband works at the building. What does he do?'

'He works for the Environment Agency.'

He shelves the pen behind an ear so he can turn the page in front of him. 'Did you know that he'd been meeting Amy Blahn?' He drops the page and his hands, now free, begin to flutter. I notice a wedding ring belting a swollen finger.

'As I said. I thought he was having an affair. I believed he was meeting someone but I didn't know who.'

'But now. Do you think he was having an affair with *her*?' He points at her smiling face still on the table.

'I don't know. It's confused in my head now. It was Michael. He was getting into my head.'

I need time to think. Before I can decide what to do, I need to see the weft and weave myself, but I can't. I haven't slept and the events of the last night are a kind of vibration that seem to shake loose everything that went before it.

'Did you kill her because you thought he was having an affair with her?'

The cliché astounds me. 'What? You mean in a jealous rage?'

'Maybe?'

'I didn't love him by then. Not after everything. I wouldn't have *killed* over him.'

'So then?' He touches the top of his head, lightly. He has thinning mousy hair and doesn't want to encourage a fall. He sits back and attempts a smile but it fails at the last. I don't like his face, I realise, now that I look closely. There is a streak of meanness there in the mouth. The features aren't even. His chin is heavy and long. But then he has this perfect, smooth, blemish-free skin which ruins everything.

'Well?' he says. 'Can you answer the question? Why were you there?'

I think about everything Michael did. How he pulled and teased at every silk string gently, so that unless you looked hard, you wouldn't see them twitch at all. It was Michael. All Michael, but I can't just tell him that. He looks at his watch and I suddenly experience a rush of control. He thinks this is slipping from him.

'Do you believe in free will?' I ask.

'Free will? As in you can choose what to do?'

'Is there another kind?' I say, a hint of vinegar in my voice.

'If that's what you're saying – that you had no free will – then –' He takes a breath to find the rest of his sentence.

It isn't what I mean at all. But it will do as a placeholder. These answers cost me something, but I hope they will buy me something more in return. 'Yes,' I say. 'But I'm not talking about me. I'm talking about you. Do you believe that all your moments are mapped out and follow inevitably one after the other?'

He considers this as he rolls the cuffs back on his pale blue shirt. All men look beautiful in blue, even him. I don't know why.

'No. I don't think I do.'

'Then think again, Detective. Really try to imagine what that would mean.'

4

Then

The man. The car crashing into the traffic lights. The whole fantastic, tragic event on the bridge hung over me as I finally walked home that evening an hour later than expected.

I should have thought of the injured people, of the blood, the agony. But it was the man's face that consumed me, the arrangement of it. And his words: 'That's why I'm here, *to save you*.' I tried to think if somewhere in my head, there was a name for him and a context, but no matter how deeply I mined, I couldn't find it.

I reached our small Victorian terrace house and unlocked the front door, keys jangling, and my heart rate picked up again. The hallway was dark and silent but still bore the scent of fresh paint from the remodelling – Russell's idea. I saw him then, his face rinsed in the light of his computer, the screen reflected twice in his glasses. He smiled when I walked into the open-plan kitchen and he hunted quickly in the fridge for a bottle of beer. He flipped off the lid and slid the bottle to me – saloon-style – over the marble top. I caught it just in time.

'Russ! Let me get my bag off at least.'

He raised his hands in surrender. 'My bad. Put way too much elbow into that.' He reached for his laptop and dived back in. 'I've got some *pomodoro* going for dinner.'

I sat down and waited for him to look up. I wanted to tell him everything, but not like this, when he was distracted by other things.

A minute later he got up to stir the sauce and then stopped dead in his tracks before crossing over to me.

'Lay. What is it?'

'I was almost killed today,' I said.

He stood me up gently and turned me to him. 'What?'

'On Waterloo Bridge. A car came off the road. Missed me by that much,' I said, showing him an inch of space between my fingers.

'Shit, Lay,' he said, looking me up and down. 'Are you okay?'

Was I okay? When I started to think about it, tears streamed. He blurred in front of me until he held me. I hid under the scent of cologne and olive oil and pepper, like a child under a blanket.

Later that night when I lay in bed, the man's face from earlier appeared in my peripheral vision, his eyes lion-like, fractured.

'Are you okay?' Russell asked for the second time that day. He leaned over so that he could see my face.

I looked across and ventured a smile. 'I'm fine,' I replied.

He touched my hand with the back of his and sunk into his pillow. 'If anything had happened to you,' he said and left the rest unspoken but heavy in the air.

The chaos of the accident played out on the ceiling as I stared at it. The blood – how dark it was on the tarmac, like hot oil. The screams running in a loop in my head, spooling out a jagged reproduction. Now there was the man himself, his face hovering at the soft edges. I held on to him long enough to see the detail. Did I know him? He seemed to know me. His face was familiar – not *known* exactly but *similar*, to someone I had there in my memory. I'd seen him somewhere before.

Sleep came in patches and in the morning, after a ragged night, I woke to find Russell had gone. He'd left everything neat and tidy in the bedroom and the kitchen, his cereal bowl washed and drained. I knew he was being considerate but sometimes he gave the impression of a man who didn't want to be seen.

I washed and dressed in a hurry and made my way into the office on the Strand. Alice was humming away across the room and smiled when I waved. My head was too crowded to speak to her, so I buried myself under the cover of a file to give myself time to arrange my thoughts.

Last night the horror of the crash and the strangeness of the man had seemed like an indelible thing. But now in this sanitised office space, the whole scene evaporated, as if the tonal greys of the walls rejected something as frivolous as a stranger saving me from certain death – the idea too silly for the dead air of a mediocre solicitors' firm.

The lights fizzed up above, setting my teeth on edge. I opened up another electronic file and skimmed some witness statements to take my mind off the buzzing. There was a part in the file where the claimant had drawn his road traffic accident as rectangles colliding on the exit of a circle. I needed Alice's help.

'Alice, can I have your cars?' I called across the room.

She looked up from her screen. Alice was often mistaken for being shy, as if that flame hair needed all the oxygen there was. But she wasn't shy. She just didn't like people much and didn't understand small talk. For pleasure she read court judgments, dissecting bodies of law into sinew and skin.

'Sure,' she said and walked over with two matchbox cars she'd pulled from a drawer.

'How,' I said, spinning my screen so that she could see, 'exactly does that car there hit that one on the front nearside from that trajectory?'

She took up the cars and began tracing the journey. 'Well, if,' she began and then stalled. 'No. That doesn't make sense.'

'Here,' I said, taking the cars. One was a red Ferrari and the other was an old blue Capri. My father had a Ford Capri once, so I always took the time to handle it whenever I could. I improvised a possible route on the desk when, without warning, the man's face returned. Just his smile at first. Then the intense eyes blinking away the sun. The vision of him was so vivid that it made me start. I didn't know what had triggered it.

Did it have something to do with the model in my hand? Did he drive a Capri? There was something there on the fringes of my memory.

'You okay?' Alice asked. From this distance I could see a silver hair working its way out of the flames.

'Yes – I just,' I said, and for a moment I almost told her everything about the evening before, but instead I handed the Ferrari back to her. 'Can I hang on to this for a bit?' I asked, keeping back the Capri.

She raised her eyebrows at me and returned to her desk, squeaking gently to herself as she did.

Who had a Ford Capri apart from Dad? There were some Polaroids somewhere – at Mum's house maybe. In one or two of them, in overexposed orange light, Dad was leaning back against the wing or bonnet of a gold Capri. But the Dad in the Capri photos wasn't the Dad I knew growing up. The one in the pictures was vibrant and mischievous. He wore a rakish grin and outlandish clothes with huge collars. But only in the photos. By the time I was ten, Dad was steadier. No flashes of danger in his eye. Just serenity. He was a man who was barely there.

On Sundays we went to the market in Chorley, just me and him. We sold cheese at the Sunday market. We didn't make the cheese but we dressed it to look as if we had. Dad bought up a few wheels every month from a local dairy and we'd carve them at home and wrap them in waxed paper. I remember the round stickers that sealed the packets. *Willow Farm*, a made-up farm with a symbol of a tree on it, in green. The real-life dairy the cheese came from was poured cement and sluiced paths that smelled sour and metallic. It was just *marketing* Dad would say, but I disagreed. To me it felt dishonest.

'Has Fry seen you yet?' Alice leaned on her elbows, a pale oval face resting on a fist. For three years I'd come and gone as I pleased, but a new manager, Mark Fry, had been drafted in to chop away the dead wood. The later I got in, the more desiccated I became.

'No,' I said.

'He's so weird,' she said and turned her attention back to the case she was working on. 'Weirdy beardy. Weirdy beardy,' she began singing quietly.

I returned to the memory of the market, turning over the car in my hand to reach it. There'd been a model-car stall – and there was a boy – the son of the stallholder. He never spoke to me. He simmered, mainly. Leaned against whatever thing he could find and drank Diet Coke.

One day, in the teeth of winter, ice biting my fingers, I'd gone red-cheeked to look at the cars. The old man wasn't there, it was just the son.

'Have you got a Ford Capri?' A din of market noise rose from the background.

He leaned forward to hear and when I asked again he nodded and then reached under the table and pulled out a box. 'Thirty,' he said, carefully unboxing an orange car and handing it to me.

'Thirty pounds?' I said, shocked.

'Fifty-four-B vintage Superfast,' he said as if the words meant something to me. 'Rare,' he added when he saw that they didn't.

I stood still for a few seconds. He waited, rubbing his chin. The muscles in his arm flexed a little as he did. He stared at me, blue-eyed.

'I've got a stall,' I said at last, which was code for asking for a discount.

He narrowed his eyes at the box and then reached under the table for a ledger. He examined it for a minute and flipped it shut. 'Twenty-five.'

He caught me looking at him and smiled. He carried on staring, but now with such an intensity, head slung at an angle, that I couldn't move.

'Just take a breath,' he'd said.

And I bought the car. He'd got into my head.

It could be him, the man on the bridge. That's how he knew me. That's why he was so familiar.

5

Now

'Resuming this interview. The time by my watch is 11;01. You're still under caution. Do you need the words of the caution repeated or explained?'

I shake my head.

'I have brought Detective Inspector Jason Omer into this interview. He's been involved in some of the investigation behind the scenes and I'll let him explain his position.'

He is very serious, this new officer, with his little round glasses. Unlike Metcalf who looks as though he has spent more time in the canteen than on the beat, Omer is trim and everything about him seems deliberately positioned. He wipes a hand over his head which is smooth and the colour of honey.

'Yes. As DC Metcalf has said, I've been involved in this investigation, following up what we describe as reasonable lines of enquiry. Something we have to do if you raise any. So, you mentioned to DC Metcalf that a person called Michael was in some way key to this case?'

I nod but don't speak.

'For the tape, the suspect is nodding in agreement. But, Ms Mahoney, if you could give us audible answers that would help. Okay. So, tell us a bit more about this Michael. Does he have another name?'

'Yes. It's Cruz,' I say and spell it out.

'Okay,' he leans forward. 'And tell us please again how you say he was involved. I've listened to your earlier interview and your words were "I thought he was an angel . . . once". What did you mean by that?'

'Maybe you should find him and find out,' I say.

The two of them look at one another. Metcalf's expression is heavy with *I told you so.*

'Well, we can run the name through the Police National Computer but we're more likely to get something useful if we have some more details. Date of birth for instance?'

I shake my head.

'Address? Phone number?'

When I shake my head again, he looks at Metcalf. 'It might return too many candidates even if I limit the parameters to London and an age range. Is there anything else you can tell us about this Michael Cruz to help narrow down our search?'

They don't know. I sit back in the chair and stare at them both. How can they not know? I assumed they had done basic investigations but they can't have.

'Check the CCTV for the building. You'll probably see him going and coming out again at almost the exact time of the murder.'

The two men share another look.

Omer speaks again for them both. 'Ms Mahoney, I've tasked an officer with checking the footage and though we still have some ongoing enquiries in relation to CCTV in the immediate environs, we have looked at the video covering the entrance of the building. There's nobody going in or out who we haven't been able to account for. Most scanned themselves in using an electronic pass containing their ID. We've cross-checked the relevant ones, in person. They are all employees. They all have firm alibis. We even see you going in. Alone.'

I tense. 'What are you saying?'

Omer pinches the bridge of his nose under his glasses. 'I'm saying that Michael Cruz, whoever he is, wasn't on that footage. So, if there's anything you want to do to help your case at this point, then we are all ears. If you can help us find this Michael Cruz, who you say was responsible for the murder of Amy Blahn, we are more than happy to facilitate that. But if not, we are ready to terminate this interview, and charge you.'

I could *no comment* the remainder of the questions. But doing that right now doesn't serve me any more. If Michael is caught and interviewed, they might make him admit what he did.

'You have to find him.'

'Then help us, Ms Mahoney,' says Metcalf, moving his chair back and forth. 'How do we find him?'

The smell of old cologne comes from one these men. Omer probably since it's a new scent in this room. It has an antique note to it that reminds me of Dad and for that reason seduces me into trusting him.

'He's some kind of corporate investigator.'

'So not an angel?'

I start at the question. 'I didn't mean it literally. He'd saved my life.'

'Okay. That's a relief,' Omer says, smiling. 'How did he save your life?'

'I don't want to talk about that. It's not relevant. No comment.'

'That's your right. So, for a job, he's a corporate investigator. I don't think we've come across too many of those. Do you mean like a financial investigator?'

'I'm not sure exactly. The way he put it to me was that he was contracted to carry out investigations for companies that had issues.' The scar on the back of my hand is irritating me. I have been avoiding scratching it because of the impression it gives them of me. It looks nervous. I rub it against my cheek instead.

'What kind of issues?' Omer taps a pen against the arms of his glasses.

'I don't know. Could be anything. Employees who were insider dealing or selling commercially sensitive information. Corruption maybe.'

'Corruption?' Omer says, dropping his pen. 'What's corruption got to do with this?'

They both stare, waiting. 'Everything, I think. I think it's all about corruption.'

6

Then

At 2 p.m., I was being 'spoken to' about the late filing of evidence in a case I was handling. It had the heavy imprint of Fry's boot all over it.

My face contracted in irritation. 'Really? We have months before trial. We can file it next month and still be okay.'

'Yes, really, Layla. We're doing things differently now. Properly. I'll have to give you an oral warning for this.'

When I steamed out of the HR office moments later, I left the door wide open in protest. It felt puerile. It *was* puerile, but it made me feel better. Back in my section of the office, Alice picked her head up to ask how the meeting had gone but then quickly curled away when she saw I didn't want to talk. I sat, clenched, in my seat, my face hot. For the rest of the afternoon, I trudged through files but as soon as the clock turned five, I picked up my bag and headed straight out.

The walk to the bridge made me jumpy. The spectre of yesterday's awful, bloodied crash clung to me all the way along Fleet Street. I should get the bus, start a new pattern of normality to try and erase the awful events of yesterday, but the thought of seeing *him* again made me repeat the day before.

At the bridge, standing at the exact spot I'd stood just twenty-four hours before, everything returned in a deluge. The BMW. The double thump as the airbags went off. The screams splitting the air. Me jittery and him holding me steady. His eyes, like raptors' eyes, tasting me.

In witness-training seminars they talked about how trauma altered how the mind laid down memory. Yesterday he'd held on to me in a way that signalled only menace. But now, only twenty-four hours later, I felt that my mind was hastily rewriting it all. He pulled me away from traffic – saved my life – he couldn't be the predator I'd believed he was.

I stayed still, waiting, as crowds of people jostled past, trampling over the bloodstains and life stains of the accident. Some commuters were a kind of clockwork and the same faces returned in a cycle. If he'd been here yesterday, he might be here again today. I needed to see him.

I checked my watch. I was ten minutes earlier than yesterday. The logical and pragmatic part of my head began to scrutinise everything I was doing. He wasn't a commuter – I'd have seen him before. And if he did turn up, then what? Was I going to ask him whether he was a boy from my childhood and expect him to remember me? I'd have been invisible to him when I was thirteen.

I stood glued to the pavement as the crowd cushioning me swept across the bridge. There were no familiar faces. I twisted to look behind me but again nobody stuck out. Within a few seconds more commuters appeared, replacing the ones who'd just crossed. I waited, scanning the men for one with the right build, the right shade of chestnut falling across his eyes.

I persuaded myself to wait until the next tranche of pedestrians and then I'd leave. I could hardly believe that I was waiting in a sea of pedestrians just to satisfy a curiosity. Was I supposed to thank him for the unnerving way he'd held me back? He'd barged into me and assaulted me away from the kerb. And now I replay it – it hadn't been exactly when the car had come. It was seconds before. He was taking credit for nothing more than chance.

So why was I still here?

I waited through two more changes of lights and then crossed. Just before I reached the pavement on the other side, I took a final look behind me. And that was when I saw him waiting to cross.

He was searching faces at the lights in exactly the way I had done. I stopped and turned to cross back over the road. A wave of commuters came now towards me and for packets of time, he faded out of view. By the time I had finally banked, I'd lost sight of him completely. I twisted back again, towards where I'd just come from, but I couldn't see him. It were as if he had misted away.

I opened the front door and dropped my bag at the foot of the stairs. Russell wasn't home. In the kitchen I poured out a glass of wine and took it to the small sofa under the window and sat back. I closed my eyes and packed the day away neatly into boxes, until the only things left were me and where I was.

I called at the puck on the countertop to play me some music and a second later Allegri was pouring out of the speakers, filling the spaces in the corners with 'Miserere Mei'.

A baited hour passed slowly until the front door scraped in the hallway. Russell, bringing a weighted mood with him.

'You're late,' I said with more edge than I'd intended. 'Is everything okay?' I added then to smooth the tone.

He dumped his bag at the kitchen door and raised his hands. 'I'm really sorry. It's been crazy at work.' He went to the fridge, passing me as he did. I caught a note of vanilla. With his beer open, he perched at the marble countertop and ran his hands through his longish blond hair.

'I'm sorry,' I said and checked my phone again for any errant messages from him – sent but not delivered. 'What's been going on?'

He laughed a little. 'Just the usual. Central government peering over our shoulders all the time,' he said, taking a gulp of beer. He shut his eyes and from nowhere I began to wonder whether he did it so he didn't have to look at me.

I chased the thought away. We sat bathed in a tense silence. He'd wanted me to ask about his job once but I'd never been interested enough in his work then. Now it felt too late to catch up.

'If it helps, I was given an oral warning about missing a deadline,' I said, watching him for a reaction but it never came. He sat like that for some time, drinking, studiously avoiding any connection. 'Russ?'

He shook himself free from whatever was bothering him. His hair standing in places. 'I'm sorry,' he said and smiled. 'Long day. Over now. So. Oral warning? Naughty girl. Or serious?'

Allegri had long been replaced by a muted Liam Gallagher. The music shifted the atmosphere in the room, giving it a nostalgic tone. Not the joy of the past, but sadness at the loss of it.

'Quite serious.' Then to change the mood I added, 'What shall we do for supper?' I got up to root around in the vegetable cupboard.

'I'm not really hungry,' he said to my back. 'I'm going to catch up on emails.'

I watched him leave, taking my appetite with him. At the counter I stared at the veins in the white granite, tracing them to their eventual ends. The surface was glassy and comforting to touch. We'd argued about this countertop. Russell insisted on the prohibitively expensive marble: *It's a natural product*, he'd said, parroting the salesman. And I'd agreed, despite the cost. Because it was Russell and Russell had the kind of charm that left its traces on you long after he'd left the room. As I ran my finger now along the pattern, it caught almost imperceptibly on what felt like a protruding grain of rock. It couldn't have been more than the thickness of a split match and although I couldn't see it, my skin snagged on it. I tried to scratch it away as if it might have been a bit of dried food but it resisted. Defiantly, not food.

Around midnight, he came down to make a snack. His face had the burned look of someone who had stared at too much light.

'Is everything okay, Russell?' I said. I hated having to ask it. I'd done this once before, with us. I'd scratched away at something or nothing, and at first it was just the lightest dusting of powder but before long it had crumbled like old plaster.

He stared back, red-eyed, for a while. His hair though long at the top was cut in a way that made him look like a boy still. He narrowed his eyes at me as if composing something but then took a breath and changed his mind.

'What is it?' I said.

He smiled. 'Lay, I'm okay,' he said.

'Do you mean that?'

'Yes,' he said. And then not unkindly, 'Despite what you did to me.'

That was three years ago, I thought, but didn't say. How long would I have to pay for it?

7
Now

'Tell us more about this man, Michael, then.'

I don't know what Detective Omer is ready to believe. Metcalf maybe, but Omer – I can't just spring this on him out of the blue and expect him just to go along with it. He waits, serene.

'Do you know anything about her, Amy, the woman who was killed?' I ask him to deflect the question.

'We know enough,' he says, I guess masking how little that is. 'We know she was murdered on the rooftop of your husband's building. We know that her two children are six and eight. They're in a terrible state right now.'

When he says that, it's a hammer in my chest. I look down as he continues.

'We know when police arrived, Amy was lying in your arms, a knife in her chest. Dead. Is there more?'

He looks up again at the red light. It is blinking. Still recording. He levels his gaze at me. Metcalf tries to join him in apparent patience, but I can see, simmering under his skin, that need to burst into rage.

I am trapped between two glaciers. I must remind myself there is danger both in saying too much and in not saying enough. There are things I need to deal with so I know how far I can go, but I can't do it from here. I need to get out. 'I can say "no comment" whenever I like, can't I?'

Omer catches himself short. 'That's your right, but –'

'But what? You don't seem very interested in hearing what I want to say. You seem to be fascinated by your own theory about what happened and honestly, I don't need to hear it. I was there, remember.'

He scribbles a note and turns the sheet over and slides it over to Metcalf. 'What did you want to say?'

'Amy Blahn. Do you know what she did for a living? What in fact do you know about her?'

Omer scouts around on the floor for his bag and pulls out a buff folder filled with documents. He riffles the pages until he finds one that he likes. 'IC1 female. Born in '79. She worked for – *e-Vinculum Limited*.' He puts the folder down. 'But that doesn't tell you who she was. That the person who shared a desk with her at work also shared her biscuits with her. Or that she and her husband, James, used to go rock climbing in the summer. Or that Amy did bath time with the kids and their dad read the bedtime stories. Or that she kept a banana on her bedside table in case she woke up hungry in the middle of the night. We know what we think we need to know about her. What do you think we need to know about Amy?'

Hearing her name repeated in this way makes me feel sick. However small a life looks, it cuts swathes of devastation when it ends like hers did. My stomach churns. I heave myself back into the room. The truth is that I don't know if what I know about her is real. I don't know if Michael lied about that too. I don't know who she really was. But the police could find out more than me – if I can push the right button.

'Do you know anything about *e-Vinc*?'

Omer touches the file on the desk. '*e-Vinculum*. Not really. The usual – but no more than that.'

'Then I strongly recommend that you find out.'

His hackles are up, not surprisingly. But he knows there is a limit to what they can do in this interview without my cooperation. They can't make me talk. I have the right to silence. It was right there in the caution that was read out at the start.

'Look, Layla. If there's something you want me to know, then tell me. You can say anything you want and if it's important we will follow it up and investigate further.'

'Investigate further? Detective, I don't see what investigations you've even started. Have you found Michael? Or even tried? I'll take that as a no. Well, until you do that, I'm *no comment*. So, you can stop the interview and do some work or listen to me shutting down your questions one after the next. Up. To. You.'

He stares at me and in that extended moment my heart is one sickening beat after another. I think I might have overplayed my hand.

8

Then

Standing at the zebra crossing, I gazed at the sandwich shop and the growing line. It wasn't even 1 p.m. and the queue was spilling onto the street. I waited for the traffic to stop before stepping onto the pavement edge. The road smelled like boiled tar. But as I was about to move forward, someone was at my side. I turned, anxious.

It was him. He'd swept his hair away from his face but everything else was still the same; the blue of his eyes was malignant. He smiled and I froze, welded to the spot.

If there was an obvious thing to say, I couldn't find it. My mind was a wheel of blank tape. I stood and stared at him as the world ground to a halt. But then through the pounding in my chest, I saw that he couldn't be the boy from the market. This man's eyes were too strong, intense. His cheekbones too sharp.

Still I stared, mute.

He raised an eyebrow, composed. Happy, even.

But in my veins, adrenaline began to course so that I felt the push of flight. I stepped away from him, my leather sandals teetering on the pavement edge – concrete under my heels but air under the balls of my feet. I tried in the stretched seconds to make sense of how I felt. I'd been searching for him and now here he was. But he was someone else, not a young boy selling his dad's toys. This man gave me the feeling of being plugged into an electric current. I felt sick.

He smiled at me, waiting for me to comment or do something. The longer I waited the greater the chasm yawning before me.

I blocked him out as a flatbed lorry lumbered towards us. I jittered, waiting impatiently for it to pass. I had been looking for him – I'd been desperate to speak to him – but now he was here in flesh and blood, I was in a racing panic. The road was clear. I took a step, when he leaned in.

'I think we need to talk.'

I quickly looked the other way for another break in the traffic and then leapt away from him and onto the road. As I crossed I looked back and saw that he was retreating along Fleet Street towards Ludgate Circus. This area was flooded with lawyers. Barristers in Middle and Inner Temple just behind Fleet Street. The Old Bailey at one end and the Royal Courts of Justice on the other. Was he a lawyer of some sort? What would a lawyer want with me? Perhaps I was being headhunted? I thought about the grey and lifeless personal injury department I'd been languishing in these last few years and doubted it immediately.

Once safely over the road, I waited for the hammering in my ears to subside. It was him. *We need to talk*? What did he mean by that?

Initially curiosity and irritation magnetised me into following him as he walked. Him on one side, me on the other, wading through a river of lunchers. But then as I drew parallel something else drove me on. Anger.

I hooked my eyes into the blazing white of his shirt and let it trawl me through crowds. He passed Middle Temple Lane before ducking behind some large black doors that led into what was known as the Temple. I crossed back over as soon as I could find a gap in the traffic and followed him. It had been a few months since I'd ventured into the Temple. It was beautiful but there was something about the place that always made me feel as if I was trespassing.

Once I'd reached into the cobbled courtyards, the sounds from the street became muffled. I stood by Temple Church, and watched him sauntering through the cloisters as if heading in the direction of the river. A stripe of sun heated the stones on the ground before me, giving them a sweet smell.

If I was quick I could catch him.

A few barristers and perhaps their clerks passed and I weaved between them and the columns to reach a shallow set of stone steps leading down into the well of an ornamental garden. Beyond it to the right a path led to a small arch and in it now stood the man from the bridge, as if waiting for someone. He raised an arm to check his watch and then leaned lazily against the wall.

I picked up my pace and then before me, the Rubicon. If I went a step further he'd see me. There was still time to turn back but not much. He rolled his sleeves, facing a quarter-turn away from me. I took the step. Crossed the threshold. He moved and then saw me.

And smiled.

'Right on time,' he said, looking at his watch.

9

Now

I am in a peach-coloured waiting room where the only sound that reaches me is the humming of the electric lights. I make small circles and with each step try to shed as much of the toxicity from the interview as I can. Within a few seconds the calm begins to lay claim to my senses and then to my body.

The overwhelming sense in this room is smell. Some rooms have eyes. Some rooms see you. You can sometimes catch them quietly observing you. Others hear. The worst ones (in my experience) touch. This one smells you. It decodes you from your scent, like an insect or an owl or some other hiding creature. It can tell when you are afraid, for instance. This room likes me, I think, and then two things happen simultaneously to ruin the silence. First, the door bursts open. And second, it propels a large red-faced man into the room.

'Layla?'

'Peter,' I say, recovering my heartbeat. 'You came.' He looks at me and for a second the last three years vanish. The air tingles. He takes half a step and then pauses before washing over me like a wave.

'Of course I fucking came,' he says and wraps me in a bear hug. Tobacco and coffee mixed with limes.

We were once at the same firm, a small generalist high-street firm with an even smaller criminal department. It was always losing money. Peter left before they finally mothballed it. I bumped into him three years ago in a bar in Soho. He'd moved to a smart corporate outfit with wealthier clients – footballers and bankers – and he was happier. We drank until the hours became small. I never saw him after that.

'So, to get to it. What the fuck were you thinking?'

'I was thinking that I didn't need a lawyer.'

'Layla, it's a pissing murder case. And you're a suspect. *The* suspect. You need a lawyer. For fuck's sake. You are a lawyer. You should know better.' He hasn't aged well. The odd streak of silver he had when I knew him has become a cloud.

'Well, Peter, it is what it –'

'Do not finish that fucking sentence. It is not what it is. Because right now what it is, is a fucking disaster.' He goes to slap his hand against the wall before changing his mind and folding it into his pocket.

'Why are you so stressed? I'm the one in here.'

He turns his bloodshot eyes at me and slowly raises his eyebrows. 'Are you kidding me? This is not a game, Lay. They're going to life you off.'

'But it wasn't me.'

'I've seen the disclosure. You were arrested on a roof with a dead woman in your lap. And a pissing Rambo knife in her chest. And. And listen to this bit very carefully, Layla. There was nobody else there. Nobody.'

When he speaks to me it is like metal on bone. And now he looks at me as if I am lying to him. 'It was a fishing knife,' I say.

'When it's in a fucking fish, you can call it a fishing knife. Until then it's a murder weapon.'

I feel my cheeks burn. It isn't being spoken to like a child that displaces me. It's the familiarity. He knows me.

'You know me, Peter. I couldn't kill a fly let alone a – person.'

'They think you could.'

'I know *they* do!' I say. 'That's why I called you. They don't believe me even though all I said to them was true.' The words come out, squeezed and compressed from my chest. I need him to believe me. I can't do it alone any more.

'Peter, how long can they hold me without charging me?'

'Initially, twenty-four hours. But they can get a senior officer to extend it for another twelve.'

'That long?' I say, shocked.

He takes a breath. 'Sit down. Tell me what happened. Everything.'

'Everything?'

'We can worry about privilege later. For now, I need the lot.'

10

Then

The sun had just dipped a fraction so that it was in his eyes. He shielded them with his hand.

'What do you want with me?' I said, collecting myself. In the air was a taste of citrus which could have come from him or from the flowers in the garden. Its sharpness was like a blade.

He put his visor hand out and smiled. 'Michael Cruz. Pleased to meet you.'

I wrapped my arms around my body, staring at his hand. 'We're not *meeting*. You're following me. Stalking me.'

He withdrew his hand. 'You followed me here, Layla. And it's not what you think.'

Suddenly I wanted to be where there were more people, and not in this secluded nook. He knew my name. The heat reflecting off the brick and stone became stifling. My head began to spin a little. I stopped breathing for a moment as I tried to keep a rein on the rising panic.

'Layla,' he said suddenly, concern blooming across his features. 'Are you okay? Let's sit down.' He reached out a hand as if to guide me to a bench. I stepped away from him and looked around for other people. Being here with him, even in daylight, didn't feel safe.

'How do you even know my name?' I said, easing backwards. It was a terrible mistake being here, hidden from others.

'You told me it just now,' he said. 'I said Michael. You said Layla.'

I thought back and was sure that I hadn't said that. I said nothing and for a second began to doubt whether this was happening at all. The light seemed too bright for reality.

He put his hands up slowly. 'I'm not following you.'

'What do you want?' I said, my voice finding purchase, as a barrister's clerk – a runner – came by with a trolley towering with briefs. He waited until she'd gone.

'I don't know,' he said. His face was contracted in seriousness. I stare at him. 'Well, not exactly. I don't know exactly what it is. But I do kind of,' he said, lowering his voice. I waited but the momentum of what was on his lips seemed to have died.

'But I'm *not* following you.' He bolted his hands together.

I began to edge away again, checking behind me as I went. There were people a few yards away. I could run or scream out if I had to.

'I'm not following you. We're – it's hard to explain.'

'Try.'

'We're entangled.'

'What?' I wasn't sure if I'd misheard. I continued to look around, scanning for clear exit routes.

'We're entangled. You and me. We're linked somehow. I know it sounds crazy but we're conjoined. Our paths are connected.'

I took a few deep breaths, keeping my eyes on him as I did. A bead of sweat trickled down the back of my neck, absorbed into the linen of my dress. He was clearly insane. 'I have to go,' I said. 'And stop following me.' I took a few steps out of the garden and quickened my pace as I returned the way I'd come. I sensed a presence behind me and I turned to see him following close behind. My heart drummed.

'Wait,' he said, touching my elbow.

'Leave me alone,' I said, shrugging him away and hurrying up the short flight of stone steps I'd earlier come down. I didn't know what I'd been thinking.

'Okay. Whatever you want. But there's no point in running away,' he said, stopping and simply calling out after me.

There were more people up there by the cloisters. I turned and faced him. He stood waiting a few metres away. 'What do you mean?' I asked. I needed to be sure what he was threatening.

'Because it'll keep happening. We're going to keep on meeting. Wherever you go. It's –'

I was near the church and touched its walls for support. The stone was grainy under my fingertips.

'It's inevitable, Layla.' And then once he'd taken a breath. 'We have to talk.'

I should leave immediately, I thought. 'About what?'

'I don't know,' he said and took another breath about to add something more but I cut him off.

'And where do you get off telling me you're there to save me?' I said, remembering what he'd said on the bridge.

He threw his hands in the air. 'Look, I don't know how this works. I just know that it does. We are being thrown together. I have to help you or you have to help me. We have to figure it out.'

'Help me with what?'

He took a few steps closer. 'I don't know. Whatever you need help with. You've got a problem of some sort – I've seen this before. It could be work or your personal life, or a problem with your husband maybe – but something. And I need to help you with it.'

'This is ridiculous,' I said, backing away. A ribbon of music from a pipe organ slipped out between the closed church doors.

Michael swallowed. 'I know it is. I can try and explain it if you'll give me the chance.'

'No,' I said, turning away. 'This was a mistake.' I fled back onto the main road, leaving him as far behind me as I could.

When I hit the Strand and the traffic and the pedestrians and the bustle of ordinary life rose around me, the whole thing began to feel unreal. Even the way he smiled and the way his hair swept across his eyes was fantastical. 'We're entangled,' he'd said, as if we were in a film.

11

Now

I have told Peter what I can. It's enough to get me through the worst of it, I hope. But I have to think about the rest of it. I don't want to tell him anything he doesn't want to know. That's something every lawyer knows – even a PI lawyer like me.

Omer and Metcalf are less than pleased to have Peter in the room. The tapes have been switched on. Metcalf rereads out the caution and then chaperones me carefully through it as if I were a child.

Omer looks at me and smiles innocently as if he is about to take a sandwich order. 'So, to bring Mr Kelly up to speed, Ms Mahoney has given us a name, a Michael Cruz, as the person who might have committed the murder.'

'Did you find –' I say, interrupting him. Peter nudges me into silence.

'Do you need to investigate that further before continuing the interview? I'm happy for Layla to be released under investigation,' Peter says, infecting his voice with a blandness it never has. He doesn't want to spook them.

'No. Actually we have investigated the name Michael Cruz. Your client's information to us was that he was some kind of corporate investigator. So obviously we have access to a large database of identities and addresses and so on. There is no Michael Cruz – it's an unusual spelling for Cruz – in that age range in the South-east.'

Peter looks at me but not for an answer. The look is a warning to keep quiet. 'I don't suppose it occurred to you that he – Michael – may not have given her his real name?'

Omer's eyes light up. 'Exactly what we thought. So, we were wondering whether there were any other details you could give us, Ms Mahoney, to help identify him?'

This time Peter is looking to me for an answer. 'I've given you a description. What else do you want?' I say.

'Blue eyes, five ten, dark hair. About forty. Yes, we have that. Anything else?' Metcalf reads this off a printed copy of my previous interview.

I can't think of any other details that might help. 'Maths. He likes maths. I mean he knows it. He's some kind of mathematician.' Then I catch myself short. They all turn to look at me.

I have to tell them something more. It's a gamble but I have to take it. 'I just remembered something. I do have his number. I'm so stupid. I thought I only ever called it from a landline but I've remembered now. I sent him a text from my mobile. Just once but it should be on my phone.'

Peter's eyebrows rise in concert with the others', but it's Metcalf who picks up the dangled thread. 'You just remembered? That seems like something that would stick in your mind.'

I know the effect isn't great but 'remembering' it even this late is better than remembering it later. 'Detective, I've been waiting in a cell all this time. I'm being interviewed in connection with a murder. It's stressful.'

Omer reaches over to pacify his colleague. 'Thank you, Ms Mahoney. That's a great help. We can look into that. But for now, can you tell us how you came to meet him?'

They all look in my direction. We have discussed this, Peter and I. This is safe ground. I can tell them about that, but how can they understand without knowing all about the madness of it? It was a sort of mesmerism. They have to understand that to understand the rest.

'Do you believe in free will?' I ask.

Metcalf shrugs his chair forward and holds a hand up to interrupt whatever Omer was going to say. 'She said that before, in the earlier interview. Why do you keep asking that?'

'Because it's all about freedom to choose, Detective.'

Omer says, straightening his glasses, 'Do you mean you had no choice?'

'In a way.'

Peter coughs and immediately lays a heavy hand on my wrist to shut me down.

'Not exactly. I mean it's how I met him. It was fate.'

'Go on,' Omer says softly as if speaking to a stray cat he doesn't want to scare.

'I didn't meet Michael, in the sense that it was an arranged or even a random meeting. It was almost – *written*.'

12

Then

At my desk later that afternoon, my concentration was shattered. His face kept coming back no matter how hard I tried to move him into a different space. By 5 p.m. I was desperate to leave work and get away from his ghost.

I texted a friend, Kate, to meet me for a drink. We'd been at sixth form together and then university and remained close as the years dragged everything else apart. I was jealous – I was a lawyer but she'd done something indulgent for a living, making expensive porcelain for Arabs and Russians. The idea alone was dreamlike.

Entering the pub, I got a strong sense of the old bank it once had been. The walls swept up high to meet vaulted ceilings. A terrace ran along a mezzanine floor, fringed with brass Art Deco railings. I pushed past a clutch of office types and walked into a vale of hot ale. I took out my phone to message Kate and saw a text from Russell.

Sorry. I'll be late again tonight.

I squeezed through the crowd and found a small table at the back. The noise gnawed at my nerves. I sat down, took a breath and messaged Kate.

I've got us a table at the back. Get me a drink in?

The din ebbed and swelled until I felt it would crash over me. I couldn't shake the man from my head. Michael. The name sounded so *benign.*

A few minutes later I saw Kate's long blonde bob swivelling in the crowd and frantically waved her over.

'I got you a pint,' she said, grinning.

I accepted it gratefully and took a gulp. She watched me, a smile playing on her lips. She knew me well enough to know something was wrong.

'So?' she said, laying her hands flat on the table, diamonds glinting. 'Is it Russell?'

Russell? No. It was this man, Michael. I thought back to the conversation but when I tried to slot the components of it back into the positions where I remembered them, they no longer clicked into place.

Kate waited for me to speak as the noise of the pub washed in again to drown out the memory of what had happened. 'Is he being a dick?'

I looked at her frowning.

'Are you and Russell having issues again?'

'No, it's not that,' I said eventually. 'I'm just having a weird day.'

She put down her drink and reached over to take my hands. 'Well, let's see if we can't do something about that then.'

I nodded and smiled through whatever I was feeling. 'Do you ever feel like you're going a bit crazy?' I said.

She looked at me in a way that made me want to cry. 'All. The. Time,' she said and then got up to buy more drinks.

I sent a message to Russell to tell him I'd be late, too. A few minutes later when I checked, he hadn't replied. But that was okay. It was.

By the time I got home, I was still dizzy from the night with Kate. It wasn't the drink – I hadn't had that much – it was Kate herself. She had a way of untangling me in a few strokes. I didn't have to talk about Michael or what he'd said. Instead she gave me her version of the life-coaching she thought I needed. How what I was feeling wasn't about anyone but me. How I needed to find the place in my psyche where the machinery was stuttering and attend to it. How the others, whoever they were, could only interact with what I presented of myself. Their reaction to me was a consequence of what I told them about me.

I clattered now through our aubergine front door and suddenly caught myself up. I didn't want to wake Russell at past midnight and for him to see me. That was what he did. He looked at me and immediately saw the battles I was waging. Whether I was winning or close to being overwhelmed. He would stroke my hair or trace a finger around my brow and bring me back to myself. When he first did that I remember how it made me feel as if I were being anointed, blessed. And that he was absorbing some of the static that followed me everywhere.

But I didn't want him to suffer what I was going through now.

As soon as I crossed the threshold, I sensed that he wasn't back yet. A flick of a switch flooded the hall with light. No shoes or coat. I slipped off my own shoes and headed to the bedroom to change. From the street the sound of bottles being kicked and students making their way, drifted up. I looked over to the neatly made bed. There'd been a time, once, when I'd have crawled into his side just to be where he'd been. I checked my phone. No messages or missed calls.

When I first met him, we didn't seem that likely. He was warm and sunny and I was prone to gloom and vapours. He wanted to march the world to rights where I just wanted to fold into a piece of space and observe it all, safely.

Kate had introduced us. She didn't like him enough for herself. *I can't vouch for him, Lay. He's my sister's friend more than mine*, she'd said, *but he's single.* I met him for the first time in a pub in Putney Village near Kate's cottage. He was sitting neatly in the corner, freshly shaved, wearing a sky-blue cotton shirt. A smart navy raincoat was folded on the seat next to him. My immediate instinct was *too cool for school.* But once we'd talked, I recognised his extremes. We were missing halves. I was a person whose hands wrung over what my mind wrought. He was a bright light. And now when I think that, it makes him sound bluff and oblivious, but he wasn't. He was kind. He wanted to know about me and where I came from. He asked about my parents – Dad especially. What it was like growing up between worlds. And I loved that – that he saw me. It never stopped surprising me that he was interested in me and loved me. And even now I had to remind myself that I deserved to be with someone like him.

But still I wondered whether he was prepared for as much fragility as I carried in my bones.

After the third or fourth time we met, he took me up to the roof of his office at 55 Broadway. They called it the country's first skyscraper. At the top it was just a space – no chairs or tables or anything to suggest anything more than just the vertical end of the building. But the views were spellbinding. I gazed out across the river. Big Ben on one side and St James's Park on the other. It felt clichéd, that view and him taking me to see it. But that's how he was, a whorl of sunlit life.

Later he took me out the back way through the fire door. Once we'd passed through a door which he opened with a twist of the Yale lever, we were standing in a narrow corridor with a fire door at the end. He pushed it and we were on the street as if we'd stepped through Narnia. I remembered it only because I'd left my coat in his room.

'I'm so sorry,' I said, laughing.

'Come on,' he said, leading me back round the front. 'I haven't got the key to get back in that other door. We have to go back through the main entrance.'

Now, pulling away the covers, I pressed my face into his pillow and searched for a trace. He was there, just, but his scent failed to return the warmth I needed. I was about to turn away, when I caught it, again. That vanilla note, from the other night. Not his smell. Not him at all.

Those words that Michael had spoken about him came drifting back. *We're entangled.* And then something about a problem I was having that he needed to help me fix. And of course I understood that he, Michael, was an aberration. That he was just as likely to be me, my subconscious, signposting dangers, but that wasn't a reason to ignore it – *him*. Michael was real whether he was warm-bodied and fleshed or just a projection.

A problem with your husband, he'd said. Why would he say that? What could be a problem with my husband? And, where was Russell now?

What would I have done if he hadn't said those words? Or if I'd been more secure? More sober? The alcohol gave me a looseness that convinced me it was the only logical thing to do. So, I did it, but only vaguely, barely tethered to an awareness of it, because of the humiliation of what I was doing.

I went through Russell's chest of drawers, sifting through the black teak drawers, looking for nothing and everything. It was strange to be searching for something unformed, chimeric, but catastrophic if found. There was nothing in his sock drawer or in with the sweaters. I slid open the wardrobe – nothing hidden there with the suits or at the back or amongst the discarded shoes. I went through drawers of folded T-shirts. Even as I ransacked his privacy, I had no inkling of what shape it would take, this incriminating evidence I was looking for. I paused. Whatever it was, I wouldn't find it in the laundered and dry-cleaned clothes.

So, I rifled through the laundry basket, shutting my eyes against the image I was cutting. Paranoid wife.

Until I found something and stalled. I held it up to the bathroom light, a shirt with white cuffs and collar but blue body. I stopped, feeling myself on the edge of a precipice. Another Rubicon. If I stepped now, there'd be no turning back.

It was nothing as stark as lipstick against cotton. It was just a smell, but it was unmistakably there. The same sickly sweet vanilla. A woman's scent. Nothing a man would go near, at least nothing that Russell would wear. I hesitated before finally balling it up to go back into the laundry. I couldn't do anything with a scent, if it even survived another night. But as I was stuffing it back into the box, I saw something. A lone blonde hair, almost gold, caught on a button. I considered it for a moment and whether it was innocent. But wrapped as it was around the second button from the collar meant that he must have been very close to her head when it came loose from her. *On the balance of probabilities*, I said to myself, engaging my lawyer's brain, it wasn't innocent. Vanilla on the bed and in his clothes. A blonde hair on his chest. And him, not even here to explain himself, but away somewhere – with someone, presumably. And me not in any position to say anything about it.

I carefully untied the hair and deposited it into the tiny useless breast pocket of my pyjamas. It was poker straight even after having been twisted around a button.

Sleep banished, I headed to the kitchen and swallowed two paracetamol at the marble top. Reflexively I ran my hand along the stone and caught the little nub of marble again. There was something tactile about the little grain. I scratched at it until my nail cracked.

Two hours had passed and there was still no sign of him. No messages or texts. Images of car accidents cascaded through my head. He could have been killed. I checked WhatsApp but his 'last seen' was switched off. He had done this once before, failed to come home, but then, he had been on a stag do and somehow had ended up in a tent on the Brecon Beacons, without a signal. And I remembered where I'd been and what I'd done, and quickly I exiled that snaking thought.

My phone was deafeningly silent, blank. No Twitter or social media notifications. A minute later my email pinged and my heart tripped.

The email wasn't from Russell, it was junk from road traffic lawyers telling me I had been involved in an accident and could have a *no-win-no-fee* claim.

For a few minutes I got lost in thoughts about Michael. I should have stayed to hear him out before walking away. He didn't know anything. He'd said *your husband* and I didn't react. He didn't know I was married except for the ring on my finger. He was a confidence trickster – using granules of detail scattered wide. He was one of those people who covered whatever grit they caught, over and over until it became a pearl. And I'd fallen for it. Sent him on his way not because he was lying but because part of me believed him. But I had no idea what he wanted. And then in my head, a whispered voice: *he knew your name.*

No sign of Russell still. The street outside was steeped in silence now. The house began to creak and make itself known in the further reaches.

A rattle in the door broke into my thoughts. My eyes flicked to the cooker – 02:39. Keys clinked and then the sound of the turning lock. I watched as Russell came in quietly, tiptoeing until he noticed the lights in the kitchen. I sat at the white granite, glaring, scratching at the spit of protruding marble again.

'You're still up,' he said, pausing in the doorway. He looked slept-in.

'You're back,' I said. He cast his eyes towards my hands worrying at the countertop. My finger was bleeding at the nail – the hand of a child. I curled the finger away into my fist and edged past him and up the stairs. I didn't want to stay for whatever explanation he'd rehearsed. In the bedroom I climbed into bed and stared at the ceiling through the darkness. The sound of the blood pulsing in my temples; the thick cloak of hot air; and me supine, unable to move. It all conspired to make me feel like I was in a coffin. A few minutes later, he was there, getting changed. I clamped my eyes tighter so I didn't have to see him as he got in next to me.

He lay firmly on his side of the bed, rigid and unmoving. For a moment, I considered reaching out a hand to him. Mostly I wanted to curl into him. I wanted all this turmoil in my head to be quelled. The space in there was too crowded. Too muddled and dark. And then as I made the decision to ease my body towards him, there it was again, the unmistakable scent of vanilla.

13

Now

'What did he say to you, this Michael Cruz?'

It's Omer leading the questions. There is no urgency to his style – he asks questions as if he has all the time in the world. He can't know that this is what I want too – to slow it all down and to let the clock tick out. He must have something up his sleeve.

'He told me that there was maybe a problem with Russell.'

'What did you take from that?'

'I don't know. I thought he was having an affair maybe.'

'So, Michael tells you that your husband was having an affair. Did he tell you how he knew that?'

'That's not what I said.'

'Okay,' he says heavily, weighting it with sarcasm. 'He told you something and you assumed from it that Russell was having an affair. Didn't you ask him what he meant?'

'No, I didn't trust him. He scared me.'

Omer and Metcalf throw one another coded looks. Metcalf picks up the questions. 'Okay, maybe we park that and you can help us with a few more relevant details?'

Peter nods for me.

'This knife. I am now showing Ms Mahoney a photograph of police exhibit NM/7 – the murder weapon. Do you recognise that knife?'

'Yes.'

'Is it your knife?'

'No.'

'Is there a reason why your fingerprints might be on it?'

I look at Peter but he's busy interrogating the picture. I'm about to answer when he speaks: 'Is that a speculative question or have you tested the weapon for prints?'

'At the moment we are just trying to clarify whether there is a reason that Ms Mahoney's prints might be on the weapon.'

Peter laughs. The sound is hollow and echoes against the furniture. 'Look, let's not play around. You're trying to trap her. So, I'm advising her not to answer that question until you answer mine. Have you tested it? Are her prints on it?'

Omer leans in to take over. 'The knife has been submitted for tests. We don't have the results yet.'

'Then *no comment*, Layla.'

'No comment,' I repeat.

'Police arrived at the scene to discover you on the roof terrace, with the victim dead in your arms. Did you see how she got killed?'

'Yes.'

'How?'

'She was stabbed.'

'By you?'

'No,' I say. 'By Michael. I don't know how many times I have to tell you this. It was Michael.' The scar on the back of my hand is itching hard – burning. I'm desperate to scratch it away but I know what impression that will make on these two. They're here just waiting for the smallest tell, some micro-behaviour that gives me up as a liar.

'Can you explain why there's no CCTV footage of the man you call Michael entering or leaving the building?'

Peter puts an arm out across me as if I am a passenger in a car and he's made an emergency stop. 'It's not for my client to speculate about that. How can she answer for footage that isn't hers and that she hasn't seen for a man she wasn't with when he left the building. *If* he left the building. He might have stayed there for hours or longer for all we know.'

Omer colours a little but recomposes himself. 'Okay. Let's – erm,' he says and then stops as if he has run out of line. 'Look, we'll be honest with you both here. We're very troubled about this victim. We've looked into her, at your client's suggestion as well. And it's a puzzle to us. She's forty-one years old. Married. Two children. No criminal record or cautions – not so much as a parking ticket to her name. Her work colleagues describe her in glowing terms. Her family and friends can't think of a single reason why anyone might want to hurt her. So we are really struggling here with why anyone would want to kill her. Do you know?'

'No. I told you. I hadn't even met her before.'

'Did Michael know her?'

'Again,' Peter says, cutting across me, 'my client cannot be expected to know if or how two people know each other.'

'Well, Ms Mahoney, do you know?'

Peter leans into me and advises me in a low voice to say *no comment*.

'He told me he was worried about her,' I say anyway.

'In what way?' Metcalf says.

'He didn't tell me at the time. He thought that she was trouble.'

'What, do you mean *in* trouble?'

I check the time on Peter's watch with a surreptitious glance. Another hour has passed. Only so many of these left surely, before they have to release me. 'No, he thought she was dangerous.'

'Dangerous how?'

Peter looks at me as if he is driving nails into my head. 'He didn't say.'

'Okay,' Omer says, pausing and writing something down. 'I think we are making progress. Michael thinks Amy is dangerous – for whatever reason. I'm guessing that you'd say that's what lies behind her murder. Let's go with that for now. What I can't work out is why they're on the roof of *that* building. Michael doesn't work there. The victim didn't work there. The only connection is you – because your husband works there.'

They all look at me for an answer. I need space to work it out now. We are getting too close to the point where I can't turn back. I have to talk to Peter, take a breath, create some room in my head to decide what to do.

'Well?' Metcalf says, prodding the table.

‘They were there because they were there,’ I say. ‘It’s the flap of a butterfly wing. Something led to it. And then, they were there. They had to be, don’t you get it?’ I smile at them, hard.

Peter holds his hand up. ‘I’d like to have a private consultation with my client, please. Stop the interview.’

14

Then

I left not giving him the chance to explain, so I could remain in the moment before the calamity. In a time when nothing had been finally decided upon by the fates.

But I couldn't shake the sick feeling of not knowing where Russell had been. And the stone under my mattress was Michael.

What had he meant by a problem with my husband? Why put it like that? Why not just say he's having an affair, if that's what he meant? If I'd stayed he might have told me the detail that I now was hungry for. But the more I thought about him, stood as he was, his shirt white-hot in the sun, the blue of his eyes piercing the haze, the more he seemed to be in a liminal space.

I needed some air. Outside in a bright shout of light, I texted Kate before making a call.

'Mam,' I said, my voice cracking.

'Who is it?' she said.

'Me, Mam, it's always me.'

'Layla? To what miracle do we owe this early morning call?' she said spryly as if she were suddenly a different person.

I didn't have an answer for her. I couldn't tell her about Russell – she'd have dismissed me – after what I'd done before. And she didn't believe in divorce, not even her own.

'Just seeing how you are,' I said.

'I'm fine, Layla. Don't worry, I haven't dropped all my marbles yet. Most of them, granted, but not all.'

I laughed along for a second and then cleared my throat. 'Mam?' I paused, hovering over the question. She'd been stable recently – no episodes – and I didn't want to change that. 'Have you ever, when you were at your sickest I mean, had the feeling that things weren't real?'

A membrane separated the silence in her world from the chaos in mine. The noise from traffic was starting to equalise. It softened and then merged with every other sound. The singing from birds high in the trees. Lawnmowers grinding. A pneumatic drill heavy and metallic on the road. And at the other end of my phone, a valley of silence.

'No, dear. I heard things, you know.'

'Not seeing people though?'

'No. Not hallucinating an entire person. Why? Are you seeing folk?'

'No, Mam,' I said quickly. 'It's okay, never mind. How are you, though?'

'Me? I'm grand. The hospital operation went okay.'

The words were like a slap. 'Operation? Mam. What hospital operation?'

'Oh,' she said, tutting herself. 'Not operation. The other thing they do. The one that's not an operation.'

'A procedure? Did you have a procedure? Mam?'

'Scan! That's it,' she said, and I breathed loudly down the phone.

'Tell me about this scan,' I said heavily, relieved. We spent the next few minutes talking in cipher about her abdominal scan and what *lumps and bumps* they were looking for. My phone buzzed lightly through the call. Kate.

'Mam, look, I'll try to drop in and see you soon,' I said and switched the call.

'Kate.'

'Lay,' she said. 'Got your message. Everything okay?'

'Why wouldn't it be?' I said.

She seemed out of breath. 'You texted. And you never text me this early on a weekend.'

'Can I come and see you?' I asked.

She hesitated. 'Okay,' she said at last. 'I'll get some coffee on.'

The taxi pulled up and I looked up to see Kate waving at me from her front door. I got out to meet her with a smile but when I reached her, my face crumpled.

'Layla,' she said, drawing me in.

I wiped my eyes as she ushered me in and opened them again to flagstones in her kitchen. 'New floor,' I said, to steer myself away from more tears.

'Oh, I thought it'd give it a more cottagey feel,' she said.

'Nice,' I said, sniffing before taking a seat at the kitchen table. It had been almost a year since I'd been here. 'Looks expensive.'

'That's not where the money went. That's the money-pit right there.'

I looked where she was pointing and saw a blue range the size of a Rover. 'An Aga?' I said.

'It takes up most of the kitchen but at least it'll keep me warm come winter. Anyway, sit. Tell me everything.' She handed me an orange china mug – one of her own creations.

I took a sip. Then another.

And then I told her about Russell turning up at dawn. About the perfume and the single blonde hair, and even as I spoke the words I hated the way they made me sound. 'I think he's seeing someone.'

She gave me a worried smile. 'I'm sure it's innocent. It'll have been a work thing or something. What did he say when you asked him?'

I hesitated. 'I didn't ask him.'

She blew into her fringe and smiled. 'Then you're probably overthinking it.'

I drained the coffee and set the mug down onto the bleached wooden table. My nerves sung from the caffeine. 'But the perfume,' I said. 'And the hair.'

She touched my hand. 'Your finger,' she said, seeing the dried blood around the nail. I hid it away into my palm. 'Let me get you a plaster.'

'No. It's fine,' I said.

She sat back again and smiled. 'So, he tried a new aftershave. And a hair? Come on, Layla. Who hasn't had a hair tangled up in their clothes before? I pick up a dozen different ones just on the way to get milk.'

Something in the pit of my stomach clenched and unclenched. 'Maybe,' I said. She couldn't know about the fear that was incubating. That he was separating himself from me. That something *was* happening and that I wasn't imagining it. A part of me even *hoped* there was someone. Nothing permanent – a one-off, like mine had been – so that finally the scales might tip in my favour for once.

I caught Kate studying me so I moved into different territory.

'Kate, this will probably sound a bit weird, but have you ever bumped into the same person twice – like a stranger?'

She contracted her brows. 'I don't think so, not in London. Why?'

'I keep bumping into this guy.'

Her eyes widened in concern, the blues lustrous and pale. 'In different parts of London? That's weird, Lay. It's such a big city.'

I nodded to myself to dislodge to the cold spear of fear that had slid in between my shoulders.

'You need to be careful. He could be dangerous.'

Russell was making us Thai curry. He knew I loved his Thai food, so it had the quality of an apology. He smiled a 'hello' as I walked in. I sat at the counter and traced the jagged edges of the nails on my right hand. I tried to avoid the raised nub of marble but didn't manage it completely. My hand began to worry at it and in the end, it felt as if I were rubbing the skin off my brain.

I didn't know how to ask him why he was so late last night without it feeling like an accusation. And I was in no place to make accusations.

'We've got a session tonight, remember,' he said, ladling out the food.

Fragrant steam from the food bathed my face. I used to welcome the therapy sessions. To begin with they felt like a redemption. And more than that an affirmation of our permanence – an act of faith. But now they felt like retribution – each visit another ritual head-shaving.

When we got there the scent of lemongrass was still clinging to our clothes. Nikki was installed in her usual place, drinking herbal tea.

'How have you guys been getting on?' she asked.

She always dressed plainly as if consciously attracting the least attention she could. 'Why don't you start, Russell? Are you happy that you're getting a good exchange of feelings between you?'

Russell nodded and smiled. 'Yes, I think so.'

She turned to me. 'Layla?' The words from that day played over and over. *A problem with your husband.* Russell had been out all night and came back smelling of perfume and covered in blonde hairs.

'Layla?'

'Yes,' I said eventually. 'It's been good.'

'Is there anything that you are feeling undermined about?'

I stood up. But then as I shut my eyes the words came.

'He came back last night after 2 a.m. No call. No texts,' I said and swallowed back everything else that had begun to bloom. 'I didn't know where he was.'

Russell stiffened but softened quickly. 'You know you could have asked me.'

I felt heat gathering under my cheeks. I didn't want to ask him these questions. 'So, where were you?'

He looked from her to me. 'I was working late at the office.'

Nikki nodded. 'Remind me what you do.'

'I work for the Environment Agency. Something came in late. I had to deal with it. That's all there is to it. What could I do?'

I wanted to leave it there, with this explanation I could work with. One that I didn't have turn over and over in my head. But the absence of detail would become corrosive later. 'You could have called. Sent a message,' I said.

'I had no signal. The meeting rooms don't all get a phone signal,' he said to Nikki.

She sat back and indicated me. 'Say it to Layla,' she said and I vibrated as he said it all again.

'Good. So now we have an honesty space,' she said, without pausing to see whether I believed him enough to justify naming the space.

He did complain about the shitty reception in various civil service buildings. But there were still landlines.

'I found a hair,' I said and immediately wished I hadn't.

I left the room just as Nikki was explaining she was giving us homework for the next session. Russell stayed dutifully and caught up with me at the car. He shook his head at me as he got in. The drive back was heavy and miserable. Neither of us spoke the whole way home. We pulled up just as clouds began to collect overhead.

'What?' I said, when I noticed him staring.

'What was all that "I found a hair" nonsense?'

'I did find a hair.'

'Whatever,' he said, kicking off his loafers in the hallway.

'No,' I said and marched upstairs to the bedroom to get the hair from the pocket in my pyjama top. But when I looked, it had gone. I checked under the pillow where I put my pyjamas, but there was nothing there either. I went back down to find him in the living room flicking through the channels.

'What did you do with it?' I asked him.

He turned. 'With what?'

'The hair?'

He shook his head. 'I don't know. I genuinely don't know what to say to that.'

I stood in the centre of the room not knowing where to turn, suddenly feeling adrift in my own home. He stared at me waiting for me to speak.

'You always do this. You raise the subject and then you run away from it. It's not a grenade. Just say what you want to say for once.'

I slammed the door and went to the kitchen to find a drink. But when the bottle was in my hand, the stereotype was so grating that I put it back down and made some coffee instead. I sat at the nub on the counter and rubbed it until I could bear it no longer and went to the cutlery drawer to find a knife. Then I remembered that Russell had a proper knife, his grandfather's old fishing knife that he kept in a tackle box under the sink. After a little rummaging, I found the mother-of-pearl-handled knife, pulled open the blade and locked it into place. I placed it flat against the granite and sliced at the nub. It slid straight over and I tried again in shorter passes. After five minutes I gave up but with a mild horror saw that the stone was scratched where I had run the knife across it. I threw the knife across the counter and watched it skitter onto the tiled floor.

As I went to pick it up I noticed something on the limestone tile. I licked my finger to pick it up and put it up to the spotlight. A blonde hair – the same golden shade as the other one I had found. And just like that one, this too, was arrow-straight.

Was this another hair that fallen off Russell's clothes? Or worse – had she been here, in this house?

15

Now

In the consultation room Peter is hunched over the back of a chair, staring down at me. He has always carried the risk of violence, I think. Hauled it around with him like a wolverine down the front of his shirt.

'We really have to deal with the knife thing now, Lay. We can't really *no comment* it.'

'But you told me to *no comment* it.'

'I also told you tell me everything and you haven't.' He wipes away the frustration that is obviously building. 'Look. *No comment* can buy us some time but it won't make it go away. It's key.'

Details of the room flow through my consciousness. I am aware of the chipped wood on the armchair I am in. And the Van Gogh on the wall, blazing yellow against the painted plaster. But I know it's just my mind tempering the tension with banality. I want to ask him why it's key but I know he's going to tell me whether I ask or not. He likes to supply answers, does Peter.

'The knife is everything. If your prints are on it and you haven't explained it in advance, whatever you say later will sound made up. If the prints aren't on it – even worse. The jury's going to wonder why you didn't deny it straight off. They will think that you wiped them off. So,' he says, straightening. 'What's it to be?'

I don't hesitate. 'Yes. The knife would have my prints. It's Russell's fishing knife. I'd used it, I don't know, a week before? Ten days? It was in the house. I used it. They don't need to test it.'

He spins around quickly so that I don't catch the expression on his face. 'Why did you have it on you at the scene?' he says, aiming his gaze at the floor.

'I did *not* have it on me. It wasn't me! Haven't you been listening?'

'Listening? Yes, I've been listening. Understanding? No. I hear you saying that this was all some guy called Michael. I don't know who he is or how you know him. I don't know why he is there on the roof with you and Amy Blahn. And now to add to all those *I don't knows* – I don't know why he has Russell's bloody fishing knife on him. But most of all, Layla, I don't know how the hell he's managed to vanish off the face of all CCTVs in the building and then off the face of the Earth.'

The colour, such as there was, has drained out of Peter's face. He is worried. Terrified. When I think about it all from here in this room, I can't make sense of it.

'Michael,' I say. 'When Michael found me, he wanted to warn me about Russell. I left before he could finish telling me what he wanted to say.'

'Why?'

'Because . . . because I thought he was telling me about Russell having an affair. But it wasn't that. It wasn't that at all.'

'Then what?' he says, coming near me now. He is holding his breath and so, I see, am I.

'I didn't know it then. But something much worse. He was telling me Amy was involved in the licencing of a really fucking dangerous chemical. And that Russell was involved.'

16

Then

I said nothing to Russell about the hair but wrapped it in some kitchen roll and placed that carefully into the pocket of a denim jacket I had hanging on a hook in the hall. It couldn't go missing from there.

Russell was downstairs watching TV. Since the following day was Sunday he wouldn't be upstairs till late. I lay in bed trying to untangle it all. The strange coincidence of Michael on the bridge pulling me back from an accident and then seeing him in Temple.

I opened my Mac and thought about searching for him but I had nothing to go on. A name – Michael – and that was it. But he seemed to know I had a husband. Maybe he knew Russell. Perhaps he worked with him. I did a search of the people in the department of the EA that Russell worked in – operations – but I couldn't find any Michaels. It might not even be his real name. I closed my computer and tried to sleep. *Entangled*. He said we were linked somehow. Maybe it wasn't Russell but me that was the connection.

The following day I studied him as he made lunch. He took a pizza from the freezer and slid it into the hot oven before quickly tossing a salad together with olive oil. He was there just an arm's length away – real. The skin on his arms and face still burnished from the summer.

On the ceiling there was a dark spot that I'd never cleaned. Every time I saw it I meant to get the stepladder and wipe it away. But I'd forget and move on to something else. Except I didn't forget – I'd left it as a souvenir and an amulet. I rewound the weeks and months and years to the moment immediately before. Russell had been cooking something complex for a dinner party we had planned for his line manager and his partner. I had been on the sidelines, rushing supplies over to him from the cupboard and beers from the fridge. It was one of those sauces that he'd read about in a Michelin book and it had taken hours of painstaking measuring out of strands of saffron and grams of truffle to get it to this stage.

I sat at the table, eating crisps and Maltesers, watching him, loving the way he moved.

'Pass me one then, you greedy sod,' he said when the sauce was shining in the pot.

I reached into the packet and lobbed a Malteser at him. He caught it with a flourish and ate it.

'Another,' he said, opening his mouth.

I tossed another one at him, and he caught it again before pirouetting back towards the saucepot.

'Give me them,' he said. 'I'll throw you one.'

'No,' I said. 'Your hands are greasy. I'll throw two – we both catch.' I stood next to him and threw two in the air but as I did the whole packet in my other hand went up too. He caught the chocolate meant for him in his mouth, just as a dozen others went straight from my packet into the complicated sauce. We both froze. He stared at the pot.

But a second later we were laughing until there were tears in our eyes.

I looked across now at him. I didn't have to step out of this reality in front of my eyes if I didn't want to. My husband here, making lunch, being himself, kind and easy company. It could remain as simple as that.

And then his phone flashed on the countertop behind him and he went rigid. He quickly swiped it off the top and dropped it into the pocket of his linen shorts. He turned then towards the oven so that I couldn't see what his face betrayed.

On Monday, I went to work as usual, alighting at Waterloo Bridge and walking across. Sunday night had been too dank and far too deep to dredge up now so I concentrated on the light instead. Summer had begun to give way to autumn. The weather was still warm but the character of the light was changing – bright white was giving way to gold and copper.

And Russell. He was still who he was. The cloak of suspicion that I'd thrown over him didn't change that. I had no reason to doubt him. He'd never given me a reason to, which was more than he could say about me.

At work I spent the morning reading new files and then at lunchtime I went to the canteen and picked up an apple and two packets of crisps. Once I'd eaten the apple I went back up and dropped one of the crisp packets on Alice's desk. She nodded her thanks and ate them semi-silently as she took a phone call. When she'd finished, she hummed to herself, interspersing the tune with falsetto squeaks, and took another call. I remembered the car I owed her. I'd give it back as soon she was off her call. But as I was thinking about this, one of the senior partners, Julianne, phoned through.

'Can you pop in to the large conference room? Now please.'

'Sure, what about?' I said.

'I'll explain when you get there,' she said coolly.

The conference room was at the other end of the office. When I got there, I saw Julianne, papers fanned out before her. Fry was next to her, looking serious.

'Have a seat.' No pleasantries at all. 'We wanted to notify you that a complaint has been lodged against you by a client.'

I sat, stunned. 'Complaint? From an insurer client?' I asked and then noticed that I was picking at the dried blood on my fingernail. I stopped.

'Not an insurer, thank God,' she said. I relaxed. Insurer clients meant half a million pounds a year in business. Client clients, *lay* clients, individually, meant almost nothing since their costs were always paid by the insurers.

'What do you need?' I asked, happy to smooth over whatever needed smoothing.

Fry peered at me over his glasses. A deep breath followed. 'This one isn't going away. He's an OBE and says he's lost his reputation by losing his case.'

I laughed. 'But even you know that ninety per cent of cases win or lose themselves.'

Julianne studied the documents in front of her. 'He said that you told him to be "flexible" about certain parts of his statement and that he was caught out in cross-examination.'

'Flexible,' I said. 'Flexible how?' I felt my colour rise.

'You told him,' Fry said, cutting across, 'that he might be better off not remembering that he swore at the other driver.'

I said nothing.

'Well?' Julianne said.

'Well what? Was he supposed to admit it? Seriously?'

Fry again. 'Yes. That's the honest thing to do.'

No lawyer would have written up a witness statement in which their client admitted swearing at the other driver. 'It couldn't have made any difference. There'd be no way of proving that he did or didn't swear,' I said. 'And if you ever went to court you'd know that judges don't care about it at all.'

There was a pause during which they exchanged glances. 'She, the defendant, had a dashcam,' Fry said finally. 'They played it at the hearing. Last-minute disclosure.'

'Shit.'

'Shit is right, Layla. We're initiating a disciplinary,' Fry said steadily. 'This is your formal notice. Interview in two weeks.'

I looked at Julianne but she had already begun to write up her minutes of the meeting.

17

Then

I left the office dead on 5 p.m. The evening crowds were as swollen as the morning's but there was no optimism there. There was more evidence of the gathering autumn: a slight chill in the air and a ponderous darkness blooming overhead. Instead of the usual route, I circled around the back of Aldwych to give myself a short extra walk. I waited to cross at the pelican when I felt a hand on my shoulder. I looked around and saw that face again. It was him. My body tensed and I felt an electric spike of fear.

'That place does good coffee. Good place to talk,' he said, pointing his chin at a grand coffee shop with gold lettering stencilled on the windows.

His face in this light glowed, giving it an unreal feel. My heart became percussive. My throat closed. 'What are you doing here?'

'We need to talk.'

I swallowed. I should run. But at the same time, I needed to know what he knew about Russell. I looked around and saw a thousand people within arms' reach. There was probably nowhere safer to be than here, cosseted by strangers. I got my phone out and shared my location with Kate. She called a second later but I didn't answer. Instead I texted her quickly to tell her it was a mistake. I was fine.

The Delaunay belonged in a Viennese courtyard. We were shown to a table in the corner and presented with an *Afternoon Tea Menu* on stiff white card. Having him this close – the heat rising off his clothes – was surreal.

'I'm sorry,' he said.

I sat and waited for him to speak.

'I wasn't following you. You should know that.' When he said it, there was something like defeat in his tone.

'I don't believe you,' I said. 'What do you want?'

He shut his eyes for a moment. 'But it's important that you do.'

'Why?'

'Because until you believe that, you won't believe the rest of what I need to tell you.'

My fists had balled so that white was showing at the knuckles. But there were people here, it was safe, I reminded myself. 'I don't know what to tell you. Just say what you need to and we can get on with our lives.'

He sighed. 'I'm a mathematician specialising in number and probability theory,' he said as the coffee he'd ordered arrived. 'I'm now in private industry.'

I stared at him. If he was deranged it didn't seem complete: the language, the tone and pace were – *normal*. But there was so little connection between what he was saying and what he should have been saying that I began to shift in my seat.

'Sorry. Back to the issue. The bottom line is,' he drew in a long breath. 'Our paths cross. They keep crossing. And they will keep crossing. It's not a coincidence, it's something else. Mathematically – it doesn't add up. I know. I've done the numbers.'

I folded my arms. This was definitely unstable. I'd seen this in Mum. The swings in logic. The changes of subject.

'You've done the *numbers*? On two meetings?' I said, checking the route to the doorway again.

'It's been more than two. Or three if you count this one. There have been dozens.'

A wave of something cold washed over me. Goosebumps appeared on my arms and my heart began to beat hard. 'What do you mean dozens?'

'I mean,' he said, 'I've seen you dozens of times. You didn't notice. But I did. It's the kind of thing I take note of. Our paths keep intersecting. It's becoming more and more frequent now. This is why you feel like you recognise me. It's because –'

I snapped out of my seat, unable to stay down any longer.

'Wait,' he said, holding out a hand. He pulled a small notebook out of his jacket and read off a page that was already opened. 'February this year. The nineteenth. You were on a train to Liverpool. I was on the same train. I noticed you because I'd seen you the month before wearing the same red coat – in Angel – at a bagel shop. Then in May I saw you again, this time at Greenwich. You were at the market. Then three more sightings in June. And July – six sightings. And now, they're happening so frequently that we've had to meet.'

My breathing had become rapid and I made an effort to slow it down before I lost control over it. I held the back of his chair, breathing. 'Because you're *following* me!'

'I swear, Layla, I'm not following you.'

I was still unsettled by the use of my name. I wondered again whether I'd told him it before. The room began to swim so I sat down again. 'What do you want with me?'

'These meetings. I think they presage an event of some kind. We are being pulled together for a purpose. We can help each other, I think. But –' he said and then caught himself.

'What?'

'It's probably life-changing, whatever it is. Or it wouldn't be happening. And there's one more thing.' He paused. 'I think whatever it is, it involves your husband.'

The buses had all been put on diversion and we were being told to find alternative ways to complete our journeys. I walked to Elephant and Castle and took a train, the conversation with Michael still ringing in my ears. It should have been two stops to Denmark Hill but in the mess, I'd managed to get on the wrong train and I was heading north instead of south. The carriage was empty – at this time, all the commuters had long gone. I sat feeling the cold evening soaking into my bones. Blackfriars Station approached but I didn't get up to change. I needed to think.

'What does it have to do with my husband?' I'd asked him.

He'd looked at me uncertainly. 'This has happened to me before – with someone else. The last time was in 2019, I remember it because I was working on a project involving chemical compounds. Wherever I went – whether it was to a café for lunch or a library or a friend's party in a bar – this woman was always there. I couldn't work it out. One day I was at a barbeque and she was there with her partner. I had spent months bumping into her. It was getting ridiculous. So, finally, I went and said hello. She was an accountant at one of the big four. Her husband, Jon, was a research scientist.'

'And?' I said, the significance lost on me.

'And I was too late for whatever it was.'

'What do you mean?'

'A few months later Jon was killed. I could have saved him, I think. I'm not sure exactly how but my chance meetings with his wife – I think that's what they were about.'

I shook my head to clear it from all this information. 'What does any of that have to do with me?'

'I don't know. Maybe nothing. But I saw Jon after that barbeque – a few days before he died. It was another "chance" encounter. He was with another woman.'

'Okay,' I said slowly.

Michael ran a hand through his hair and it glided smoothly back into place. 'I've seen the same woman again. With your husband.'

18

Now

'Resuming the interview at 14:19. Have you had sufficient time to consult with your solicitor?'

'Thank you. My client would like me to read a prepared statement to you on her behalf about the knife. I'll read it into the record. *The knife in question is a fishing knife that belongs to my husband, Russell. I have in the past had cause to handle the knife which is usually kept at home and I can confirm that my fingerprints are likely to be on it.*'

Peter puts the paper on the desk for the officers to peer at. Omer picks it up and studies it further before smiling at me.

'Thank you, Ms Mahoney. That's very helpful. So, following on from this prepared statement, we do have a few questions for you. Firstly, you say that the knife is kept at home. Can you tell us how it ended up at the scene of the murder on the roof of 55 Broadway?'

Peter gives me a neutral look that I can't read. If it's dangerous to answer, I expect him to say so but he keeps silent. 'Russell took the knife with him on a fishing trip,' I say. 'He'd left his bag at the office when he got back. The knife would have been in there.'

'And Michael must have taken it?'

'Yes.'

'Are you sure?'

I hesitate. 'No. Yes. Look, I don't know for sure. But I assume so.'

Peter rapid-clicks his pen on and off. He seems to be heading to a crux. He wants to interrupt but he's calculating that damage against the damage of not interrupting.

'Remember you can say *no comment* to whatever questions you like,' he says – more to them than me. He won't meet my eye.

'So just to summarise this part. You go to the office to see if your husband has returned from his fishing trip?'

I nod.

'We really need to hear the answers for the tape.' Omer smiles blandly when he says this.

'Sorry. Yes.'

'Why couldn't you call him or wait for him to come home?'

'Because,' I say and then slap my hands on the desk. I take a breath and try to compose myself. 'Because as I said, he wasn't talking to me. I didn't know when he'd be back.'

Omer makes a small note on a sheet of paper. 'But he was back. You turned up at his office and he was back. Luckily.'

'Luckily? I don't know what you mean by that.'

'Okay then, coincidentally. He happened to be back. When you went there.'

'Yes.'

'But you didn't know he'd be back.'

'No. But I knew he was due to be back around then.'

'How?'

'He had to come back eventually,' I said, raising my voice.

'So back to my question. Why didn't you just wait for him to turn up at home?'

'Because I wasn't sure he'd come home.'

'Why is that?' Metcalf asks.

'No comment. I've told you already. I'm not going over it again.'

Omer raises his hand a touch to indicate that he will take the next question. 'Then this Michael. Why was he there at the office?'

'You'll have to ask him.'

'We will if we ever find him. But until then what's your explanation for him being there?'

'I don't know for sure. The thing you have to understand about Michael is that he would just turn up wherever I was. I never arranged it. I never knew it would happen or when it would happen. I'd be somewhere – crossing a road, buying lunch – and he'd be there.'

'He was following you?'

'No. At least he assured me he wasn't following me. He said we were *entangled*. That our fates were intertwined.'

Peter looks at me, his brow concertinaed into a frown. He is warning me in a way that won't be picked up on the audio.

'I'm not understanding,' says Metcalf. 'You told us he was investigating corruption or something.'

'He was. That's what he told me – later. But it was the fates, for want of a better word, that were putting us in each other's paths.'

'That's what he told you?'

'Yes.'

'And you believed him?'

'Yes.' I look between them and see them exchanging looks. Even Peter has buried his eyes under a saluted hand. 'Look, I know it sounds mad. But when he explained it to me, it sounded less mad. It sounded – plausible. And the more he spoke about it, the more it just sounded like a fact. It was just how life arranged itself.'

'Then explain it to us,' said Omer. 'The way he explained it to you.'

'If you want to,' Metcalf says, smirking. 'I mean, in the next few hours, once this interview is over, we have to decide about charging you. So. Up to you if you think you have anything to say that could help us decide that.'

I open my mouth to say something but he interrupts me. 'I mean you've said you think there was corruption. But you still haven't said what that was.'

19

Then

I alighted at the next stop just as the sky, bloated with rain, burst. I changed for a train going in the other direction. By 9.30 p.m. or so I was home, pulling off my damp boots in the hallway. Russell was not there. I made some tea and threw on the shawl that I kept on the kitchen sofa. The smell of damp from my clothes hung heavy in the air.

I asked the device to play Hans Zimmer. Gothic strings mingled with wild drums and horns. The music seeped into my body until I could feel the cells untangling.

Michael had seemed plausible even if what he was saying was crazy. I mean I didn't believe in his fated connections, but *he* seemed to.

I tried now, in the security of my house, *home*, to shake him free. But he'd already inveigled himself into my head. When my thoughts became intrusive, I had to deal with them immediately, before they became embedded. My mind could bend and twist my sanity if I let it. I needed distraction. I rooted around the cupboards under the sink for Russell's bag of tools. In the black-and-yellow rigid canvas bag I dug around until, under the hammers and spanners, I found what I was looking for.

The track ended and seamlessly merged into Faithless – 'Insomnia'. The words pounded over the bass: *I can't get no sleep*.

I took the tool over to the countertop and felt for the nub of marble. It was there still, like a raised scar. I passed the metal file from one to the other hand to get used to its weight. Russell had used it once for filing down the end of a metal bolt when the summer had made the wood swell and stopped a lock from fitting.

I levelled the file against the stone and rubbed. The steel grumbled briefly against the granite before slipping off and crushing my fingers between the handle and the top. I shook off the pain and tried again and this time got more purchase. Back and forth I went passing the tool over the surface, harder and harder. After a minute I stopped to examine the results with the tip of my finger. The nub was still there – scratched but essentially whole. I went back at it, using more force, and continued for some minutes. But when I examined the surface again, there was no change. I wasn't making a dent. I screamed under my breath and just about held myself back from flinging the thing out of the window.

By the time I went to bed at past midnight, Russell was still not back. What was he doing? What stopped him from letting me know he was going to be late? I didn't need to hear any excuses; just the information would have been enough. After Michael and everything he had said to me, I worried that something might happen to Russell. I thought about this man, Jon – now dead.

Over the years Russell had spread to fill all the spaces in my mind. When he wasn't physically with me, I felt desolate and cut off from the world, so having him in my head made me feel *held*. I thought he felt the same about me, but I was beginning to doubt it.

I slept on and off, some part of my brain leaving a channel open for the sound of his steps in the house. Then somewhere deep into the night, I heard the door go and my eyes snapped open. Footsteps. Bathroom. More steps. In the bedroom now. Undressing. Then a heavy, slow wave of movement as he folded himself into bed. I caught the sickly scent of vanilla but overlaid this time with his usual peppery perfume.

Kate had said it could be a new aftershave and maybe it was. But there was no new bottle on the dresser.

In the morning, Russell woke early and moved around lightly as if keen not to wake me. He'd never been this quiet. If he woke first, he'd go and make a pot of coffee and we would unfurl together sip by sip. But today, it was as if he was escaping. I checked the time on my phone when he was in the bathroom and saw that it was just after six. Why was he up so early? When he returned from the shower, I turned in the bed and waited as he dressed. He left and soon after I heard the door thunk. He'd gone without breakfast.

I went through his drawers again to see if there was something I had missed and then checked under the bed. And then deep into the centre, with a jolt, I saw a small black shape. I lay flat against the floor and reached as far as I could. My fingertips caressed plastic which was just out of grasp. I took an empty hanger from the wardrobe and swiped under the bed until it came sliding out. It was a phone. A small, new, but cheap phone. My pulse flickered as I switched it on. It blazed into life before asking for a passcode. I stared at it. There were numbers that were meaningful to him and I tried every combination until the handset locked. Why did he have what could only be described as a burner phone?

I dressed and went to the kitchen. My nerves thrummed but I forced myself to sit at the counter, waiting for the kettle to boil. New scratches on the white surface seemed to vibrate in the early light, deep and ugly. I turned away. I didn't want to drink my coffee here. I threw on my denim jacket and grabbed my keys to leave. But then as I did, I remembered that this was the jacket in which I had put the stray blonde hair. I teased it out of the top pocket and dropped it carefully onto the granite into a shaft of low sunlight coming through the roof light. When he returned, he'd see it. And if it meant something more than a stray hair, I was sure he'd get rid of it. I wondered who the hair belonged to. Was it the same woman who had been with Jon? Was that what the phone was for – to communicate secretly with her?

At a café near work I ordered coffee and did my best to shutter the low rumble of conversation at the tables. I closed my eyes to ease the pounding in my head. After a minute my phone rang.

'Mam.'

'Thank God for you,' she said, her voice brittle.

'What are you on about?'

'You're not dead then? I had visions of you lying dead under a car or something.'

'No, Mam. Alive and well. Are you okay?'

'Grand. I'm grand. How are you and how's that husband of yours?'

The chasm that lay between her Russell and mine gaped. For a moment I considered just telling her exactly how it was. That he was coming home late and leaving early. That I believed he was seeing someone else, and that he might be in danger somehow. But most of all, since she'd asked how I felt, I wanted to tell her that I was being held together by two silk threads.

'Fine, Mam,' I said eventually. A tear threatened my eye. 'I'm fine. Russell too.'

'Good.' And then after a beat she said avidly, 'Oh, you know you were asking me, the other week here, about seeing people?'

'Yes,' I said slowly.

'And you asked me if that had ever happened to me. Well I had a think about that. I think there was a time. It wasn't anything concrete – it was more a feeling.'

'What kind of feeling?' I said, tensing.

'Like I was being watched out for.'

My heart suddenly started to skitter. 'What do you mean, Mam?'

'Oh, nothing, love, I'm sorry to even mention it. It was that time though when I first got all the visions. It was mixed up in all that and the voices.' The line crackled at the end of her sentence.

'No, Mam. Not the voices. This is new. You've never said anything about this before. What was this feeling like you were being watched over?' I said, trying to keep her on track as the memory of her time in the hospital came back to me.

'Oh, I don't know. It sounds silly now. Never mind it.'

'Mam!' I said, my voice tightening.

'Okay,' she said, wheezing. 'It was – well do you remember when I was in hospital, down in Southampton?'

'Yes. I remember.' She'd been sectioned after a manic episode.

'It was then. When I was there in Southampton, that's when I saw him.'

'Him, who?' I said, holding my breath.

'He never told me his name. But he was beautiful so he was,' she said, trailing off.

'You have never ever told me about this,' I said. 'Who was he? Did he just turn up at hospital? What did he say to you?' The low murmur of early diners began to get louder. Raucous shouts from the back. Laughter over the top of it. I held the phone tight to my ear, the glass pressed right up against my face.

'No, dear, he didn't say anything. I mean I was in no state to even hear him speak with all them medicines they were giving me. Anyway, that was all it was,' she said breezily, and I could tell from her tone that she was preparing to put the phone down.

'Wait, Mam.'

'Yes?'

'What did he look like? Can you tell me that at least?' It seemed important to know this.

'What did who look like?' she said, being lured away again by confusion.

'The man,' I said. 'The beautiful man you were just telling me about. In the hospital.'

'No, dear,' she said, recovering the thread again. 'There was no man. He wasn't a man.'

Now it felt as if I had lost the reel from which the conversation had unwound. 'You're confusing me, Mam. What do you mean he wasn't a man?'

I didn't know what I expected her to say in the gap before she said what she said. But it wasn't what she did say.

'He was an angel, love. A guardian angel.'

20

Then

I spent some of the lunch hour in a small conference room on the phone to the GP. I didn't know whether Mum was getting worse. Was this something to worry about on top of everything else? The doctor told me in a soothing Kildare accent that she'd keep an eye on her and promised to pay her a home visit in the next few days to check on her. I wanted to go myself but the idea of going there in the strung-out state that I was in at the moment didn't seem like a good one.

I returned to my desk for the rest of the afternoon. Alice was in her usual pose – curled up in her swivel chair. She squeaked as she read through some case law.

'Do you have my car?'

'What?' I said before remembering. I scrabbled through my bag in search of it until my fingers touched hard metal. 'Sorry, I must have left it at home. I've just been dealing with a lot right now.'

She unfurled and padded over in her stockinged feet and then stood a couple of feet away from me. 'Do you want to talk about it?'

'No, it's nothing serious. Just Mum. She's not that well.' I felt tears gathering but didn't have the energy to be fussed over by Alice. I made an excuse and left the room. Before I knew it, I was heading down to the ground floor and out of the building.

With irritation I realised I'd left my bag and keys at my desk so I couldn't go home. Instead I jumped on a bus and headed to Trafalgar Square for the National Gallery to clear my head.

I paid for the exhibition of Artemisia with my phone. A large, graphic canvas in sumptuous blood-like velvet and lit with swathes of gold caught my attention. I stared at it. *Judith Slaying Holofernes*. I remembered this from school. Artemisia. The only woman from that era painting pictures like these. The image was shocking even now. Two women in the act of driving a sword through a man's jugular.

But I found it calming. The two women seemed so rational – bored almost. As if they were putting out the rubbish. A job to be disliked but found to be necessary.

'I like it better than the Caravaggio.' The voice made me jump. I recognised it.

I looked around and saw him there, arms folded – his brow crushed in a frown. 'I told you it would keep happening,' he said with his palms up. He moved to stand in front of me.

I circled quickly away from him and made for the exit. 'Leave me alone.'

He took my elbow and spun me round. 'I'm not following you. Look,' he said and fished out a paper ticket and flapped it at me. 'I bought this weeks ago.'

I stared at the ticket and couldn't fathom it. I didn't understand. It wasn't possible.

He smiled, seeming to read my thoughts. 'I know. It seems improbable. But then probability is strange.' He sat down on a bench. 'Do you know the birthday paradox?'

I said nothing. The way out was straight down the steps. There were security guards at the entrance to each room. He continued talking.

'The birthday paradox. Take a roomful of people – what are the chances that two people will have the same birthday? Logically the answer is one in 366 if you include the leap year. But using probability theory, if you had just seventy people in a room – *seventy* – the probability of two people sharing a birthday is 99.9 per cent.'

He sat back, as if whatever he had said was an answer to something I had asked.

'I think I'll go now,' I said.

He stood too but continued. 'Some things that look and feel like coincidences really aren't. They fall squarely within a probability paradigm. But this,' he said, standing in front of me, 'isn't within a factor of probability that's explicable mathematically. We keep meeting. It's not coincidence. It's something else.'

I looked at him carefully. Whatever he was saying, he believed it. 'So, I'm supposed to accept you're not following me? That you're here because of something to do with you seeing my husband with some woman you saw before?' My voice hissed in the velvet hush of the gallery.

'All I know is that it's true. I have no reason to follow you. But now that we have met it's obvious that we are supposed to. It has something to do with that woman and your husband. I can't see any other connection. And if I'm right about the processes that govern our decision-making or apparent decision-making, then we are heading for some kind of catastrophe.'

'Why do you care?' I said, suddenly flaring.

'I don't. Believe me. But it's happening right in front of me and I can't escape it. Jon was killed. One minute he was crossing the road and the next he was knocked down by a passing motorbike. The rider's helmet smashed through his face.'

I turned to walk away. I'd heard enough but he held me back by the elbow. 'I saw it happen,' he said. 'With my own eyes.'

21

Now

'Processes for decision-making? What did he mean by that?' Omer shows no hint of slowing down or veering off-track. It feels innocuous, what he is doing. He moves slowly across the ground but he is a tank. Everything under the track is being ground into dust.

'He meant that there's no freedom – to choose. Everything is inevitable. We are cause and effect.'

Metcalf lets out a laugh that ends in a bark.

'Doesn't matter whether you believe it. It's true,' I push. 'Everything is cause and effect. Every one of the billions of stars and planets – every single one is just cause and effect. They exist in their current states because of the things that happened beforehand. Do you think you're immune from cause and effect, but whole galaxies aren't?'

Metcalf bristles. 'If you're saying I can't choose for myself, then you're mistaken.' His arms fold, one over the other and he stretches out his legs.

'However you want it, Detective. I'm not trying to convince you. But think about it. Don't you do what you do, because of who you are? And isn't *who* you are because of *how* you are inside? Or what happened to you from outside? You do what *life* programmed you to do. Me too. Everyone does. We don't choose. We just react in the only way we can, given who we are.'

Omer smiles. He seems impressed. 'Can we maybe get off the metaphysical stuff and stick to the nuts and bolts?'

Metcalf leans across the table and sweeps the files and pens straight onto the floor. Peter shifts in alarm. 'Like that. I chose to do that.'

The room stops. For a moment it appears as though everyone is caught in a glare of light.

'You *think* you chose it. That is all it is,' I say, recovering from what he's done, uncertain whether he's proved or disproved what I've said.

Peter coughs. 'I think it might be a good time for us all to have a break.'

The tapes are stopped and within moments we are back in the room we were in earlier.

'What are you doing?' he says after shutting the door.

'I don't know what you mean.'

'All this free-will bollocks? We are in a murder interview and you're giving them all this crap about how we don't make choices?'

I take a breath. It's been hours. My eyes are heavy. My head hurts. What I want more than anything in the world is to be home in my bed, asleep. 'It's real, Peter. Whether you want to believe it or not. It is real.'

'No,' he says. 'I'm not interested.'

'What choices have you ever made that weren't triggered by another one? You came here. Because of something that I did. You had a fag on your way in because of the fag you had before that which increased the addiction. And because of the one you had, you'll have the next one. Everything is presupposed by something else. Name one thing that you chose independently of everything else.'

He looks ready to blow but I see how he is controlling his breathing so that I am not subjected to it. 'You don't get it, Layla. You think you're saying something clever about free will. You're not. All you're saying is that you killed her but it wasn't your fault.'

A wave of heat comes from nowhere into my face. 'That is not what I said.'

'No. Not in words. But it might as well have been.'

The room tingles like the aftermath of a crash. There is a whine in my ears and I stop so that it can dissipate. But it won't. It lingers until it makes itself clear. It's my mind coming to the sickening realisation that he's right. All I am trying to do is to tell them what happened and what Michael was saying to me. And then I consider it again. Has he been spiking me all along? Did Michael know I'd say this and in saying it, that I'd sign my own death warrant?

'Peter, it wasn't me.'

'Then, Layla, you have to stop acting as if it could have been.'

I push off from my seat and pace around the room, my arms flapping. 'All I'm doing. All I'm trying to do is to tell the truth here. Michael. Michael Cruz murdered her and they're doing nothing to find him.'

Peter rubbed the stubble on his chin. 'Well, you can hardly blame them when you haven't given them very much to help locate him.'

I throw my hands up to my head. 'I can't give what I don't have!'

He takes a breath and lets it out slowly. 'If we can't give them a candidate, we have to give them something to prove it wasn't you. And in case I haven't made this clear enough, Layla, there's a charging decision coming. And if they decide to charge you, that's it. We're done. We can't turn back the clock.'

The things I have to do once I leave here are mounting. And I have to speak to Russell, face to face. I can't stay here. I can't. 'But I can be bailed if they do charge me, right?'

'What? Tonight? Okay, this really is my fault and I feel like I haven't explained it to you at all. If Bin Laden was sitting where you are and the CIA were questioning him, he'd have more chance of being bailed. Look at me.'

I raise my eyes to meet his, my heart beating out the seconds.

'If they charge you, you won't see home. Again. Ever.'

I feel as though I have fallen down a sheer cliff. 'What shall I do, Peter? Help me.'

'Tell them. Tell them about the corruption you suspected.'

22

Then

On Sunday it wasn't until we were in the car heading for our session with Nikki that I remembered that I hadn't done the 'homework'. So now, as Russell drove, I tried to come up with examples of communication 'corridors' that were blocked, but I couldn't think straight. The events of Tuesday were still turning in my mind.

After seeing Michael at the gallery, I'd run out and quickly stumbled down the steps, my head spinning. But the fresh air swept my skin as soon as I hit the bottom step and again, in the bright light of day, I wondered if he could really have been there. People didn't just turn up like that speaking about hit men on motorbikes and probability theory – looking like he did, polished by the sun, teeth like pearls.

And as I left I'd turned for a last look at the steps sweeping up the building like a conductor's arm. He was putting on his sunglasses and came skipping down. My heart scurried as I circled round to the plinth on the left of the square and melted into the crowd. He crossed Trafalgar Square and headed towards Charing Cross. I took a deep breath and followed. There were so many people in this part of London, it would be easy to disappear.

At the mouth of Charing Cross Station, he entered without a backwards glance. I put my head down and carried on, pushing forward, resisting the urge to turn back. At one point, right in the middle of the concourse, he stopped and spun around as if sensing me watching. I hid quickly in the doorway of a station shop, and watched. He checked his watch then ordered a coffee and carried it to a wobbly aluminium table. He steadied it with a fold of paper or card under the leg and then sat before dialling a number he appeared to be reading off another small card. I couldn't catch what he was saying but he seemed suddenly grave. A second later he'd drained his coffee and was hastening towards the barriers.

'Wait,' I called out, running.

He turned back towards me, smiling. I did what I could to control my heartbeat. 'What did you want to tell me? Why did you follow me in there?'

He put his hands on his hips and stared up at the void. 'I keep telling you. I'm not following you. But what you have to realise is that it's not an accident. We're being brought together to make a change happen. I didn't act quickly enough with Jon. And I'm terrified that if I miss my chance with you, someone else is going to die. Maybe one of us. Maybe Russell.'

Commuters washed around us as if we were rocks in a river. Something wasn't right and for a second, I couldn't put my finger on it. And then I did.

'I never told you his name,' I said.

He sighed. 'Okay. I think I should go,' he said.

'Wait,' I said, holding him back. 'I'm trying. But I don't know what you're saying. Not really. It all sounds like voodoo to me.'

He stared for a second and then smiled. 'Trust me, I know. It *is* voodoo. Einstein talked about something called *quantum entanglement* as "spooky action at a distance". He discovered that if you observed one particle here, then another entangled particle, even light years away, would instantly change its properties. As if they were connected by a mysterious communication channel. It doesn't make sense. But it's true. Not just true – it's a scientific, provable fact. We are connected. Something in your world and my world and your husband's world is affecting the others. And on it goes down a chain. We have to find out what it is.'

'Or what?' I said, my head fizzing with this.

'I don't know. Someone dies. Or many people die. All I can tell you is that on my best hypothesis, it has to do with my company and your husband. Has he got anything to do with the chemical industry?'

'No.' Russell had never mentioned chemicals – not once. 'And if it is to do with him, then why are you and I the ones who are so –' I groped around for the word, 'entangled?'

'Maybe because I can't get him to do what needs to be done. But you can.'

'Which is what?'

'Until we know how he and I are connected, I don't know. You'll have to do some digging,' he said before he checked his watch again. 'I have to catch this train,' he said, and ran.

Once his train had vanished down the line, I circled back to the little table where he'd sat. Lying on the surface was a small white card, *e-Vinculum* it said, and underneath in small letters was the word *Industry* and under that in even smaller letters, *Chemicals, Polymers, Gas, Oil and Markets*. There were no other details. On the other side was a telephone number scrawled in biro. I put it into my pocket and was getting ready to go when I saw a sleeve of white under the table leg. I stooped to collect it. It was the entrance ticket to the gallery. I was about to throw it away when I remembered and checked. With a pang I saw there was no date on it at all. Just the name of the exhibition. He could have bought this after seeing me go in. Not weeks ago, as he'd said.

When I'd returned home, Russell wasn't there. But he'd been home. His water bottle and trainers weren't there so I guessed that he'd gone to the gym. There was a coffee mug on the counter – still warm.

The hair I'd left on the counter had gone.

When he came back from the gym, we hardly spoke. The missing hair stretched taut between us. I didn't know what to do to touch him. He was there in the room, skin still golden, just an arm's length away, physically, but in every other way he was in another dimension. What could I say to him about a missing hair? It was too tenuous to come between us. But if he was in danger – real danger – I had to find a way to reach him and get him to talk to me.

And now we were on our way to another session. An ambulance siren shattered whatever peace there was in the car until it wailed into the dispersed traffic. I glanced at him. He looked worn out. Whatever he was doing was ruining him too. I blinked and I was back in the counselling session.

Nikki was dressed completely in different shades of grey as if the threat of colour was an insult.

We spent a few minutes talking about how the last week had gone (Me: *Not good – Russell was back late every night.* Him: *Am I not supposed to work now?*). We hadn't done the homework. She explained that she wasn't there to grade us but to give us a chance to make our own breakthroughs. I could have set her on fire.

'Why don't you tell Russell how the last week has been for you?' she said, straightening her dress before gazing at me with round eyes.

'I don't know,' I said. 'It's been lonely.' I felt like I was watching him as a speck on a distant shore as I sank beneath a gluey sea. 'He hasn't been back before midnight any night this week. I worry about him.'

She looked at me in a way that made me long for a normal human reaction. 'Do you worry about him or is it suspicion we are talking about here?'

Russell laughed. 'I've been working.' He turned from me to Nikki. 'There's a kind of emergency on at work. The PM's Office and the whole Cabinet Office have been called in to try and get a load of transitional legislation in place to deal with a Brexit issue at the EA.'

'And does the PM specifically ask you not to call your wife?' I asked.

He reddened. 'If they say there's an emergency and it involves all twenty-two departments, then it's an emergency.'

Nikki looked at me. 'Is there space in your perspective to accept this explanation?'

Although I was staring at the floor I could feel her eyes hooking into me. I waited until I heard her cough.

'There was a time once he had me come to meet him after work at his office. They have a roof garden that they hardly use. He took me there and gave me champagne in a coffee cup. And we watched the birds gathering in the sky. And we were happy. *He* was happy.'

I remembered the building now. The stone reliefs by different artists – the winds, North, East, South and West, blowing beautifully between windows. But it was the statues, Day and Night, I loved best.

And the legend that surrounded them. How the artist had to cut away an inch and a half of stone penis from the statue to cool the public outrage at it.

Nikki looked up as if she'd missed everything I had just said and turned to Russell for a cue. He looked sad.

She turned to say something to me when I felt a swell of anger. 'He's got a secret phone for God's sake.' I blurted it out just like that. They stared at me as if I'd gone crazy.

In the living room, later that evening, Russell put his laptop on the carpet and finally spoke to me. 'Layla, I promise you that I am not having an affair. I'm not that kind of person.'

I blinked, surprised at the directness of it. 'You mean me. That I'm the kind of person who does that.'

He hesitated. 'Maybe I do mean that. I've given you no reason to doubt me, despite everything.'

'Just say it. Just say the ugly words. You never say it. I had sex with another man. I did. I hate that I did. But it was one time. You have to forgive me for it now. Or there's no point in this.' I wanted him, more than anything else, to see that one fact. That we could recover if only he'd let us.

'Is that what you want?' he said. 'I don't think it is. I think what you want is the opposite of that. You want me to keep punishing you. Again and again.'

'What?'

'That's what this is about, isn't it? All the accusations about the late nights, the hairs and now, what, a secret phone? You're pushing me away, because you hate yourself. I get it. It was a one-off. A drunken mistake with a work colleague. But you need to forgive *yourself* and not sabotage us.'

I didn't know who he'd become. 'No. I want you to be honest about what you're up to. And – wait –' I said, holding him off. 'If it's nothing, then I want to understand why you have a burner phone under your bed and why a complete stranger is warning –' My voice cracked.

His eyes widened. 'What? What complete stranger?'

I took a breath. I wasn't sure enough about Michael or what he was saying to tell Russell about it. 'Nothing.'

'Come with me,' he said, getting up and taking my hand. The warmth of his touch ran all the way up my arms so I was reminded of Russell from years ago. He led me carefully into the bedroom and stood by one side of the bed. 'Under here?'

I nodded but I already knew what was coming. He bent his knees and grasped the edge of the bed with two hands and raised it to waist height. I peered under. Dust hung like stalactites from the underside. But no phone – only the wire coat hanger and the marks I had made in the dust. I couldn't have imagined it.

And now I wished desperately he hadn't done that.

By doing it, he'd pulled the boards from under my feet so that I no longer even had the certainty of my own ground.

From the street below, a car revved its engine in anger and I went and looked out to see a small hatchback surrounded by teenagers. Steam billowed from the exhaust.

I climbed into bed and curled up. Russell got in next to me and stroked my hair. With my eyes closed I could be anywhere – not just in space but in time. So back I went into childhood and back further still until I was just a flicker of a golden heartbeat in a womb.

And then the scent of vanilla came floating up from his pillow and I was suspended again from silk threads. I couldn't bear to look at what would be racing up to meet me from the ground when they snapped – either destruction or worse, a wretched, broken survival.

23

Now

'We are resuming this interview. The time by my watch is 16:23. Present are myself DC Omer Smith; DC Metcalf; Peter Kelly, solicitor; and Layla Mahoney. You're still under caution. So, Layla, have you had the time you need? If you do need to stop the interview again for a consultation, just let us know. Is there anything you'd like to add before we start with our questions?'

Peter leans forward and steeples his arms. 'We'd like to reiterate that we are concerned about your lack of ability to trace Michael Cruz, given the assistance Layla has offered with his description and his employment and his number. And we'd also like to make the point that it was my client who called the police to the scene.'

Omer is nodding throughout this. 'Yes. So, we're still completing our investigations re Michael Cruz. So far, we haven't turned up any footprint at his employer's – *e-Vinculum* Ltd. He's certainly not on their permanent staff. We'll find out later today, hopefully, whether he's a subcontractor of some kind. The number you gave us was from a pay-as-you-go SIM. There are no details registered to it and it's no longer in use.'

Peter makes a note in his pad. I lean over to read it. He's scribbled the words 'Burner phone'.

'So, moving on to the 999 call. We're just going to play you it now.'

The other detective, Metcalf, presses a key on a laptop and the sound arrives, loud and urgent, adding drama to a room that doesn't need it.

Emergency. Which service?

Ambulance. Come quickly. There's so much blood.

Where are you?

There's blood all over. Oh my God, she's not breathing –

Madam, you have to stay calm. Listen to me. Listen to me. Where are you? I will send an ambulance but to do that I need to know where you are.

Oh oh. What is it? The EA building. 55. 55 Broadway. London. I'm on the roof terrace.

There is a burst of static and it is that that plunges me straight back to the exact moment that is playing out in front of us. I know what took place. But in this room, I'm the only one who knows how it all happened. Peter has his eyes shut and is concentrating on every screamed word of mine colliding with the calm of the operator.

Okay, help is on its way. I have your number here ending 283. Is that the number you're calling from?

Yes. That's it.

Is it someone with you who needs the help? Tell me what's happened.

A woman. Oh my God, I think she's dead. I think she's dead. Come quickly. Leave now.

Madam, is the person breathing?

What? Er no. I think she's – wait, no, she's not breathing. I don't think she's breathing. You have to help me.

Put your ear to her mouth if you can. Tell me if she's breathing.

I can't tell. I can't tell.

Can you check for a pulse?

There is a pause.

Can you just check for a pulse for me please?

Then my voice finds its footing again. *I can't find . . . Oh my God, I think she's dead. There's a . . . a . . . a knife in her chest.*

Okay. We've sent an ambulance. I want you to wait with the injured person till help arrives. Stay on the line. You said there's a knife in her chest?

Yes.

Listen to me, madam. Do not touch the knife. It could be holding the wound closed. If you move it, it could cause more damage.

Oh my God. She's bleeding all over me. It's on my hands.

You're doing really well. Anyone there with you yet?

No. Oh wait. Yes, they're here. Someone's here . . .

The silence is brittle, bathed in static. For a second nobody moves until the recording is switched off. The two police officers shift in their seats. Peter's face though is washed in relief.

'Well, it's obvious she was reacting genuinely to what was happening. To me at any rate. You can't be saying that was manufactured emotion?'

Omer's face remains set. He blinks slowly as if nothing surprising has happened. 'So, we understand, of course, that it must have been a distressing experience. Whether you were responsible or not. Believe me. We see this all the time. Husbands kill wives. Wives kill husbands. It's always a shock to the system.'

Peter huffs as if it's a tiresome, petty point that Omer is scoring. 'But this isn't husband and wife, is it?' he says.

But Omer isn't interested in points. He's after something else.

'The operator in the 999 call advised you clearly not to touch the knife. Did you hear that on the recording?'

'Yes, I did.'

'Did you remember her saying that to you at the time?'

'Yes.'

'And did you touch the knife?' he asks slowly. His pen is poised as if the ink of whatever I say will dry indelibly.

'No.' And then I remember. 'I mean, as I said before in my prepared statement, I did handle the knife earlier. At home.'

'Okay, but not on that day?'

'No.'

'And you say that Michael was the one who stabbed her with it?'

I look across at Peter. How many times was he allowed to ask the same question? 'Yes.'

'Was there anything unusual about the way he used the knife?'

'No. I don't think so. What do you mean?'

Metcalf rustled a stapled document he was holding. 'Well, the thing is we've had the lab results back on the knife. Just a short-form report.'

'And?' says Peter. 'Don't you think you should have given us the heads-up about that before resuming the interview?'

'We didn't feel the need, since your prepared statement admitted that Ms Mahoney's prints would be on the weapon.'

'So, what's the issue?' Peter presses.

'The issue is that there weren't any prints on the knife.'

The words hang in the thick air of the small dark room. Peter seems disturbed by the news but I can't understand why.

'I'm sorry, Detective. Why is that – *significant*?' I ask. 'I didn't touch it that day so of course my prints won't be on it. Or might not be.'

Omer shifts in his seat and pinches the bridge of his nose under his glasses. 'Because there were no prints on it at all. They'd been wiped off. The knife was clean.'

Peter wipes his face with his hand, releasing some eau de cologne into the air. He holds up a hand to ward me away from any further comment.

But I can't see the problem here. Peter has obviously not understood what I am saying. 'He obviously wiped the knife clean. I mean he would, wouldn't he? To avoid getting his prints on it.'

The silence is a blanket.

'While it was in her chest?' Omer asks quietly. 'Are you saying he wiped the handle after he stabbed her. While it was still in her chest?'

The air is stale and heavy. All eyes are on me, waiting. 'No,' I say. 'I don't think that happened.'

'Then how?'

I think I can tell them. I first have to ask whether there's anything to lose. Then whether answering causes more danger or less. That's what I have to do with each question but the effort of this measuring has become so exhausting. Each answer, like Russian roulette.

They are still looking at me, waiting.

I spin the barrel and pull the trigger.

24

Then

Morning.

Russell left early again. The sun had barely licked the horizon and he was up and out of the door. Later, as I waded through the bedroom getting ready, I considered the paucity of Russell's traces these days. Nothing was left out. His night clothes were all hidden away. Everything was in its place, out of view. He'd always been like this but today the lightness of his tread stung. As if he was telling me that he could leave without a trace too.

I checked under the bed again but the phone wasn't there. Last night I'd made sure he was asleep, that there was the faintest curl of a snore on his breath and on one of those breaths I slid out from under the covers. In the hallway I found his leather satchel where he kept his laptop. I knew his password. We knew one another's passwords – we were married – how could we not? The home screen invited letters and numbers and I typed them in. The screen wobbled a refusal. I tried again. He'd changed his password.

It was something and nothing. Something he could explain and nothing that I could complain about.

Now in the kitchen the scratched countertop and I glared at one another. I touched the protruding nub and had the urge once again to scrape at it. Instead I Googled how to polish out scratches in marble and ended up hiring an orbital wet sander on a tool-hire website. It would be here on Saturday and I could spend the afternoon putting the damage right.

As I left the kitchen a clothes brush caught my eye on the small round dining table. It was one of those things that was usually left gathering dust in a drawer. But here it was now, out – brazen. I picked it up and rubbed the velvet top to tease out the fluff. Then I pulled at the bristles to drag out any hair but it was clean. But Russell must have used it and he must have had something on his clothes that needed brushing off. So where was the evidence of it and who had Russell been brushing his clothes for? He wasn't a preener. He was effortlessly handsome. Never needed to iron his shirts. *I'm damp when I come out of the shower and my body warms the creases away*, but the truth was that you didn't notice his clothes. You noticed *him*: lean, golden, cool. So, why this brush, on a Wednesday?

Though it felt exactly like the paranoia I was afraid of, I went to the sensor-activated pedal bin and waved a hand over it. At the top was a cirrus wisp of brush debris. I took it in a cupped hand to examine under the roof light. There were long hairs in with the mix of fluff which I winkled out. Gold-blonde. I tucked them carefully away into a kitchen towel and put the tissue into a pocket of my bag before I left for work. The evidence was mounting but I didn't need it as evidence. I just needed to recover some sanity.

The office had a dismal feel to it and almost as soon as I arrived, I wanted to leave. I buried my head in a case, reading what I could, until lunch crawled round. When I came back from the shops, Alice waved at me from her desk to get my attention. 'Fry was looking for you. He said three-thirty.' Her dress, forest green with panels of copper, together with flame hair gave her the look of a Klimt. She tucked her feet beneath her on the chair and swivelled as she hummed.

Then I remembered the disciplinary interview. In the mess of the last few days, I'd forgotten it was happening today. Not that it mattered now. I'd decided to fall on my sword. I had no choice. There was the dashcam recording of the client swearing and the statement that I had drafted for him, denying the swearing. And on top of that I'd admitted it to Fry and Julianne. At least the client wasn't an insurer – that was a saving grace. It was one client, one set of fees. Once I apologised, they'd give me a final written warning.

I texted Kate to ask if she might be around this evening for a drink. She replied immediately.

Can do a quick coffee at 5-ish if that's any good? So sorry can't stay. I have my sister over so – and then she added a yawning emoji.

I don't mind if Anna comes with, I replied but she brushed off that suggestion in such an odd way (*Anna isn't feeling up to coming out*) that I felt sure she was lying about it.

When 3:30 p.m. came, I called across to Alice, 'Wish me luck.'

'Luck,' she replied with a half-smile and turned back to her work. She was rocking lightly and squeaking just on the border of audibility. But then as I left the room I heard her calling after me. 'Oh, Layla. The car,' she said but she trailed off when it was clear I wasn't coming back.

The panel consisted of Julianne Cook, Mark Fry and Pritti Kumar, one of the partners I liked almost as much as Julianne. I nodded at them as I walked into the large conference room and took a seat. The balance of power in the room was reassuring. Fry was the odd one out, the rest of us, friends or if not friends, trusted colleagues. Women. If we weren't comrades we at least were the same tribe.

'Hi. Can I just say something,' I said, as they shuffled pages. They looked up and waited. 'I want to say that I accept the allegations. And I apologise for the lack of judgment I showed. And for the damage caused to the firm's reputation.'

As I spoke I concentrated on the two women. They knew me. I worked hard. I was good at my job.

Fry looked at me from over his glasses before taking them off and pointing at me with their arms. 'This is very serious, Ms Mahoney. It's more than just the firm's reputation at stake. This is an existential crisis,' he said, his eyes bulging as he spoke.

'I'm not sure I follow,' I said slowly. 'Existential how?'

'Well, for one this is a breach of your professional code. We probably have to report you to your professional body for misconduct.'

'What?' I said, shocked. 'I'll be struck off.' I felt heat creeping up my body.

'If we didn't report you then we, each of us,' he said, pointing his glasses now at Julianne and Pritti, 'would be guilty of misconduct too. And I don't need to tell you that without partners, there's no partnership and no firm.'

I tried to catch the eyes of the two women who *knew me* but their eyes had fled. 'You can't report me. Please.' My voice, plaintive and unrecognisable.

Fry laid his dry hands flat on the table. 'Well, to be frank with you, Ms Mahoney, we are going to have to think carefully about it. Now that we have your admission we don't at least have to go through the formality of proving the breach, as it were. The only question is what we do. We'll come back to you in the next week or so, but as you can see, the easiest thing for everyone, by far, might be for us to report you to the SRA and dismiss you for gross misconduct. It's the only way the firm survives. Garden leave from tomorrow,' he said, and I watched, shell-shocked, as they filed out of the room.

25
Now

Silence is a weapon.

The detectives wait, quietly.

A beat.

'You don't have to say anything remember, Layla,' Peter says too late just as I have started to speak.

'I think he was wearing gloves,' I say. 'Maybe that's why his prints aren't on the knife.'

'In September?' Metcalf says and then splutters as something catches in his throat. He reddens at that.

'I expect that if you've determined to murder someone, you don't much care whether it's quite the weather for gloves,' I say but immediately regret the tone.

Omer writes something down and then ticks something else off on his paper. 'You know, Ms Mahoney, we haven't talked much about Russell in all of this. We've heard more about Michael than about your own husband.'

'Is that a question?' Peter asks seriously.

'You've told us that you went to the building to meet Russell, or rather to see if he was there. But when you got there he'd already left – is that it?'

'Yes,' I say, unsure where he is going with this.

'How did you know he'd left?'

'Well, when I got to his office, I opened the door and saw he wasn't there.'

'But his bag was there?'

'Yes.'

'And what you told us was that Russell had taken the bag on a fishing trip and that that must have been where Michael got the knife from?'

I run through the sequence in my head, looking for traps. 'Yes. It must have been.'

'But to be clear, Russell had gone by the time you got there?'

'Yes, I said that already,' I say, looking at Peter.

'Okay, well, we have done a search of Russell's office and the thing is, Ms Mahoney, there is no bag.'

Omer waits.

'Okay,' I say. My throat has become parched suddenly in this air-conditioned room. What the hell happened to the bag? I cough away the anxiety. If they see it matters to me, they will tighten the rope. 'And?' I say as steadily as I can.

'And – my question is – where is the bag that the knife came from?' Metcalf asks, leaning in.

I'm trying to understand this quickly. The pieces aren't falling into place properly. The bag was there when I'd been there earlier. It had to have been there when Michael got there. 'Well, if you've searched the correct office –'

'We did,' Metcalf says bluntly. There is dandruff on his jacket and it has the effect of bringing me back into the room in a mundane, solid way. 'We ordered the building to be sealed as soon as you were in custody and started the search. The search-book tells me: no bag in your husband's office.'

'Then Michael must have taken it. Find him and you'll find the bag.'

Omer slides his paper across to Metcalf who nods at whatever is written there. 'Did he have it with him when you saw him on the rooftop?'

'I don't know.'

'You never mentioned anything about him having a bag with him,' says Omer.

I hike back through my memory of what happened. 'Then he didn't.' I have to be careful now. 'Or he did but I didn't see it.'

Peter cuts across me. 'Where is this leading?'

Omer ignores the interruption and keeps his eyes glued to me. 'So then by your reckoning, he killed Amy Blahn with a knife that he took from your husband's bag, from your husband's office, and then returned to the office, what, to steal the bag?'

Peter, who has been tensing in his seat for the last few questions, finally snaps. 'That isn't a proper question, is it? You're asking her to speculate. Frankly anyone in the building could have taken that bag before your search reached that room. It's an enormous building.'

Omer takes his glasses off slowly and places them on the desk. He fiddles somewhere under the desk and brings up a small cloth and begins to wipe the lenses. 'It's not speculation exactly, is it, Mr Kelly? It's just the logical extension of what Ms Mahoney has said. I'm just making sure we've understood it correctly. Have we, Ms Mahoney? Understood?'

I take the cue for what it's worth now and mumble a reply. 'No comment.'

Peter shakes his head gently. 'It's time for a break, Detective. We've been going a while now.'

Omer checks his watch. 'Sure. But just one thing before we break. How did you know he'd left? Russell, I mean?'

The muscles in my arms begin to burn. Why do they keep asking the same questions? They are trying to trick me into an error. 'Because he wasn't in his office.'

'But you thought he would be?'

'Yes. I did.'

'They told you at reception he was in his office?'

I cast my mind back. 'I think they said he was away from his desk.'

'Not that he'd left?'

'Yes. They didn't say he'd left.'

Omer straightens his tie. 'So, given that his bag was still there, how did you know he wasn't just away from his desk?'

I stop. How did I know? And finally, the answer arrives. 'His things. He'd taken his stuff. Like, I don't know, his keys, laptop. Phone. There was no phone there.'

'It couldn't have all been in the bag?'

'I didn't look in the bag.'

'So how do you know the knife was in there?' All of these questions from Omer peppering me now.

'I didn't. I assume it must have been because how else did Michael get it?'

'Then all his things, his keys and laptop or whatever you were talking about, might have been in the bag too. If you didn't look, you couldn't know.'

'I don't know,' I say, confused by these questions that feel unconnected and sly.

'And he might still have been in the office. Maybe he'd gone to the loo? Or gone for some water?'

'No,' I say. 'He wasn't there. He'd gone.' I am conscious that my voice has become sharp.

'How do you know that?' Omer asks softly.

'Because,' I say and suddenly there are tears. They have been pooling quietly somewhere behind my eyes and now the dam has burst.

'Because what?'

'Detective, that break?' Peter says urgently.

'Because what, Ms Mahoney?'

I have to tell them but I am not sure what that will mean for me. I look for something to help focus my thoughts but all I can see now through this veil of tears is the room in blur. And then when I shut my eyes and the tears cascade, it's no longer the room that falls into view when I open them, but the rooftop. And the blood ponding over my fingers as I hold her in my arms.

'Because,' I say, wiping my eyes. 'I did look in the bag. There was no phone. No keys. Just his dirty clothes.' They all stare at me in silence. 'And his fishing knife.'

26

Then

Kate was waiting with two lattes. She half-rose, her limbs willowy, to air-kiss me on the cheek and sat down again with a furrowed glance. 'How was the disciplinary?'

'God,' I said, holding up a hand. I took two sips of coffee and waited for it to hit my bloodstream. 'They've suspended me,' I said at last.

She reached over and took my hands and the touch of her skin on mine, soothing, brought tears to my eyes. I hated crying when I what wanted most was to be composed.

'It'll be okay. And you know what, so what if they sack you? You'll get something else. You're the smartest person I know.'

I released myself from her hands. 'Thanks. I don't know if I can go through it all again. Start again from nothing. I'm so tired –' All the moving parts of my life were drifting apart and I didn't have the strength to pull them together again.

I looked at Kate, her open face gently freckled across the bridge of her nose. How removed it was from all of this. I cut myself short. 'Can we talk about something else?' I asked.

'Sure,' she said. 'Hey, I just remembered you shared your location the other day.'

'Sorry. I thought I'd seen this guy again but I was mistaken.' I didn't want to tell her about Michael. Not yet. 'How's Anna?'

'Anna? What do you mean?' She pulled a strand of hair over her ear.

Her puzzlement was genuine. I held her eyes a beat but then let her go. 'Your sister. She wasn't feeling up to a drink – is she any better?'

Realisation dawned across her face. 'Oh, sorry. Yes! What am I like? A million miles away. Yes, she's got a migraine. But you. What are we going to do about you?' she said and started rooting through her handbag absently, probably for lip balm.

'We've been seeing a counsellor,' I said. There was a crash of dropped crockery from the back of the café. A stream of laughter escaped from behind it. 'For months now.'

Kate looked at me wide-eyed and held a hand over her face for a moment. 'What? Seriously?' she said. 'Because of the affair?'

I smarted at the use of the word 'affair'. It was one time – a mistake. 'I don't know if we're going to make it,' I said and then stopped. I stared at Kate's hand. She hadn't been looking for lip balm but a tiny roll-on. 'What's that?'

'It's an essential oil,' she said, handing it over. 'Rub it on your wrists. Stress relief. Try some.'

I twisted it in my fingers as my mind raced on. I rolled the cool ball against my wrist. The scent filled my nose with a cloying sweetness. 'Vanilla,' I said. 'I never had you down as vanilla.'

I searched for any trace of discomfort in her face but there was nothing. She nodded guilelessly. My stomach turned. I endured the next few minutes of bland conversation with a smile.

Vanilla.

'I'm just going to pop to the loo. Won't be a sec,' she said brightly, after finishing her coffee, and got up taking her phone with her.

My mind tumbled darkly at the possibility. Kate and Russell? Though she was the one who had introduced us, she'd seemed almost apologetic about it. She knew him through her sister and refused to vouch for him. *I hardly know him – so it's no problem if you don't like him, Lay. He's a bit of a brat.* And over the years if they happened to be in the same room, Russell would often just leave. It couldn't all have been an elaborate act. Had they started off ignoring one another but then something sparked? Isn't that what always happened? Steel struck flint again and again until suddenly there was fire?

I saw she'd left her bag. The hum of voices that had been indistinct became now untangled strands of conversation that I could make out. The crowd became a gathering of individuals, and each one made me self-conscious about what I was about to do.

I stood up casually and pretended to check my phone, turning a few steps in each direction and back again. But when I sat down, it was in Kate's seat, in front of her open bag. I reached in and found her hairbrush. It was a round compact one with a mirror and collapsible plastic bristles on the inside. I quickly picked at the caught hairs and fumbled them into my pocket and then returned to my own seat just as she came into view.

I sat patiently through ten minutes of Kate's life-coaching. *You need to focus on what you want for yourself*, until she made her excuses and left, trailing smiles as she went.

The scent of vanilla clung to me all the way home. I couldn't shake it even though by then the smell was mainly in my head. Kate. It couldn't be Kate. She didn't like him. They weren't at all similar. He was energetic and driven whereas she was arty. He hated what he saw as all the pseudo-psychology she spouted. At home I ran straight to the bedroom and pulled away the covers to expose the pillows. I buried my face into the one on his side. The vanilla was there. I smelled my wrist. They smelled the same.

I rang Russell but it kept going straight to voicemail. I had to speak to him now about this. It couldn't wait till after midnight when he got home.

By ten, I was so exhausted by the thoughts clawing around in my head that I had to do something to shut them down. I took a bottle of cognac to the bedroom, my head drenched in thought. *Kate and Russell. Why didn't I see it?* The floor beneath me began to shift. I sat on the bed to stop the room from moving and when it finally did I climbed in and unscrewed the bottle and drank mouthfuls before lying back against the mustard velvet headboard.

I covered my eyes against the light that was suddenly everywhere. My thoughts crackled until the noise made me numb.

When he finally made it home, I was asleep. I managed a bleary attempt at consciousness when he walked in but I was too thick with alcohol to force myself awake. Instead I just lay there on the fringes of sleep, aware that he had picked up the bottle. He smoothed the covers over me and crawled into bed. I fell almost immediately back into a jagged, black sleep.

In the morning he escaped before I could talk to him. In the folds of sleep, I'd resolved to confront him, before it drove me completely mad. But he'd gone and I was left there in bed, staring at the ceiling long after he'd slammed the front door. When I finally emerged from bed, I was still raw from the booze.

I dressed and went into the kitchen to force down some toast. The scarred countertop stared back at me. The nub was protruding still from the scratches, a bluff in a stormy sea. I couldn't wait for the sander so dug out Russell's tool bag again. I found a chisel and a hammer and took it to the counter. Carefully angling the chisel against the slub of rock, I struck it hard with the hammer. At first it simply slid over but then when I hit it again, it caught and the tip embedded minutely in the stone. I struck it again, hard. The nub splintered into the air. I looked down at the top. The blow seemed to have pulled away a whole seam of stone with it so now there was a deep gouge in the Italian marble. *Shit.*

I put the tools away and covered the crevasse with some books so I wouldn't have to look at it.

I swiped my keys from the table and paused. In the course of the night – in the tumbling uncertainty of it – something did crystallise. I had to find Michael. Michael knew something. He *was* following me.

As I walked to the front gate I noticed something glittering just on the other side of it. I stooped to pick it up. It was a thin silver chain. It could have been dropped by anyone, I knew that. But there was something indecent about it being there on my paving stones first thing in the morning. There was nothing distinctive about it. If you lost one of these, you wouldn't be able to say it was yours with any certainty. I placed it carefully on the front doorstep. It could be mine, for all he knew. There'd be no reason for Russell not to return it to me or leave it somewhere for me to see.

If he was innocent.

27

Now

'Just to be clear on this. You saw the fishing knife in Russell's bag but you didn't touch it?' Metcalf is rigid with excitement.

'That's right,' I say slowly. I can't avoid this admission because it's the only way that I can convince them that what I am saying is true.

There is a pause and for now they seem satisfied by this. 'Okay. I see. I'd like to just ask you a few questions about what's going on in your life right now,' Omer says solemnly.

'How is this relevant?' Peter cuts across, but there is no commitment to his own objection. He seems worn out.

'We're just exploring motive,' Omer says. 'It's up to you, Ms Mahoney, if you want to answer.'

I nod and for once I'm not asked to make my consent audible.

'You'd lost your job recently?' Metcalf says, looking at a sheet of paper.

'I was suspended.'

'How were you feeling, in yourself, about that?'

'I don't know what you mean,' I say.

'Were you depressed? Or angry?' Metcalf says, raising his voice too much.

'You mean did it make me want to kill a stranger on a roof?'

Peter stifles a smile and raises an eyebrow at them both as if to say *you did ask.*

Metcalf scratches his forearms, leaving traces of dust and red. Omer signals to him that he's going to take over. 'You've already told us a bit about your relationship with your husband. That you thought he might be having an affair. Did that make you angry?'

'It didn't make me happy,' I say. And I think this is true. I wasn't angry about it. The anger, if there had been any, had long since burned away.

'We've taken a statement from Russell and he doesn't seem to share your views about the marriage.' Omer asks the questions softly so that it feels like he's tossing grenades underarm as if to a child.

Russell? I don't know why I am surprised – shocked – by this. Of course they would have taken a statement from him but still the news unravels me. I blink the shock away. 'You mean he doesn't agree he was having an affair? I could have saved you the trouble, Officer, and told you that myself. He was denying it. Always denying it – that was the problem.'

'Then what made you think he was having an affair?'

'Is this important?' Peter asks. His hands are in tight fists.

'According to your client it's the reason she went to his workplace. To confront him. Wasn't it?'

'Not exactly,' I say.

'But you were going to his place of work unannounced for a reason,' Omer presses on.

'Well, yes. I needed to speak to him. He was coming home late, sometimes so late I'd be asleep. He'd leave in the morning before I woke up. He wouldn't take my calls and I'd had enough.'

'So, you turn up at the office. They let you in at reception and then you go to his office – his room, but he's not there.'

'Correct.'

'But he's left his bag. You've seen his knife in the bag. But his phone and keys and whatever else aren't there. And you're as certain as you can be that he's gone?'

'Yes,' I say, exhausted by the repetition of these questions.

'Leaving his bag and his fishing kit?'

'Yes.'

'Why would he do that?'

'How am I supposed to know what he's thinking, Detective? I can't read his mind when he's talking to me, let alone when he's ghosting me.'

Peter raises an eyebrow at them in warning.

'Well, did you not wonder about it at the time? Like, why has he left his bag here?'

'Not really. Maybe he didn't want me to see what was in it? Maybe he had, I don't know, something incriminating in there? A pack of condoms, a pair of knickers, I don't know. Maybe he just couldn't be bothered to carry it home on public transport,' I say and I am only just on the sane side of shouting.

'And this Michael guy didn't have it with him on the roof?'

'The bag? No. I've said that already.'

'And you can't account for why it wasn't in Russell's office when we searched it?'

'No. I can't. Maybe Michael took it after the stabbing. Maybe someone else took it. His actual office doesn't have any locks.'

Omer and Metcalf look at each other, waiting. Finally, Omer nods. Metcalf takes a sheet of paper dramatically from an envelope and slides it over to me. 'When police went to see Russell at home today, the bag was there.'

A veil of blood rushes under the surface of my skin. I can't understand what has happened. 'Then he obviously came back for it,' I say, trying to hang on to information which is now slippery through my fingers.

'We checked the CCTV. He didn't come back. He says he took it home when he left,' Omer says solemnly.

'Then he took it with him.' I click through the options in my head. 'He could have gone to the loo. Perhaps I saw it then. And he came and got it before he left.' I'm trying to put this together quickly but at the same time make sure there are no holes left open.

'The thing is, Layla, we have checked the time of your 999 call to the police. It was at 20:39 and lasted around three minutes.'

'And?'

'And,' Metcalf says, elbowing in, 'Russell left at 20:18. In other words twenty minutes beforehand.'

'Sorry, I don't understand the point you're making,' I say. The sound of a door slamming, metallically somewhere in the belly of the building, reaches me. And it's that more than anything else that has happened that frightens me most. The idea of being buried here or somewhere like here, for years.

'The point he's making, Ms Mahoney, is that Michael could not have got a knife from a bag that wasn't there when he came in. On the CCTV, you can see Russell carrying the bag.'

My face feels suddenly cold. It's such a stupid mistake. My eyes begin to flutter in alarm and now my throat is tightening. To control the rising panic, I take hold of the edge of the table and squeeze until it leaves a ridge in my palm.

Peter glances at them before reaching across to pick up the witness statement. 'If you're going to spring statements like this on us, then I'm going to advise *no comment* till we have had a chance to read them.'

Omer smiles softly. 'I think your client looks as if she could use some time. Do you want to break now?'

Peter sees my face and nods. 'Yep. Now is good.'

28

Then

I traced my usual route to work despite being suspended. I had to speak to Michael and find out what he knew about Russell. I didn't know where he was but since he was in the habit of stalking me, I figured he'd turn up. I waited on the bridge for ten minutes but he didn't appear. Then I walked slowly to my office building and back again. Once I'd trailed my usual lunch spots, I walked, deliberately, to a nearby café, scanning the streets as I went.

It wasn't till I'd sat down with my coffee that the absurdity hit me. He'd almost persuaded me that when one of us needed the other, our paths would magically cross. But sitting here in a café at a table strewn with empty sugar sleeves and coffee stains, the idea of some mystical connection felt foolish.

I put the name 'Michael' and the word '*e-Vinculum*' into my phone and searched. The company's website was showing as 'under construction'. A small part of the website was functional and told me all about the sectors it operated in – *agriculture and feed, power/energy, cleaning and detergents*, and *water treatment* – but nothing at all about the personnel. I searched for a 'contact us' button but found that there were offices up and down the country from Hove to Runcorn and everywhere in between. Without a surname, there was no chance of finding him, if he even worked there.

There was still Russell. He was still there to be asked and though I was sure he would slip from under the questions, the least he could do was face them while I watched him and read his reactions for some small truth. If I couldn't ask him whether the vanilla he smelled of these days had rubbed off from Kate's skin, I could ask him why he smelled different. I could ask him why he'd changed his password on his laptop. I could ask him why he wasn't coming home at night.

By four, the light was spread thin and silver. I'd spent as long as I could here. I got up to go home but then couldn't bear the idea of all the chaos that filled the spaces between our walls. So I stopped at a pub on the way.

Being alone in a pub full of people felt like the end of something. My life was assaulting me from every direction. I took a seat at the deep mahogany bar and ordered a glass of white wine. The noise was warm and muted and it should have made me feel better than it did. From behind me I caught the tails of conversations as they drifted through the cushion of sound around me. Every strand of it seemed to do with me. I heard names spoken: Michael, Kate, Russ. Then strings of words that carried other meanings for me. *Chemical. Freedom. Divorce.* I finished my drink then ordered another. Every sip now conspired with every other atom in the air to absorb me into its skin so that I felt as though I were consuming the entire room. I typed the words 'Environment Agency' into my phone and clicked on the few tabs but the Agency didn't have a public interface the way that businesses did. There was no obvious list of people to scroll through. If Michael knew Russell, it wasn't something I could find out from Russell's work website. I gave up and went home.

As I approached the front door, I was cycling through the conversation I was going to have with Russell when I remembered the chain. I checked. It wasn't there. I walked close up to the step and crouched down, shining the light from my phone into the dark crevices. I opened the door and even though I knew from the missing chain that Russell was home, I was still surprised to see him there in the living room, watching TV. To look at him, it seemed as though nothing could be wrong. His face was a lake, not a muscle rippled even when I came in and sat down heavily next to him. The scent of vanilla hung thick.

'We have to talk,' I said.

He lowered the volume and waited, saying nothing.

'I don't care if you're seeing someone or not. I just need to know. I mean it would be fair.'

He folded his arms but still said nothing – staring out ahead.

'Can you not just please tell me? I'm entitled to know.'

When he turned to me his face was set hard. 'Why are you asking me when you've clearly already decided? You think I'm having an affair. Does it matter what I say? You'll still believe what you want.'

My heart began to kick and I focused on the patterns my foot was making in the carpet. 'Why am I finding blonde hairs everywhere, Russell?'

He shifted and repositioned himself so that he was looking into my eyes. His skin shone pale now as if it had been under a stone. 'Are you? Are you really finding hairs everywhere?'

I thought of the wrapped lone hair in my pocket and knew what he was doing. He was making me ridiculous. 'Did you pick up the silver chain?'

His eyes turned before blinking in surprise. 'Wait. That was you? You *left* it there. What? For me to hide it away somewhere?' He threw up his hands. 'This is exactly what I mean. And for your information, I picked it up thinking *you'd* dropped it. Here,' he said, teasing it out of his pocket and letting it fall into my lap.

It sat there like a silver worm. The TV muttered, jolly and overexposed, through the adverts. I thought about what Michael had said, about how Russell was somehow at the centre of it all.

I drew a breath. 'What are you working on at the moment?'

He looked as if he'd misheard but when I repeated the question, he simply frowned. 'What? Why?'

'Just. Am I not allowed to know?'

He sighed deeply. 'Nothing. Transitional provisions. Brexit. All of that crap if you're really interested.'

'What about chemicals?'

He frowned. 'Chemicals?'

I nodded but had nowhere else to go. 'I just want to know what you're doing,' I say over my quickening pulse.

'Layla,' he said, turning off the TV, 'I'm happy to spend all night every night telling you about my job. Really, I am. But that isn't what you want to know. And until you tell me what that is, I'll never know.'

Before he left the next morning, Russell made a point of stretching out the silver chain along the counter, leaving it in a perfect straight line. Neither of us spoke. He picked up his leather bag and walked to the front door and shut it behind him.

I took my phone into the bedroom and scrolled through it on my bed. Steel light washed in through the net curtains as I searched through the entries until I found the one I wanted and dialled.

'Stef. It's Layla Mahoney. Yes – so sorry to bother you without warning. Do you happen to know the number of a good tricho expert? Hair analysis – that sort of thing?'

'Hi, Layla. Tricho? Just a sec, I might have a number on my phone,' he said and hummed while he looked. 'No cigar, sorry. But, I can give you some names from the register of experts we use if that's any good?'

He sent some names and I chose the one with the glossiest website. It had experts across a dozen specialities from blood spatter to DNA. The trichology expert, Dr M. Kashiff, specialised in hair-strand analysis to test if people had consumed drugs. I called him and asked whether he could do an analysis of hairs to test whether they were from the same person.

'Can you do it quickly?'

'Sure,' he said brightly. 'Just send them separately packaged and clearly marked. I'll turn it round as soon as I can.'

After I ended the call, I took the hair I'd scraped from Kate's hairbrush and the ones from the clothes brush and put them into a couple of ziplock freezer bags. On one I wrote 'KATE PEEL' and on the other 'UNKNOWN'. Looking at them they seemed identical. The light seemed to hit the strands in the same way. Kate's hair felt more delicate but then the other sample had been raked through a clothes brush.

When I got the report, I'd know for certain. I already knew. But I'd know in a way that mattered – I'd know independent of my own mind.

I slipped out to post the package. And then as I walked back, in the grey light, I thought about the day stretching out in front of me. I needed to do something to take me out of my head. It had been three months since I'd seen Mum.

I took the train. I didn't want to drive all the way to Havant by myself, the way I was feeling. I had the sense that if I were on the road travelling at seventy, then something reflexive might take me over for a second to plunge me into the barriers. It would be quick and painless. I couldn't afford to give myself that power.

The train wasn't busy so I slipped into the first-class carriage. The seats were large and the compartment hummed gently in its own silence. I lay my head back against the headrests. A second later the doors behind me swished open, startling me upright. Why was I so skittish? Michael. In the deep spaces of my mind, I suspected that he might be on here too. As the train pulled away, I threaded my way through the carriages, swaying, glancing left and right for signs of the man. But he wasn't there.

I reclaimed my seat and connected to the Wi-Fi, and checked the *e-Vinculum* website again, this time the 'Our People' section was up and running. I typed in 'Michael' and waited for the results. It was no use. The company had hundreds of employees across tens of pages. The few *Michaels* it did turn up looked nothing like him. Had he told me his surname? If he had, I'd forgotten it. I stopped. I'd been assuming that the card he'd left on the table was his own and that he'd used it to write down a number. But it was more likely that someone from the company had given him the card with the number scribbled on it.

A trolley came offering complimentary snacks. I shook my head at the woman but took some napkins. I unfolded one carefully onto the Formica and made a list of the days I had seen Michael.

1. Bridge – where the accident had happened
2. When I tracked him into Temple
3. Café in Aldwych
4. The Gallery

I looked for a link but couldn't find one other than the one I didn't want to give oxygen to – me. But the more I stared the more obvious that link became until it had so crystallised that I screwed the napkin up and threw it across the carriage.

The train rocked and hummed through the countryside. What was solid beyond the glass vanished no sooner than it had been glimpsed. I thought again: that the only connection between those occasions – and the locations – where I had seen Michael, was me. There weren't impossible coincidences at play here. All there was, was me. He could only ever be where I was. Whether it was on my way home or at a gallery, I was the common factor. Maybe he didn't exist after all and we hadn't had any of the conversations I believed we'd had. He'd never rescued me. He wasn't a phantom guardian or this metaphysical presence set on Earth to save me. He *was* me, the incarnation of my insecurities. That was all. He was just an avatar.

But the card in my bag was real.

Then was there something in my own life that did connect to *e-Vinc*? I didn't know the company. I was sure that I hadn't worked on any cases that involved a chemicals business.

I fished out the card from my bag and stared at the number. It was a mobile number.

29

Now

'What the fuck, Layla?'

'What? What did I do?' I say. Peter is swirling around the room, his face reddening by the second.

'Russell's bag. Why did you lie about seeing the bag?'

'I did see it. Just because those idiots can't make sense of it –'

He scratches his head and then leads me slowly over to the chair in the corner. There is foam spilling out from an arm. 'Layla, you know what these idiots are doing, don't you? They're sitting you down in a chair, tying leather straps around your arms and right now they're soaking a sponge to put on your head. And in about an hour from now, they'll be fucking *Green Mile*-ing you. Do you understand? This is a murder case. It's your life.'

His face is creased in desperation. He is crouching on the floor next to me, his arms either side of me on the arms of my chair. I stroke one of them until he drops his head and stands.

'Bit dramatic that, Peter.'

He smiles. 'Okay. But we have to do something here. They're running out of time. They either release you under investigation or they charge you with murder. And I can tell you this for nothing. Unless something fucking dramatic happens in the next few hours, they will charge you.'

A sudden vision of the woman crashes into my head. She is lying back in my arms, mouth gaping. There is blood bubbling up from her chest. I'm trying everything in my power to fend the images away but the more tired I get the harder it is. I stand and join Peter in pacing the floor. It's been a long night – almost a full day now since it happened.

'How much longer can they keep me here?'

'Another twelve hours,' he says, checking his watch. 'Just under.'

I can't believe it can be that long. He sees the look on my face.

'If you're lucky. If you're unlucky they can go to the Mags and get another sixty hours.'

Peter is reading the witness statement he's been given, so I return to my seat and close my eyes. It's only a few seconds later that they're forced open again.

'Fuck, Layla. You need to read this.'

I look down at the statement at the part that he is pointing to and a lump forms in my stomach.

30

Then

As the train pulled in I held my breath and dialled the number on the card, withholding my number as I did. The number connected and I held the phone close to my ear as the train drew to a halt and the doors opened. Once I was on the platform, when it was clear no one was answering, I ended the call.

By noon, I was standing outside the door to Mum's bungalow, still numb from the journey. I shook off the fatigue and studied the house. The brick-laid drive was showing weeds and the windows needed a good wash. After a deep breath I rang the bell. Mum opened the door with a surprised look on her face, which wasn't reassuring since she was supposed to be making us lunch.

'Love,' she said. 'Come in. I was just about to get some food on for myself.' She was dressed for winter though the sun was still warm.

Inside I saw how bad things were. The edges of the floors were thick with dirt where Mum couldn't reach with a vacuum or mop. The cooker had ground- and burned-in residue, just out of the immediate eyeline. When we were growing up, Mum had been scrupulous about keeping a clean house. She claimed it was the Irish in her but lately I wondered whether it was less about the Irish in her blood and more about the chemical balance in it. As she bustled about I took a slow waltz around the house. There were forgotten objects Easter-egged around the place. A coffee mug behind the Yucca. A hairbrush in the dish rack. A slipper under a sofa cushion. I picked up what I could without being seen and rehomed it all. It wasn't at the level of real alarm, more a flag. At home, these past few weeks, I had done minor versions of the same things – taken the TV remote control into the bathroom or misplaced my keys – but seeing it there before me in its full-bloomed state was seeing my unfurled future.

'Are you taking all your medication, Mam?' I asked her once we'd eaten the soup-and-sandwich lunch she'd made. We were at the small tiled kitchen table, severed by a long triangle of light.

'You know they make me feel foggy if I take them all the time,' she said, as she made a swipe at some breadcrumbs scattered on the tile. 'But I take enough.'

'Enough? What's enough? You need to take them all!' I said.

She worried at a stubborn red stain in the tile glaze with a ridged thumbnail. The similarity didn't escape me – her life and mine, echoing. Then, as if shaking herself loose from a dream, she stood up and smiled uncertainly. 'Tea then?'

'Mam, promise me. The meds. You'll start taking them. Properly.' I turned in my chair as she walked past me to switch on a plastic kettle the colour of old newspaper. She put her hands up by her ears to make it clear that she didn't want to hear any more.

'No, I'll not promise any such thing. You don't know what they do to you. They eat your brain up. I'm like a zombie at the end of it. Can't do nothing for myself. I'm just sitting and vegetating like a –' and she hunted for the right word and turned to me as she groped for it but came back empty. Her face had crumpled and as her eyes became glassy, I had a vision of her then as she might have been as a child – frightened. 'Like a bloody turnip,' she said finally.

I ushered her to the living room and sat her down on the sofa while I returned to make the tea.

By the time I had come back, Mum had relaxed a little but was still a bit jittery. She was rubbing her fingers back and forth across the brown velour of the sofa. When she got like this the only thing to do was to spend some time grounding her. She liked tea. She liked having familiar objects around her. Older things – anything more recent didn't work. Her stable memories were from ten or more years before. Enveloped in them, slowly she'd return.

She gazed up at me from the sofa and smiled uncertainly.

'Do you want me to do some tapping?' I asked. She'd responded quite well to energy tapping in the past. I wasn't completely convinced by it when I'd first heard of it but I saw it working with her. Just a few taps around her face with my fingers restored her equilibrium.

'No thanks, dear.' She picked up her teacup and smiled.

I went around the room to gather some of the older objects to help her become centred – a tiny crystal ornament from the mantel, an old lap blanket, a coin purse – and gave them to her. She looked at them, puzzled, but handled them as though she was aware that was what she had to do.

'I know,' I said then, seeing it on a shelf under the TV, 'what about the photo album? I haven't seen these in a while.'

I got up and retrieved it. The thick green padded cover flung me into a childhood memory of being stretched on the carpet, poring over the images, hours at a time.

'Here, Mam, look,' I said, opening the cover. The film had come away from the photographs, the glue loosened by the years. The first page had two pictures together of Mum and Dad shortly after their wedding. In one they were in a park posing by a rose bush. In the second, they were standing by Dad's gold Ford Capri. Dad was tall and slim and wore his hair long and swept across his jaw, a handlebar moustache draped over his mouth. Mum, tiny next to him, her dark honeyed hair flicked away from her face in feathers. She leaned into him – held him – as if without him she might blow away. Both were squinting at the lens in a shaft of sunlight. She put a swollen finger now to the peeling plastic. Remembering.

'He hated that car,' she said.

'What?' I said, surprised. 'He loved it. He loved that Capri.'

She laughed softly and turned her gaze towards me. 'No.'

I dipped into my bag and found Alice's toy Capri. I really should have given it back to her but having it with me gave me comfort. More than a talisman, almost a thread that connected me to Dad. I showed it to her. 'This one. He loved it.'

She smiled again. 'Ach. He only said that once it was gone. The thing was always leaking oil and what have you. The time of it,' she added. 'He loved the time of it. We were still young and free. And then when you came along, he had to sell it to get baby things. He was worried it wasn't safe for you. He preferred the Princess. Horrible wobbly thing but he liked roaming you around in it.'

'And you too, Mam.'

'I don't think that's me you're remembering.'

Then suddenly her face changed. A mask descended and whatever there was behind her eyes a second ago had retreated. She looked at me with a stranger's eyes. 'You,' she said, pointing a finger at me. 'You!'

I stood. I hadn't seen her like this before. I'd heard about it from the carers who dropped in an hour each evening but had never witnessed it. She took her teacup and flung it into the middle of the room. For a second I froze, not sure what to do. Then I hurried into the kitchen to get a cloth. When I returned Mum was staring into space. I dabbed at the stain in the carpet and tried to reassure and settle her at the same time.

'It's okay, Mam,' I said. 'It's just tea. I'll get you some water. Wait.' In the kitchen I tried to find a clean glass but there weren't any in the cupboards. I found one in the sink and washed it hurriedly as loud thuds sounded from the living room. When I got there Mum was sitting at the coffee table trembling. The glass that sat on top of the wood was smashed.

'Oh, Mam,' I said and stroked her arms and her back. 'It's okay.' There was blood on her hands where shards of glass had caught her skin.

I sat with her, soothing her for the next fifteen minutes or so. Slowly she emerged again to take her place behind her own eyes. She smiled as if seeing me for the first time as I fussed around her, clearing away the glass.

When I returned from disposing of it, she was holding the photo album. 'Layla, oh, look you got the picture album out.'

'Oh,' I said, and because I couldn't think of anything else to say, I took it from her gently and quietly turned the pages.

There was Dad again. I hesitated, watching for her reaction. She seemed okay. She smiled at the picture, remembering it. I did too, conscious that I was remembering him in a stylised way. Looking back into my childhood, now as an adult, I knew that the memories weren't real. They were constructions. In my recreation of Dad, he always took me to and from school. He always walked me so that he was traffic-side on. But my rational brain knew it wasn't true. It was true sometimes. But he was, as everybody is, flawed. He was ordinary, but a real person.

He always smiled in my memories. I wondered about Mum and how she remembered him. Did she see him in the same simulated way that I did? How did she cope in that wilderness of time when he was gone?

The pictures of him were grounding her now when a second ago they'd derailed her. They were putting her world into order and soon after her mind followed the crumb trail from the past into the present. Tentatively at first but then more firmly. When we were towards the end of the album, I saw some photos that I had seen before, but didn't know in the same way. They didn't follow any chronology. There was an old black-and-white one of Granny from Kildare which I loved, mixed in with more recent graduation pictures of me.

'Are these new?' I asked.

'Oh, those. Yes. I found them in a bag of your things from uni when I was clearing out the understairs' cupboard.'

Me and Kate grinning at the lens, mortar boards balanced, scrolls being brandished. We were both beautiful then. But between then and now, something had happened to me. I turned the page. Me as an awkward thirteen-year-old holding a blurred hand to the camera.

'Is that Kate?' I asked.

Her face clouded over at the descent of some memory. I tensed briefly but she brightened again. 'Katharine? Well. I suppose,' she said and then her tone changed. 'You were so shy then. But bold when you needed to be!'

I had been both shy and wild at one stage, as if trying each before I had to choose who to become. I felt all the memories seep in. I turned the page. And stalled. It was a picture of Dad in Chorley Market. I think I remember taking it. He was smiling, patiently waiting for the flash. As soon as I saw it I understood why I took it. In the background, behind Dad, was the boy from the matchbox car stall. I took it out from the album to get a better look. The eyes, narrowed as I remembered them. Hair still long and swept over the brow, but glossier in the sun. Foolish to think now that he was Michael. But that wasn't what had alarmed me. It was the girl in the corner of the picture. A wisp of blonde hair. Was it Kate? It couldn't be. I didn't know her then.

'I do miss him though,' she said when I shut the album. 'Your father. No matter what he did. I can't help missing him.' Her eyes travelled in her head until it seemed they found focus again. 'How's your friend? Kate, is it? Always smelled so nice that one. Very fragrant.'

'She's fine, Mam,' I said, getting up to put the album away.

'Has she got a boyfriend now?' Mum asked, smiling.

'I've no idea, Mam. I've no idea.'

31

Now

'Why would he say that? Why would Russell lie like that?'

Peter's face is displaying as little as possible. If he has a police station face, that's the one he is showing me. 'I was hoping you'd tell me.'

He reads out the passage. '*I have been asked by the police whether I have recently been fishing anywhere that involved an overnight stay. Although I have spent the last couple of days with my brother, it didn't involve fishing. I have been asked whether I have a pearl-handled fishing knife and can confirm that I do not.* He's lying or you are.'

'He is! Why would I lie?' I start to say until he gives me a look to say *who has a better reason than you?* 'Look, I don't know why he's lying but he is. If I could speak to him for a minute, we could clear this up.'

Peter rolls his sleeves up to expose his meaty forearms. A steel watch dangles heavily off the end of a wrist. The door opens and a woman in a tabard looks in apologetically before spirting away again. 'You can't talk to him. He's a witness.'

'But if he knew how important this was, I'm certain he would change his statement. He doesn't even know what's happening with me. I called *you*. I haven't even told him where I am.'

Peter colours a little and then loosens his collar. 'I'm sure he's got a pretty good idea by now, Lay.' He stares out of the window but there is nothing to see there except the brick of the building opposite. He sighs extravagantly. 'So, what are we saying now – when we go in?'

'The truth. That he's lying.'

I think about the last few weeks and the way he has been towards me. It's been there, but only dripping, acid gnawing away at our connective tissue. The hairs. The chain. I wonder now whether he planted them all.

'And what's his reason for lying going to be?'

'I don't know,' I say. And honestly, I don't.

'Okay, wait, let's get this right before we go in. Is there any way to corroborate what you're saying about the knife? Are there pictures of it anywhere? Where did he get it from? Maybe there's a receipt or an email or bank statement. Something.'

'His father gave it to him; it belonged to his grandfather,' I say. 'He's dead now but his brother's still alive. He'd be able to confirm it. They fought about it after his dad died.'

'Okay, good. Anyone else know about it or seen it even?'

'I don't think so. It was a stupid knife. He kept it in his tool bag usually.'

Peter takes a blue A4 notebook from his bag and makes a note before staring into space. 'The thing that worries me is why he is saying that it's not his knife. Does he hate you that much?'

'Maybe he does,' I say, and for the first time I am wondering exactly that.

32

Then

When I got back there was a letter on the doormat. I ran into the kitchen with it and took Russell's fishing knife from the counter, sliced through the envelope and read. It confirmed that I'd been suspended and put on garden leave. Fry had wanted me cut away from the moment he arrived. I put the letter straight into the recycling bin.

Russell wasn't there but he was still with me as I paced the living room, corroding my sanity. Him and Kate. The vanilla. She always smelled nice, as Mum put it. Not exciting or spicy but 'nice'. Nobody expected to be undone by something as bland as vanilla – not Kate, not me. I wasn't sure whether I felt more betrayed by Kate my best friend or my husband. And then it came to me as a question: was she the woman Michael had seen him with?

I had to speak to him. I called the number on the back of the card again, withholding my own number. It rang a dozen times and for the whole time I held my breath. Finally, on the thirteenth, it was answered.

'Hello?' I said after a beat. The line was silent. 'Hello?' I ventured again. A second later the line went dead. I called again but the phone was switched off.

I tried to conjure an image of Kate and Russell together but it wouldn't quite coalesce. He was too entwined with me and my memories of us together for him and Kate to be a viable image together.

Then before I knew it, I was calling her number. It didn't connect. They had to tell me about the affair eventually. But I couldn't wait any longer, for the sake of my head. I needed to talk to her because if she knew, if she understood how deeply bereaved I felt about it, she'd give way. I knew she would. I was sure I couldn't survive it if he left me now. In a year or two perhaps I'd feel stronger, more able to withstand it. But not right now. She had to let him go.

I looked out of the front window and saw his car parked outside. I threw on my coat and left. In my coat pocket was the smooth gloss of the Polaroid I had taken from Mum's house. A minute later I was driving for Kate's cottage.

The dark clouds above seemed to portend something more than weather. Raindrops spat on the windscreen behind a rumble of thunder. I drove quickly and as I did I turned around in my mind what I'd say to each of them. Something about his cowardice and her betrayal. My oldest friend. I had *confided* in her. The thought made me queasy. The horn from a bus blared, making me jump at the wheel. My tyres skidded momentarily from under me. What was next? Did I tell him not to come back? Was that what I was supposed to say to him or was that just one of those analogues from TV? I wondered whether that was what I was becoming, a person who learned how to be from TV.

I pulled up outside Kate's cottage and banged on the door. A few seconds later it opened but then stuttered abruptly as a chain grumbled across the gap. There in the stretched space was Kate's surprised face. She looked different somehow.

'Oh,' she said and then paused, and shut the door. I waited. A minute passed before the sound of the chain being unhooked and the door opening. 'Everything okay, honey?' she asked.

'Can I come in?' I said. She never called me 'honey'.

She nodded and opened the door wider, making way. I marched straight into the hall and noted the doors. The kitchen door was ajar. I glanced in and saw a frying pan on the electric rings and two plates nearby. But the living room door was shut – that's where he'd be. I strode in, Kate on my heels.

'Is everything okay?'

The room was empty. A faint glow in the fireplace where the last of a fire sputtered. 'Not quite cold enough for a fire, is it, Katharine?' I said lightly.

'What's going on? Who brought you?' she said, following me in.

'The fire,' I said, pointing at it and smirking.

'Last night. I lit it last night. It's just the embers,' she said. 'What's this about?'

I stamped back into the hall. 'I have to use your loo,' I said and started climbing the stairs. She watched from below as I reached the landing. Instead of going into the bathroom, I went to her bedroom door and pushed it open. Empty. The bed was neatly made. A starburst clock on the wall showed it was just after 2 p.m. I checked the second bedroom at the back of the house. Also empty. But then as I pulled the bedroom door to, I heard the noise of the front door clicking shut. I raced across the landing and then downstairs. I pushed past Kate through the front door back into the street.

'Where did he go?' I shouted, scanning the road up and down.

Kate stared at me. 'What? What is happening?'

I stood in the middle of the street. There was no sign of him. He'd gone.

'Just calm down for a second. Come in and we can talk about it,' she said, edging towards me in faltering steps.

'I *know*, Katharine,' I said, and then raising my voice to a scream, 'I *know*.' I searched my pockets for the Polaroid. When I found it, I looked at it and then threw it at her feet. She stared at me in shock. Or fear. Without waiting for an explanation, I got back into the car and realised that I was holding the fishing knife in my hand. I must have taken it out of my pocket when I was looking for the photograph. In the rear-view mirror, Kate was standing in the road, the Polaroid now in her hand. Her expression changed as she finally fathomed the meaning of it.

I called Russell repeatedly that afternoon but each time he left the phone unanswered. Finally, just after lunch, he sent a text message:

Kate called me. Are you okay??? I'm worried about you

I didn't know if I was okay or not but there was no peace to be found in the house. Russell's message burned a hole in my stomach – Kate had called him. So now, though he wasn't in the house, he was here in my head – with her. Even when they were apart, my mind conspired to bring them together. I didn't even know where he was. And that question was still plaguing me – what was the connection between Russell and the man who'd been killed – Jon? Michael knew more than he'd told me.

I pulled up the *e-Vinculum* website and looked at the different offices. The ones in the north could be discounted. I doubted whether Michael would be so freely available in London if he were based in Runcorn. There wasn't a London office but the southern one was in Hove. I grabbed my briefcase and the car keys and left.

The light outside had a fractured, split quality about it. One half of the sky was golden but as I turned a corner, I saw that the remainder of it was dark and brooding. It was the kind of day that sometimes blew down trees but on others, gave up rainbows.

Whenever I headed south I could feel the tidal pull of vast open water. I knew that magnetic, gravitational pull was because of Mum and Dad. They'd taken me to see the chalk cliffs once in Seaford. I remember everything and nothing about the day. The details had all been bleached out by time, but the sensations were all there, bubbling. I was ten or eleven. All I remembered was being there, in the open, in the warmth of a perfect blue day. The air was as soft as cloud. And the day had this quality of timelessness that I have never, since that day, ever rediscovered. It was as if I'd stepped into a dimension where time had stopped. For just those few hours.

After around two hours of driving, I could see the sea on the horizon, separated from the sky by a line.

I followed the satnav on my phone until I reached the *e-Vinc* offices and could park nearby. The building looked more like a large detached red-brick Victorian house than the registered offices of a large multinational chemicals company.

Inside, the ground floor rooms had been knocked through to make a large foyer. The space was dominated by a huge sandblasted glass screen fizzing with colour. It seemed to tell the story of the journey of the elements from exploding stars to gold mines.

The receptionist glowed, her skin the colour of sunlight. 'Morning. Oh, look at me stuck in the past as usual. Afternoon!'

'Hi,' I said, pointedly placing my briefcase on the glass-tiled floor. 'I've got an appointment with Michael.'

'Just a moment,' she said and examined her monitor. A trace of jasmine lifted from her ringletted Afro. 'I'm so sorry I didn't catch that. Michael who?' She looked back at me and smiled.

'I know this sounds silly but the surname has just fallen out of my head. I'm so spacey at the moment.' I smiled back at her to disguise the bluff.

She narrowed her eyes at me. The fixed smile danced a little on her lips now. 'Any idea what department?'

'No,' I said, shifting on my feet. 'He didn't say. But how many Michaels can you have?'

'The system doesn't search under first names I'm afraid.'

I exhaled loudly. 'I've come a long way. If there's any way that you could help? Maybe you know him? About five foot ten, brown hair, blue eyes, good-looking?'

She flushed with embarrassment. 'Sorry,' she said. 'If you have his number you could call him? Or if you can tell me what it's regarding, I might be able to help narrow it to a department?'

'He's a scientist, I think.' I was sure he'd mentioned something about science but now, here, in the moment, I couldn't be sure.

'Analytical chemist? Chemical engineer? Nanotechnologist? Biotech? Geoscience? You'd have to be more specific. There's a lot of departments.'

I stepped back onto the pavement. The air was heavy with salt and the sound of gulls cracked overhead. I walked in the direction of the sea and within minutes I was at the beach.

I crunched across the deep shingle and sat just out of reach of the surf as it broke on the shore. The wind blew fiercely off the water, bringing a taste of sea. The panorama – of sea and sky – returned me to that childhood memory. I was sitting, staring out to sea and eating sandwiches. There were sandcastles I think. And Dad helping me pick out pebbles for decorations. Mum was somewhere too, but in the image, she was faded.

A sadness dropped over me. The perfection of a moment when it bled into my life always had this effect. I wonder what I could have done differently to change things. And then, if I had made some other choice, who that choice would have changed me into. I used the sound and rhythm of the waves to quiet myself until it felt as though I had stepped free. The thing gave me a feeling of giddiness, as if the threads had been snipped away but instead of falling like a puppet, I'd become suspended in air – hovering precariously between states.

I got to my feet, rubbed the shingle from my jeans and trudged back towards the car. What was I thinking anyway? How did I expect to find him without a full name? I cast my mind back, sure that he'd told me his surname. It was Michael – something short, maybe just a single syllable long – but it had gone.

The building that housed *e-Vinculum* Ltd stood silent in front of me. I peered through the windows for any sighting of Michael, but of course he wasn't there.

Maybe he was never there, but my head had never taken me that far before. Somewhere under dust I have memories of hearing voices deep in my ears. No sentences. Just words, belched out in such a way that I couldn't tell whether they were commands or accusations.

I got into the car and leaned into the seat and rubbed my eyes. It was a long drive back and I hadn't eaten anything all day. I thought of going to a pub for some food, but as I turned over the ignition, a shadow loomed over my passenger window making me jump. And then it tapped on the window insistently. Quickly I locked the doors. The hand knocked again urgently. I lowered my head to get a look at the person but they – *he* – was too close to see his face. I lowered the window a fraction, letting a gust of sea air blow in.

'Layla, it's me,' he said.

I lowered the window a little more until the whole of his face became visible. But by then I already knew who it was. The scent of sandalwood ribboned in.

'Michael,' I said.

33

Now

'We want to go back over a few things if we can, please.'

I wait for Omer to say what he wants but he takes it so slowly, pausing at each step, that the muscles in my arms have gone rigid with tension. I have to get out of here and I don't know whether them 'going back over' things is just a way to stretch things out so they can apply to the court for more time. I think about whether there is another way of getting what I need done. There's Peter but – although I trust him – he'd never do it.

'Okay, so this is the picture we have built up so far. I just want you to see it like we are seeing it. We have a dead woman in your arms with a knife in her chest. You say you have never seen the woman before but you have seen the knife. You claim it belongs to your husband but he says he's never seen it before. You're on the roof of your husband's building – but your husband's nowhere in sight. And the man you say killed her doesn't appear to exist or can't be found at any rate. What we can't seem to work out is why you are on the roof in the first place – any of you. Amy Blahn, you, Michael – if there is a Michael. Why are you there?'

There's no way of explaining this that doesn't sound contrived or crazy. But I have to. 'Do you remember I was telling you about free will? In a way we were there, all of us, because of that. One thing led to the next and each successive thing. I can't tell you why we were there without winding it all back. And then the question is, how far back do we wind?'

Metcalf swears under his breath and pushes back from the table. Omer holds up a hand to try and pacify him but the rage in Metcalf is almost palpable. 'This crap again?' he says and leans back against the wall, glowering.

'Okay,' Omer says, turning back to face me. 'Let's start with Amy Blahn. Why was she there?'

I blink in surprise at him. 'Haven't you asked Russell about that?'

'Right now, we're asking you. What can you tell us about it?' Omer says.

I look at Peter, who nods at me to continue. 'She worked at *e-Vinculum* – the chemicals company. Michael told me that she was trying to get approval for a chemical compound that he'd developed –'

'Wait a second. A compound that *he'd* developed. I thought you said,' he flicks through his notebook. 'Yes. You told us earlier he was a corporate investigator. Now he's developing chemicals?'

'I don't know. That's what he told me – I'm not the police. I didn't investigate him.' I notice that my voice is becoming jagged and I stop to smooth the edges. 'He spoke knowledgeably about chemicals and compounds and molecule chains. I assumed that he was an investigator *because* he was familiar with the industry. Otherwise how would he know if anything was going wrong?'

Omer seems satisfied by the answer for now though the look on Metcalf's face betrays more scepticism.

'Okay. Amy was trying to get approval did you say, for a chemical? And that is Russell's area at the Environment Agency?'

'No, it isn't. He deals with compliance and regulatory matters. He doesn't get involved in actual approvals or testing or anything like that.'

'So then going back to my question, why was she there?'

I trace the scar on my hand with a fingertip. 'I'm not completely certain. I'm only going on what Michael told me. He said that she was looking for approval for a chemical that wasn't safe. It was never going to be passed but she was talking to Russell about how it could be. I don't know. He was suggesting that she was bribing him or – compromising him somehow.'

The two detectives exhaled at the same time. It was late and they had a glazed-over look about them. From the street below, I could hear the screech of an animal – a cat probably.

'Michael told you this?'

'Yes,' I say.

'Did you know if it was true?'

I pause. 'No. Not for certain. When I asked Russell about work he was always cagey. I never really knew anything about what he was up to.' I think about the times I could have asked him but wasted the chances. And then I think how when I did finally ask, he shut me down.

'But you believed him. Did "Michael",' he does speech marks with his fingers, 'mention Amy Blahn by name?'

I shake my head. 'No. He didn't know her name.'

There is a sea of crumpled brows. 'Then how did he know who she was?' Metcalf says, supplying the question.

'That's the point, Detective. He didn't. He didn't know who she was.'

34

Then

Michael waited for me to speak but I was trapped in indecision. I couldn't have him in my car and yet I had to speak to him. Finally, I leaned over and opened the door. The scent of coffee and sandalwood followed him in.

'You came to see me,' he said, smiling. 'They told me,' he added, indicating the *e-Vinculum* building. 'How did you know I worked here?'

I steeled myself and started the car. 'I didn't for sure,' I said, my knuckles blanching on the wheel. 'And they didn't for sure either,' I added. 'They didn't seem to know who you were when I went in asking for you.'

'Clara? She's new. She hasn't got the hang of all the names yet.'

He was so close that I felt sure he could hear my heart racing. If he resisted me here, on a deserted high street, I wouldn't be able to get him out. Who would know if anything happened to me?

He'd saved me from a horrific traffic accident. If he'd wanted me dead, maybe I'd be dead already. 'We need to talk,' I said. 'Put your belt on.'

I drove to the beachfront. It was a short drive and a minute later we were standing on the promenade, staring at the sea. People, friendly and polite, nodded as they passed, pulling dogs along on long leads. The waves ahead rolled in the darkening sky, threatening.

'Tell me what's going on. Who are you and what do you want with me?'

Michael walked a little away from me and leaned against the iron rail running along the walkway. His hair blew extravagantly in the breeze. 'We make industrial chemicals. Polymers, non-polymers, petrochems.'

'Go on,' I said. There was a gravity to what he was saying that filled me with dread but I needed to hear it.

'And I make some of the products. That's who I am.'

'You said you were a corporate investigator.'

He frowned and turned back towards the sea. 'Look, it doesn't matter what I do formally. What matters is what I've found out. What matters is Russell. He's being leaned on to approve a dangerous chemical.'

'A chemical? He has nothing to do with chemicals.'

'I don't know all the details but this is real and I think he's at breaking point.'

My heart tumbled into a ravine. 'What do you mean?'

He looked around and then back into the sea as the air blew fine spray into our faces. 'If that chemical gets approval then we are in a world of trouble. A lot of people will die.'

I tried understand what he was saying but my brain was stuttering at the way what he was telling me didn't match anything that I knew about Russell. 'I don't understand what you're trying to tell me.'

'The way that bond is formed makes it so strong that there's no tearing it apart. In other words, it won't degrade. Ever. And when you ingest it, and you will, through your skin, through your lungs, in your food, it will kill you. It causes cancers – all kinds of them,' he said and stopped. He stared at me, as if waiting for me to catch up.

I opened my mouth to ask a question that I couldn't formulate. There was too much here to try to make sense of. The idea that once it escaped its box, there would be no way of containing it ever again.

He shifted between feet. 'Look. The important thing is the woman he's meeting – you have to find out who she is. And you have to do it soon.'

35

Now

'I don't understand. What do you mean he didn't know who it was? How would he know what she was doing if he didn't know who she was?'

Omer is losing his cool now. I think it's the late hour. The lack of fresh air. These electric lights. All of it is getting to him. It's a dangerous game, I know. I want him to crack but when he does the pieces have to fall the right way up.

'He was aware of her. He knew that she existed and that someone was trying to get this compound approved. He just didn't know who it was. It's a big organisation.'

'And what? He was appointed to investigate that? To stop it being approved? That doesn't make any sense to me, Ms Mahoney. The company could just have withdrawn the product.'

I nod. 'That's what I thought too initially. But I hadn't understood what he meant when he told me.'

'Which was?' Omer says, leaning forward.

'That the company itself was behind it. The company wanted it to be approved and they'd sent her off to do the dirty work.'

Omer stands up and rubs his forehead. 'Sorry, maybe because it's late and I'm not all there, but didn't you tell me that Michael was a corporate investigator for the company?'

'I did. But he wasn't investigating this for them. This was something he was doing on his own initiative. He was whistle-blowing, I think. I don't know anything for certain. As I keep reminding you, this was just what he was telling me.'

There is a collective sigh and Peter takes the opportunity to check his watch and wonder out loud whether they might want to call it for the night.

'We'd prefer to keep going for a bit if you're feeling okay, Ms Mahoney. The clock is ticking on the detention as you know and then we'll have to apply for an extension. But if you need a short break, we can accommodate that.'

My head is aching now but all I want is to be able to go home and sleep in my own bed. If I tell them I want to end the interview here, then it's a certainty I'm staying the night on a concrete one.

'No. Let's carry on.'

'Okay. Just want to switch subjects now, if I may. To repeat myself, we haven't spoken much about Russell in these interviews. You've told us that he wasn't speaking to you and that seems to be your answer to why you happened to be on the roof last night.'

'Questions, please,' says Peter. He has his head in his arms now on the table like a boy in a classroom trying to get some sleep.

'The question is, why he wasn't speaking to you? Had there been an argument of some kind?'

'No. No argument. He just wasn't engaging with me. I tried on multiple occasions to get him to talk. About us. About the affair I thought he was having, but he wouldn't.'

'No reason?' Omer says quietly.

'No reason.'

'You hadn't done anything to him?'

He can't have told them that. Not now. Not after everything. Not knowing where I am now, in a police station. He loves me. The rope that binds us to one another is dozens of strands thick. I call to mind his sunlit face. He won't have.

'No,' I say. I am emphatic. I have to be. It's the one gamble I am happy to make.

A silence gathers. It's heavy and soft like a duvet, filling all the gaps where noise might hide. I look between Metcalf and Omer. They're waiting for something and then I see what it is. It's Peter. They're waiting for his attention. They want him to lift his head so that he can hear what they're about to say. A second later he does exactly that and tilts his face to look at the two detectives.

'She said no. So, let's move on,' he says.

Omer reads off a sheet in front of him. 'Can I ask you how you got that cut?'

My heart clatters in my chest. I touch the raised skin on the back of my hand that never healed as well as I thought it would. 'It was an accident. Chopping vegetables.' I hold my breath as I speak.

'Wasn't there an incident with Russell?' Metcalf says.

'Incident' is still a neutral word. An accident can still be an incident. 'No.'

'No incident where you went at him with a knife and stabbed him in the stomach?'

The room crashes so violently that I want to block my ears with my hands. I can't believe he has told them this.

'Did Russell tell you that?' I ask. My voice falters but I recover it.

'Did it happen or not? You can see why it might be relevant?' Metcalf continues.

'No. Well, he did end up with a wound but I didn't *go* for him like you're saying,' I say, improvising something as quickly as I can.

Peter is holding up a hand to stop things but it's no use. The momentum is with the police and I can't just leave it here now, like this – hanging. On tape.

'But you did stab him with a knife?' Omer cuts in.

'It wasn't like that!'

'Then what was it like, Ms Mahoney? Tell us.'

Peter slaps a hand down on the table. 'Just hang on a second. What's the relevance of this question?'

Omer answers. 'Well, your client has been arrested on suspicion of murder – committed with a knife – and this is another occasion on which she stabbed someone with a knife. I'm not sure how it could be more relevant.'

Peter stares but the logic of that statement is hard to resist.

'So?' Omer says, looking at me. 'How did it happen?'

'I was cutting vegetables.' The memory of that evening comes flooding in. I was in the kitchen chopping vegetables. The air between us was thick and sour. We'd been arguing since the minute he'd walked in. I remember how red his face was at the tops of his cheeks. Those spots burned into my memories because of how unusual it was to see that colour in his face. How beautiful in a way it made him look. And I remember how sad it made me that his beauty only rose to the surface in anger. He'd been so angry. So angry.

The men wait for an explanation but we all know that no matter how I phrase it now, here in this dark, serious room, it will sound weak and hollow. I still can't believe that Russell told them this after everything. Peter will be furious with me for not doing as he'd told me to do. To assume that Russell wouldn't try and help them if he had the choice. But Peter didn't know about us – the depth of our entanglement. How much the suffering bound us to one another as much as the love once might have.

'I was chopping vegetables. He came up behind me and surprised me. I turned and the knife caught him.'

'And then did it catch you back?' Metcalf says, sneering.

Peter makes a move to intervene but I stop him. 'Yes, it did. He reacted by pushing me and the knife away and I was caught by the tip. It wasn't a serious injury in the end.'

'His or yours?'

'Neither. It was just unfortunate.'

Metcalf rubs the back of his hand against the edge of the table. 'Just seems like you've got an unfortunate habit of sticking knives into people.'

'That's it,' Peter says. 'It's late. We need a break. Everyone needs some sleep. Let's draw stumps.'

36

Then

Once Michael left, I sat in the car and thought about going home. The darkness had set in now and the prospect of a long drive made me go cold. I didn't like driving in the dark at the best of times but the idea of going home just to be there, rattlingly alone, made me even less inclined to start the car. I thought about what Michael had said, but now that he'd gone it sounded absurd, and at the same time, he was so certain about what he was saying.

My phone lit up the cabin as a message came through from Russell.

Spoke to Kate again. She's worried about u. I am too. Best to give u some time to yourself. I'll stay at Sam's tonight.

I called Russell's brother and after a few rings he answered.

'Sam, is Russell there? It's Layla.'

'Russell?' he said and then floundered. 'Um. Yeah, he's just um –' and then came the sound of him shouting for Russell. 'He's just dealing with something. He says can you call him on his mobile in say ten or fifteen minutes?'

I hung up. There was no point in chasing Russell now that he was hiding. He'd deny meeting any woman and deny responsibility for what was happening to us, and our problems would become the child of my unstable mind.

He had to be with Kate right now. I picked up the phone ready to call her but an image of her cut across my mind. In it she was holding the picture and there was a look of horror across her face.

If I called her now it would just entrench the idea that I had lost my mind.

He'd told me I was sabotaging us, as if I needed destruction in my life to survive. But it wasn't all true. It wasn't all in my head. However much I might have craved destruction, I wanted us to survive – thrive even. But I had no way of following the thread back to any kind of redemption when the starting point was so occluded. How did I know what we needed saving from when he refused to admit what was happening? Refused even to throw it on the scales.

The drive back was a haze and when I finally pulled back into my road, I was exhausted. As I got out of the car the interior lit up and I saw that there was a receipt on the passenger seat with writing on it. I picked it up and saw a string of numbers under the name 'M. CRUZ'. That was it – the name he'd given me and that I'd forgotten so easily. I looked again. He'd left his number. I folded the paper and slid it into my purse.

At the front door I paused to wonder whether Russell might have come home after all, but the absence of lights in the house answered that. I headed straight to the bedroom and curled into the duvet. Within moments I was asleep and lost in a tangle of confusing, chemical dreams.

In the morning I was woken by the sound of incessant ringing on my phone. It was work – and there were several missed calls. I sat up and pressed redial.

'Hi, it's Layla,' I said to James, our receptionist. 'Someone tried to call me but they didn't leave a message.'

'Just a moment,' he said and I waited as he transferred me. 'Hi, Layla, it's Hana. HR. Just wanted to tell you that the panel has made its decision and wanted to know when you were free to come in for it?'

'I can come in tomorrow,' I said.

'Actually, they wanted to know whether you were free to come in today at around four?'

I agreed. She didn't give me any kind of clue about what the result might be but then I'd have been surprised if she knew or cared. I was so exhausted that I didn't have the mental space to humour my anxieties about it.

As soon as I put the call down, the doorbell sounded, making my heart leap. Ever since Michael crashed into my life, I was constantly on the edge of a blade. But it wasn't him – it was just the delivery from the hire shop. I took the heavy sander from the teenager who'd brought it and lugged it to the kitchen and put it on the counter. Earlier I'd superglued the chipped rock back into place but now it protruded by another millimetre. The scratched marble vibrated under the white glare of the spotlights.

I had some time.

I put the machine carefully over the scratched area. They said to start with the most abrasive sanding disc. I loaded on the right disc and carefully pressed the button. The machine made a thunderous noise and skidded immediately out of my grip, bouncing hard across the surface and stopping only when I released the button. It hadn't made a dent. I took it again, tighter this time, and pressed the button. The motor screamed and as I held it to the marble, sparks flew. Again, it wanted to spin away from my grip and even though I pressed down hard, it dragged me along with it. Finally, in frustration I unplugged the machine and put it away. This time the counter was a beach of powdered grit and stone. What had begun as a small circle of scratches was now a three-foot stripe of scars and gouged rock.

I slid to the floor and sat, buzzing not just from the machine but also the havoc it had wreaked. I calmed myself down. I was late. I had to get ready for work. It was okay, I told myself, I'd call the original kitchen fitters. It wasn't the end of the world. They could probably polish it out.

Out on the street I noticed that the weather had turned with a purpose. The leaves had shed all at once from the trees so that there were carpets of rust along the paving. The sky was a flinty grey and the memory of summer had misted away like fog.

I pulled my scarf close against the cold as I crossed the bridge. A familiar metallic tang lifted off the river reminding me of that day when I first saw Michael. How much had changed since then. Russell and I had begun to corrode. And now Kate. I cast my mind back to that last meeting. I didn't have enough information yet to put her reaction into context. That look she gave me, was it guilt or was she genuinely perplexed? I'd know when the results from the hair-strand test came back.

When I walked into the office, Alice, in a smooth-knitted navy dress, rose to say hello. I remembered with a guilty pang her toy car still lurking at the bottom of my bag. I rummaged around for it blindly but for some reason I couldn't find it even when I looked a second time.

'Layla,' she said and came to hug me. She held on tight.

I prised myself slowly off. 'It's okay, Alice. No one died,' I said, laughing a little.

'What happened? Are you back now?' she asked, cocking her head.

'I don't know. I'll find out at four,' I said, looking at my watch. She smiled and padded back to her desk in her stockinged feet. Her pumps were draped around her neck on a pink brief ribbon.

Only Pritti and Fry were there when I walked into the meeting. Pritti smiled apologetically. Fry remained inscrutable, his hands like meat on the table in front of him. Pritti looked down at her papers.

'Layla. Look, to cut straight through it, we have thought long and hard about our decision and have made a number of findings which we will run through with you now.' She began to read from the letter that she had in front of her. It explained how every breach of the code had 'on the balance of probabilities' been proved. Finally, she looked up. 'But we give you credit for your admissions and feel that due to your record we can deal with this with a final written warning. But we have to warn you, Layla, that this means that any further incident, however minor, puts you at risk of dismissal.'

Back in my office my head began to spin with noise. It was a horrifying clashing sound. I pinched the skin between by thumb and forefinger and then lay my head on the desk and tried to block out the din. It was so stupid to have been so worked up about this.

Alice came over and rubbed my back and made soothing noises. I smiled and released her so I could leave. They'd let me take the rest of the day off to get myself together. I pulled on my scarf and turned to go when something caught my eye. It was a Post-it note on my screen.

'Alice, was this you?' I said, pulling it off. She shook her head. I read it.

Meet me at Waterloo Bridge. I'll be waiting.

I turned it over but there was no name anywhere.

37

Now

'I don't know why you wouldn't tell me about stabbing Russell. When I asked you – the first fucking question I always ask every client is if they've got any previous –' He slaps his hand against the wall now and then faces me.

'Convictions. You said convictions. It didn't go anywhere. I wasn't charged with anything. They can't use that, can they?' I didn't see how they could. No jury had decided I was guilty of anything to do with Russell.

'Don't fucking even do that, Layla. This isn't a game. You knew it was important that you'd knifed someone in the stomach – your husband of all people. And, yes. Yes, they can use it. It's reprehensible behaviour. Bad character. It's admissible. For God's sake, Layla.'

A swell of tears surface and I curse them. 'So, what now?'

He stands panting heavily until finally he catches his breath. 'Now you get some rest. They want to recommence the interviews in the morning.'

'Okay,' I say. 'Is there any way I can get home for the night? Just for tonight?'

Peter shakes his head. 'Even if you weren't living with a prosecution witness, it would be impossible. You'll have to make the best of it I'm afraid but I'll see you tomorrow morning. Try and get some sleep. You'll need to be better than you were today if you want to see daylight in the next twenty years.'

The tears come again but I wipe them away hurriedly. 'Can't we just carry on and get it over with?' The thought of enduring a night here is only made worse by the thought of a sleepless night bleeding into a wretched morning.

'No. We all need some sleep – them and us. Also, I want to check out your brother-in-law. See if I can't get a statement from him about this knife, before someone thinks about getting to him first.'

The news surprises me. 'You think he'll help?' I ask.

'Why wouldn't he? It's such a small thing.'

'What if he lies?'

'Then we've lost nothing. And if I have time I want to drop in on Russell. I want to know why he's so intent on shafting you.'

My heart drops a beat. 'You can't talk to him, Peter.'

'You can't. I can. There's no property in a witness. As long as I'm careful not to pressure him in any way so no one can accuse me of attempting to pervert the course of justice.' He is so sure of himself that I can't bear to be the one to stop him.

'I don't mean that, Peter. I mean I don't want you to.' I say it and then hold my breath. I don't want to explain. I just want someone for once to do what I say.

'Layla. There's a limited amount of information that they will have given Russell. He might not know how serious this all is for you. Maybe he thinks there's no way anyone's going to charge you, his wife, with a murder. Maybe he thinks he's helping you out by denying the knife so it's not connected to you. I don't know. But trust me on this, Layla, we have to act now. If they charge – and it's looking highly likely right now – then there's going to be no way out of this until your trial. And that could be a year, two years away. You'll be stuck in a prison on remand. And whatever you might have heard about women's prisons, they're no joke.'

I hold Peter's arm gently while I search for a way to tell him. 'I don't trust Russell. I don't trust him not to make this worse for me in any way that he can. You don't understand what he's really like.'

38

Then

I threw the Post-it note in the bin. Michael didn't know where I worked and even if he had found out, he wouldn't know where my desk was. But who else would leave a message like that? He didn't have my number. If he had to get hold of me, this was how he'd have to do it.

I reminded myself of what he'd said about finding out who the woman was Russell was seeing. I didn't know how I could possibly do that. Russell worked in the operations department of the EA and was dealing with some transitional regulations to do with Brexit, but that's all I knew about his work. It was completely possible he'd told me more about it in the past but that I'd glazed over. How was I expected to find a woman I had neither met nor seen nor had any details whatsoever about? I didn't even have her name.

I Googled the words 'Brexit' and 'chemicals' and 'regulation' to see whether anything came up. What I saw was pretty opaque. There was an organisation called REACH – the Registration, Evaluation, Authorisation and Restriction of Chemicals – which regulated all chemicals in the UK. Or it had. It was an EU body but we were out of the EU. Maybe that was the transitional arrangement he was dealing with. From The EU to the UK. But how did that connect to *e-Vinc*?

I typed in '*e-Vinc*' and after some rabbit holes found a forum that talked about *e-Vinc* trying to develop new versions of previously banned chemicals. Was it something to do with that? I had no idea, but I doubted it. Russell didn't deal with anything like products. All he did was draft frameworks of rules.

I could call Michael – I had his number. If he could give me something more to go on.

'Alice, did you see who put that note on my screen?' I asked again.

'Sorry, no,' she said, immediately turning back to her work. 'I've been in and out. What is it?' She chewed the top of a pen, her eyes being pulled repeatedly from me to her case.

'Nothing,' I said. 'Probably a mistake.' I unzipped my bag to retrieve the number and keyed it into my mobile. But then just before I dialled I thought again. I didn't want him to have my number. I didn't even know who he was beyond what he'd told me and had no way of telling whether any of it was true. I picked up the work phone and dialled. I listened to my heart flicker in time to the rings. Eight rings and no answer.

I readied myself for the journey home. Why the bridge of all places? It had the feeling of an ambush. Or perhaps it really was all as dangerous as Michael had said. I reassured myself as I walked. I was early so whoever it was, they wouldn't be there yet. And there'd be other people all around at this time. It was safe. Still – better not to take the risk.

I pulled up the Uber app and looked for a car. Demand was high – a ten-minute wait for the nearest one. I was about to make the booking, when my phone rang from a withheld number.

I hesitated. The phone continued to ring. Finally, I answered it.

'Layla.' Kate's familiar voice. 'Can we meet?' she asked.

Relief rushed through me, followed quickly by embarrassment at our last meeting. She didn't sound good. There was something fragile about her tone. And she'd hid her number. My mind began to whirr. Perhaps she was with Russell. Her phone had died and she'd had to use his. And now she wanted to meet me and I knew why. She wanted to get ahead of the guilt and confess it all, in a public place, in a small controlled explosion.

'Sure,' I said. 'Jacks? Twenty minutes?'

Jacks was an odd place, a kind of café dressed up as an old gentleman's club. It was drenched in hunting and shooting paraphernalia. One entire wall was given over to watercolours of hunts, alongside replicas of vintage shotguns and rifles behind glass cases.

I looked for Kate and found her installed in the window, watching over two steaming cups. She stood to meet me and then sat down. Her look was different from the last time I'd seen her. The jeans and tight polo neck had been cast away in favour of a soft pink cashmere dress.

'About the other day,' she said, smoothing her sleeves. I squeezed into the space opposite her. 'Is everything okay?'

There was no guilt in her eyes. Just concern. Maybe Russell was right – it was in my head. 'I'm sorry, Kate,' I said. 'I don't know what that was all about. The disciplinary and Russell and Mum with her issues – I think it all became too much. I'm sorry.'

'Russell called me,' she said. 'He's worried about you too.'

I didn't know what to make of that. 'I'm okay now,' I said. 'I think the stress of the last few weeks just, I don't know, tipped me over some line.'

She smiled. There was warmth in it but also a note of confusion in her expression. She exhaled, relieved. 'As long as you're okay.' Her hand reached out across the table and squeezed mine. And just like that I was transformed into the gauche teenager that I always became in her presence.

I told her about Michael. Not everything but enough. I wanted to reach her and for us to find ourselves again in one another. I told her how I'd driven to Hove to track Michael down at his office.

'Bloody hell, Layla,' she said, eyes round.

'I know. I don't know what's happening to me. I feel as if something is driving me slowly off the edge of a cliff. I'm taking these risks that I'd never take. Russell's hardly around. And then when he is, he clams up. And there's work,' I said. 'I'm back for now but I don't know how long I can keep it up.'

She looked at me uncertainly. I wondered whether she was upset that I hadn't apologised enough for the outburst at her house.

'And, you know, turning up like that at your place,' I added.

She batted off the comment and then took a slow sip of her mint tea, the scent billowing before me. 'But speaking of that day. The photo. What was that all about?'

The Polaroid. I cringed. 'I'm not sure I know any more. At the time I thought you were trying to make me lose my mind. And seeing you in that picture from years ago threw me I guess.'

She stared at me until I felt self-conscious. The room hung momentarily in silence as if waiting.

'What were you doing in Chorley Market anyway? Did I take you?' I said to fill the silence.

She dipped her hand into her handbag and took the picture out. She handed it to me, gravely. 'It's not me, Layla. Look at it. She's way too old in that picture to be me. And that's – isn't it?'

'Sorry what?' I said, not hearing what she'd said.

'Your dad.'

I took it and studied it. 'Sorry, I thought you said – Yes, that's Dad.'

'He looks about thirty in that picture.'

I looked again. She was right. It couldn't be her. In this light it didn't even look like her. There was a fizz of blonde hair, but everything else was wrong. The girl in the picture was older than Kate would have been. And though Kate today was long-limbed and willowy, she hadn't always been fully in charge of her own body then. The girl in the picture was a woman. I put the Polaroid face down.

We sat for a few minutes waiting for the charge in the air to dissipate. Ragtime jazz pumped through tiny speakers making me feel even more dislocated than usual.

'So what did he say, this Michael?' she asked after a while.

'I don't know, Kate. He seemed to think that Russell was in danger.'

'That's worrying, isn't it?'

I was afraid she might overreact but I pressed on. 'It is, and I'm not sure I trust him. There's something not right about him. The worst thing is how I keep bumping into him. Out of nowhere. I mean, here, in London, is one thing. But Hove?'

'Didn't you say you went there specifically to find him though?'

I drained my coffee. It wasn't exactly what I'd meant. 'True,' I said. 'Can we talk about something else? How are you?'

Later as we left the café, I checked the time. Someone was there on the bridge waiting for me. 'An early drink? If you're free?'

'Go on then,' she said after a beat. 'Where?'

'There's that bar on the corner of Waterloo Bridge.'

39

Now

'Layla. Fuck. Shit. Let me just sort these papers out a second. Sorry. Okay. How are you? Did you sleep?' When he enters any room, this is what Peter does. He dominates the space so that there's barely enough room for the air.

I blink away the fatigue and nod. 'I've had better nights but I think I was so tired that I managed some sleep.'

'The noise – did it reach you? From out there?'

A chanting that had started up early this morning. I couldn't make it out clearly except for the words *NO RELEASE*. 'No. They'd gone by the time you'd left. Only turned up again this morning.'

He smiles. 'I told them that they'd taken you away for the night. They dispersed quickly enough after that.'

He sits next to me on my concrete bed and gets out his phone and starts to scroll. He's made notes.

'They really hate me,' I say as he finds what he's looking for.

Peter nods. 'Today. Tomorrow maybe. Then they won't know who you are any more. It's women for some reason. They always come out for the women. I think they hold you to a higher standard.'

I'm not sure whether he means me as a woman or as an Asian woman. But either works. People expect more of women. And more still from Asian women. Maybe they want me to be weak and biddable. But even if I am that, they won't see my vulnerability, only the destruction that I might wreak. I turn their worlds inside out. He sees my face drop and puts his phone away. 'Come on. We need you back in the game.'

'Okay. I'm here,' I say and muster a smile. 'Any luck with Sam?'

'Well there's good news and bad news on that front. The bad news is that he wouldn't speak to me.'

'And the good?'

'That he hasn't spoken to the police and looks as if he has no interest in speaking to them.'

'Can you be sure?' I say, because I know how thick the blood is in that family. I've seen Sam covering for Russell.

'I think so. He wanted me to tell you he wasn't getting involved on either side. Which is as good as we can hope for.'

I nod. There isn't much I can do about it from here. Keeping a person locked up isn't just about confining you. It's about removing every possible way of communicating with anyone else. It's a kind of torture to soften you. 'What's the plan for this morning then?' I ask because I can't think of anything else to say.

'Before we get there – there is one thing you should know.'

'What?'

'I went round to see Russell.'

'Peter!' I say and stand up so that my anger has room to swell.

'Don't worry. That's not what I wanted to tell you. I didn't speak to him. I couldn't, as it happened.'

'What do you mean?'

'When I got there the boys in the white suits had taken over the gaff.'

'What?'

'Scenes of crime officers. They were conducting a search.'

'But is that normal?' I feel my pulse begin to race. What were they looking for? I scanned my memory for any speck that might incriminate me somehow.

'Yes and no. Doing a search, yes, that's pretty standard. But SOCO? Doing a forensic search at a *crime scene* is one thing. But I can't see why they'd want one at your place. Can you?'

The thought of a forensics team wandering through my house in paper suits adds to the surreality of the last day and a half and does nothing for my panic. Maybe it was standard procedure.

'Can you?' Peter repeats, causing me to look up. 'I'm asking. Can you see a reason why they might want to do a forensic search?'

I shake my head. 'No. I can't.'

'Suppose we'll find out soon enough when we go in,' he says and checks his watch. 'Five minutes.'

'What are they going to cover – do you know?'

'Not really. But they don't have long to do it,' he says. 'Less than an hour now.'

Less than an hour. The thought of an end in sight makes my heart jump. 'What should I do? *No comment* or?'

Peter puts his briefcase softly on the floor. 'As before, Layla. I don't like *no comment* interviews; they make juries suspicious. And your case is suspicious enough. Dead body in your arms. It's not a *no comment* case. But. As I told you yesterday, it's fine to go *no comment* to inadmissible or inappropriate or irrelevant questions. I'll step in when I see them. But the real question is, what's your objective here?'

'What do you mean?'

'I mean if you're protecting yourself in case the thing goes to trial, then we go one way. But if you're trying to persuade them not to charge you at all, then we go another.'

'The second, of course,' I say before he's even finished.

He sighs. 'It's not as simple as that. I don't think we've got much chance with the evidence as it is. But if we were somehow going to convince them not to charge, the only possible way we could do that would be effectively proving it wasn't you. In this interview. And that entails telling the police things that might end up putting a rope around your neck if it goes wrong. It's a really risky strategy. The police are up against the clock. They charge or release when the time is up. But that means we are too. We've got a limited time to make them believe it wasn't you.'

'But it wasn't me.'

He looks at me dead in the eyes. 'Convince them.'

40

Then

From the bar on the corner of Waterloo Bridge, I kept an eye out for Michael but saw nobody. I wondered whether he saw me but couldn't approach because I was with someone. At one point at just after six I strained my eyes and could have sworn that I'd seen a ghost in the mist rising off the river. A ghost who looked like Dad. But then I blinked and he vanished.

We stayed out and drank, Kate and I. She talked and I listened until we'd wound back time twenty years. That fancy dress party we'd held that one time. How I'd bought us both identical wigs and how under them we'd looked the same. When she left, I was sad to see her go. But then we hugged and I couldn't shake the sense that there under the pears and freesias was a thread of vanilla.

When I got home, I was surprised to see Russell – in the kitchen. He looked up from his saucepan but didn't say anything. I skirted past him to get a drink from the fridge, suppressing the anger that was building at the sight of him.

'How was it with Sam?' I asked, taking a seat at the ruined counter.

He took his bowl to the table and chewed sullenly. For a few stretched seconds, I thought he wasn't going to speak. The heat rose on my skin until my face began to writhe. Finally, he swallowed.

'Fine. He told me you called.' There was the glow like sun on his cheeks still. His eyes, forest-green lights, twinkled as if nothing could be wrong.

'But you didn't call back.' It was more statement than question. The smell from his food began to make me feel hungry.

'Don't,' he said.

'What?' I said, beginning to flare.

'This. I don't have the energy tonight. You were checking up on me so you wanted me to call back. And because I didn't, because I wouldn't *behave* by calling you, I'm getting this.'

For a second I thought about what he said. I wasn't trying to control him. All I wanted was a chance to escape my head. I just needed something – an admission, a concrete denial. Something I could process, but instead all I was getting was this – this refusal to commit to a position.

He picked up his fork and carried on eating. Then after a mouthful he pointed it at the countertop. 'Any chance of getting that seen to?'

'The fitter is coming next weekend to polish it out,' I said, lying.

He laughed. 'Polish it out? Really?'

'Fuck off, Russell,' I said and got up to make some food. I rooted around for an onion to chop for an omelette. In the drawer I found a small paring knife.

He got up from his food and stood behind me. For a minute he said nothing but I could hear his breath deciding between words.

'Layla, I'm worried about you. About your mental health.'

'No. No, you don't get to make this my fault,' I said, half turning around to face him. 'You just have to answer your bloody phone!'

'Kate – *your* best friend – she called *me*. Do you know why? Because she was worried about you. *I'm* worried about you.' His voice was loud and I could hear the drink in it.

I was silent then, and turned back to the chopping board as I waited for the tide of his anger to peter out.

'I thought you called her,' I said but he continued as if I hadn't said anything.

'I was in the middle of a meeting. Talking about fucking policy and approval protocols with counsel and I get a call from a hysterical Kate worried about you! Poor her.'

'Poor her?' I said. 'Really? Whatever you like, Russell. Whatever you like.' It wasn't meant to mean anything. I had just run out of things to say. 'She's fine,' I wanted to say. 'I just saw her and she's fine.' But I said nothing.

I continued to dice the onion at the chopping board. Russell stepped closer and was now right behind me as I leaned my weight on the knife to take the end off the onion. He tried to spin me round, holding me by the left elbow. 'I'm trying to talk to you!'

I turned abruptly, the knife still in my hand. He was close. Too close. And as I twisted round, the blade went straight into his waist. He leapt back in shock to find the knife still dangling in his stomach, an inch up the blade. Without thinking, he pulled it out and sliced my hand. Blood trickled down onto the tile from the back of my hand where it had cut the vein and joined with blood from him. The blood mingled on the floor like a pact. He stared at me open-mouthed.

41

Now

The same people in the same places gives this the feeling of a play. As if I'd miss them if I never saw them again. What I want most is for them all to pull back the curtain, step forward and take a bow. All their stage make-up smudged quickly clean. Hair tousled, brows glistening with exertion. And smiles all round, to show me they aren't any longer villains and heroes – that they were just acting.

'Just to advise you that we made an application to the Magistrates' Court for a warrant of further detention and they granted it,' Omer says after repeating the caution.

I look at Peter to see whether I have understood. My heart thuds as he speaks.

'How long?'

Omer looks at the clock. 'We have about six hours.'

Peter takes the piece of paper that Metcalf slides over to him. Once he has read it Peter pats my arm. 'It's fine, Layla. It could have been thirty-six hours.'

I can't believe that they can do this without telling us. And then it hits me. To get the extra time they will have told the court that they need it to make further enquiries. Who are they talking to? Russell?

'Have you ever had mental health issues?' Omer says after a short pause. He says it as if he is asking me whether I have had a decent breakfast. Is that what they are investigating? If so there's nothing in the system about me. I've never complained to doctors about any of the strange things that I might've seen or heard. I think that's true. But like everyone, I've been upset sometimes when I've talked to my GP. When I thought I was depressed. But that's not the same at all.

'No.'

'Any history in the family?'

It's still casual, the tone, but it feels tense on this side of the question. As if the answer will detonate.

'That's a big question. Depends what you mean. My mother has vascular dementia. It's not a mental health condition as such but does have – *components*.'

He ventures a half-smile and even that changes his face from that of an accountant to one of a human. 'So, what I'm getting at is whether there's anything that could be classed as a psychosis? Have you seen things or heard voices?'

'No.'

'For the time that you were on the roof garden until emergency units arrived to the scene, do you have a clear recollection of events?'

'Yes,' I say, catching the edge in my voice.

'You had an understanding of the quality of your actions?'

'What do you mean by that?' I ask. I turn to Peter who translates it.

'He's asking you whether you were insane. If you didn't know what you were doing was wrong, then you could have an insanity defence. He's heading that off. Aren't you, Detective?'

Omer flushes a little at the criticism implicit in what Peter has said. 'Not at all. I just want to make sure that you were aware of what was going on around you and that you perhaps hadn't had an episode or hallucinated any part of the events.'

Peter smiles and shrugs off his jacket. As he does the scent of deodorant dusts the air. He rolls a sleeve and looks Omer straight in the eye. 'If she was hallucinating, how would she know?'

'That's not exactly what I said.'

'Can we move on? Ms Mahoney isn't raising insanity.'

Metcalf smiles in a way that makes me go cold and I wonder what is at the heart of his cruelty. Is it intrinsic or did something happen to him?

'Okay,' Omer says. 'We will move on. We took a statement from a work colleague of yours, Alice Cook. There are a couple of things we want to ask you about her statement.'

I hear the words but my mind is still a few minutes behind in the conversation. I don't want to lose the chance to tell them about the ghost. It has implications. I know that. Once I tell them it will set off all kinds of pandemonium. But if I don't mention it now, then what? It will seem contrived and invented. I remember a thing from the dusty corners of my law school criminal law about recent fabrication. If I mention it later, it will seem like a lie.

I look across at Peter who has his head cocked, waiting for the questions about Alice. But it's not Alice he's interested in. What he wants is the information about the search so that he can reassess where we are and what my chances of leaving here are. He occupies most of the space at this desk with his body leaned over it. For a second I feel as though I could curl up against the side of him and use him as shelter. Maybe that is what I am doing after all. There is a question but I haven't heard any of it. They are all now looking at me. The three men compressing all the space there is in here into thicker and thicker blankets of warm, stale air.

I can't rely on anyone – Russell has made that clear to me. I had one plan in my head and now under the bright light of this new day, I see the colours fading. I have to bring this round to my advantage. I look across to Peter and lay a hand on his arm. As he keeps telling me, these men are here for just one reason, to put me down.

'I think I need to tell you about the ghost.'

They stare at me. Peter is about to say something to interrupt me but I squeeze his forearm to stop him. 'It's okay,' I say. 'I have to. They'll find out and it's better this way.'

42

Then

I raced to the bathroom to wrap bandages around my cut. It didn't seem serious but the spurting blood made me dizzy. I left Russell downstairs. He'd torn off his shirt and held it against his wound to help staunch the flow. It wasn't deep.

'What the hell, Layla,' he'd said as I'd hurried out of the kitchen.

'Go to A & E, Russell. It needs a stitch,' I said, heading upstairs. I was applying pressure to my hand when I heard him thump upstairs to rattle around his cupboards for some clothes before returning downstairs and slamming the front door as he left.

An hour later and I was sitting on my bed, wound cleaned and dressed. Russell wouldn't be back for hours yet if he was at the hospital.

In the mess and tangle of the bottom of the wardrobe, I dug around until I found what I wanted bundled into an old pair of tights. I smoothed it all out and then shook it free. The bandaged hand throbbed and bloomed in places with blood. In the mirror I watched myself as I pulled the wig over my head. I don't even remember now what I bought it for. Was it *that* fancy dress party? All I remember was that I'd gone all-out and bought us both real ones, not fancy dress ones. I'd kept them both. In the mirror all I saw was a cascade of blonde, like a waterfall. When I wore it back then, I felt transformed. There were no sidelong looks with unasked questions about where I was from. I could pass through unmolested. Now I just felt invisible, as if I could fade away from sight.

From the bed I stared at the window, the new hair liquid on my shoulders. In the darkness, the window felt like a one-way mirror. A glimpse into secret lives. I got up and stood right against the glass so I could look out. The bandage on my hand burned and I held it against the coolness of the window to soothe it. Below a woman was rushing into her car. In the distance, if I turned my face flat to the glass, I could make out the rise of the road and on the horizon the jagged glass peak of the Shard.

Russell came back from hospital in the early hours. I had left the curtains open and could see crimson streaks cut into the sky. He hobbled pointedly into the bedroom, unbuttoned his shirt carefully and dropped it to the floor before making his way to the bed. I saw the small wadding covering the few stitches he must have had.

'What did they say?' I asked, sitting up. He said nothing but instead bent stiffly to pull the covers back.

'Russell?'

'I was lucky. It didn't penetrate past the muscle. Another inch would have been a problem,' he said, climbing in awkwardly.

'What did they –'

'Three stitches. Dissolving,' he added.

'I'm sorry,' I said quietly.

He sighed as he pulled the covers carefully around himself. 'It's fine. It was an accident.' But he said it as if it was anything but.

I got up and left so that he could sleep without being disturbed by me. I'd started the night determined to ask him about the chemicals and the EU and what connections he might have to Michael. I'd wanted to ask him about the woman, but all that was in ruins now.

In the morning I took a different route into town. Instead of approaching Waterloo, I took a bus that went across Blackfriars Bridge, and from there a short walk across the Embankment and up through Temple would take me to the Strand. It was nicer but the journey added about ten minutes. As I walked I thought about Russell and how quickly it had free-fallen. Last night we were only a hair's breadth from disaster. We could have killed one another.

I don't know whether it was that – the different journey – or what was happening with Michael, but the world felt displaced somehow as if everything were slightly off. Not physically, but *dimensionally*, as though I were a few minutes into the future or the past. I shrugged off the sensation and concentrated on my breathing until every part of me was vibrating in tiny waves.

When I got off the bus, I was calmer. My adrenaline levels, stable. The intrusive thoughts were at bay. And as I walked along the Embankment, I felt vague and almost peaceful for a change as though I was coming to a resolution about Russell. What happened last night made me realise that whatever I suspected him of lived in a world that hadn't yet been made. It didn't mean that he wasn't seeing someone else or that he wasn't lying to me: it was simply that those things hadn't been uttered into existence yet.

At that precise moment, walking with the river just beyond my peripheral vision, I tripped on an uneven pavement slab. I fell, lurching horribly forward. The blood rushed into my face as I snapped through the air, anticipating the pain from an abrupt meeting with the pavement. And then, just as I had surrendered in that split second to the sickening thud of contact, something happened. I felt myself being magically pulled back to my feet, as if being rewound on a reel of film.

I looked around at the person who had pulled me up. At the sight of him, the blood drained from my face.

'You?' I said, gathering myself. I rubbed myself clean of the debris that hadn't made it to my clothes.

'You didn't come to meet me at the bridge. I thought maybe you might. I phoned your office and left a message. Did you not get it?'

I stared. 'What are you doing here?'

'I wanted to see you. And if Mohammed won't come to the mountain, then the mountain must come to Mohammed. You look shocked. What is it?'

'You?' I said again. His face was different. On the surface. But underneath, where the eyes lived, it was the same as it always had been.

He stood smiling at me. The bright morning sun gave his skin a square of gold light. 'Come on then,' he said, holding his arms out. 'Give your old dad a hug.'

He took my hand as he had when I was a little girl and we walked through Middle Temple Garden. There was a locked iron gate to negotiate but we bustled in just as a resident was coming out. She looked us up and down and smiled. She knew we didn't belong, but in that English way, would rather see strangers trespass where they didn't belong than appear racist.

The garden, laid out on classical lines, still held the soft charm of an English country garden. There were hidden spaces behind raised terraces. A bench posed out of the sun under an old mulberry tree. We made our way there and sat without speaking and breathed in the scent of still dewy grass. He seemed old and young at the same time. His smile was gentle but oddly fixed.

It was thirty years since I had seen him. I needed to see where he had begun to fray for the memory to hold together. I searched his hands. Were there small liver spots there on the backs? How were the fingernails. I searched for the grime of entropy in him. Thirty years couldn't pass without taking their toll.

'How are you?' he asked me repeatedly.

'I'm fine. Dad. You're here.'

He continued to smile and then stroked my face. I was fighting hard against the certainty that he wasn't real. He couldn't be. I gazed out towards the river and tried to enjoy the sensation of the sun on my back. That feeling of warmth reminded me of a time deep in the past. It transported me to a childhood whose details I couldn't remember. But the feeling was tangible. It was that feeling of warmth and safety. We were all innocent then.

And then I blinked and I was here in the office.

I went to Alice's desk and pulled up a chair.

'Everything okay?' she asked quietly.

'I think so. Do I seem okay to you?'

She tugged a few strands of copper hair into a point and sucked the end. 'Compared to what?'

'To me. Compared to how I normally am.'

She considered this for a moment. 'Compared to how you were a month ago? Not really. But compared to how you were, say a week ago? Yes. Definitely more normal. What's going on? Is Fry bothering you?'

'What? Oh, no. It's nothing.' I got up to go but then felt so dislocated that I sat back down again. 'If I was being mad, you'd tell me, wouldn't you?'

'Ha,' she said, amused. 'That would be ironic.' And then began to squeak softly to herself as she turned to her papers.

43

Then

As soon as my hours were done, I went home. The journey was quick and uneventful and my thoughts kept returning again and again to Dad. I should call Mum. There were things I had to speak to her about. If I'd hallucinated him, I'd done it in breathtaking detail. But maybe that was how it worked when you became 'florid' as Mum had in the past.

Through the small glass rectangles of the front door, I saw a light was burning. Russell was home – if he'd even left. I lumbered in and saw the day's mail neatly stacked on the small cabinet. He must have made it as far as the hallway at least. I thought about him stiff-bodied from his stitches, but he'd done it to himself. I didn't have the space in my head to assume responsibility for another layer of guilt.

I shuffled through the envelopes. Junk mail, bank statements and then something more substantial in a buff A4 envelope. I sat on the stairs and tore it across the top. Inside was the expert's report on the hair samples. Quickly, I folded over the top of the envelope and shoved it into my handbag. I didn't want Russell to see it.

In the kitchen I saw his remains – toast for breakfast and a can of soup for lunch, the cookery of an invalid – but no Russell. I dragged a bottle of wine from the rack, opened it and then took it away to the living room to read my letter. There were two sealed bags returning the reference samples and along with them a report. I skimmed through the stuff about reference samples and methodology, and went straight to the conclusions.

I read it and then, not quite believing what I'd read, I read it again. And a third time. I was in the process of reading through the earlier sections carefully when Russell pushed open the door and came in. I stuffed the papers into my bag. He was rigid – all the softness was gone from his body.

'I'm going away on Friday for a long weekend. Fishing.'

I looked up at him. There was soup on his trousers. He swiped at it when he caught me noticing. It left a small heart-shaped stain.

'You okay to fish?' I asked.

He closed his eyes as if trying to control what he wanted to say. 'Should be by then. Anyway. It's mainly standing around.'

Silence whined in the stale air. 'Who with?'

'My brother,' he said, cutting his eyes away from me.

'Does he know?' I asked tartly.

He left the room, shaking his head. But a minute later he came back. 'And I've called someone to deal with that mess you made in the kitchen. I hope you've got cash because they'll want cash.'

When he left the room, the silence in it began to hum again. Sometimes that meant trouble for me. I had to focus to keep the thoughts at bay. To fight the swell, I returned to the report and puzzled at the conclusions again. The hairs didn't match. They were different. These weren't Kate's hairs I kept finding. It wasn't Kate that Russell was meeting. But it was someone. The analysis showed that Kate's, which they referred to as the reference sample, was naturally blonde of Caucasian origin. The other was dyed blonde, but of South Asian origin – possibly Indian.

He didn't know anyone else of Indian origin, in London. Why was that hair in my house, in my kitchen, on a clothes brush, on Russell's shirt? It couldn't be a friend or a neighbour. Could it be a work colleague of Russell's? I used to know them when we first got married. He talked obsessively about them. The ones who had been there too long and wouldn't make way for the new ones like him. The ones who were new or annoying or ditzy or lazy. There were none who this hair could belong to. I thought back to that day where I'd crashed his lunch at the restaurant. That woman, who he said was counsel, was she Asian? All I remembered about her now in the haze the memory was glazed in, was that she was beautiful. Intense. But I'd have remembered if she'd been Asian, like me. She was tall and her cheeks were ruddy as if she'd been slapped. I didn't remember her face clearly.

It made it all the more likely that he was having an affair. There was no innocent way for the hairs to have inveigled themselves into his clothes and onto our kitchen floor.

The thought of it, the secrecy, the betrayal, the life behind the scenes, began to claw away at me. I could feel it making its way deeper and deeper into my head. Soon it would take hold and when there, disperse into tiny hotspots, impossible to pick out.

I ran from the room and raced through the house, looking for him. He was in the bathroom, shaving. Shaving in the morning made his face look slippery and for years now he'd shaved in the evening. He was naked from the waist up. The wadding taped to his stomach was stained maroon in places with dried blood.

'I know about the woman,' I said. He coloured for a second but disguised his discomfort with a scrape of blade against his cheek.

'Woman?' he said, dropping his razor into the basin.

'The Asian one.'

He turned back to his own face and washed it carefully in the mirror. 'Layla, I think you need to go and see somebody. And while we're on the subject. Can you please stop going through my things?'

'What?' I said confused.

'My things. Don't think I haven't noticed you moving things around.'

'Like what?' I said.

'Don't,' he said. 'My watches. One day they're there and the next they've disappeared. And my sock drawer. Why am I finding random cufflinks in there?'

'Well, it's not me.'

'Then who?'

'I don't know. The cleaner might have done it,' I said and immediately wished I could take it back.

'We haven't had a cleaner for a year,' he said.

'I know, I know. I didn't mean recently but maybe then, a year ago.' I didn't remember moving his cufflinks or anything that I didn't put back in its place. I weighed up the possibility that he was trying to make me doubt myself, but gaslighting wasn't his style.

He replaced the towel and rubbed his face. 'I'm really worried about you, Lay.'

I went downstairs driven by hunger gnawing at my insides and rummaged for something quick to eat. A packet of crisps, some nuts, anything. In the back of one of the kitchen cupboards was his bag. I reached in and saw his fishing knife. I didn't remember putting it back there.

I opened the blade and ran my thumb along the edge, and felt a quiver of energy. The possibilities that lay balanced on that steel edge were infinite. Life and death.

I looked at it for a whole minute before replacing it and going up to the bedroom. I needed to be as far away from it as I could be. And then as I sat on the bed, I heard a tiny buzz from somewhere near Russell's wardrobe. If I hadn't been perfectly still, I'd have missed it. Training an ear for Russell's footsteps. I leapt to his closet and began swiping as quickly as possible through his hanging clothes. The sound of the pump from the shower was still vibrating through the floor. He wasn't a person to linger under the water, I had to hurry.

A second later the pump turned off. Frantically I thought about what he was wearing yesterday when he went to the hospital. The sound of footsteps now came from below as he walked up the half-flight. Whatever he'd worn most recently was likely to be at the far end of the hanging rail. There was a cotton jacket there. I patted down the pockets and froze. It was the burner phone – the phone he assured me he never had. A message had come through. And then just at that second, Russell was on the landing pushing open the door. I dropped the phone back into the pocket and closed the wardrobe door. I was breathless. I needed cover so as he came into the bedroom, I raced towards the door so that we bumped into one another. I panted out loud.

'For God's sake,' I said and left the room. Once down the stairs I doubled over catching my breath.

But I'd read the message. I just couldn't believe what it said.

I sat at the kitchen counter trying to make sense of it and more than that, the fact that Russell had lied to me. It was his phone. Of course it had been his phone. I had seen it under the bed but the way he had denied it had made me believe that I couldn't trust myself. I'd trusted him instead. I thought about the message that had flashed up from an unnamed contact.

Meet me tmrw on the roof. 7.30 x

44

Now

'The Ghost?' Omer says. The tone is a mixture of boredom and frustration. He wants to get on and knows I am interfering with his custody time limits. I've decided that this is the only way out right now. Once the clock runs down the police have to get an extension. And according to Peter, they need to justify the further detention to the court. All I can do now is to make sure they can't justify it. I don't like taking risks but I have to give explanations where I can safely, and let the time run out where I can't.

'Well, not like that. It's not a pseudonym. I thought I'd seen a ghost.'

Omer nods impatiently. 'And can you tell us what the relevance is for this investigation?'

I lean back a little in my chair and add a flash of disbelief to my expression. 'What you said. About hallucinations. I thought I should mention it.'

He smiles as though I have played a chess move he'd not expected but is nonetheless impressed by. 'So, you hallucinated that you'd seen a ghost?'

I nod seriously. 'Well, it wasn't a real ghost.'

'Okay then, tell us about the ghost if you think it's important.'

'There's not much to tell. It was broad daylight. I was walking into work and I thought I saw the ghost of my father. He spoke to me. He was as real as you.'

'I see,' he said.

Metcalf is simmering. He elbows his way into the exchange. 'Is there anyone we can confirm that with?'

'What? That I saw a ghost?' I say with more mischief than I expect.

He colours and when he speaks he is more than normally abrasive, 'I mean did you tell anyone about it?'

'My mother.'

'I see,' Omer says, wrapping up this line of questions. 'Well, we will just have to see whether you intend to run an insanity defence but for the moment there's nothing that makes you feel like you can't continue?'

I flick an eye at the clock. There's a careful balance to strike. 'I feel fine. I just wanted to be sure that I told you. I know I didn't really see a ghost. I know there are no such things as ghosts. But I know that I believed at the time that it was a ghost.'

Peter gives me a questioning look and makes a note in his book. I smile lightly at him to assure him I'm okay. That I'm not a killer and that I couldn't ever be one.

'Can we move on now to the statement that we took yesterday from your work colleague Alice Cook?'

'Is there any disclosure?' Peter asks.

'No. It's a short point really. We went to see her to ask about you and what your movements were when she saw you last. We can go through that later but when we asked her how you were over the last few weeks and days and if you'd been behaving strangely, she said some interesting things.'

'Did she? Is this about me asking her if I seemed mad to her?'

'Sorry what?' Omer again.

'I asked whether I seemed like I was acting normal to her. Is it that?'

'No. Not that. Ms Cook told one of our officers that you had asked to borrow a toy car from her that she keeps for recreating car accidents. She said that you kept refusing to return it to her even though it had sentimental value to her.'

'No, that's not –'

'And that when you finally did return it – well.'

'She was most upset,' Metcalf added. 'Our officers said she was crying when she gave her statement.'

There's a pause in which I hold my breath. I don't know how much else she has told them. My throat is dry and I try to swallow some moisture back into it. I am terrified it's going to give me away.

Peter looks up and searches first my face and then theirs.

The room is fizzing with energy drawn from the silence. Outside the noise of sirens and distant reversing trucks filters up and tries to dilute the tension in here.

My heart beats out the seconds in double-time. I wait. Is it coming for me, that next question, or did she take pity on me? She would have been aware that the police were investigating a serious crime – a murder – and that I was a suspect. Would that make her more or less likely to help me?

'Why did you do it?' Omer asks.

I feel relief but hope that when I exhaled I didn't signal it too obviously. 'I didn't.'

'You know my next question.'

'I don't know,' I say. 'It can only have been Russell. But did I see him do it? No. Do I think he did it? Probably.'

'Why? Can you think of a reason why he might do that?'

'That's what he's like. That's what he was doing to me. He was moving things around or hiding things and pretending he wasn't.' And now he was telling police things like I had stabbed him.

'It's funny you should mention hiding things. He told officers that that was what you were doing. You were hiding his cufflinks or what have you and putting them in different places. And that, in his words, you were becoming paranoid. He was worried about you.'

Peter stiffens and then bangs the desk with a fist. 'Come on, Detective. I've let a lot of this go. But you can't just make comments like that. Ask a question. That's what Ms Mahoney's here for. Not to hear what her husband thinks of her.'

'It's just that to me, looking at it, I would say neutrally, it looks like you're not completely in control of your anger – causing criminal damage to property. Would you agree?'

'No, I would not.'

He lets a breath out through his nose. 'Let's park this for a bit because I'd like to deal with something else, please. I went over the answers you gave us last night and I just want to be sure about one thing. You said you'd never met the victim before?'

'That's right.'

'And you stand by that?'

'Yes,' I say, feeling something coming towards me.

'You had a good look at her on the night of the murder and again, just for the tape, you'd never met her before that day?'

'Never.'

'In the course of the search at your house yesterday, officers uncovered a couple of interesting things. There was a forensic hair-strand report – recent – found in your wardrobe. You'd commissioned an expert to analyse two hair samples.'

He pauses and waits for an answer.

'What?' I say, trying to keep the colour in my face as it sinks to my throat.

The detectives exchange looks. 'Well, Ms Mahoney. The obvious question is, why were you doing a forensic hair analysis?'

Peter turns to look at my reaction. I don't know how to answer this question. There is too much to explain and these police officers won't understand how Russell had driven me to this.

'No comment.'

'The hairs weren't a match.'

'Okay,' I say.

'To each other. But one was a match.'

'What do you mean?' I say, puzzled. 'They weren't.'

'One belonged to a Ms Kate Peel according to the labelled strands and was not a match to the other.'

'Exactly,' I say.

'But the other was a direct match from the victim.'

'It can't be!'

'And I want to know, how you had it if you'd never seen her before?'

I throw my mind back to the report. The one hair sample was Kate's. I knew that. But the other was South Asian, the report had said. It had to be a bluff.

'It couldn't have been a match.'

'But it was. We had the lab run a quick analysis. It'll take a few days to get the full report. But the short-form report is clear. It's a match with a 99 per cent probability.'

'It can't be,' I say, looking at Peter. I turn back to Omer. 'If you have the report there, you'll see that the expert said that the one I was unsure about was from a person of South Asian descent. Indian probably.'

Omer looks at his papers and nods. 'That's right,' he says, his face blank. 'We found hairs on the victim's face and hairs that weren't hers.'

Peter stands up and is furious. 'Are you serious, Detective? Suggesting that they were the victim's hairs and now admitting that they're not! I've got a good mind to report you for that.'

Omer colours. 'Well, I think I said hairs *from* the victim. In any case the point is that they're hairs that had somehow been transferred to her. And those hair strands were an exact match for the very ones Ms Mahoney had tested.'

'What?' I say.

'And sent off to a lab two weeks before she was killed.'

I think about how I stroked her hair when I was holding her. Tears begin to swim in my eyes and I dab them away with the back of my hand. I haul myself back into the room. There's no time for this. I need to concentrate.

'How did these hairs find their way onto the victim's face and clothes?'

'I don't know,' I say. 'Maybe they came off me onto her. When I was holding her.'

Metcalf shuffles his chair forward. 'Maybe. We don't think so, though. It's much more hair than we'd expect in secondary transfer.'

I frown at him until Omer picks up the baton. 'There's over fifty per cent more hair than we'd expect if it just came off your head. But it's not your hair. If you've picked someone else's hair up on your clothes and then transferred them onto her, we wouldn't see anything like the amount we have.'

I shake my head. Lost. The room, the detectives, even Peter, feel like they are bobbing on water and receding so fast that I can't keep them in view. I can't give them an answer. So there's a limited amount they can do with that line of questions. But we will circle back to it eventually. I have to get out. I try and catch Peter's eye but he's making a note and I don't want to be too obvious about it.

'There is one other puzzling thing. When you were arrested, you were wearing a lanyard. We have it on your property sheet.'

'What about it?' Peter asks sternly.

'Well. We were just wondering why the lanyard had someone else's name on it. Did you give that name to them when you got your pass?'

'No comment.' I give Peter another look but now he's focused his attention on the detectives.

'You chose an interesting name though, didn't you?'

'What do you mean?' Peter asks.

'Well, as Ms Mahoney no doubt will tell you, Kate Peel, the same name on the hair sample that she sent off to the lab.'

Peter has finally asked for the break I've been telegraphing to him. In an interview this long, he says to the police either he gets coffee or he is leaving and heading off to a Starbucks. They laugh good-humouredly at that and show us into a room with a coffee machine. As soon as we are alone, I take Peter by the arm.

'You took your time.' My heart is racing with what I need to say. With what I have to run by him.

'I wanted to wait for a convenient time. They were asking you some pretty interesting questions about hair-strand testing that you organised and stopping an interview at the interesting bits is a bit like sending up a flare. I hope you're not going to tell me we have something to worry about here.'

I drop his arm. 'No. I've remembered something. I don't know why I didn't think of it earlier.'

'For crying out loud, Layla.' He takes a deep breath and the raises an eyebrow. He holds both for a second. 'Well?'

I run the events through my head to make sure I have them right. 'Michael. I think there's a way that I can prove he exists.'

Peter widens his eyes. 'Pissing hell. I'm your friend in this, Lay. Me. I'm the one you can tell shit to.' He rubs his face. 'If you don't trust me –'

'I do. It's not that. It's just the CCTV of the building that reminded me.'

'What about it?'

'It's not the only place in London to have CCTV.'

'No. But if you're expecting traffic cams or CCTV from the street to pick him up, it's not that simple. Most places don't keep CCTV for very long. Some not more than twenty-four hours. And if you're thinking of shops with street-facing CCTV, the quality is usually shit. That's if they're working.'

I nod anxiously, waiting for him to finish. 'No. Not the street. I'm talking about a building. A hotel. I went with him to a hotel.'

'You did what?'

'Not like that. Look it's a long story. But a week ago I went to a hotel around the corner from Russell's offices with him. It's the Plaza. They'll have cameras, surely.'

He takes out his blue notebook. 'What day?' he asks and then notes down the answer. 'Apart from the entrance did you go into any other public areas?'

I think. 'A lift.'

'Okay, that might be good,' he says. 'Where did you go?'

'To the hotel bar.'

'Great. There should be a lot of people then who might have seen you. Layla, this might be the thing that makes the difference.'

I cast my mind back. I'm not sure how to explain all this to him in a way that doesn't make it sound stranger than it is. 'There were only two people there. I think they were on honeymoon.'

'What kind of hotel bar has only two people in it?' he says, puzzled.

I swallow and remind myself there's nothing odd about this in itself. 'It was windy.' He stares at me as if I have gone crazy. 'It was on the roof of the hotel.'

He absorbs the information and begins to pace. And then after a while he nods to himself. 'Okay. That's fine. But listen to me. We go in. You answer your questions about the hair strands. And then – only when I say do you raise this. Understood?'

'Yes.'

'I don't want anyone to think you're trying to dodge any bullets. Come on, let's go. We have a lot to get through and I want them to get these enquiries underway as soon as possible.'

45

Then

In the morning, as soon as the light pierced the curtains, Russell was up and out of bed. He winced as he moved but he was better than the day before. Before I was out of the shower, the front door had slammed and he'd gone. Still damp, I checked his wardrobe. The jacket that the phone had been in was gone. I dressed quickly but then felt unwell suddenly – I was having my heart palpitations. My palms became clammy and my face ran cold as the blood dropped out of it. I sat on the bed. Just a few minutes to breathe. The night had been hot and dizzying. My dreams, what I remembered of them, had been flash-cards of unconnected images. Michael. Work. Kate. Hair strands. And then Dad and the strange encounter we'd had. The way he'd smiled at me and taken my hand. And the message on a burner phone in Russell's pocket. All of it percolating in a soup through the night. When I'd woken, it had left me feeling groggy.

I looked across to Russell's clean bedside table. His side of the room, everything of his, free from any memory of him. His cologne, cream and hair-wax, tidy on the chest of drawers.

Just me, in disarray.

I thought back to Dad. As a child, in my memory he was always smiling. He'd been tidy too. Not obsessively like Russell. Some of his clothes would always be out and unfolded, waiting to be rehomed. There was always a jacket on a chair. Scraps of paper littering the bedroom, or the kitchen table. Mum picking up after him. But even so he wasn't really untidy from what I remembered. I'd had an uncle who was more obsessive. Dad's brother would get up early every morning and wipe his car down from top to bottom and poke around in every tiny grill hole for hours. There was something in that obsessiveness that unnerved me. I wondered now whether the compulsive cleaning was hiding something else. A Sisyphus-like penance for something. And Russell – what was his neatness concealing?

I pulled open a drawer and saw his pants neatly stacked, socks in rolls down one side. I reached in with both hands as if to toss a salad and jumbled them all up. Then the drawer beneath. I didn't know what he'd meant about the cufflinks. I wasn't hiding his things or whatever else he thought I was doing with them. But now he had mentioned them, I checked those too. A pair in the shape of miniature crossed daggers came into my hand. They were beautiful. Lifelike. I put them in my pocket. They felt comforting – a piece of something he'd worn close to his skin.

There were jeans and trousers in the drawer, again neatly folded and smoothed. From the top I took some mustard chinos and patted them down for objects before rolling them into a ball and throwing them against the wardrobe. They thumped heavily, before sliding down, inert. I picked them up again, shouted out: '*Coward! Coward! Coward!*'

I couldn't untangle it. The affair and this business with the chemicals. I couldn't even begin to understand what it meant for me, what it said about who I was until I knew *who* he was. I plunged my hands into the trouser pockets but they were empty. I considered leaving them there on the carpet as I made my way to the door. My tiny vandalism. But then would follow all the insinuation of madness. I scooped them up and folded them back into his drawer.

The text didn't say where, but it had to be the roof of his building. The one he'd taken me to. He was seeing her tonight.

I left without breakfast. At the bus stop I rummaged for my purse but then saw the toy car had returned to my handbag. I glanced at the shining blue metal, nestled between my purse and hairbrush, puzzled.

On the bus I tried to order my thoughts. I couldn't follow Russell. My office was a little lax about security, but his, because it was under the umbrella of government, was a different proposition. You couldn't get through the turnstiles without a pass.

At Waterloo Bridge, the wind blew across the water so that when it hit the pedestrians it washed them in Thames mist. I shivered. The sky was slate and the cold was beginning to gather from all corners. It felt as if we had barely tasted summer. My head began to pound as I rounded Fleet Street. I needed coffee.

On Bell Yard I took a left and headed to a coffee shop that sold espresso shots out of a window. As I ordered I took out my phone. I thought about Dad. He was dead. When I saw him, it wasn't his ghost I was seeing. Ghosts didn't appear in front of sane, healthy people. What was happening to me was medical. A visual and auditory hallucination.

'Hi, Mam.'

'Who is that?'

'Me, Mam. Always me. Have you got time for a chat?' I said, paying for my coffee.

'Layla,' she said as if she had called me. 'Are you okay? Not injured? Or dead?'

'Mam. I saw Dad in a – *vision*.' I paused to let the words sink.

'Okay,' she said and then mumbled along to herself. 'Who's that now?'

'Dad,' I said, gulping hot coffee as I paced. 'It was a hallucination.'

'Oh,' she said and was silent for a minute. I pressed the phone hard into my ear for sounds of any tears. 'What did he say?'

'Nothing much. He seemed so real, though. I walked with him a while through some gardens nearby. We sat on a bench. Told me he was staying at the Savoy but not much else. He said he missed me. I could even smell him.'

'Always smelled nice so he did – your dad. What was he wearing?'

I cast my mind back. 'I don't really remember. He was dressed quite modern – young. He had a suede bomber jacket on – I think,' I said, crossing the road and entering my building.

She was quiet. 'It's been so long,' she said at last. I reached the door to my building and jumped into the lift. For a minute the call cut out.

When I got into my office area, Alice waved from her desk, mouthing something. I put the phone against my chest.

'I have a telephone hearing in ten minutes. Is it okay if I use the room?' Alice asked. I nodded and returned the phone to my ear. Mum was back on the line.

I dropped my voice. 'It seemed real, Mam. Really real.'

'I know, dear,' she said.

I felt tears gathering behind my eyes. 'How did you cope? I don't know what to do.'

There was silence on the line and suddenly I regretted burdening her with it. 'It's okay, Mam,' I said. 'I'll call you later.'

'Layla,' she said then. 'Be kind to yourself.'

I sat at my desk and faced Alice who had now started to squeak to herself, the phone still to my ear. I fished cock-handedly into my bag for her car. I didn't know why I had held on to it for so long. Maybe Mum telling me that he'd hated the Capri had reminded me to return it. The phone was slipping so I pressed it hard into my face with my shoulder. I found the car at last and walked to Alice's desk and dropped it gently on her papers. *Sorry*, I mouthed in apology.

'Mam, I better go. I'll call in a few days.' I said, and ended the call. I turned on my computer to check my diary and then began to gather a few things I could take into another room while Alice did her telephone hearing.

'How long are you listed for? Five-minute job or forty-five?' I asked, gazing into my computer screen.

She didn't answer and I wondered at first whether it was Alice being Alice. I turned to her expecting to see her twisting pencils into her hair. She was staring at the desk in front of her. I stood to get a better look and ran over towards her with my hand over my mouth.

'Oh my God, Alice,' I said. 'I don't know how that happened.'

46

Then

The car was bashed in.

It looked exactly as if it had been run over by a real car and crushed. I was horrified and ran over and picked it up. 'Alice, I'm so sorry.' I turned it round in my hand, shocked.

Alice was crying. Her face was pomegranate and hot tears steamed down her face.

'I'll replace it, I promise,' I said and went to hug her.

She pressed me away, wiping her face with the back of her hand. 'You can't,' she said. 'It's not replaceable. It's from my childhood. You knew that.' She picked up the ruined car and left the room.

I chased after her. 'I'm so sorry, Alice. I don't even know how that could have happened.' I raced through the last few days but there was nothing that could have accounted for that kind of damage. It had to be Russell. 'Alice, come back. Please. You have your hearing in a minute. Look, come back. I'll fix it. I promise.'

She turned and stalked back to her desk, her eyes pointed to the floor. I took my bag and crept out.

The smell of diesel rose off the tarmac as I headed out up Chancery Lane. I crossed the road into the 'fields' opposite and found a bench. A streak of autumn sun painted everything with a glow of copper. How on Earth did Alice's car become crushed like that? It had to have been Russell, but why? Was it to punish me? To make me feel as if I were losing my mind?

If I got some tools from somewhere, some pliers maybe or a screwdriver, perhaps I could improve it a little. I could prise the roof up, get it so that it looked more like its usual shape. I dropped into Robert Dyas and searched for a tool that might help. The screwdrivers all came in packs of six or seven and the pliers seemed too big for such a small car.

'You could do worse than a Swiss Army knife,' an assistant said and showed me a red one with ten or eleven tools attached. 'One of these might work?'

Back at the office I waited until Alice left to get her usual afternoon coffee. She seemed about to ask me if I wanted anything but then caught herself and changed her mind. I waited a few minutes and then went gingerly to her desk and picked up the car. It had a deep dent in its roof but the rest of it seemed okay. I turned it slowly around and underneath it was intact save for a small shard of glass between the wheel and the body. I inserted the end of a blade into the opening and flicked the glass out. Then I turned the car again and wedged the knife into the Perspex windscreen and flipped it out. Then I chose a larger blade and shoved it inside the opening so that I could lever it up to the inside of the roof.

But no matter how hard I pressed, I wasn't able to push out the dent. It needed more force because it was made from cast metal. I swapped the tool for the large cutting blade and gave it one final push, using all my strength to force the blade upwards. At that moment I heard a faint humming noise. It was Alice coming down the corridor. In a panic I snatched at the knife and felt it slip out of the car. The knife flew through the air and landed an inch from her feet. She stood stock-still in the doorway, her mouth dropped open. Before I could say anything, she left the room, her face blotched red.

I sat at my desk for the rest of the afternoon, vibrating with what had happened. I couldn't process it. And there was still everything else circling that needed attention. There was still Russell.

At 7:30 this evening he would be on a roof meeting the woman. It had to be the rooftop of his building. Whether he was having an affair or any other secret meeting, that's the place he'd choose. If I could be there, to see it for myself, I might pull myself out of this crippling darkness. Or at least begin to face the slow journey out. If Michael was right, this woman was connected to him and to Jon and to some kind of catastrophe. But I didn't know if Michael was right. I didn't know that Russell was meeting a woman at all.

I took out my phone and went to Google Maps to remind myself exactly where it was and then zoomed in closer and closer until I could see the rooftop. The image was old. The trees lining the road were spiky and undressed by winter. Seeing the building on street-view reminded me how impressive it was. There was something solid and squat about it that gave it a Churchillian feel. As if the man himself had been transformed to Portland stone, to watch over the palace. I'd forgotten how much I'd loved it once. How Russell had taken me to the rooftop a lifetime ago.

I dialled Russell's number and waited for him to pick up. I could start by asking him why he'd done that to Alice's toy car. He didn't pick up. I had to speak to him, now. And if he wouldn't answer my calls, what other choice did I really have?

I found Michael's number and dialled it from the landline. My heart thumped when he answered.

'Michael?'

'Who is this?'

'Layla,' I said, looking around. The office was deserted.

'You found my number in the car? I was half-wondering whether you might have missed it. I didn't think you'd keep it if I gave it to you.'

I thought about this and he was right. Or might have been right. 'I need to speak to you,' I said.

'What's it about?'

'Trust me,' I said. 'You're not going to want to miss this. I'm leaving now. Meet me at Russell's building.' I killed the call and realised I'd been holding my breath.

I grabbed my things and rushed towards Temple Tube station. A gale had started up and I was glad to tap through the barriers into the shelter of the station. Within a minute I was on a Tube to St James's Park, just a few metres' walk from Russell's building. It was almost seven by the time I got there. I gazed up at the edifice. The *Winds* winked at me and suddenly tears were flowing down my face. What was I doing here?

I continued to stare up at the building. He'd told me once about plans they had to sell it off to make luxury apartments. I hadn't cared at the time, but now seeing it again, the idea felt like a sacrilege. I headed back towards the station to find Michael, keeping my head bent against the wind. Then near the entrance I saw him. He was wearing jeans and a tan motorbike jacket.

He smiled at me through narrowed eyes, surprised to see me here. 'What is it?'

I ushered him down a side street. 'It's Russell. He's meeting the woman this evening.'

He stared hard at the ground. 'How do you know?' Then he seemed to think better of the question. 'Forget that. What time and where?'

'Half-seven, I think,' I said, dropping my voice.

'Do you know where?'

I hesitated. 'Do you have an accessible rooftop on any of your buildings?'

'What?' he said, furrowing his brow. He swept his hair back with a hand and waited for me to explain.

'I know he's meeting her on a rooftop. I think it's the rooftop of his building. But I can't be sure. It could be one of your buildings.'

'We have roof gardens on some of our buildings. But we have no offices in London. The meeting place has to be here. There's only one way to be sure.'

We circled round the building until we were opposite the entrance. Through the doors deep into the building were the glass barriers that restricted entry. There was no way I could get in unnoticed.

'I'm not sure how I get in,' I said, indicating the entrance with a look.

'Can't you say you're meeting your husband?'

'I could. But you don't think they might call him and tell him I'm here?'

Michael tugged at the neck of his white T-shirt and gazed around. Then his face changed. 'We don't need to get in.'

I stared at him. First his hands and then shoulders, neck and face. Eyes. I had to ground what I was seeing to be sure he was there. The idea of him seemed too vivid for reality. And yet the redness on the skin of his fingers or the twist of his eyebrows was too mundane to be other than real.

'C'mon,' he said, turning and heading left away from the traffic. 'I have an idea,' he said and smiled.

47

Now

'Do you want to tell us why you have a sample of hair matching the hair strands found on a woman lying dead in your arms? If you knew her, that's something we might understand. But you said you'd never met her before.'

Omer is poised for the answer but Peter interjects, 'To be clear we aren't talking about her own hair.'

'But the question remains, Ms Mahoney. How did you get it? And why were you sending it off to a lab for tests?'

Peter is studying his hands. He knows I have to answer this question. If I avoid this one it's only going to entrench them in any charging decision.

'I found the hairs on Russell's clothing. I thought he was having an affair with my friend. I needed to be sure.'

Metcalf lights up. 'Wait, you're telling us you found a hair on your husband's clothes and immediately thought he's having an affair and then immediately went and got forensics on it. I'm not being funny, Ms Mahoney, even we don't move that fast.'

I am aware of my hands being balled into fists so that the knuckles appear buttery. 'It wasn't just one hair, Detective. They were turning up all over the place. On the floor, in the bin, wherever I looked I seemed to see these long blonde hairs. One was wrapped around his shirt button. I mean, how could that have got there? Of course I was suspicious.'

'I don't know. But sending off for a forensic examination? That seemed normal to you?'

'I didn't know what else to do.'

'You didn't think of asking your husband about it?' Omer asks softly.

I look from one and then to the other. 'Of course I did. But he denied it.'

'And so, are we now getting close to an explanation for why you're on the roof of his building? You went there to confront him?'

The lights flicker overhead as if in warning. 'Yes,' I say.

'And when you find that he's not in his office, you go looking for him?'

'No.'

'You're angry. You go looking for them. And then you find them – or Amy at the very least.'

'That's not how it happened.'

'And you see this woman with this long blonde hair that's been plaguing you and you stab her in the chest.'

'No!'

Peter leans forward and taps on the desk with a finger. 'Detectives. The deceased was a brunette, wasn't she?'

Omer's face twitches. 'Yes, she was. But the point we are making is that your client saw her husband with another woman. And well –' he says, turning now to me, 'you'd be surprised at how often we see this.'

Metcalf picks up the thread. 'We do understand, you know. I mean if I caught my wife with another man, I don't think I could say for certain that I wouldn't lose my cool. We're all capable of doing things in the heat of the moment.'

'There was no heat and no moment,' I say firmly.

'No, Nick, I agree with Ms Mahoney about that. I don't think we can fairly categorise this as a spontaneous act of jealousy.' Omer's face has relaxed into itself. He is calm, serene almost.

In the space he leaves I know that something is waiting to leap out. 'Okay, then,' I say to defuse whatever is coming. 'Can we move on?'

'I mean it's not spontaneous, because of the knife. When you went in there, you went in with a knife. It was already in your possession. This wasn't spontaneous. It was premeditated.'

'I did not go into that building with a knife. I already told you. The knife was in Russell's bag. I saw it there. Michael took it from the bag. How many times?'

'You weren't in the habit of carrying knives around, Layla?' Peter says then in order to underline the point.

'No,' I say, laughing a little at the suggestion. 'I've never carried a knife about with me.'

'Okay,' Omer says, then straightening. 'It might be time for you to see this statement.'

When I see the name on the top of it, my heart sinks.

Peter reaches over and reads it, but as he does he holds up a hand.

'My client recalls that she went to a hotel with the man – Michael. It's the Plaza. You might want to take these details down and see if they still have the CCTV.'

Omer looks up at me, surprised. He hasn't expected this, I see now. He hasn't expected Michael to be real.

48

Then

As I followed him on the pavement, I had a moment of déjà vu. 'Wait,' I said. The sun had stained the sky orange. Something in the darkening light was signalling something to me but I couldn't quite grasp it.

He stopped. 'We haven't got long,' he said. 'There's a hotel around the corner.' He looked back at me and then broke into a run. I hurried with him until minutes later we were at the glass doors of a hotel. The name PLAZA stood in huge silver letters above them. He pushed his way past the doorman and went straight to a bank of lifts and began jabbing at the buttons. We stood, catching our breath. There was an unreal quality to everything. I began to question whether I was having an episode. His eyes were so blue that it worried me.

I could sense the shift when it came. When warnings came from everything and from every direction I knew my brain was having trouble filtering. As if I were in a bit of Truman madness. Wherever I looked people were pointedly turning away from me. But then, I was in a hotel, people did that in hotels. The lift doors opened and Michael beckoned me in. I twisted the scab on the back of my hand to shake me into the moment. He stood in the lift – alone – holding the doors open.

'Layla.'

'Where are we going?' I asked, stepping slowly in alongside him.

'There's a rooftop bar. I know this place. And I'm pretty sure there's a view of 55 Broadway, the building you want – London's first skyscraper.'

My head began to spin but I pulled myself back into the present. We climbed floor after floor, running through the lights. The scent of cologne drifted off Michael as he scratched his neck under his T-shirt. We glided smoothly upwards until finally the doors pinged open. As they parted, a large hotel bar emerged into view. I scanned it and saw that it was pocked with a few customers busy at their laptops or phones, nursing drinks. A doorman in a black suit casually guarded the entrance to the rooftop. Michael checked his watch and paced up to the glass doors.

'I'm a guest,' he said. 'Just showing her the view.' He smiled and the doorman pulled the door smoothly open.

Outside the wind assaulted us in gusts. It was much higher than Russell's building which meant that we would have an elevated view if he was there. I walked straight up to the glass balustrade and leaned over to get my bearings. The air slapped at my face – it tasted of metal and earth and left me breathless. The park was directly ahead so his building would be around the back. I started for the rear, skirting around the perimeter until I could see the huge blocky building sitting fat and immovable in its pen.

There were no drinkers out here; the winds were too rude. But an Asian couple was standing against the glass taking selfies. They smiled at us in solidarity as their hair whipped across their faces. I smiled back and carried on around until the terrace stopped short. Michael was close behind me and together we peered over the edge.

'Can you see the rooftop?' he asked.

'Maybe. If I leaned right over. It's just out of view.'

Just then he bent his knees and looped an arm around my waist. 'Hold on to the edge,' he said and hoisted me up. My heart kicked, terrified. A shriek escaped my lungs but was drowned by the wind. 'Can you see now?' he shouted against the buffeting air.

I held tight to the edge of the glass until my fists turned white. His arm was tight around my waist. If he let me go now there would be no chance of surviving. Slowly I relaxed my grip and leaned over. Down and to the right was the flat roof Russell had taken me to. There was nobody there. The only thing to be seen was a pair of metal boxes housing fans that looked like air-conditioning units. I could make out letters in red on one of them. Just as I was about to signal to be brought back down, I saw a figure emerge from the left into view – a woman. But not the Asian one I had been expecting. This one was tall and firmly white. Her hair flickered in the wind.

'Anything?'

'Yes. Just a little longer,' I called out over my shoulder. She was around a hundred feet away so I couldn't make out her features. She might have been anything between twenty and fifty. Her long raincoat gave nothing away. I could see her check her watch and look around her, the tails of her buff-coloured coat clapping behind her.

'Okay,' I shouted back against the wind and Michael gently lowered me. 'There's a woman, but he's not there yet. Maybe give it a minute?'

He nodded and pulled away at the collar of his jacket to straighten it. 'Do you recognise her?'

I shrugged my shoulders and felt tears gathering in the wind. 'No. Maybe you do?'

'Let me look,' he said and leaned right over the balustrade. He studied her for a minute to make certain. 'No,' he mumbled. Then he looked into my eyes and read something in them. 'What?' he said.

'What now?' I said.

'I'm not sure there's much more we can do from here.' He turned in the direction we'd come from. 'At least it doesn't look as if Russell is having an affair with her.'

'What makes you say that?'

'He'd have turned up,' he said, as if it were nothing. I'd wondered whether Michael had nudged me into seeing an affair where there wasn't one. He'd raised my suspicions and fuelled all my hesitations and uncertainties until they'd become truths. But on the other side of that equation was everything else. The hairs on his clothes. The chain on the step. The scent of vanilla on his clothes. The burner phone. Those things, whatever they were, were more than a question of being nudged.

But some of what Michael brought vanished like wraiths when you grasped them. Something else bothered me. 'I asked you to meet me at Russell's building.'

'Yes. And I would have,' he said.

'Except I didn't tell you where he worked.'

He didn't hesitate. 'You told me he worked at the Environment Agency. I Googled it.'

I looked at him but he wouldn't meet my eyes. The sound of birds high in the sky made everything mundane and quotidian. That was good. It was real. 'You know who she is.'

He opened his mouth to reply but I filled the space before he could.

'And you know more than you're telling me. I call you on no notice and you come without a second's thought. You didn't even ask me what it was about. You just dropped everything.'

He pulled back from the edge and plunged his hands into his pockets. His hair flailed in the gusts. 'I told you,' he said, shifting between feet. 'There's a connection here. We need to get to the bottom of it. People could die.'

I laughed without trying to hide the ice in my voice. 'You keep saying that and yet you've given me no reason to think that's true. It's my own fault. I've just gone along with whatever you've told me. Mysterious connections and some nonsense about quantum entanglement that's all you've given me.'

He gave me a look I couldn't read and after a minute, to fill in the dead space, he leaned over the glass and stared down below. For a few moments he said nothing. When finally he spoke, there was a note of resignation in his tone. 'Okay. I do know more than I'm telling you at the moment. But you have to believe me, it's for your own safety.'

'Then,' I said, walking away, 'you can do it without me.'

'Layla –'

'No,' I said, shrugging off his hand. 'Look at me. I'm on a rooftop bar with someone who I don't know, spying on my husband for a reason I don't understand. So, you either tell me something or I'm done.'

A second later something caught his eye and he sprang to life. 'I think I can see someone.'

Despite it all, I rushed to the edge. It was Russell. I could tell from here just by the coat – the silly one that he wore whenever he felt the slightest chill in the air. It had fur trim around the hood. Without asking, Michael lifted me up for a better view. The woman saw him and raised her hand. They kissed quickly on the cheek and then started having what seemed to be a serious conversation. A minute later she reached out and held his hand. In the intimacy of that touch was everything. They continued to speak; small touches decorated everything they said. A hand on the small of her back. Her fingers touching his arm. The way in which their heads were turned.

'Enough,' I said and Michael lowered me back to my feet. I felt dizzy. I sat on the ground to get my breath.

He stooped down to me after a beat, apologetic. 'I'm sorry,' he said.

I was still reeling from what I had seen. 'Do you know her?'

He shook his head. 'I don't recognise her from this distance. I could really do with getting closer.'

I hugged myself against the wind that was blowing up from the traffic below. He continued to stare at the two of them, watched them until they'd gone.

'How did you know she'd be here?'

I thought about the message on his pay-as-you-go phone. 'Why should I tell you anything when you've told me nothing?'

He turned me by the elbows to face him and held me tightly. My heart fluttered in alarm. 'This is serious. You have no idea what's happening here.'

'So tell me.'

When he said nothing, I pulled out of his grip and walked off towards the entrance as he jogged up behind me.

'Wait,' he called.

'Not until you tell me what's going on.' I felt him stop in his tracks. I turned.

'Okay,' he said, holding his palms up. 'I know what she's doing but I don't know who she is. I need to find out as soon as possible.'

'What do you mean?'

'I think she's sleeping with your husband.'

'Why do you care?' The sound of a dropped spoon or fork scattered the silence.

He sighed and ran a hand through his hair. 'She was doing the same with Jon. After a while he wouldn't play ball so she threatened to tell his wife. And when that didn't work, well – all I know for sure is that Jon's dead.'

My dress flapped in the wind. 'But why? What the hell is this all about?'

He turned away and then faced me again, his hands spread. 'The chemical I was telling you about – polymer really. It's deadly. It's going to destroy lives –'

'Michael.'

'Sorry. She's the one who's behind it. We think she's applying pressure to your husband to get it licensed. She used Jon until she couldn't and now she's using your husband. I know I have said this before but if that bond makes it into our eco-system, it's game over. You have to find out who she is. I've tried. She's very protected. But it has to be you, Layla, and you have to find out *now*.'

'Fuck you, Michael,' I said, and walked away.

49

Now

'We've made some preliminary enquiries,' Omer says, reading from his laptop. 'The cameras at the Plaza on the ground floor are all pointed in the direction of the reception desk. There are none by the lifts. And,' he says, scrolling, 'the only ones on the rooftop bar are facing the serving area. Did you or Michael buy a drink?'

'No,' I say, and then lean forward. 'How can there not be cameras in a hotel?'

Omer smiles. 'Privacy, apparently. Some guests don't like to be seen coming in or out. But you probably knew that, Ms Mahoney.'

Peter looks up and glares until Omer puts his hands up.

'Let's move on, shall we?' Peter says.

Omer nods. 'This is from the statement of Katharine Peel. She describes how three weeks ago you turned up unannounced to her house. She says that you were acting strangely and that as soon as she opened the door, you barged your way in and started searching through the house,' says Metcalf.

'Is this at all relevant to this investigation?' Peter asks, eyebrows lofted.

'Of course it is. Ms Peel says that you were aggressive and difficult to reason with.'

I try to hang onto the present but I am being torn away by what Omer has said about the hotel. I was sure they'd find him. It's a hotel for goodness sake. How can there not be cameras? And then it dawns, from what Omer accused me of. Michael knew that. He knew the cameras wouldn't pick him up. That's why he suggested it.

'I'm sorry,' I say. 'Can you repeat the question?'

Omer coughs. 'Ms Peel. Her statement. She says you were aggressive with her.'

'I wasn't aggressive,' I said. 'I was upset, yes. But I thought she was having an affair with my husband.'

Metcalf scratches his neck which makes it come up in red streaks. 'In your mind, is everyone having an affair with your husband?'

'That is not called for,' Peter says firmly.

Omer takes over. 'She also says that after throwing a picture of a stranger at her, you pointed a knife at her. Which she took as a threat.'

'What? No!'

'I mean it only stuck out to us because in her telling of it, it was a distinctive knife. Pearl-handled, she described it as. She's been shown a photograph of the knife used to kill Amy Blahn and she's made a positive identification. It's the same knife.'

I stare at the table. Why would she claim that I'd pointed it at her? It was in my hand by accident. 'I didn't point it at her at all. It happened to be in my pocket and I was looking for a photograph and it got mixed up with it.'

'You know that having a lock knife in a public place without a reasonable excuse is an offence. Why were you carrying a knife at all?'

'It was an accident.'

'It accidentally fell into your pocket? When you were about to confront a woman you believed was sleeping with your husband?' Metcalf says.

My face began to pulse with heat. 'Of course it didn't fall into my pocket. I'd just been using it for something else. I didn't intend to take it with me.'

'And yet,' Omer says, picking up the thread, 'the very same knife ends up in the body of another woman you believed was sleeping with your husband?'

Peter swallows and I know that he is trying to control his 'tells'. He knows the interview has taken a disastrous turn but does not want to let the detectives know what he is thinking.

'When I went to Kate's, I didn't remember I had the knife with me. And I didn't point it at her. I wasn't aggressive with her at all. And I can only think that she's saying all this because she actually is having an affair with Russell. Did you think of that?'

'Well, she denies being in any relationship with your husband,' Omer says.

'But she would, wouldn't she?' I reply, trying to muster as much calm as I can.

'I don't know. Would she? She has nothing to gain by lying.'

'Unless she *is* having an affair with Russell,' I say and then wish I hadn't. 'She remembers things differently from me on this.'

'Differently?'

'She's not remembering it as it happened. It was an accident having the knife in my hand.'

Omer and Metcalf lean back in their chairs and confer in heavy whispers. A second later they lean forward again apparently agreed about something.

'Okay. Let's do that now then,' Omer says to him quietly. 'Now, Ms –'

Something in that sentence makes me smile. And the strangeness of that itself makes me smile all the more. It's the '*now*' that triggers it. And although I know it looks terrible, *will* look terrible, I can't help myself.

'Something amusing you, Ms Mahoney?' Metcalf asks.

'No.'

'Go on. I think you should share it. We're only in a police interview and you're only being interviewed as a murder suspect.'

'It's nothing,' I say and try to straighten my features.

'Well, if you want to leave it there on tape – laughing for no reason – that's up to you.'

I pause but cannot seem to remove the smile from my face. They are all looking at me. 'You said "now". There is no *now* objectively. There's only *my* now and *your* now and all of our individual nows. Time isn't universal like that.'

'You've lost me,' Omer says.

'Time moves at different speeds for everyone. It's a fact. I checked.'

'Is it? And what's your point?' Metcalf asks.

I want to say that if we can't be sure of at least that one thing, that simplest of things, the moment that defines our lives – now – then surely nothing can be certain. Instead I shake my head and look at my hands.

Peter leans forward to the detectives. 'I think it's time for a break, gentlemen, isn't it?'

They nod silently, switch the tapes off and seal them.

50

Then

We sat facing one another over a dinner of noodles and stir-fried vegetables. Russell was showing me how debilitating his stiches were by sitting rigidly at the counter. I was counting the ways in which I could ask him who he had met on his roof without setting him off. The more I spelled it out – *I saw you from the rooftop of a nearby hotel with a man who keeps following me* – the more mad it sounded. In the end I said nothing and later when we went to bed, we lay down together as stiff as dolls in a box.

He woke when the morning was still dark.

He'd packed a large bag the previous night and now having dressed, he picked it up from the foot of the bed and heaved it over his shoulder.

'When are you back?' I shouted out before he had started down the stairs.

'Early next week,' he said, continuing down. The only words he'd spoken to me this morning. I thought again about Michael and what he'd said before I stalked off. That she was sleeping with Russell. That she'd done it to somebody else and that he'd ended up dead. I hadn't even bothered Googling that. *Jon*. It wasn't anything to go on.

I followed him and stood behind him on the stairs, arms folded like a cliché, watching as he pulled on his wax jacket.

'What?' he said.

'Where are you going again?' I asked. He was about to leave but I needed to pull him back in so that we could talk.

'I told you. Norfolk,' he said, dragging the zip up his coat. 'Broads.'

'Norfolk Broads,' I said, rolling the words around in my mouth. 'Good fishing there?'

He looked back, irritated. There was a smudge of colour flushing his pale cheeks. 'Pike,' he said and then opened the door to go.

'But –'

'What?' he said, turning back and heading straight into the kitchen. He returned with the waste bin and went to empty it outside into the large green one. He came back and did the same with the recycling. He saw me waiting. 'What is it?'

I started back up the stairs and a few steps up I looked back round. 'Doesn't matter. I thought that if you were fishing –'

'What, for God's sake?'

'You might want to take your fucking tackle box and rods.'

He stood there dazzled by his foolishness. 'Crap,' he muttered and limped off again into the kitchen.

'And don't forget your precious fishing knife.'

By the time he'd slammed the door, I was back in the bedroom, staring at the drawn curtains, watching the light filter in around the large grey rectangles like Rothkos in a gallery. The light around the edges, a glimpse of apricity, hope after darkness. A hint rather than a promise.

I knelt down at his bedside table and pulled out the drawer. It had a few sleeves of paracetamol and some muscle spray but nothing else of interest. Then I moved on to the cabinet underneath. Passports and other bits of paperwork – receipts mainly. I didn't know what I was looking for but I went through each of them.

The bottom of his wardrobe revealed nothing but neatly stacked jumpers that he'd get out closer to winter. I searched everywhere there was a drawer or a space to hide something but nothing leapt out. He was neat so it was easy to search. And that gave me an idea. He kept neat plastic folders for all the bills and life-admin paperwork that we generated. They were in a cupboard under the bookshelves in the living room. I took each plastic folder out and riffled through the pages without result.

Eventually I went back to the bedroom to check the pockets of his coats and jackets – after finding the phone I didn't think I'd strike oil twice but there was nowhere left to look. When I got to a navy wool jacket that he hardly wore, with brass buttons, my hands stopped. There was a lump in the inside pocket. I plunged my hand in and felt a package in paper. When I pulled it out I saw a thick envelope. I opened it, eyes wide.

It was full of £50 notes.

I emptied it onto the bed and counted. £3,250. What was he doing with that much cash?

I sat on the bed and thought for a second and then took out my phone to send a message.

WE NEED TO TALK

I sent the message and then dropped back onto the bed and shut my eyes. A wave of tiredness swept over me so that it felt as though the blood was being pulled from my head and out through my feet.

The last thing I remembered before I fell asleep were Michael's eyes – his expression telling me I didn't know what I was getting into, and feeling now that he was right.

When I woke it was nearly noon. I called in to work to say that I'd been feeling under the weather. I waited as the call was transferred to the HR manager. 'We'll need a note from your doctor if it's longer than forty-eight hours,' he said and hung up.

At the bottom of my own wardrobe, I caught a wisp of blonde and I crawled over and grabbed the wig. I stripped off. I stared at myself in the mirror, naked, with this shock of dead hair raining down my back and shoulders. It made me feel disconnected from myself. I stared at my face, her face, and saw someone I recognised but not somebody I knew that well. This woman in the mirror felt free and gave me a rush inside as if I were falling through the air.

Then I dug out my raincoat, almost identical to hers, and put it on over my naked skin and wrapped the belt around tight. In the mirror it was as if I had captured her. She looked at me – we studied each other. We crossed our arms and then flicked the long curtain of hair back over our shoulders. I stepped further away from the mirror until I was standing on the landing and peering through the bedroom doorway at the mirror. At this distance we could be the same person. Identical but for the colours of our skin.

The doorbell rang.

I opened the door to a thickset man with power tools in a heavy canvas bag at his feet. It was only as I caught his look that I realised I was still wearing the wig and the coat.

'Here about the marble,' he said, looking away.

I thought for a second before coming to. 'Oh, the countertop,' I said, tightening my coat around me and leading him through.

He gently placed his tools onto the tiles and began to size up the damage.

'Can you polish it out?' I asked, pulling the lapels close.

He looked at me as if I were crazy. 'No. We'll have to replace that whole length there. You could turn it upside down and repolish it but then you'd have that bullnose on the wrong side. It wouldn't really work. But,' he said, brightening, 'we did have some in stock, that colour, or near enough. It's in the van. You can have a look before I fit it.'

'No. It's fine. Just do what you have to,' I said and left him to it.

After showering I went to the kitchen, my own hair damp, to see what progress he'd made. He had taken a huge circular saw to the existing top and cut it away from the supports. The large, white, damaged slab stood tilted against a bank of kitchen units. Dust lay in sheets everywhere. A pack of latex gloves spilled its contents on the floor. He looked up from his saw when he saw me and pulled up his visor.

'Can't carry it safely away like that so I'm going to have to cut it into two lengths. We'll try and salvage some and knock it off the cost. But it won't be much. A couple of hundred maybe.'

A couple of hundred sounded like a lot and I wondered exactly how much the full length was about to cost me. 'Okay. So that will leave me with how much to pay?'

The figure was eye-watering. I sighed and left him to it and then went upstairs to change. As I put the wig away, I thought about how to find her. I had to stop her before it was too late, before she got to

Russell in a way that I couldn't undo. I sat on the bed and opened up my Mac. I did a search of the *e-Vinc* sales team. It seemed to be a small team. A dozen names came up but none of the photos matched the woman I'd seen. One had a missing picture and under it was the name S. Hussain. It didn't fit with the woman I had seen. White. But then, I considered myself – Mahoney. A white name over brown skin. I searched under her profile and saw that she was an account manager for *the largest blue-chip chemical company in the world*.

I dialled the number on the website and asked for Ms Hussain from sales. A voice asked me what the call was about.

'I'm from ICI,' I said, saying the name casually. 'I'm calling from accounts.' I could only hope it sounded plausible as I held my breath and the line went silent. I wondered whether this was the same woman I'd seen at reception in Hove when I went looking for Michael. I prayed she didn't recognise my voice. She came back on the line telling me to hold before transferring me.

'Hello?' a voice said over the line, shaking me into action.

'Hi, I'm calling from ICI. We're having a review of some of our data. We've not got a record of you as our sales contact. Is it you?'

There was a pause on the line before an alert reply. 'Oh, you should do – it's definitely me. You might have had John Wooler, but he's left now.'

'Excellent,' I said. 'I'm seeing a few clients this week to update my list. Can I just check where you're based?'

The line went silent for a second. 'Not anywhere specifically. I'm on the road a lot. This week I'll be in London. Next week I should be back in Hove.'

I didn't want to waste any time. 'Perfect. I'm in London Monday. Perhaps we could meet for a coffee?'

After checking her diary, she agreed to meet me at a café near Victoria Station. 'How will I know it's you?' I said before winding up the call. I checked your website but –'

'Oh. Yes. My picture's not up yet. I'm Asian, I suppose. Five feet tall and shoulder-length hair. I could send you a picture if helps?'

'No, that's fine,' I said. 'I'll find you' – and then before she could ask me what I looked like, I hung up.

It wasn't her.

I had just ended the call when my phone rang. Mum. I wanted to let it ring but after what happened when I saw her last, I had to make sure she was okay.

'Hello, dear,' she said.

'Mam, is everything okay?' A loud rumbling noise that put my nerves on edge had started up in the kitchen. I needed to get out.

'Yes. I needed to talk to you about something if you have time.'

'Of course. What's it about?' I said.

'Your father,' she said and then went silent. 'There's something you need to know.'

51

Now

We are in a different consultation room and Peter has stripped off his jacket and rolled up his sleeves. The tie has come off too. This room is peach. There is a window and when I peer out I can see a line of pigeons perched on the roofline opposite. They are there as if they have been arranged a finger-space apart. There is something menacing about them.

'Hitchcock,' I say aloud.

Peter, who is sitting with his head in his hands, looks up at me. 'What?'

'Nothing. Those birds feel like Hitchcock,' I say and nod out of the window.

He stands up and leads me by the arm to the sofa where he had been sitting. 'Sit.'

I sit and for a moment he says nothing. He stares at the floor and taps a foot rhythmically on the thin carpet.

'Can I ask you a question, Layla?'

'Sure.'

'How long have I known you now?'

'On and off? About nine, ten years.'

'Okay. And in that whole time, I don't think I've ever seen you behaving like this. And I need to know what we're talking about here. Is this the stress of the situation? If it is, then that is completely fine. I understand. It's as close to life or death as we get in our courts.

Believe me, I get it. But if it's something else then we need to talk about it.'

I take a breath but it gets stuck in my throat. Am I acting strangely? I usually have a sense of that – some warning when it happens. 'What do you mean?'

'This business about there is no "now" or whatever that was.'

'But it's true,' I say. 'Time is totally relative. Everyone has their own tiny watch that they run by. The fact that we all follow one clock-time is a kind of convenience. A device.' He raises his eyebrows at me. 'It's true!'

My voice echoes in the room.

'Layla, I don't care. I don't care if it's true. You sound crazy. That's all it is. That's everything. Crazy.'

'What, so facts are crazy now?'

'No. I didn't say that. I said it *sounds* crazy.' He looks away and then looks at me again. 'Even to me. It feels like someone else has walked into your body. Just now when you said Hitchcock out of the blue – don't you see it?'

I stand up and head back to the window. The birds are gone. 'But it was like something out of a film. Am I not allowed to say things that I think any more?'

'Not when they're so disjointed from what we're talking about.'

I let that sink in. We both seem to. 'So, what next?'

'Nothing. We've had a break. They're going to carry on with their questions.'

I nod and offer him a smile. He takes it and stands. 'But I'm keeping an eye on you. I don't think you're psychotic or anything but stress can do things to people. Even stable people.'

Maybe he's right. Maybe I have pushed it too close to the edge so that I have strayed into crazy. But I have to show them how hard Michael had knocked me off my axis. I didn't start off crazy – he's done it to me.

Back in the interview Peter smiles at me and then turns to the officers and motions to them to carry on. The caution is given and after the long beep and the introductions, we begin again. Omer rubs the bridge of his nose.

'Just to continue with this line of questioning. We were talking about you and knives. Going back to your colleague Alice Cook's statement now. You told us that you weren't a person who carried a knife. However, when officers took a statement from her, she was quite clear that she saw you with a knife at the office.'

My heart races at this. I hope she hasn't said any more than this. 'She's got it wrong.'

'Wrong? You mean she's lying?'

'No,' I say. 'But she's not remembered it correctly. Or hasn't seen what she thinks she saw.'

Omer looks down at the paper in front of him before lacing his hands together. 'According to her she remembers it very well. And she saw it very clearly.'

Peter interrupts. 'Then it's her recollection against Layla's, isn't it?'

Omer nods. 'She says you threw the knife at her and the blade only just missed her.'

I shut my eyes. Alice. Oh, Alice.

52

Then

Saturday. Michael called from a withheld number, telling me that he had received my message.

'You said we needed to talk.'

'We do,' I said. 'But first I need more than I'm getting from you right now. You think about it. If you want my help – and you clearly need it for some reason – then I want to know everything that's going on. If you can do that, great. Let me know. If you can't, then I'll do whatever I need to.'

I hung up without waiting for a response. There were still a lot of questions for him to answer. I still didn't understand who he thought this woman was – not necessarily her name – just who was she? Did she work for his company, and if she did, why couldn't Michael just tell them what she was up to? But most of all, I didn't know why he was getting involved. When he called back I was in the car driving to Mum's. He could wait. Mum couldn't.

Within two hours I arrived at her house and I banged on the door repeatedly until she opened it. She squinted at me in the low light, surprised.

'Layla. What are you doing here? Are you okay?'

I kissed her impatiently on the cheek. 'Can I just come in?'

Inside, the bungalow smelled of soured meat which caught me by surprise. 'Mam? Are your carers still coming around?'

'Oh, just in the evenings to help with a meal and a bit of this and that.'

I tailed her into the living room. 'And they're treating you okay, are they?'

'Oh, Layla. Stop headaching me now will you please.'

I sat down on the sofa and spread my fingers on the brown velour. I remembered when this was new and now it felt like a relic.

'Will you have a tea?'

'No thanks, Mam. Come and sit. I want to ask about Dad.'

She sat down next to me and looked at me uncertainly. Her eyes were watery and on the edge of tears. 'What is it, dear?'

'Dad. You told me something on the phone about Dad. I need to talk to you about that.'

She patted my hand. 'You know I don't like to, Layla.'

She'd called me and had said that she had something important to tell me about Dad and now that thread had slipped through her fingers. 'Tell me again how he died.'

'Ach. Really, Layla, you want to go over that now, do you?' She looked away and began to fuss about the coffee table. The glass hadn't been replaced but the wood underneath was still intact. She started polishing the surface with a cloth.

I took her hand. 'It's important. Please.'

She sighed and leaned back against the velour. 'Well, all's I know is when he went back to Pakistan. Karachi. When was it now? Ninety-three, I think. Anyway, he was doing good for a while. And then I got a call from the brother out there that he'd had an accident. A bus or something. He was in one of them tuk-tuk things and him and it went under the bus wheels.'

I studied her. There was sadness there but I couldn't translate any more than that. 'You spoke to me on the phone yesterday, Mam. Do you remember?'

She glazed over for a minute before regaining her footing. 'Course I do. I invited you for lunch.'

'No, you didn't invite me for lunch. I came because I wanted to speak to you about something. You said something about Dad.'

'Did I?'

'Yes,' I said, shifting in my seat so that I was facing her. 'I told you I saw his ghost. And then yesterday, you called me.'

'Did I?'

'Yes. Don't you remember?'

'I don't know. What did I say?'

'Mam. You really don't remember? You told me that Dad was alive.'

The sun receded leaving fiery streaks on the sky. My life was becoming circular. Me driving along the South Coast, reluctant to return to my empty house. Russell, God knew where. I knew he wasn't with his brother but I called Sam anyway. He didn't answer. Perhaps he felt it was a trap and there was nothing to be won by picking up. He wasn't a bad person, Sam, but perhaps this – me calling and him having to pretend Russell was with him – made him one when he didn't deserve to be.

I continued driving until I was somewhere I had never been before, a village called Saltdean. I parked and walked along the beach which was thinning out even as the darkness dropped like a cloak. The mood changed with the light. The families had packed up, shaken sand from their shoes and gone. In their places came the young men, trawling up and down, cigarettes with lit ends, leading the way. After a few strides I made my way back to the car and leaned back into my seat, eyes shut. White noise filled the cockpit so quickly that I became alarmed. I opened my eyes but everything remained as it had been. And then my vision began to blur and glow. I'd had similar feelings before the onset of migraines. An aura in front of my face, blotting out whole vistas.

There was nothing to do but to wait it out. I couldn't drive like this. I saw the glowing green cross of a pharmacy up ahead and I made my way there. I got a couple of packets of co-codamol and a bottle of water, paid and left. I had intended to go straight to the car when I saw the light of a small supermarket a little way along. Hunger began to claw at me then so I went in for some food. The aisles were too bright for my eyes and so I weaved through them, fingers fanned across my face. My headache was now in full flow, pounding. The pain expanded like the ripples on a pond – exploding and then receding momentarily.

I hesitated by the wine bottles. I didn't want to drink because that would leave me stranded here, in the depths of nowhere. And the price of drinking would be more headaches when I woke up. But the pain was too heavy, too sickening to be helped by pills alone. I paid for a sandwich and a half-bottle of cognac and made straight for the car. The pain was no longer a wave. It was now hammering so that my fingers shook when I tried to unscrew the bottle top. I took a long draught, the sharpness at the back of my throat lost in the crippling migraine.

On a quiet spit of sand, I sat and shut my eyes. The sea air blew hard, taking the edge off the nausea. Something to do with the salt in it felt healing. I breathed deeply, willing the pain away. Then I remembered the bag in my hand and dug in to find the pills. I snapped out two and washed them down with the cognac. Then slowly I eased myself back and lay on the sand.

The waves lapped. As they did I started to feel more and more disconnected from something essential in me. The pain had receded but the thoughts, which it had been shrouding, began to emerge in its place.

She said he was alive. That Dad had contacted her to say that he was alive. When they'd separated, he'd returned to Pakistan, his birthplace. Then a year or so later his family had contacted her without telling him. They'd said he was dead. Amongst themselves they'd decided it would be easier all round so that when he remarried there'd be no baggage of an ex-wife and a daughter in England.

'And you knew he wasn't dead?' I'd asked in shock.

She'd blanched. 'No! Not then. Later. Much later I found out he was alive.'

'And you didn't tell me?'

Her eyes became glassy. 'I didn't want to break your heart all over again.'

Even now I wasn't sure whether she was being lucid or not. What difference would it have made anyway? He spent my childhood over there while I was here. In a sense, he was dead either way. Maybe I was better off not knowing. I thought back to seeing him in the gardens. When we had been walking, it had just been the two of us. There was nobody that I could rely on for corroboration of his presence. I considered the irony of that. A city as crammed as London and not a human in sight. Had he spoken to anyone else? If he had would it have been real or just another layer of hallucination? But he was there and I had seen him, if he was alive. If I'd known that at the time, I wouldn't have doubted it for a second.

The sound of waves crashing in the dark, its significance, began to make me vanish. Its certainty. Its roiling vastness was obliterating. Sea. Air. And nothing between them but me.

What was death anyway? I felt a kind of relief at the innocence of it. Death was uncomplicated. At best it was a gate on the other side of which was nothing or something, but which definitely was not this. And then I realised I wasn't afraid of it. It was a kind of compulsion, I saw now, pushing, pushing.

The pain of the headache had become entrenched. I lifted my head off the sand to snap two co-codamol out of a sleeve and swallowed them with a draught of cognac. I was vaguely aware, through the veil of throbbing pain, that I had taken some already. But it seemed so easy at that moment to just step off. It didn't feel monumental – but natural. I took another mouthful of drink and put my head back into the sand.

I dipped my hands into my pockets to find my phone. When I drew it out I saw there were no missed calls. Nothing from Sam or Russell. I went to my favourites and dialled Mum, my head a kaleidoscopic swirl.

'Hello, Mam.'

'Who's that?'

'Me, Mam. It's always me,' I said and laughed. I struggled to sit up and popped another two pills into my mouth.

'Everything okay, dear, is it? You're not dying?'

'No, Mam. Not dying, or dead.' There was a rustle on the line as she waited for me to speak. 'I just wanted to make sure you were all right.'

'Are you okay? You don't sound right, dear.'

A dog barked somewhere a mile away. 'Just a headache,' I said and took another swig. 'You're not afraid, are you, Mam?'

'No. Of what, dear?'

'Anything, Mam. I don't want you to be afraid of anything, Mam.'

I looked for another two co-codamol to take but the sleeve was empty. I found the other and pressed two more free. The headache had settled to a sick, dull ache. I put them on my tongue and looked for the bottle in the darkness. The only light now was from the moon glittering off the sea.

53

Now

'It's not painting a great picture, is it, Ms Mahoney?'

Peter sighs loudly. 'Detective, can we try to leave the speeches for lawyers at the trial?' He has obviously decided that there will be a trial. They will charge me. I thought I had managed to negotiate a way through this, at least until they had to go to the Magistrates' Court for more time. But they must think they have enough.

Omer nods, apologetic almost but not quite. 'Okay. Maybe I can summarise and Ms Mahoney can comment. You are found on the roof of your husband's building with a woman who's been murdered. She has a knife in her chest. You tell us that it's a knife belonging to your husband and that he left it in the office. He tells us that he's never seen it before. Your friend, Kate, is shown a picture of the knife and she says that not a week ago you turned up at her house with that exact knife. And now there's Alice Cook, your work colleague. She's told us that you caused criminal damage to her possessions and that she saw you with a knife, and that you threw it at her. And that's not to mention what you did to your husband. With a knife.'

I am about to answer – I need to say something to kick off an avalanche so this mountain of evidence begins to cascade away – but he stops me with a hand.

'And just before you comment. The woman you are with up there is a woman you suspect your husband of having an affair with. You have hairs tested in a lab which turn out to be an exact match for the hairs she had all over her. But your defence is that someone else killed her. Someone who can't be found anywhere. Who can't be seen on CCTV. And who doesn't appear to work where you thought he did. I have to say, Ms Mahoney, it doesn't look good, and we would love to hear what you say about it.'

'You have. You have heard what I say about it. I've answered every single one of those points. And Alice. Alice is lovely and everything but she's not all there. I don't mean that in a bad way. But she misread what was happening. I was trying to help her. To fix her car. And you can check my bank account. I bought that knife – a multi-tool really – from Robert Dyas that day. It flew out of my hand. By accident.'

Omer makes a note.

'When you got to the office to find Russell, why didn't you call him instead?' he asks.

'Because I was there to talk to him face to face.'

'Did you speak to anyone on the phone? Anybody call you?'

'No. I don't think so. You can check my call history.' There is something coming but I don't know what it could be.

'Looking back now, are you saying that the victim, Amy Blahn, was there on the roof because she was supposed to be meeting your husband?'

'I don't know. I guess she must have been.'

'Ms Mahoney, we've checked into Amy and you were right about one thing. She did work for *e-Vinculum.* So, what was she meeting your husband about?'

'I can only tell you what Michael had told me. She was trying to get a chemical compound licensed.'

'But Russell's job has nothing to do with chemical approvals, does it?'

'I don't know. He wasn't very forthcoming. He refused to answer me whenever I raised it with him.' My heart is racing now and it is giving my voice an edge of guilt.

'Well, we *have* checked. With him and his employers. And there's nothing to suggest he would have had any sway with approving chemicals.'

They stare at me, eyes as if in suspension fluid. Floating. 'Well, I didn't know that.'

'If he had made plans to meet her, he would have to get her into the building, wouldn't he? Russell would have had to let her in. Or make those arrangements?'

I weigh the damage that any answer can cause. Though I have been doing it with every one, there are so many now that I feel as though I'm trying to pick up scattered sugar. 'I guess.'

'But the question for you, I suppose, is, why, after making all these arrangements to meet her and to get her a pass or whatever it is, into the building, he then didn't stay around to meet her?'

The walls are beginning to vibrate a little now. It could be a migraine. 'Have you tried asking him?'

'Well, here's the interesting thing, Ms Mahoney. We did. He claims that your mother called him to say that you were about to kill yourself. Or that you were already dead. Care to comment?'

I laugh under my breath. 'If you knew her you'd know that she was always saying that to me recently. For some reason it had got into her head and she couldn't seem to shake it.'

'Is that true, Ms Mahoney?'

'Yes, of course it is. Why would I lie about that?'

Omer smiles but there is no warmth in there. 'Maybe you wanted him out of the way so that you could be alone on that roof with Amy. She was expecting Russell but you turn up instead. And Russell – well, he's miles away because you together with your mum have sent him on a fool's errand.'

'And how exactly do you think I managed that? Did I call my mum and tell her to tell Russell I was killing myself?'

'Did you?' Metcalf asks.

'What? You think Mum called Russell but not an ambulance?'

'Mothers have been known to do stranger things. Maybe you'd told her it was a ruse.' Omer again.

Peter spreads his hands on the table and I see now for the first time how tightly wound he is becoming. 'What evidence do you have to support that?'

'Well, we have checked Ms Mahoney's call records and we can see missed calls from her mother three times within ten minutes of Ms Mahoney entering the building. I'd say that would put you, Ms

Mahoney, on your account, in his – Russell's – office. And Russell on the roof or on his way to the roof to meet Amy.'

'Sorry, I don't see what you're getting at.'

'What I'm getting at is that you know that Russell is meeting Amy Blahn. And you need him out of the way. I'm not saying you decided to kill her there and then, but you were going to warn her off. And your mother was the perfect vehicle. She was already worried about you taking your own life, you said. And it's a simple step, isn't it, to get her to call Russell and to warn him that you were going to kill yourself?'

'Have you asked her?' Peter's voice is sharp.

'What?' Omer looks up puzzled.

'Her mother. What did she say?' Peter says firmly.

Omer tugs at the top button of his collar. 'We have an officer there as we speak taking a statement from her.'

'Well, don't you think, Detective, that we should wait until we have a statement before you start asking Ms Mahoney to speculate on something that might not have happened? And while we are on speculation. You've told us about missed calls to Ms Mahoney. Were there any calls between them that connected?'

Omer fumbles at his papers and shakes his head. 'Not that I can see.'

'So, let me get this correct. You're suggesting Layla spoke to her mother to tell her she was dying and then told her to get Russell home immediately and yet there are no calls on her call records to suggest that could even have happened?'

Peter's eyebrows are raised and he has the look of a headmaster telling off a child. The two detectives are gaping for words until Peter stands up and calls for a break. 'We can have it in here if you can just switch the tapes off.'

54

Then

I was now in the car. The last minutes were in a blender, lost to detail, but still there in an amalgamated way. He had hoisted me up and started patting me down for my car keys. So now he was in my car driving me home. My eyes felt heavy as soon as the car warmed up. I didn't know how was it possible to sleep when all my energy was fighting against my own urge to stop my life. I forced my eyes open to look at Michael.

'Did I call you?' I said, checking my phone through the fog. There were no calls to his number.

'You haven't had enough pills to be sick sick,' he'd said. 'But if you're thinking of doing it again, let me tell you, it's not as easy as drifting off to the pearly gates in a gentle sleep. It'll get into your liver first and then you'll die. Painfully. Even if you got yourself to a hospital, you'd be in excruciating pain till you died.' When I didn't react he said, 'Jump under a train. Quicker. Less pain.'

He'd said it just like that – compassionately. But without crossing any lines.

'Why do you care?' I said.

'Because. Because of all this crap. I'm linked to you,' he'd said. And it was that – the banality and repetitiveness of this thought that sent me, finally, to sleep.

When he pulled up at my house, I woke to him patting my arm. Startled, I jumped before piecing together what had happened. I saw my house. And Michael in the driver's seat. He knew where I lived. Had he checked the satnav?

'Thanks,' I managed. 'I won't invite you in.'

He nodded and handed me the keys and climbed out. The air was chilly, but the sun was coming up, I could see the glint of it on the horizon.

'Can I ask you a question? The truth?'

'Fire away,' he said, holding the collars of his leather jacket closed.

'What were you doing there? On a beach in the middle of nowhere?'

He thought for a second. 'I could ask you the same question.'

I started to speak even though I hadn't collected my thoughts properly. But I didn't have time for any more of this.

He sighed and looked at me with sadness. 'Look. Whatever you were there for doesn't matter exactly. You were there because you were there. The same for me. I was there because I was. Would you feel better about it if I said I was visiting my mother or I was there for work? Or something else? Whatever took me there, took me. In my mind *I* don't have to explain the coincidence, any more than *you* do.'

I hesitated. 'You'd gone to see your mum?'

He sighed. 'It doesn't matter. The fact is we're connected. I tried to warn you about it. It won't stop until it is – *satisfied*. It'll keep happening. Just decide when you want to get it done.'

I started towards my door but he held me back by the elbow. Just as he had done that first time. The scene came crashing back. 'You said in your message that we had to talk.'

I rubbed my eyes and tucked a strand of hair behind my ear and remembered. 'You still haven't told me what you know.'

He considered this. The early light gave him a ghoulish look. He sighed. 'The connection is *e-Vinc*. As I said, we make industrial chemicals. And chemicals, as you can appreciate, are extremely tightly regulated. For good reason. You don't want the wrong ones out there.'

'So, what's wrong with that?' The sun began touching the horizon with faint orange light. The air tasted of dew.

'Well, some dangerous chemicals are really good chemicals. Some of them, what we describe as long-chain PFAS, are really very good. I mean they are almost super-powered. When these were first developed, it was like the industry struck gold.'

'How do you mean?'

'Imagine a chemical that can do everything. That's a PFAS. You spray this thing onto anything and it's waterproof. I mean properly waterproof – you can't get a drop of water past it. You paint it onto a pan – you can fry an egg on it dry and it'll never stick. You've got metal components that corrode – put some of it on and they won't any more. You want to make almost anything, from semiconductors to the coating on your phone or the packaging for your cornflakes, waterproof, it does it.'

'I'm sorry, I don't see the problem.'

He shook his head. 'Ha. The problem is that it made the industry millions. Billions. Until it didn't.'

'What does that mean?' I said, struggling to keep up. The tiredness was being moderated by the adrenaline that was now in my system but the two things were arguing.

He sighed. 'It killed people. The run-off from the chemical plants contaminated the water supply. Everything in touching distance died. Not instantly. But a lot sooner than they would have. Cancer mainly. You know it's true. Cancer is everywhere now. And it's a lot to do with this chemical.'

The words hung in the air between us like stones.

'So, what does all that have to do with Russell, with me, with you? They banned it, surely.'

'That specific chain, sure. But they, we, are always making more chemicals. We used shorter chain molecules at first. But they were dangerous too. And the regulatory body, REACH, was on top of it unusually quickly. Shut it right down.'

I breathed again. 'So, that's good.'

'It was. But REACH is an EU body. We'll be out of the EU. And so, the UK is going to be doing its own policing. But frankly, it doesn't have the database that REACH has. So there's a frantic effort now to negotiate a licence to use the EU database. But until then they need transitional arrangements in place.'

I rubbed my head. The pain was building now like a wall behind my head. 'You're losing me.'

'There's a hundred new chemicals a week all needing approvals. They're all in a holding pattern until someone designs the right process to decide what goes through and what doesn't. I'm sure you can imagine, there's a lot at stake here. Some of the more ruthless businesses are seeing this as an opportunity to exploit an incomplete system. If they can get a chemical through the new filters in the system then it could mean billions.'

'But how do they do that?'

'Well, they "help" design the system. Unless you've got twenty experts across twenty different scientific and chemical engineering disciplines, you'll never be able to catch it.'

'You mean rig the system so that it lets your chemical through –'

'– before the REACH database comes through. And by then it's too late to stop it.'

I wrapped my arms across my body against the cold. 'You still haven't said how this affects us.'

'I think the woman we saw is trying to rig the system. With Russell.'

I laughed. 'I wish you'd told me this at the start. Russell doesn't deal with chemicals or filter systems or databases or whatever you think he does. He writes compliance documents to do with –' I said and stopped.

'Brexit?'

I hesitated. 'Yes. But not chemicals. Law. Minor bits of regulatory stuff. Secondary legislation.'

'You're wrong. But if I'm right and this woman is working on getting this product through – and succeeds – then we're all dead. And I'm not being dramatic. We won't be able to avoid it. When it's out, it's everywhere. And it never breaks down. The bonds are too strong.'

'What I don't understand, Michael, is who you think she is and who you think she's working for.'

'I thought that was clear,' he said slowly. 'I think she's working for us. For *e-Vinc*. The company is corrupt.'

He levelled his eyes at me, waiting, but I didn't answer them. I turned instead to go into the house.

'Now, you. You said you had something to say.'

I looked at him and then at the house. The lights were all out. Russell on his invented fishing trip. Michael looked anxious, jittery even. The poise he'd carried around like a cloak, nowhere to be seen. I took a breath. 'I found cash. Lots of it.'

'How much?'

I told him the amount.

'It doesn't seem anything like enough money to bribe him – though for all we know he went and bought a load of crypto with most it and this is all that's left. How did he explain it?'

'I didn't ask him. He's gone away,' I said. 'And I'm too tired for this now.' My eyes were heavy and swollen with exhaustion. I turned away to go inside.

'Wait. If he's away, this is the perfect time.'

'To do what?'

'Search. You need to find out who the woman is. Find her and I can expose what she's doing.'

'I did search. What do you think I've been doing? Except I don't know what to look for. And you haven't told me.'

'Look, Layla, I'm sorry. I'm sorry that you're in this and I'm sorry that someone is getting ready to unleash this – toxic mess into the world. And I'm sorry I don't know how to help you more. And the truth is, I don't know what to look for. I just know that I have to stop her.'

I looked at him one final time. 'Why do you? Call the police. Tell them everything you told me.'

'I can't.'

'Why not?'

He stared at the sky as if coming to a decision. 'Because I helped develop the compound.'

55

Then

The smell of wet earth hit me as soon as I walked into the kitchen. There was building dust everywhere. The fitter had tried his best to sweep up but had left a film of wet marble dust over every surface. The new countertop, though, gleamed in the light – polished and cleaned of every speck. I ran my hands across it searching for nubs and was disappointed not to find any. He'd left a box of latex gloves at one corner on the top, spilling its contents. Underneath was what looked like an invoice but I didn't examine at it.

In the bedroom, through the exhaustion, I searched again through Russell's things for the name of a woman and for traces of more money. Money was the easiest thing to focus on. There might be a receipt for something somewhere – maybe a Bitcoin transaction. He wasn't the kind of person to blow thousands on a thing. No, he'd be more cautious. He'd have invested it somehow or banked it in a separate bank account. Russell did everything electronically so there'd be no paper statements. If only I could get into his phone – I was certain I would find something there.

After an hour, I'd found nothing. In the bedroom I sank to the floor and willed myself to think. If this woman was trying to license a chemical or somehow influence the approval process what *physically* would that involve? Documentation of some sort – containing some kind of chemical blueprint maybe? Or a formula? And perhaps if it was illicit, they wouldn't want an electronic trace. Maybe his phone didn't have the answer. Maybe it was on paper somewhere? Like the cash. Untraceable.

Russell never brought paperwork home. Occasionally I printed reports or witness statements on paper because I found them easier to amend. But Russell always worked digitally. There had been nothing in his pockets or drawers. We didn't have a shredder. I checked the recycling bin.

But it contained just a few empty food cartons that I'd put in there myself. Then I remembered how he'd emptied the bins before he left. Outside the blue one was empty. It must have been collected already. In the dawning light I peered into it. There were a few stray cardboard sleeves and some plastic film along with the remnants of some torn envelopes. And then, stuck to the side, I saw two pieces of photocopy paper. I leaned in and pulled them out. The first read:

THE INDUSTRIAL CHEMICALS APPLICATIONS
(LICENCE APPEAL PROVISIONS) (REVOCATION)
(NO. 2 ORDER) (2013) 2013 NO. 1192

Underneath there were numbered paragraphs dealing with 'Legislative Context', 'Territorial Extent and Application' and then a paragraph headed 'Matters of Special Interest to the Joint Committee on Statutory Instruments'. The rest had been torn off. The second piece had a partial graph showing 'behaviour over time' and nothing more. I put the pieces in my pocket and headed inside.

I had to go to bed. Exhaustion had descended. I slept as soon as I hit my pillow. The alcohol, the pills and everything else thrown together, sent me into a deep sleep.

When I woke it was past midday and the room was flooded with cloudy light. I tested my head, and found the pain had gone. I thought back to the night – the pills – Michael, and I wondered whether he had been there. It didn't seem plausible that he'd found me on a beach by chance. He'd either followed me, or I'd called him and later deleted the call. Even as I was wondering what was happening to me, I felt as though some enormous tidal wave was pulling me deep into a sunless ocean.

It was Monday, but I called in sick again. Nothing was right. Wherever I looked something was out of place and needed to be tidied or disposed of. But then when I picked up the object, whatever it was, I couldn't think what to do with it. In the kitchen for instance, I saw the invoice and the gloves and went to do something with them but then stalled because there was nowhere for them to go. I remembered the pieces of paper and pulled them from the pocket of my jeans and looked at them again but I couldn't make anything of them.

I called Kate but her phone went to voicemail. I then rang Mum but ended the call before she picked up.

When we last spoke she'd told me Dad was alive but I wasn't sure whether I trusted these new truths of hers. I wasn't even sure of my own. The idea of it made my mind scatter like marbles on a floor.

I cast my mind back to him and whether he occupied air in the same way as a fleshed person. I willed my brain to help me resolve it. He was there, but barely, exactly like a ghost might be. The fact he was alive didn't mean that I had seen him. That thought began to eat away at me until I began to wish I'd taken a picture of him. I could still smell his warmed skin but a memory wasn't proof. Memories stretched across aeons unfixed by time.

An hour later I was in an Uber travelling across London. When I got out I was standing in front of the Savoy, staring at the Art Deco building. The door was guarded by a liveried doorman and even before I had revolved through the doors, I felt inadequate. The chess-board floor moved beneath my feet. I squeaked my way to the front desk and gave my father's name.

'Which room, madam?'

'I'm not sure, but could you tell him his daughter is here.'

She muttered something in French to her counterpart before turning back to me. 'I'm sorry, madam, but we cannot confirm whether any guest in particular is staying.'

I found myself sighing. 'I'm not asking for confirmation. Just ring his room, please, and tell him his daughter is here. I'll wait for him in the bar.' The idea that I might be asking for someone who might have been dead for decades or if alive had never been here made the floor slide from under my feet. I held on to the desk edge.

She made a note with a pencil. 'The American Bar?'

I had no idea. 'Yes please,' I said and then turned uncertainly towards the doors through which I'd entered.

'To your right, madam,' she said, smiling lightly.

The American Bar was carpeted in dark rust with swirls of pale yellow that made patterns like slices of brain. Ahead a thousand spirit bottles stood arranged on mirrored shelves behind a curved bar. Jazz piano played somewhere deeper in the room. I was shown to a small table by a white-jacketed man who skirted elegantly around the few tourists nestled in pockets here and there.

'Madam?' the waiter said, placing a menu card down.

'Martini,' I said, glancing at it.

'Vodka martini? Olives?'

I nodded and he hurried away and reappeared with it moments later.

I sat sipping my martini in a daze. An hour ago, I was on the sofa at home and now I was in a place once frequented by Ava Gardner and Oscar Wilde. I stared at the angry red line of the scar across the back of my hand.

I didn't know if he was alive. Mum's dementia wasn't the kind that had clean lines of lucidity and forgetfulness. There were textures of reality in her life. Some darkly shaded parts had beams of light scattered through it. But the light and dark sometimes mixed so that what she was left with was neither memory nor invention but a blend of both.

If she'd discovered he was alive when she said she did, I'd have been around twenty. By then most of the pain had been done. It hadn't healed, but the pain itself – the pain of living through the days – had gone. Those mornings at school where I'd huddled under a tree overcome by tears. The misery of Sundays which held nothing for me but my mother, caught under the weight of her depression. I remember walking in on her once and seeing her on her knees, sobbing as if the world had burned up everything. We'd lived those days of my mum and I pulling each other through endless summer weeks. The pain had been done. So maybe she was right. By the time I was twenty, there was nothing to be gained by the truth. It didn't have the power to save either of us. All it would have done was make me feel that the effort of all that pain had been wasted.

Or perhaps it was just more texture from Mum's mind. Maybe he had died all those years ago in Pakistan. Or died recently. And I was seeing ghosts.

I took an olive from my drink and wondered whether things would ever get back to normal. It didn't seem possible. Pieces of my life were floating away like ashes from burned paper. Too small to hold on to. Too fragile.

A different waiter oozed into view and gently placed the bill on a silver plate. I left it there for a while untouched. 'It's a message, madam.'

I picked up the note.

Mr Khawaja says he will be there in a minute. Please stay until he arrives.

The name sent an unexpected spike of electricity through me. That name of his. I'd never been allowed to use it as a child – it drew too much attention. I'd always had to use Mum's name. With my light colouring, I could just pass.

Khawaja. I rolled the name around in my mouth. My father was alive. Had been alive all this time.

Even before the plate was spirited away, I saw him entering the bar. He was dressed in a dark green sports jacket, white shirt and navy tie. He scanned the room until he caught sight of me, and he waved as he came in.

'Layla,' he said and kissed me on both cheeks. He beamed as he sat. 'I'm so glad to see you. I wasn't sure whether you'd come.' His face was the same one I'd seen at Temple a week ago. Lightly drawn. Faded.

'I thought I was seeing ghosts.'

He extended a hand towards me but I leaned away from it. 'Well, as you can see. I'm firmly not a ghost. I'm in London to meet some hospital managers about taking their old wheelchairs and so on off their hands. We can really use them in –'

'Dad, I thought you were dead,' I said and watched his face fall.

'You have to believe me, Layla. When I found out that she had told you I had died, I was furious.'

'She told me that your family called her to say you had died. She didn't know you were alive.' A swell of anger rushed in.

He reached out again for my arm. 'Layla, I spoke to your mother regularly. I made it very clear to her that I would leave it in her hands and your hands. Whether you wanted to have any contact with me. I didn't want to force it.'

I took a mouthful of my drink and studied his reaction. There was never any booze in the house when we were growing up. He noticed but said nothing.

'Have you got time to take some food?' he asked.

'No.' I gathered my things and stood up. 'I don't know why I came. I just wanted to know if I was going mad.'

He stood too and stretched out a hand to my arm again. 'Layla.'

'Why did you leave, Da—?' I stopped short. I didn't want to call him that but didn't want call him by his name either. 'Why did you leave us?' There were tears coming and I wiped them but as fast I did, more came in their place. I sat down again and dried my face. When I looked up he was still standing.

'It was complicated, Layla.'

'It's not complicated. I was your daughter. You left me with her knowing what it would do to her.'

He sat back down in his seat and stared at the patterns in the carpet. The piano changed from jazz to something bluesy.

'How could you leave *me*, Dad? I was thirteen.'

He called a waiter over as if he were in a cheap restaurant, hands flailing, and asked for a whisky 'on the rocks'. The waiter returned with the menu. It seemed to baffle him. 'Black Label,' he said. When the waiter had gone he spoke. 'I never meant to leave but – it was my mother's funeral. I had to. And then you know your mother and I had been having problems. And the UK never felt like home. But being there felt like home. I called your mother so many times asking her to come for a visit. To come for a few weeks and see what the life was like.' His eyes lit up as he spoke. 'There was sun. There were gardens around our house as large as the local park here. And fruit trees. So many trees with oranges this big.'

A waiter came with his drink and set it carefully on the small table.

'I wanted you both to come. We could start again.'

The bar was beginning to fill for the pre-lunch crowd. 'What was so bad about here that you had to leave your own daughter? I can't –' Tears threatened again.

'It wasn't you, Layla. I never wanted to leave you. This country didn't want me. Whatever I tried it would just spit me out. I didn't blame it for that. That was its nature. Then at least. It's changed a lot since,' he added. He took a sip and grimaced and I wondered whether he'd ever had any alcohol. 'But I knew that since I had left that I couldn't dictate terms. It was up to your mother whether she wanted you to come.'

A waiter hovered nearby and took my glass when the silence made space for him. He asked quietly if I wanted another and hastened away to get it.

'But you know I grew up. I became an adult – what, twenty years ago? It wasn't her business after that. You could have called me.'

'I could have. Yes. But I didn't have your number, Layla, and whenever I called your mum, she said you didn't want to talk to me. Wouldn't give me your number. And then she became ill. Well, you know that.'

My head was reeling from all this information. I got up to leave. 'I have to go.'

'I also came to see you. I found you on the Web, and your law firm. I left a message for you. I needed to see you. Before it was too late.'

The alcohol was making me feel warm and hazy now. The room moved a little under my feet. 'It is too late,' I said. 'Dad.'

56

Now

'Ms Mahoney, we want to go back to the knife and the fact that no prints were found on it.' Omer has the kind of energy that slow releases throughout the day so that there's never a dip. He seems the same as he first walked in. Nothing tires him out. Metcalf though – and Peter – are fraying at the edges. 'Do you recall that your answer about that to us was that the assailant – Michael – was wearing gloves?'

'She said he might have been wearing gloves,' Peter says immediately.

'Yes,' Omer continues. 'Because that was your only explanation for there being no traces of a single print. But we do have some good news. The crime scene investigators found some gloves at the scene. They were thrown over the terrace by the murderer.'

'How can you be sure they belong to the murderer?' Peter again.

'They are covered in the victim's blood. There's no other reasonable explanation.' Peter nods and Omer continues but now he is looking intently at a report. 'I'm showing you photographs of the gloves. Exhibit NM/8 for the tape.'

'Okay,' I say. He shows me some bloodstained gloves that have been balled up and then opened up picture by picture.

'Did you see him wearing these? They're a kind of latex glove.'

'I can't be sure whether those were the exact gloves but, yes, similar. The blood gives it away though. I guess.'

Omer nods. 'Yes. Only –' he says and stops while he finds his place on the page. 'We have had preliminary results back that tell us there is some DNA on the outside of the gloves. Could any of that be yours?'

There is only one answer I can give at this point. 'No.'

'The more puzzling thing is that there is no trace of any person's DNA on the inside of the gloves. Can you explain that?'

Peter interjects. 'Does she need to? Because from here it looks like she's told you the killer wore gloves and you found some gloves worn by the killer. And what you seem to be saying is that there is none of my client's DNA on the gloves. Doesn't that rather blow your case out?'

'Not exactly. The killer wore those gloves. That seems certain. But she can't prove without some other forensic link to the gloves that it wasn't her wearing them. She can't rule herself out, can she? Can you, Ms Mahoney?'

'She doesn't need to rule herself out. That's called the burden of proof, Detective. It's your job to prove she was wearing them, not the other way around.'

Omer looks at Metcalf and then back at me. 'Well, you see, Ms Mahoney, we think we can prove that you were wearing the gloves.'

Peter sits up. 'What do you mean?'

'Well, these gloves weren't just examined to determine the blood match. They were also tested to see what make they were.'

'Why?' Peter asks, but I know what he doesn't.

'Because of the gloves we found at your client's address.'

'What?' Peter says, looking to them and then to me for confirmation.

'Yes. There was a box of latex gloves found in the kitchen, in the cutlery drawer.' Omer blinks benignly.

Peter looks at me and I nod. 'So, what? How do you know it's the same brand?'

'Because of the thickness of the latex – not latex strictly – but nitrile. The ones in Ms Mahoney's house and the bloodstained ones at the scene have an unusual spec in that they are 5.75 mills thick. It's quite rare apparently.'

'Rare? As in the guys who made the box that you say was in my client's house – what, did they make just the one box?'

Metcalf coughs. 'No, but they sell a limited quantity of that type. In fact, that particular thickness they don't even make any more. They stopped making it a year ago.'

'That doesn't mean that they're rare,' Peter presses.

'Why have you got nitrile gloves in your house, Ms Mahoney?'

'They were left by the man who fixed my kitchen countertop.'

'And just to be clear. You don't carry these with you for any reason? For work or anything else?'

'No.'

Omer makes a note. 'So, if you had them with you on the roof, that would have to be, shall we say, premeditated?'

'I didn't have them with me on the roof.'

'And you didn't wear them when you were killing Amy?'

'No.' There is an edge to my answer. 'And if I had been wearing gloves, surely my DNA would be on there. You don't have an answer to that one, do you?'

'Not yet,' he says. 'But we're working on it.'

57

Then

I spent the rest of the day after seeing Dad at home. I didn't want to move from the sofa. I just sat and stared at my hands. I had missed it all. All that suffering that Mum had held tight to herself. Or maybe she hadn't held it that tightly. Perhaps she'd left it out for me to see, but I'd been too self-absorbed to notice anyone but myself.

That would be the start of another undoing, because that's how I had to be seen now. Selfish, self-obsessed.

In the middle of the night, I woke on the sofa and went to the bathroom and threw up. My stomach was a knot. The whole space in which I existed was toxic. I had to get away from my head somehow and be free of the poison. I took myself off to bed and allowed the feelings to consume me a little more, hoping that eventually I'd disappear.

In the morning I felt both too unwell to go to work and too unwell not to. Staying home seemed the more dangerous option, so I dragged myself in.

When I got there, Alice looked up but then turned away. I began a smile for her but then allowed it to die on my lips.

I was relieved when the working day was over and it was time to go. Before I left I wanted to call Russell. He'd said that he'd be away for a week but had been vague about exactly when he was coming back. I didn't know which day of the weekend he meant. And now the more

I thought about it the angrier I became. He'd transformed me into this creature that only cared about licking its own skin.

Last night I'd had a dream that I was being dangled out of a window a hundred stories up. That was how I felt.

I couldn't live like Mum had been living all these years: in a wilderness without any clue about what had led her there. Whenever I had asked her why she and Dad split up, she always said it was Dad's decision and that he never really explained why. He wouldn't be drawn on it. And now Dad himself was saying only a little more than nothing. He had a sense of not belonging but everyone had that. Nobody belonged anywhere. That was why everyone complained endlessly about their own pain and turned it into currency.

I wasn't any different. If Russell ever told me what it was he found difficult about me – what my failings were – I'd be thrust into that pain myself. And I knew the mechanical separation of flesh from bone that that would start. I could hear the judder of the engine, even thinking about it now. But in the end, it couldn't be worse than what was already happening. Though my brain hadn't started to fillet me yet, it was dancing around with knives in its hands, sharpening, sharpening.

I picked up the desk phone and dialled Russell's work number. If he wasn't there, I'd go. I'd find a way in somehow – I was his wife after all.

'Hello,' I said. 'Can I speak to Russell?' I kept his surname out of it so that I'd appear familiar.

'Sure. Just a second, I'll put you through. Who shall I say it is?'

My heart flipped. He was there. My mind raced and before I could think of a neutral pseudonym, 'Kate' leaked out.

'Okay,' the voice said and then the line rang. My heart began to thump. Maybe that didn't mean he was there but that they were checking. A minute passed and then the phone was answered and back came the distinct sound of Russell's voice. 'Hi, Kate.'

I slammed the phone into the cradle, my breath heavy. The hum of my computer fan filled the air, as if trying to make everything feel normal.

I could go anyway. See him. Confront him about it all. I checked the time. In thirty minutes or so he'd be getting ready to leave. I might see him with someone and I could confront them both. Find out what the hell he was doing with this woman and her chemicals.

I jumped on the Tube and headed to St James's Park. Russell was connected to everything, it seemed in that moment. He was at the centre pulling at the strings. When I thought about it, he was the one who'd brought Michael and that weird energy into our lives. This woman he'd been meeting – that was on him not anyone else. Even whatever was going on with Kate and even with Alice, it was Russell who'd been responsible. He couldn't have known it was Alice's car when he destroyed it, but that didn't mean he wasn't culpable. It all tracked back to him. Whatever Michael was, whether he was a clear warner or, as I was beginning to suspect, a placeholder for my own worries, he wasn't responsible. It was all Russell. Michael was just trying to do something about it.

Within twenty minutes I was standing again outside the monolithic building. A chill descended as though the warmth were being sucked out of the air.

'Finally.'

I looked round. Michael. He stood to my left, arms folded. He was smiling. The blue of his T-shirt was bright cobalt under the black of his leather jacket.

'Michael,' I said, unsurprised. His sudden appearance made me doubt again that he was there at all.

'They're in there, aren't they?' he said.

I took hold of his arm and squeezed. He smiled again, amusement playing across his features. 'What?' he said, puzzled.

'Nothing. I can't trust myself to know if you're here or not,' I said more to myself than him.

'What are you talking about?' he said, concern descending over his features.

I ignored the question. 'Why are you here, Michael?' People were trickling out of the building wrapped in coats.

'You know why.'

'Piss off,' I said and headed towards the door.

'Wait,' he said. 'You need to get in and I know how you can.'

My throat became tight. I checked at the extremities of my senses. I looked for the warning signs: did I feel as if I were the centre of the world? Was everything a signal or a message meant only for me?

I wasn't sure any more.

He walked towards me. 'We can get in without being seen. I've been inside.'

I was overcome suddenly by fear but more than that, anger. 'What were you doing in there? Did you go to find Russell?'

A gust of wind blew hair across his eyes. 'No. It's more than just the Environment Agency in that building – a few different manufacturing companies have their registered offices there. Even chemical companies.' He smiled. 'I know how to get you in.'

Here he was distorting the air again – interfering with the pattern of things. I stared at him. His eyes shone. 'I'm not sure he's even in there,' I said.

He moved closer. 'Did you find anything more? Wait,' he added, 'you did. You found something. What?'

I thought back to the scraps of paper. 'You were right. He is involved in something.'

'Where is he now? He's up there?'

I hesitated. 'I don't know. Maybe. He hasn't been home.'

The air blew across his face, making his hair flit. 'Why are you here? What brought you here – specifically?'

I hesitated. I stood there shaded from the wind for a minute by his body. A wisp of some scent from his neck reminded me of Dad. My shoulders dropped and I relaxed. 'I thought he might be with her. I –' I started but the rest of the words misted away. There were enough of them but I'd run out of energy to drive them out.

Michael nodded slowly as he listened, as if he were trying to unpick some complicated problem. Finally, he looked up. 'Come on,' he said and led me round to the back of the building.

He pointed out a door along the wall where people were smoking. 'When they go back in, we can slip in too. No cameras either,' he said, looking up.

I remembered the time Russell had brought me down that exit. 'We can't. You need a key to get through the second door.'

'Not if we push through behind them.'

'No. I can go in through the front door. I'm not a criminal. I don't need to sneak through back doors to see my own husband.'

Michael gave me a small nod. 'I'll come in with you if you like?'

I patted myself down as if I had mislaid something. 'Why?' I said.

He seemed to freeze for a second and then a look of concern washed over his features. 'I need to know if she's in there and what she's said to him, Layla. And how far along has this gone.'

'No,' I said. 'I'll do it. I'll find out.'

He stood looking at the door and then turned to me. 'How are you going to do it?'

'I don't know yet.'

We walked back around to the front. I thought again about everything that had happened these past weeks. 'I'm just going to tell him straight. She's dangerous.'

He bit his lip. 'Do you think he'll listen?'

I considered this. 'He might. If you have something, some evidence that I could show him, then he'd listen.'

He smiled.

'What?'

'I can send you the chemical specs but they're going to be meaningless to anyone but a chemical engineer. Look. You go. Find out whatever you can. If you don't get anywhere, then so be it. I'll be waiting down here for her. If you can't get it from him, I'll get it from her myself.'

'Do you think she's in there?' I said.

'I don't know. All I know is that if he's rushed back here without going home, I'm suspicious. I know that they were getting very excited about something in the boardroom earlier this week. It has to be to do with this.'

I took a deep breath and walked up to the entrance. Inside a steady stream of people with passes were walking unhurriedly through glass barriers that slid open like London Underground stiles. Off to the right was a reception desk staffed by a middle-aged woman. I approached her and smiled. 'I need to see Russell Becker.'

Without looking up, she asked, 'Have you got an appointment?'

'No, but he's expecting me,' I lied. 'Kate Peel,' I said and drummed my fingers on the table in faux impatience.

She looked up, pale grey eyes behind gold frames. After taking my details she dialled a number and after a minute said, 'He's away from his desk but you can go up if you know where you're going? Second floor. Two-eleven.' She handed me a plastic pass on a lanyard with the name Kate Peel freshly printed on it.

I walked as if I came here every day, straight through the barriers and up to a bank of lifts on the left. One came in seconds and I got in and punched 2. I breathed out as it climbed.

I knew him. He loved me. If I could sit down with him alone for a few minutes and remind him that we were once the ones who were entangled. Our individual lives had collided with one another's and changed them forever. Whenever he moved he pulled me a little in the trail of his gravity. He didn't know how serious this was. When I explained it to him, he would see. The phone, the secret meetings, the money he was taking from them – in cash – were proof enough that there was something dangerous about the chemical, or if not proof then a warning.

The lift doors opened onto a deserted corridor with identical doors alongside leaded windows. The walls were creamy travertine. I walked slowly, touching the smooth stone until I came to a water fountain sunken into the wall. There was a notice warning against drinking it. Along the length of the corridor only two offices had any lights burning inside. Small white plaques marked with numbers were the only thing that distinguished one from the next. The light to 2.11 was one of two that glowed. I knocked gently. My heart was in my mouth.

There was no reply so I knocked again. As I waited I began to cycle through the conversation that I was about to have. My mind raced ahead. What if she was there? And if she wasn't, would I have to fight past his denials, past his excuses and explanations? *Why can't you just be honest? Who is she? I saw you on the balcony with her.*

The door remained shut. I knocked again. And when there was no answer, I pushed it open and went inside.

58

Now

'We may have solved the problem about the gloves, Ms Mahoney.'

I don't say a thing. I wait for Omer to say what he wants. That is where we are now. He is saying what he needs to say to tick all his boxes, and I am laying down the foundations of my defence where I have answers that will work. There's an unexpected peace from accepting this part of it at least. They're going to charge me, that much is clear.

'We almost missed it, didn't we, Detective Omer?'

Omer nods. 'Yes. The sergeant picked it up actually when he was booking your property in. Can you see that there on your property sheet?' he says, pushing a piece of paper at me. 'In your coat pocket there was a pair of leather gloves.'

'Okay,' I say slowly.

'Well, that's it, isn't it? If you wore those gloves and then the nitrile ones on top, then the murder gloves would have no prints. No DNA.'

'In the early autumn?' I say.

'Well, why have you got them in your pocket?' Omer asks without missing a beat.

'Because they were in there from last winter,' I say just as quickly.

Peter wades in, his arms up. 'Hold up. Let's get back on track. Detective, your theory about double-gloving goes just as well for the murderer, Michael. He could have done the same.'

'He could have, it's true. But Ms Mahoney told us that she was quite sure he was wearing latex-style gloves. She didn't say anything about him wearing leather gloves underneath.'

Peter sniffs derisively but I have come to read that sniff in a different way. It means he is struggling for purchase.

'But,' I say. They look at me. I pause. I let the tape play on because there is power that I hadn't appreciated in letting the silence expand to fill all the spaces. They don't like it. It's suffocating. 'Isn't this all mere speculation? Guesswork?'

Peter smiles a small smile. He stands and stretches as much as he can in this small room. The air is stale and I can tell he wants to leave and smoke and come back again when he's less fried.

'It's funny, isn't it, Ms Mahoney? In all my years as a police officer, I've never heard an innocent person say that something I put to them is speculation. If they're innocent, they usually just say I'm wrong – not that I'm guessing,' says Omer.

'Then you're wrong,' I say. 'It was Michael. I keep telling you that.'

'But there is one problem with your version.'

'What's that?' I ask.

'He's not there on CCTV, is he?'

It's time to play my last card.

'Detective?' I say. 'About that. The CCTV, I mean. Did you check if there were any cameras at the back? By the fire door?'

The silence is heavy. 'Yes,' Metcalf says sullenly.

'And?' Peter says, flat.

'There are no cameras there.'

I nod and rub the scar on my hand. 'There you are then,' I say. 'Hard to spot a man on the film if he doesn't walk under the camera.'

'Unless he's a ghost?' Metcalf says.

I close my eyes against the insult he tries to feed me with his expression.

'Well, you've told us how you had hallucinated the ghost of your father, Layla. That must have been a strange experience?' Omer is leaning forward ever so slightly to encourage me to confide. He smiles gently.

'It was,' I say.

'Must have been traumatic, having to deal with his death. And you know we are very aware of how trauma can affect people. It can make them act in ways that they'd never dream of acting otherwise.'

'Really?' I say, unable to conceal the sarcasm.

'The harm can be catastrophic.'

'Where are you going with this?' Peter asks gruffly.

'You didn't tell us, Layla, how your father died.'

The question throws me. Not so long ago, I thought he *had* died. 'Under the wheels of a bus. In Pakistan. His rickshaw was crushed.'

'And how old were you when this happened?'

'Around thirteen,' I say automatically, welcoming the opportunity to talk about it with someone. He didn't die, but I'm in this alternate truth now. I know this story well enough, I've told it to myself for years. Everyone I know can back this version up.

'Must have been tough to hear that about your dad.'

I say nothing.

'Did you ever get yourself some grief counselling or therapy?'

'No,' I say. 'We survived. We just took each day as it came. Some were worse than others.'

Omer nods slowly as if he understands all the layers and colours of grief. Maybe he does. 'What was he called? His name?'

I stall. That question is loaded with ordnance. 'Maqbool,' I say.

'He didn't use another name? An English name?'

Peter catches the expression on my face but he can't stop them here. It feels like the wrong call. He doesn't want to draw attention to it too much. 'Can you tell us what this is about?'

'Sure,' Omer says. 'We asked Kate Peel and Alice Cook whether they had ever met or heard about a Michael associated with you. They both said something quite curious.'

Peter looks at me and then back at them. Omer meanwhile waits for me to spill the beans myself but I'm not sure what beans he thinks I'm carrying.

'They each said that the only Michael they had ever heard you talking about was your father.'

It takes me a second to realise what they mean. 'Mike. And it wasn't his real name.'

'But he did go by that name sometimes?'

The space here in this room becomes like a thing squeezed. 'It was the seventies when he came over here. They didn't understand Muslim names. Someone where he worked just told him one day that he couldn't say "Maqbool", that his name was going to be Mike. And it stuck.'

'Only, we have your father, who went by Mike, and this Michael who is turning up out of the blue. Saving your life at one point, then ruining it at the end.'

'What's your point, Officer?' I say.

'No point as such. Just wondering whether there's some trauma playing out here. I'm not an expert but it seems like you've resurrected your dead father in order to punish him for what he did to you. For dying. For leaving you alone.'

Peter slaps his hands on the table and grumbles loudly before Omer holds up his hands.

'It's okay,' I say to Peter before turning to Omer. I take a moment to consider what I am about to say. I think I have to come clean. 'Except he's not dead any more, Officer. I saw him a week ago. In a hotel bar.'

Peter drops his head into his hands and groans. When he comes up for air, his face is red.

59
Then

Inside, the office was much as I remembered from the time I came here five years ago. We'd dropped by on the way to dinner because Russell needed to collect some papers. His desk was white and his chair grey, devoid of personality. There was nothing personal in the room at all. No trinkets. No framed pictures. No mugs or anything that could remind him of home. As I absorbed the neutrality of it, I wondered whether it was now more than that. That he didn't want *her*, when she came in, to be reminded that he had another, messier life.

I sat in the chair and spun to look out of the window, but it was a narrow gimlet opening with glass an inch thick. There was nothing to see outside and nobody looking from the ground would be able to see even a glimpse of life within.

The desk was clear. A monitor that sat at one end of it was dark. Around the room nothing else seemed out of place. For a second I began to wonder whether he'd even returned when I noticed the bag he'd packed for his trip. It was there, stuffed under the drawer side of his desk – the only clue that he'd been back at all.

I hooked it with my foot and heaved it into the light. The bag looked untouched by mud or anything that suggested fishing. I undid the zip and inside found it packed tight with dirty laundry and nothing more. Along one side was a zipped pouch that opened to reveal Russell's grandfather's pearl-handled fishing knife. I opened the blade. It was clean and smelled more of polish than fish.

If he hadn't been fishing, where had he been? His smell escaped from the opened bag, making my heart drum. I tipped out the contents and rummaged, looking for something that would answer that question. But I found nothing. His shaving bag offered no clues either.

From the bag or from somewhere in the room came the faint scent of vanilla, throwing me once again into a haze. I turned back to the desk. The drawers seemed to hold nothing interesting. Russell didn't keep junk. Each drawer was neatly arranged with pens or paperclips and highlighters. But then as I shut the drawers again, I caught a glimpse of something black and gossamer stuck between the drawers at the back. I pulled it free. I could hardly believe what I was seeing. Though I had suspected him, deep in the folds of my mind I'd suspected my sanity more. I picked them up with a forefinger and thumb. Tights. Worn, not new. I pushed open the narrow window and threw them out.

My throat began to tighten and the urge to get out of the room became overpowering. I opened the door, breathless. Then something else caught my attention: a sound at first – whirring – and when I looked, a small light under the desk. It was his computer. It was switched on. I tapped at the keyboard and the monitor came to life. If there was a sleep function, it had either not been set or Russell had left the room just seconds before I'd come in. On the screen was a calendar open to the current date and month. Today's date was circled in red. There was a single entry.

A. B. on roof.

There was no time given for the task but his last meeting finished at seven o'clock. I checked the time at the top right of the screen. 19:09. He must have only just left.

The roof. I had to get to the roof.

I ran out of the door and straight to the bank of lifts where I jabbed at the button impatiently, waiting for the lift to come. A minute later the doors opened and I stepped in. Art Deco mirrors were framed by dark copper lit from above. I immediately looked to see whether there was a marker on the buttons for the roof terrace but there was none. I pressed the uppermost button and waited as it climbed slowly through the numbers. Just before the top floor the lift pinged and the doors opened. A man in a grey suit smiled bashfully at me. He had the air of someone who worked here. He was relaxed, and familiar enough with the lift to be able to press G without looking at the buttons.

'Silly question but I'm meeting someone on the roof terrace and have no idea where it is,' I said. 'When I get out of the lift, do I turn right or left?'

He smiled again. 'Depends which terrace you want. There are three.'

Three? My heart sank. And then something occurred to me. I had seen it from the hotel bar. 'Which one is the lowest?'

'Oh, you've passed it,' he said, without having to think about it. 'You want the roof gardens on the tenth floor.'

I looked at my watch. Time was racing. I pressed 10 and waited for the lift to reach the top floor and begin its descent. But when the doors opened, they stayed open. We waited. The seconds ground out slowly. Nothing. I jabbed a finger at a button and then several buttons but still nothing happened. The man blinked at me. A few seconds passed. The opening gaped at me, beckoning me out.

'Are there stairs?' I said.

'There's a fire-exit stairway on the other side of the corridor. Not sure it'll be any quicker though. It'll get going soon enough.'

I dashed out of the lift and when I got to the other end of the corridor I pushed the door but found it was stuck fast. A fire door – locked! I cursed my luck and ran back to the lifts only to find the doors closing. I screamed out under my breath and punched the buttons. An agonising five minutes later I heard the lifts grinding near. The doors opened with a ping. The same man was inside.

'I tried to send the lift up to get you but it wouldn't go up unless I stayed inside pressing the button.'

I looked at him puzzled.

'You seemed like you were in a hurry.'

We stood awkwardly as it began dropping down floor by floor. It was 19:29 by the time it halted finally at the tenth floor.

'Bye,' he said kindly. 'You can't miss it. It's just past the function suite.'

The doors opened to reveal more travertine-lined walls and dark wooden doors with leaded glass panels. I scanned the walls and thankfully, there was a sign showing the way to *The Roof Terrace*. I quickened my pace until I saw the door that led out onto the roof space. Through the glass I could see only sky. If Russell was still there, he must have walked around the corner to the other side.

I leaned against the double doors and walked through. The wind blowing at that height had surprising strength considering the calmer evening air on the ground. There were low lights embedded in the floor near the balcony walls. A couple of them buzzed and flickered as I skirted them.

I continued right and walked slowly, quietly, along the paved path until I reached the first corner. There was nobody there at all. I pushed on and slowed again at the next corner. I pressed flat against the stone walls and peered around. Still nobody. My heart was thumping in my chest but I took a breath and moved on, repeating the same dance I'd just done until the next corner. The views over the low balustrades beyond were dizzying. I felt a creeping panic but managed to hold it at bay.

At the next corner, I stopped and looked.

I saw him.

And her.

60

Now

'Can we have that break now?' Peter says.

Metcalf gathers his things but Omer seems to remember something. 'Sure. There's just one small thing I want to ask you about if I may?'

'You may,' I say, folding my arms.

He is reading off a tablet. 'Officers spoke to a Mr Sasha Harlan. Do you know him?'

'No,' I say. 'Should I?'

'He works at your husband's building,' he says, laying the tablet flat.

I rack my brains for the name but it means nothing to me. None of Russell's workmates are called Sasha. 'I don't know him.'

'In fairness, he doesn't know you,' he says, picking up a pen to doodle a note on a scrap of paper next to the tablet. 'But he remembers seeing you around twenty minutes or so before the murder. He says you were looking for the roof garden. You shared a lift.'

I swallow and suddenly remember the man in the lift. Was this what they went to court to get extra time for? 'I *was* looking for the roof. I've told you that already. I was looking for Russell.'

'That much we get. It's just that he told us you were . . .' He searches the statement for the word he's looking for '. . . frantic.'

All the eyes in the room are drilling into me. 'He's mistaken. I wasn't frantic. I was – normal. Calm.' His word against mine, surely. There wouldn't be cameras in the lift.

The detectives trade another look before Omer continues. 'Also, as I said, he puts you in the lift about twenty minutes before the murder. What were you doing in those twenty minutes?'

That question punches straight through me. If I was standing I'd slide down the room into a sea. Peter's face begins to muddle at the edges and I am finding it hard to hang on to the moments. How have they managed to do this – to find twenty minutes – just like that?

I grit my teeth hard. 'He is wrong about the time. I went from the lift up to the roof. That was it. There is no missing twenty minutes or any minutes.'

Peter leans across to me and touches my hand softly. His eyes are flickering in thought. And he finally resolves what he is trying to puzzle out. 'I'm assuming, Detectives, that, this Mr Harlan, didn't mention a knife?'

Omer coughs lightly. 'Well, he didn't recall one.'

'And no mention of gloves?'

He shakes his head.

'But you're confident that he saw my client either immediately before or shortly before the murder?'

Omer blinks rapidly. 'Well – there's twenty minutes to account for.'

Peter rubs his meaty arms and leans forward. 'But that's just a question of what the time happens to be. Or whether the guy's watch is telling the right time. This Mr Harlan is either right or wrong about the time. But you're not suggesting, are you, that my client went up there and came back down, got a knife and some gloves or what-have-you and went back up again?'

'She might have had them with her. In her handbag, maybe,' Metcalf says acidly.

Peter doesn't miss a beat. '*Might have. Maybe this, maybe that*. Not exactly the rigorous standards we expect here, Detective?'

Omer leans back and smiles. 'We are just asking the questions. If Ms Mahoney has answers to give, then she can give them. It's her chance to say what she wants to.'

'Then ask some questions, Detective. Different ones. She wasn't frantic. She told you that.'

'Why would Mr Harlan say you were?'

'How can I know what was in his mind?' I say.

'Well, we know what was in his mind. He's told us. You were frantic.'

Peter cuts in again. 'Frantic? Really? Do we have more than just that word?'

'Sorry?' Omer says.

'Frantic how? Was she running? Screaming? Shouting? How was she frantic?'

Omer buries his head in the screen. 'He doesn't say. He just says she seemed "frantic".'

Peter leans in. 'Detective, I'm not sure what your point is here. This was before any murder. What reason would she have for being – *frantic*?'

'That's why we are asking.'

'Okay and she has answered. So, stop the tapes. Let's have our break now. In here is fine if you can leave us for a few minutes.'

61

Then

My heart pounded in my chest. This was it. He was here. She was here. I was here. All the players on one stage ready to rise and fall and scatter. The light was failing now so that the views which moments before had been washed in gold were now spotted with electric light. I moved towards them slowly. The words weren't ready in my head but it didn't matter now because whatever I said, however raw and unplanned, would at least – at last – bring us to a conclusion. That was all I had wanted for so long. An ending.

I edged nearer, keeping my shoulders close to the wall. If I could catch any of the conversation between them then it might keep them from dissembling afterwards. I couldn't handle more denial. I was about to take another step when my phone buzzed low in my hand. The light from the screen glowed like a lamp. Quickly I put my hand over it and turned it off. Thankfully it had gone unnoticed. Neither of them looked my way; they were too far away still – two figures – one just out of focus. She was facing away from me and he a few paces behind her was doing the same. Talking to her back.

A few steps more and I could make out Russell's back. He was in casual clothes – a dark fleece that he rarely wore at home and jeans. I looked beyond him to the woman he was talking to. Blonde, almost golden, arrow-straight hair. There was something familiar about her in the way it fell. Splinters of their conversation drifted towards me before being carried away again on warm thermals. The tone was serious – decisive almost – as if a turning point for whatever it was they were in.

As I rounded the corner and drew nearer, it suddenly became clear that she wasn't talking to Russell and he wasn't talking to her back. No. She was talking to someone directly in front of her. Russell, like me, was in the shadows. This was another person she was in conversation with. And now there we both were, unseen by the woman and the man she was talking to. And me, unseen by Russell.

I eased towards Russell until I was standing next to him. He shifted his body a fraction towards me as if to acknowledge me but didn't turn to face me or say anything. He stared at the back of the woman's head. The cool scent of citrus came up from his body, mixed in with vanilla.

The man she was talking to muttered something at her that made her turn around to face us.

Her face was small and attractive and framed by the waterfall of blonde hair. As soon as she saw us, she blanched. 'Who are you? This is a private conversation,' she said, blinking rapidly, nervous. I looked into her eyes. Some parts of her were familiar and yet all wrong somehow.

'Is it?' I said and for a flash, her expression, caught in anxiety, lost its confidence.

Russell, who I felt turn to me in surprise as I spoke, shifted. He strode to stand next to her and then two things happened at once. The first was that her face began to coalesce with a realisation as he stepped closer to her. The second was that mine must have done the same as I realised something about him too. It wasn't Russell who we were looking at and who had moved towards her. It wasn't Russell who had been standing next to me in the shadows. It was Michael – wearing Russell's clothes.

The blood immediately froze in my veins. 'What are you doing here?' I asked.

'I looked for you in Russell's office,' he said coolly. 'You were gone. I'd have preferred it if you'd gone hunting for the conference rooms. But – Well. We're all here now.'

The woman and I both stared at him, her confusion as deep as my own. Behind her the man she'd been talking to stepped into view. It was Russell in his work suit. He saw me and faltered.

'Layla, what the hell are you doing here?' he said.

I couldn't speak.

'And who's this guy?' he added. 'What are you both doing here? Who are you?'

Michael peered at the woman who was now trying to hide her face behind her hands. 'You're Amy Blahn,' he said, taking a second look. 'Of course it's you under there.'

The woman's expression turned into one of horror. 'I have to leave,' she said to herself and began to march towards the entrance. Her face was set, rigid. But before she could get far, Michael pulled her back by her arm. She jerked in surprise and then terror. Michael's hands were in latex gloves. I froze and watched as she tried to shrug him off. But she was being held fast. A look of dread crossed her face and I remembered when he'd done that to me. Prevented me from crossing. I thought he'd saved my life. But when I saw how he was smiling at her, my stomach twisted. He moved swiftly round behind her.

'Let her go,' I said, snapping out of my rigor. 'Michael, she's scared. Let her go.'

He continued to smile but said nothing. Russell was bolted to the ground open-mouthed. He was blinking rapidly as if trying to force his body to move.

Amy began a scream but Michael reached a hand around to cover her mouth, smothering it. Whatever sound she managed to squeeze from her lungs became lost to the winds as Michael pulled her back to his chest. Then in alarm I noticed him reach for something with his other hand, which he now brought languidly towards her ribs. It was a blade. I stared at it, eyes wide, as with a thud I registered the pearl handle of Russell's knife.

He tightened his arm around her neck so that her knees buckled. She tried to cry out but the sound died in her throat as he squeezed her neck.

'Stop!' I said, lunging forward. I clamped my hands hard around his arm. He stiffened and tried desperately to shrug me off but I hung on. His arm was rigid and no matter how much of my weight I threw onto it, I couldn't move it.

It must have been the sound of Amy's feet scraping on the concrete that woke Russell up. And then there he was, his hands too gripping Michael's arm, yanking with all his strength.

Michael shifted position so that he now had both hands gripping the knife. But his arms were wrapped around Amy's neck so that with each second he held on, the closer she became to being strangled. I called out. 'He is killing her! Get the knife from his hand.'

Russell shifted his grip so that his hands were now on Michael's, trying to pry his gloved fingers off the handle. Michael twisted away but the weight of us both on him was too much. Slowly the knife was forced away from Amy's neck and the blade turned down towards Michael's waist. Michael grunted and pushed Russell's hand back away from him and for a minute they were suspended in a perfect stalemate. The knife quivered between them, pointing now towards Amy's stomach. She cried out and then desperately began to twist her body away from the pointed blade. Michael kept his arms wrapped around her, squeezing hard. The blade hovered in the gap she'd made and was now touching his stomach.

'Let her go!' I shouted and tried to loosen his grasp on her.

Amy continued to struggle and wriggled downwards to get out of his grip. I bent down and put my arms around her legs to help drag her free. She managed a few inches so that the knife which had been at Michael's waist height was now level with Amy's chest.

Realisation dawned across Michael's face. And then the world slowed. Michael stopped fighting. Russell, who had been pushing the knife towards Michael with all his weight, suddenly felt the resistance cease. He stumbled, and as he did he followed the blade as it plunged through Amy's chest. I tried to pull her out of Michael's arms but it was too late. The knife went through her. I heard myself scream.

Michael coolly pulled the knife half out until a pool of blood bubbled through. Once he'd made sure that the blade hadn't stemmed the blood flow, he pushed the knife back in.

We froze there for a moment, in the wind, three living, one now nearly dead.

She gasped suddenly for breath. I turned to her in shock and watched as she raised her head and dropped it. And then finally lay still.

'Michael?' I said in disbelief. The words barely whispering out.

'I'm sorry,' he said, pulling his bloodstained gloves off. Underneath, his hands were as white as the gloves he had balled and thrown over the side. And then I realised with a sick jolt that he had another pair of gloves on underneath. 'Prints,' he said when he noticed me looking. 'On the way out.'

My whole body began to shake. 'Oh my God. Oh my God,' I said, my face burning and wet with tears. 'What have you done?'

I crawled over to Amy and cradled her head in my lap. 'What did you do?' I screamed again at Michael.

He looked at me blankly before brushing his clothes down. Then he knelt down so that his face was inches from mine. 'I didn't do anything. I wasn't here.'

'What?'

'I'm sure you don't want a witness to what he just did,' he said, looking over at Russell, who had dropped to the floor and was leaning against a wall.

Then without another word he turned and walked calmly towards the exit, leaving us alone.

62

Now

The tapes have been switched off and now without the others here in the room, it feels as though the tension of the last hours finally has room to evaporate away.

'How did you know to ask whether the witness saw me in gloves or with a knife – what if he'd said yes?' I say.

He rolls his sleeves up tight where they have unravelled. 'Because they'd have opened with that if Harlan had even hinted at it.'

I nod, glad to have Peter here with me. I lean back into the chair and feel a sigh escape. 'How long left now before they decide about charge?'

He turns his head and makes his joints crack. 'They're making a decision now, probably. I'm afraid if you're asking me, I don't think it's going to be what you want to hear.'

I sink a little further into my seat. Of course, I suspected this. 'What will happen now?'

'Well, if they do charge you they have to consider bail but – Well, it's a murder and realistically they're not going to risk letting you go.'

'Risk? Am I a risk?' I blurt it out before I have been able to think about it.

'Even if you're not a physical risk – which let's be honest, when you're looking at a murder with a weapon, unprovoked, is going to be hard to avoid – they still have media risk. They don't want to take the flack for releasing you. They'd rather a court made the mistake of releasing you than them.'

'Mistake?'

He colours a little and I feel sorry for him. 'I mean if they released you and you ended up killing someone when you were out.'

My mouth drops open.

'I'm not saying that will happen. Of course I'm not. But they'll be thinking it. It's damage limitation from their point of view. They wouldn't want to take the risk.'

We sit in silence as the weight of that disperses in the room. When I look up again he is running a thick hand through his hair. It's not preening. It's almost the opposite. He's making himself look as he feels. Dishevelled. 'So then what happens to me?'

He turns his head to the floor. 'Remanded overnight to the Magistrates' Court. Then another chance for bail forty-eight hours after that from the Crown Court.'

'How likely is that?' The gravity of this and my life as it begins to look now and over the next two days suddenly hits me in a way that it hadn't before. It's not an intellectual proposition now. It's really happening.

He shakes his head slowly but says nothing else.

I take him by the arm and shake him. 'Peter, I can't stay in a prison for a year waiting to be tried.' I can't be in prison a year. Or a week. There are things I have to do.

'Well, let's get to the end of this last bit and see where we are.' He sits down, chin in his hand.

There is a knock at the door and we turn to see Omer in the glass. He beckons Peter who gives me a look of puzzlement and eases towards the door.

'Can we have a private word?' Omer says, cracking the door an inch.

'Without my client?' Peter says, looking at me.

'Initially, yes,' he says and opens the door fully to let Peter out. Whatever he is thinking, Omer, it shows on his face as something that has no light in it at all. I can see through the glass the men are discussing something now. Peter runs a hand through his hair again and loosens his tie yet further. He shakes his head and after a minute he looks at the floor and nods. It doesn't look good at all.

Time has stopped. There is nothing in here to mark it. No windows. The digital clock that was counting out the minutes and seconds of the interview has stopped. My watch and phone are away in a locker somewhere. There is only me and the muffled world outside. I wait. I can do nothing else. The scar on my hand burns. I turn my wrists up and stroke the skin on the forearm. It is smooth and delicate like silk. It is so thin there that it is a wonder that it doesn't split at every minor daily assault.

There is nothing around to scratch at it. It's not that I want to kill myself. I'm not suicidal. But I do want to cut the skin – just enough to let some blood rise to the surface. Enough to send a rush of chemicals through my body. I pull my sleeves back down and sit clutching my hands one to the other. Come on, Peter. Let's get this done now, I say to myself. I stand back up, restless, shifting from one foot to the other until the door finally opens. Peter comes in first.

'I think you should sit down, Layla.'

'What is it? Are they charging me?' I ask and feel the tears pricking.

The officers come in and take a seat. They sit with their hands in their laps.

'What? What is it?' Fuck, I think. It's something terrible.

63

Then

Russell was swearing quietly to himself. 'Fuck fuck fuck.' When he finally looked at me, it was with horror. 'Oh, fuck, Layla. What did we do? She's dead. I stabbed her.'

I clamped my eyes shut and tried to think but Russell was swearing, muttering, as if broken in the middle of something. I had to think. I needed space.

Russell knelt next to me and continued to mumble swear words. 'Fuck. I am so fucked, Layla.' His eyes were red, streaming tears. I reached a hand across to his face to try and soothe him. Under my fingers his face quivered.

I shut my eyes trying to think of a plan. The air had wisps of vanilla in it as it rose off Amy's face.

'Russell,' I said finally, laying her gently down. 'Who is she?'

He continued to mumble erratically until I stood him up and shook him. 'Russell, it's important. Listen to me. Who is she? Who is Amy B –'

'Her name is Amy Blahn,' he said, coming to.

'Who is she? Why were you meeting her? What were you involved in?'

He turned to me with an expression I couldn't read. Confusion maybe. 'Involved in?' he asked. 'Nothing. I'd met her a few times. She wanted to report on a dangerous product. She was very nervous about it. Wouldn't speak to anyone but me.'

I let the words sink in. 'A few times?' I asked, trying to understand. 'Are you sure?'

'Yes, I'm sure.' He wiped his streaming face with the back of a hand. 'Why does it matter?'

'I need to know,' I said firmly, holding his face so that he couldn't turn away. The police could be here soon. Time was moving and we had to move with it or be lost to it.

'She wouldn't trust me at first. She wanted to be sure I could keep her name out of it,' he said. When I didn't appear to follow, he added, 'She was a whistle-blower.'

My heart was a dropped brick. 'A whistle-blower? I thought –'

'You thought what, Layla? What? What did you think when you brought a murderer into my building?' Even in this light I could see that the colour had drained from his face.

'He told me that you were being used by her. That she was trying to get a chemical *approved*.'

He looked to be in shock. 'How many times, Layla? I don't get involved in approvals. I write bloody protocols.' His voice so loud now that I worried it might carry.

Adrenaline began to swim through my veins. 'But the tights. I saw the tights in your office.'

'Tights?' he said in confusion before it dawned on him. 'Layla! *Your* tights. They were for –'

The rest of what he said washed over me. My tights. And as soon as he said it, I knew. They were mine, though I didn't remember ever leaving any at the office. Something clawed away about them – a half-memory. 'You have to get out of here. Now,' I said, looking around towards the exit.

He opened his mouth to say something and then closed it again. His head lolled on his chest and for a second I thought he'd passed out.

'Russell!'

He looked up with narrowed eyes. 'I can't leave, Layla. She's dead. I have to stay.' He sat down again and circled his arms around his knees.

'No,' I said. 'You have to get up. You have to go home.' My heart began to race. There were police coming this very second. There had to be. Someone might have heard something. Michael might have called them on his way out.

'What am I going to say when anyone asks? It's in my diary that I was meeting *A.B.* here today. They'll know it was me. There are cameras all over the front of the building.'

I turned this over. 'You were called away.'

'Called away – where, home? And by who?'

I thought about what he was saying and he was right.

He'd been right about all of it. I'd got everything so wrong. He'd been trying to make me see him. He'd tried to reach me and save me from making a huge mistake. But he'd always done that – not rescue me – but held my hand through the fires.

'Call Mum. On your office line. Tell her that you heard from me. And that you think I'm about to kill myself.'

'What?' he said.

'Trust me,' I said. 'She always thinks I'm dead or dying. Her dementia isn't good. Call her. She'll try and call me and when she can't get through, she'll call you again. And that is what called you away. You were worried about me.' I touched his face and looked into his eyes until he understood what we had to do.

'No, Layla, I can't just leave.' Tears washed down his face.

'You have to,' I say. My voice is cased in desperation. 'You have to go now. It's our only chance. When the police come to see you at home, you tell them that was the call that took you home. I'll wait fifteen minutes before calling the police. Give you some time.'

He pulled himself to his feet and paced out a circle. The tears had subsided and he seemed calmer, before suddenly breaking down again. I stood and reached out to him and put my arms around him and waited for him to stop.

'Go,' I said. 'You don't have much time.'

He started to move off in the direction of the entrance but turned. 'What are you going to do? What will you tell the police?'

'The truth.'

He looked at me, puzzled.

'I'm going to tell them it was Michael.'

He tried to smile through it but couldn't find the strength. 'We can both tell them that. We both stay, Lay.'

'No,' I said. 'I'm not sure they'd ever find Michael. But if you're here, there's no way the police don't suspect you of this. And I know you, Russell. I love you, but you won't withstand it.'

He looked at me and I saw the depth of his eyes. 'You won't either,' he said.

'I'll be okay. I'm a lawyer. I can persuade them about Michael. But not if you're here. If you're here they'll think I'm trying to protect you.'

'But you are. I was the one that pushed the knife in.'

I sat and cradled Amy's head once again. 'It wasn't your fault. But they won't believe that.'

He crouched next to me. 'You go,' he said. 'I'll stay.

'No, Russell,' I said, getting to my knees, 'you have to go. There's no time. Go.'

He hesitated for a second. 'But my DNA – isn't it going to be everywhere?'

'Maybe. But there's going to be DNA from a hundred people. It only matters if they're looking for you. You're not on a database. They can't match it to you – unless they already suspect you.'

He nodded and then stood straight and turned slowly away.

From below the sounds of the street traffic rose and melted one into the other. I pulled Amy's head onto my lap and stroked her face as gently as I could. Tears gathered and then flowed.

I cried until there was nothing left but the smallest kernel of self-knowledge. That I didn't think I would have exchanged my life for hers if I'd had the choice. And I was saddened unbearably by that thought. I reached down and kissed her head. Then sat back and counted into the night sky until I was sure at least fifteen minutes had passed. And when I was sure, I reached into my pocket and took out my phone. There were six missed calls from Mum. One, cleverly, from Russell.

'Emergency. Which service?'

'Ambulance. Come quickly. There's so much blood,' I said. I knew there was going to be a recording of this call. I'd heard many of them in the cases I'd done. It wouldn't be hard. It was just a question of letting go. At last, I could let go.

'Where are you?'

I could hear my voice cracking. I sobbed. 'There's blood all over. Oh my God, she's not breathing –'

64

Now

'I'm very sorry, Ms Mahoney.'

'You're sure?' I ask quietly.

'Yes,' Omer says.

I exhale and look across at Peter who nods. 'What happened?'

'Officers went round. Knocked on the door. There was no answer and eventually they forced the door. Paramedics were called. And a doctor pronounced death. She said she very likely had a heart attack.'

I nod repeatedly to myself. Peter lays a hand over mine.

'Can I go now? See her?'

Omer and Metcalf whisper to one another and finally Omer looks at Peter. 'In the circumstances, we can RUI to return in a week. We have to refer this case to the CPS for a charging decision and we want to take a few days to follow up some last things.'

The letters RUI play on a loop in my head. I've forgotten what they mean.

Peter thanks the officers in a way that leaves me in no doubt that they are doing me a favour. The grief I am feeling though is too muted and overwhelming for me to thank them.

'But it will be a condition of bail that you must live and sleep at a different address from your husband as he is a potential prosecution witness.'

And then I remember. RUI. Released Under Investigation.

Peter agrees for me and then manages all the details. Within an hour I am standing on the street behind the police station waiting for

Peter to hail me a cab. Though the crowds have mainly dispersed, a few of the more persistent voices have remained behind to fling hate in my direction. Even from here I can hear the reedy chanting of the last few determined voices. I wonder how I must appear to them. I haven't slept or washed and whatever tears I have shed have dried on my face. Guilty. I suppose I must look guilty.

When Peter arrives a few minutes later in the cab, he gets out and directs the driver to my home address.

'I've spoken to Russell and he's agreed to stay with his brother for the week,' he says, leaning in. 'I'll swing by in the morning to drive you to the mortuary.' He shuts the door on me but I climb back out of the car and embrace him. I'm not sure what I would have done without him.

'Go on home, Layla. Get some rest. Call me in the morning. I've paid the driver.'

Now I am outside my home staring at the front door. It has only been hours but time has warped so much that it feels longer. I think I have assimilated the idea of being kept in custody so firmly that I have already begun to inhabit an alternate life. The police returned my keys but I am still in police-issue clothing that is so thin that it does nothing to keep out the cold night air.

Russell has left the hallway light on so that my key finds its slot quickly, and then before I know it I am inside and I am stilled by the feeling of sanctuary that overcomes me. I have never known this place as a place of refuge. Recently it has been a cold harbour. A place to berth but not a place that I could be happy or safe in. I head for the kitchen where Russell has left the lights on – for me or just because he was in a hurry to leave. I sit at the counter and touch the smooth white marble. The kitchen is pristine. The mess has vanished. In just two days everything has been cleared away and wiped clean. Whatever disarray the search had caused, Russell has seen to it.

The heaviness in my stomach about Mum feels lighter. I don't feel the guilt about her that I have been expecting to feel my whole life. She was alone when she died and I'm sad about that. But she was getting worse and every time her memory failed, she lost a particle of who she was.

I can't remember the last time I ate. They offered me something boated in plastic in the cells but I couldn't even look at it. In the fridge there is a loaf of bread so I make some toast and eat it at the counter. The room buzzes in silence. The house is beginning to feel hollowed out again. That feeling of asylum is already spiriting away. There are echoes in the hall and the landing upstairs is creaking and the house is covered in ghosts all over again.

I wash my plate and boil the kettle. Tea is a better choice than wine. If I start along that road tonight, it will lead me to places from which I won't be able to find my way back.

The kettle boils, filling the space around it with steam. As I pour it out I am sure that I see a face materialising behind the cloud.

'You're here?' I say. I'm not prepared for this at all. He is supposed to be away from here. There are things to do and I haven't gathered together how I feel about what he's done to me.

'On my way out now,' Russell says. There is a bag in his hand that he places gently down. He steps towards me and wraps me softly in his arms. 'I'm sorry about your mum.'

I pull back from him and stare at the bag. It is the same one that was at the office. The one the police claimed wasn't in his office. 'You took the bag?'

He begins to interrupt me but I am not in the mood to be stopped. 'I've been in an interview being grilled about a bag that I told them I had seen in your office and you took it? What were you thinking?'

He shifts between feet. 'I didn't know what you were going to tell them. I thought I should take it or it would seem strange that I'd left it there.'

'But the plan, Russell! You'd heard I had died. You were rushing off to check if I was alive. Why would you take the bag?'

He runs a hand through his hair, still the colour of sand. 'I wasn't thinking straight. I'm sorry. What did you tell them?'

'Doesn't matter now. They're going to charge me now probably,' I say, and the realisation of that strikes me harder than I was prepared for.

'They're charging you? Have you got a solicitor yet?'

'Yes, I have,' I say.

At first, he glosses over whatever I'm holding in the tiny muscles of my face. And then he sees it. 'Peter? You used Peter? After –'

In my breath is everything that's happened in the last day. I let it free. 'I think we have more to worry about than that right now.' I blink away the tears. 'It might have been fine, Russell, if you hadn't been so determined to ruin me. I don't know why you'd do that.'

'What do you mean?'

I can feel my legs trembling under the weight of everything my body has gone through. 'The knife. I told them that Michael had taken the knife – your knife from your bag. But *you* told them you'd never seen it before. How do you think that looked?'

'I thought I was *helping* you. I didn't want them to know it was my knife. I didn't know how *that* would have looked? That you had taken a knife with you from home? Why would I be trying to ruin you, Layla?'

I sit back down. Russell looks as worn out as I feel and he sits too so that on our stools we are as if strangers drinking at a bar. I cycle through the interview. 'You told them about me knifing you. Did you have to do that? It just seems like I am sacrificing everything to get you as far away from this as possible and you are not on my side at all.'

He goes to the fridge and takes out two bottled beers and opens them. He slides one across to me. 'I didn't tell them about that. They must have known about it from when the police were notified by the hospital. It's there in the system. I didn't tell them anything. Read my statement if you like. There's nothing in it that goes against you.' And then as an aftershock he adds, 'I *love* you.'

We sit like that, side by side, drinking beer until he finishes. The events of the last two days are a tangled weave. I have trouble unpicking the strands. 'Who was she? Amy?' I ask at last.

'I told you. She was a whistle-blower. Her company had licensed a highly toxic product. She wanted to warn us that the hazardous materials reports had been altered to get it through the application.'

'I thought you didn't get involved in licensing chemicals,' I say, but I know what is coming.

'I don't. That's why she came to me. She felt she could trust me. I couldn't tell you about her. She was paranoid about being followed,' he says and then stops and laughs bitterly at that. 'Not paranoid enough.' He gets to his feet. 'I better go. I don't want the police to know I'm here.'

I think quickly. 'You taking the car?'

'Yes. Why?'

'I need it to go and see Mum in the morning. Peter said he'd drive me but I think I'll go alone,' I say, but I need it for something far more urgent.

He shoulders the bag and looks at his phone. 'I'll get an Uber. There's one in two minutes,' he says sadly. 'We need to talk. Maybe in a couple of days?'

'Maybe. But maybe it's too late for talk now.'

He wipes his face with a hand. 'The man. Michael or whatever you called him. I need to know what's going on, Layla. I don't even know who he is. Is he coming back for us? Do we have to worry about him, Lay?'

I exhale. 'I don't really know, Russell. And that's the truth.'

He hesitates as if picking over his words. 'But if he goes to the police. And tells them it was me?' he says and the fear etched into his features makes me feel a hesitation about him that I'd never felt before. I see now that he only cares for himself. I wonder how I'd missed that all these years.

'I doubt that very much. He was there to kill her, whatever actually happened. He's not going to say anything.'

He turns sadly towards the door but then stops to rummage in his bag. 'Before the police came, I put this in the car. Wasn't sure what was on it. Thankfully they didn't search the car.' When he stands up he has my laptop in his hand.

I suddenly remember there was a search. There were forensic teams here. 'What did they take?'

'Not much, in the end. Some papers. A box of those disposable gloves the workman left. They were looking for a Swiss Army knife. They weren't here long. Did upstairs in less than five minutes – spent most of their time in the kitchen.'

'Thanks,' I say, and take the laptop from him. 'There's nothing on it, anyway.'

'No,' he says. 'But I wasn't sure. At the time.' He looks at me now as if he doesn't know me. And I think, when I return the look, mine must be the same. We are strangers.

65

Then

As I held her head, I stared again and again at her face. I recognised it. Not exactly, but it felt as though some of her features were familiar. Even with the blood drained from her face, I saw that she was beautiful. The beauty would have moved Russell more than he'd have expected. But that was true of us all. The dying of it before our very eyes was always what made it hypnotic. He'd have seen it and wanted to capture it – save it.

And then as I stroked her brow, I saw her head move, and I realised at last what made her so familiar. She was wearing my wig. Russell had smuggled the other wig for her to wear. That's why he had my tights – I'd kept the wig in them. She must have been terrified of being recognised by someone from her company. That accounted for the secretive meetings on the roof. It was clandestine but now as she lay lifeless in my arms, I saw that it had been justified.

I worried about the wig. It was another piece connecting Russell and me to her. I knew Russell. If asked directly, by the police, he would explain immediately and say that he'd taken my wig to disguise her. And then he might be arrested for her murder and if he was I knew he'd break. He could hide from me and my questions but he wouldn't manage it with the police. Carefully I peeled it back away from her scalp and turned it inside out and gathered it into a ball. I peered over the edge of the balustrade and found an area on street level that was lined thick with large refuse bins. I could drop it there. If I was lucky it could go unnoticed there for weeks. Perhaps by then I could find a way of getting to it. I watched it fall over the edge until with an almost silent, muffled thud, it landed.

When the police arrived with the ambulance service, they did so en masse. Scores of them. They stomped across the roof pavement, radios cracking with static, torches lit, voices stern and confident. Armed.

I was handled swiftly into cuffs and as I was led off by two female officers, I saw the paramedics gathered around the dead woman, still hopeful that there might be life to be cajoled from her.

'Sit down over here,' one officer said, after taking me inside the building to a bench by the door. 'I can loosen your cuffs a little if you like.'

'It wasn't me,' I said then, registering my wrists shackled in silver. 'He can't be far. You have to act quickly.'

She walked off to a quieter spot and spoke into her shoulder radio. The other officer with me pressed a button on her chest and smiled apologetically.

'Body-worn camera,' she said. 'We have to record everything now. We're just waiting for transport to take you down to the station.'

I stared at her. 'But the man, don't you want to seal off the building or streets or whatever it is you do? He'll get away.' I began to shake, at first just a shiver but then my whole body fell into convulsion. Sweat started pouring down my neck.

'It's just the shock. Don't worry. Try and breathe normally,' she said before addressing a police officer who had been writing in his notebook. 'Tom, can you get her a foil blanket from the paramedics?'

After a few minutes the same officer stood me up and led me towards the lifts. 'Brace yourself when you get out there, love. There's press.'

'Press?' I said, shocked.

'Government building. Police. Sirens. Dead woman on a roof. Word gets round quickly I'm afraid.'

At the police station I was processed and offered the right to see a solicitor. I declined and spent the night in the cells waiting, going slowly mad. Every half an hour someone opened the hatch to check I was still alive and then vanished only to reappear just as I'd finally fallen asleep. In the late morning, following an offered but untaken breakfast of microwaved curry, I was brought into the interview suite to be questioned by a police officer who introduced himself as Detective Metcalf.

'I don't need a solicitor,' I said when he asked again. 'I am one.'

He nodded quietly to himself. He seemed perfectly neutral about my refusal. But I should have had Peter there from the start. At one point early in the interview, Metcalf leaned across the desk and eyed me.

'You've been arrested on suspicion of the murder of Amy Blahn. What can you tell me about that?'

'It's not a great question, is it, Officer? Do you want to be a bit more precise?'

'Did you murder her?'

'No.'

'Do you want to tell us what you were doing with her on that rooftop? And how she ended up with a hunting knife in her chest?'

66

Now

Once Russell has gone, it takes an effort to separate his ghost from my skin. He is there within me. My love for him, I see now, changed me – altered my cells – so that when he is near I can't move freely. To lose him I shower and scrub myself hard with a rough sponge, sloughing off the skin. Still flushed from the hot water, I dress in jeans and a dark hoodie. In the bottom of Russell's wardrobe is a selection of caps that once he was in the habit of wearing. They made him seem insouciant and bohemian. I find one that has a peak to keep my face in shadow and I grab the keys and get into the car. Just as I start it up I remember something and dash back into the house. I take my backpack and place it on the table while I look for the torch. I am sure there is one in a kitchen drawer. After rattling through the first couple, I find it behind a pile of takeaway menus. Next, I am back elbow-deep into Russell's tool bag. I take a small screwdriver and a tube of superglue and wrap them in a carrier bag. I look up at the roof light as the first drops of rain begin to pock the glass.

I pull my cap low and drag the unused bike out of the bike shed.

Cycling like this, I feel freer than I've felt in years. The night air is scented heavy with dew and earth and washes over me as I ride. The rain stopped before it started which is a relief because I need to be at least a couple of miles away before I start searching. I am somewhere near Clapham before I ease off the pedals and start to scan the streets. It's not long before I see the Audi. It's almost identical to Russell's in every respect. Ten minutes later I am cycling back with its number plates in the carrier bag.

It is 3 a.m. by the time I have swapped those plates with the ones on Russell's car. As I turn the ignition, my eyes are stinging from exhaustion. The traffic at this time of the morning is sparse and deep into its own rhythms. The traffic lights all play to my advantage and let me flow effortlessly through the streets. Just before 3:40 I am parked near the back of 55 Broadway down a narrow street, St Ermin's Hill. I had checked a street-view map on my laptop and from what I could tell the wig had landed there – somewhere. Even in the low light I can make out a queue of large blue and black bins that must serve the entire building. I pull Russell's cap lower over my eyes and take my torch out and dance the beam across the lids and down the sides of the bins but cannot see anything that looks like a wig.

There's nothing for it but to roll up my sleeves and poke around. I step back to gaze up at the walls of the building. There are no cameras here so that is something. There is nobody around and even the main road is only thinly dusted with traffic. I won't be seen.

I take the handles of the first bin and tug it out from the wall. It takes all my strength just to shift it a few inches. In the end I simply lift the lid and look inside before quickly checking around the sides. No wig. I run my gaze along the row of bins. There are twelve of them in total. I take a breath and methodically check each one. It's only been just over two days. It can't have been moved already. And even as I am forming this thought, the obvious conclusion is scratching away behind my eyes. The police have already found it. They are already comparing it with the hairs found in my home in the hair-strand report.

By 4:15 I am sitting on a step and catching my breath. The wig isn't here. I think again about what might have happened. Either the police have it or someone else found a wig, liked it and took it away. Only one of those options works for me but there is now nothing I can do about either.

I make my way back to the car and climb in. But just as I am about to turn the ignition the passenger door opens and a man gets in. My heart ricochets. It is Michael, though the trademark smile is for once, nowhere in evidence.

'Get out,' I say, as firmly as I can. The bird at my chest flaps in terror.

'Just drive,' he says and pulls the seat belt across. 'Do it and you never see me again.'

'And if I don't?' I say, trying to control my rising fear.

'I have the wig,' he says, pulling a golden ball from inside his jacket. 'When I was waiting for the police to turn up, I saw it sailing over the edge.' He replaces it and leans back in the seat. 'I'm guessing it's yours. Russell gave it to her to wear. Why else would you have tossed it over?'

I don't answer but stare at him in shock until he waves at me to get moving. I turn the key and put the car into gear. As I drive he tells me how sorry he is about everything. He is insistent about how there was no escaping it. He talks of inevitability and though I'm listening I am only half-listening. My attention is focused on getting him out of my car and putting as much distance as I can between us. The man is dangerous. Yesterday he killed a woman.

'It's hundreds of millions of pounds,' he says. 'There is no practical way of stopping a wave of that magnitude. It comes and it will flood you, whatever you think of it, whatever you plan for it. It will not stop.'

'Where am I going?' I say, my voice faltering. I am heading vaguely in the direction of my workplace. I need to wade in familiar water.

'The Tubes will be running again in a few minutes. Any one will do.'

I drive towards the river. There are stations along the way that I can stop at easily enough. Temple Tube station isn't far and if drive there I can park nearby. 'What is it you want?' I say.

'It's simple,' he says. 'Make sure Russell says nothing about what he may or may not have heard from Amy.'

'And?'

'And nothing. That's it. If he talks, then I'll have to make it clear to the authorities that there may be an alternative explanation for Amy's murder.'

'What do you mean?'

'I know you didn't tell them that Russell was the one who killed her. They've only arrested you – so far. And that means you've been lying to the police.'

The Embankment is clear of traffic and I slice through without any trouble. Michael has taken his phone out and is busying himself with it, the light of the screen giving his face a vampire glow. I have to glance at him over and over to convince myself that he is here with me in the car. The sandalwood cologne he is wearing is heady and sends me into a memory of something childlike. It's disarming and I cannot let it do that to me.

'Maybe. But you'd never go to the police and put yourself in the frame for murder,' I say, manoeuvring around a line of parked cars.

I look across and see the smile is back again. 'Well, I wouldn't do it in person obviously. But I'd find a way of making them look at Russell. I still have his clothes, remember. Steeped in her DNA I'm sure.'

I look at him but don't say anything.

'Oh, and I have a tendency to make videos of memorable moments. There's a nice one here of you with Amy. And,' he says, showing me the screen, 'is that Russell in the background?'

My heart drops. He'd recorded it after he'd left us. He must have filmed us from around the corner where I'd first seen them.

He sees the look on my face. 'I'm not sure how you talked your way out of the police station. But if you like your freedom, you'll keep your mouth shut.'

I have to know how much ground I have to move in. 'What if I already mentioned you? To the police?'

'Of course you did. But you don't know me. Nobody knows me. Tell them everything you can about me – I don't mind a bit. But if Russell tells anyone what Amy told him, it's over.'

'They know about *e-Vinculum*,' I say at last.

He nods but isn't surprised. 'There are millions of compounds. They all have unique identifiers. Without knowing the precise formula, it's a needle in a haystack. *e-Vinc* makes a thousand applications for licences a month. That one formula is invisible, buried in with the others. You need the formula. You can't do a thing without it. But Russell knows it – I'm sure she'll have given it to him. Tell him to keep it shut.'

I pull into Temple Place, swing the car around to the left park by the kerb. Michael checks his watch. It has gone five. The Tubes are open. He steps out but before shutting the door, he leans his head in for a final look. 'Don't be a hero, Layla. The men who control the business – they'll stop at nothing.'

He catches the scepticism in my eyes, pauses and locks his eyes onto mine. I hold my breath just waiting for him to go.

He pulls the wig from his pocket and throws it on my lap. 'Don't fuck this up, Layla. It's over.'

67

Now

I watch his back retreating into the distance down the steps and towards the mouth of the Tube, whose gates are only now being pulled open. Then before I know what I am doing, I have left the car and am pacing after him. I realise still have the wig in my hand so I push it deep into a pocket and pull the cap down over my head as I break into a run.

I have a sudden image of life as it must now be, yawning ahead of me. There is just me. Everything else has been ripped from my hands. Mum has gone. Russell has reduced himself to dust in front of me. And once the news of this murder has percolated through the news cycles, I will have no friends and no job. That's if I'm not convicted. The idea of a life in confinement is so nebulous that my mind can't even process it. For a terrible moment I can't tell whether I am chasing Michael now in fear or desperation. When he leaves finally, and disappears to wherever a person like him goes, what will be left to me, except me? The one person I realise I cannot be with.

'Wait,' I say, as I draw near to him. He turns at the bottom of the stone steps leading to the station. Though he sees me rushing after him, he doesn't stop or slow down. He carries on as before. For him this part of the story is done, but I race on. I catch him just as he is passing through the barriers. I have left my purse at home so I am forced to duck under the barrier like an errant child. 'Wait,' I say, scrambling through, my arm outstretched. He doesn't turn. He takes the stairs down to the platform and I follow, almost tripping as I go. Under the curve of the tunnel, the board shows seven minutes to the next train.

'Wait,' I say, panting as I reach him. 'I need to know something.'

He smiles his infuriating smile. 'Go on, Layla. Last chance.'

'It was you all along. Russell wasn't having an affair. It was you. You were manipulating me into believing that he was.'

He laughs softly. 'Hey,' he says, palms spread. 'All I did was give voice to whatever was in your head. I didn't create the problems in your marriage. They were already there. You already suspected him. I was just helping you to believe in yourself.'

'But he wasn't doing anything wrong.'

He smiles and half turns away before turning back and narrowing his eyes. 'You believe what you want to. I didn't force you to do anything you didn't want to do. You always had a choice.'

And then it's my turn to laugh. 'A choice,' I say and nod to myself. 'That was the problem, wasn't it? Choice. I always had a choice. And it always got in your way.'

'Until it didn't.'

'Until it didn't,' I say. 'That's why you tried so hard to get me to believe that there were no free choices. That everything was just a domino-fall caused by the previous domino.'

A veil of discomfort drops over his features. He looks at the board. It hasn't moved on from seven minutes. 'Who knows really? Aren't you here now because of the person you are? Aren't you making the only choices that Layla can make, given her character and her upbringing?'

'But I have the power of choice. It's the one thing you couldn't control. So, it was the thing you worked hardest to undermine.'

He flares at this. 'Why are you here, Layla? Why did you go back to the building just now? Because of a thing you did two days ago, when you threw a wig over the wall. And everything since that moment to this one, was caused by the millions of moments in between. You don't have a choice, Layla. You never did. It was always an illusion.'

There is the slightest tremor developing now in his hand. It is shaking but if I happened to be looking elsewhere, I'd have missed it. I know he doesn't believe what he is saying. 'You're afraid. You're afraid of choice.'

'You don't know what you're talking about.'

'No,' I say. 'I do.' The platform is still deserted but for the two of us. The time has started to tick down again on the board and has flashed up three minutes. An announcement comes across the tannoy about the next train not stopping at the station. 'If there is no freedom to choose, you wouldn't have to warn me off. I would do what I would do anyway according to your theory. But you're afraid of my agency. So, you're back to what you do best. Manipulation. You have to manipulate me into doing what you want me to do. That's what you've been doing all along.'

He shakes his head. 'Look, I've said what I need to say.'

'I see through your crap, Michael.'

He swivels round as if checking for listeners. 'Fine. Do you know what? Believe what you want. But if I am warning you, it's because I'm the same as you. I'm a victim of my own game of falling dominoes. I have to warn you. I don't have a choice. It might not be necessary to warn you. But I have to do it because of who I am. And who the hell knows, maybe the warning is the thing that makes you do the next thing that leads to you making sure that Russell shuts the fuck up about what he's heard. And honestly, I don't give a fuck either way. The scientific fact is: you have no choice. All you have – all any of us ever have – is the illusion of choice. Because it feels good.'

The sound of the approaching train chases a blast of hot tunnel air that makes his hair flick across his face.

'It feels good to choose. So the brain tricks you into thinking it's a choice. Because anything else is depressing. There are no choices, Layla.'

The train rushes to the mouth of the tunnel. Michael narrows his eyes at me.

'Don't fuck around with these people, Layla.' He catches the defiance in my eyes and swallows. 'Did you never stop to think how I always knew where you were?'

I don't reply but am holding my breath.

'It's them, Layla. They have so much money to throw at every problem you can't even begin to calculate it. They watch you whenever they like. They can find you wherever you go. You'll never outrun them.'

The heat of the tunnel comes rushing up in a blast as the train races forward. He turns to watch it and as he does I reach into his jacket. He steps back away from me towards the track. For a second he stumbles. 'Give that back,' he says, pointing to the phone in my hand, and moves towards me. The train has almost drawn level with us when I run at him and with all my might, I push.

68

Now

There is so much adrenaline pumping through my veins that I am shaking. The train races on through the tunnel not deviating from its track an inch. I wonder if the driver has even seen him. Just then I hear the train screech to a halt in the darkness of the tunnel. Shit. I turn and run quickly up the stairs but before I get onto the concourse, I hastily pull the cap lower. In a second I am crawling under the barriers again. A member of the station staff sees me and calls half-heartedly before turning back to his free newspaper.

My heart is racing. There are cameras in the station but they won't have picked up my face, hidden under the peak. I must get as far as I can from the station. Luckily, I know this area – its rat runs and the hidden cobbled corridors of the Temple. Within a minute I am deep in the belly of the Inner Temple just as it starts to wake. Barristers wheeling flight cases are making their way across the stones – their faces serious – mirroring mine. I pick my way through them, head down, and walk out onto Fleet Street. A few minutes later I am panting outside a coffee shop, queuing for a coffee. I want to blend into a group and it's as good a place as any to take stock. My breath comes out in deep gasps. But slowly by the time I am at the front of the queue, it settles into its usual flow.

Only when I have ordered do I realise that I have no money – no phone. Nothing to pay with. The girl behind the counter smiles at me when I apologise and try to cancel my order. 'On the house,' she says and begins to bang and rattle at the coffee machine.

I thank her and take my coffee and try to reorganise my thoughts. The car is close to the Tube, and I cannot leave it there much longer. I have no idea what the police will make of it all. Will they be called immediately? Or will it be an ambulance, or the fire service? I carry on walking with my head down. Around the corner there's a bus stop with a slippery plastic seat. I perch on the end and sift through the possibilities. I have to get the car. If the police note it being there or need to move it for any reason for ambulances or whatever, then the number-plate swap might not be good enough cover for long. They'll call the person it's registered to who is sure to tell the police their plates have been stolen. I have to take the car away now before any police arrive and swap those plates before the owner wakes.

The coffee is now coursing through my veins so that together with the adrenaline, it's just enough to see off the effects of a night without any sleep. I lower my cap in the reflection of a bus window. I wish I had my phone but the police have it still. And then I know what to do. One thought has triggered the next.

The Temple is the perfect place for what's next because there are almost no cameras and plenty of hidden corners where nobody comes. I head there quickly and find a nook under a long run of stairs and take off my sweatshirt. Though the shirt is black it's lined on the inside with light-grey fleece. I turn it inside out and slip it back on. Then I reach for the cuffs of my jeans and roll them up to just below the knee, taking care to tuck the rolls under. From a distance they'll just about pass for Capri pants. I stare down at my trainers which are white as snow. Anyone watching on CCTV will spot those immediately. I slip them and my black socks off and then drag my socks over the trainers and press the edges under the opening. I put them on. They look strange up close but on a camera, they'll pass for black trainers. There is nobody about. I take the wig from my pocket and pull it on. I can't check how I look but I know how much this wig changes me. I check that I still have the phone and that it's switched off.

I head back to my car and thankfully, there are no police yet, but the station entrance is already thick with commuters waiting to be allowed in. I quickly get into my car and drive, avoiding the main roads where the most cameras are. I'm certain that the smaller roads are less risky than the major ones.

The traffic is heavier now but even so I am at Clapham before the worst of the commuter jam. The street is still empty as the light begins to colour the sky. A dog-walker passes and smiles as I coast along looking for the car. It's exactly where I'd left it, but now in the growing light, its face looks as though it's had its teeth removed.

I pull in behind and get out of the car. Within a minute I have superglued the plates back onto both cars. With luck they'll never notice the missing screws. When I drive away, my pulse is still ripping blood through my veins.

I charge into the house, strip off and jump straight into the shower. My legs give way under the flow of hot water so that in the end, I simply sit cross-legged on the shower tray and let the water run over me like hot rain. I stay until my skin has puckered at the fingers.

Once I am clean and dressed, I raid the fridge for food and am so grateful to see that Russell has left me some croissants. He never eats them himself so I am touched by the gesture. It's the only sliver of affection or concern he has shown me in days, and I feel as if I might collapse under the weight of it. I take large mouthfuls, salted by tears, and eat in a heaving mess until there's nothing left in the bag. And then I go to my room and sleep.

Hours later I wake, drenched in the sensation that I have woken after a long flight. I am hungry again which takes me by surprise because the memory of those croissants is so heavy. I drag myself to the kitchen. For some reason only breakfast is appealing to me, so I have bowl after bowl of cereal washed down with cold milk. And after that toast and coffee. By the time I have cleared everything away, the daylight is beginning to leak away again.

On the sofa I reach behind to where the landline is and I check the messages. There are missed calls from Peter and Russell as well as from work. I listen to the message from Russell. He's changed his mind about talking to me. He thinks it might be best if we don't risk my bail. A steam-head of something like betrayal in that message but I don't have time to disperse it. The message from Peter is next. He is renewing his offer to come to the mortuary with me to take charge of Mum's body. It's not something I feel like I can face right now but at the same time I can't face it alone. I open up my laptop and send him an i-Message and ask him to come by tomorrow morning. There are things I need his help with now that I know there is a high chance of me being charged with Amy's murder. I need to sort out the mortgage and the bills and maybe even Mum's will. When I sit back and think of the sheer volume of administration that I have to abandon at almost no notice, it sends a sheet of panic through me. And then Michael's face slams into view. That smile. Did I kill him?

Although he doesn't want to talk to me, I need to talk to Russell. I have to tell him about Michael – at least that – and then he can wash his hands of me if he wants. The image of Michael's smiling face is now replaced with one of his face caught in surprise as he fell backwards. He has to be dead. I don't want to check the news because of the threads that will lead to me. I try to blink it away but it is still imprinted on my mind. And now too, its companion, the sound of a train dragging his body over the lines and it thudding deep into the tunnel. I didn't know that I was going to do it. It wasn't an act of defiance. I wasn't proving my freedom to act or trying to shatter my way out of a paradigm. It was just the only rational thing to do. He'd always be there in the shadows, exerting his influence – if not on me, then on Russell. There'd never be any way for Russell to escape. Michael knew what Russell had done. He had his clothes. Once the chemical was out there, he'd have no reason to protect him. He'd have been a loose end. The chances of Russell now, with all that's happened, being able to argue self-defence or accident, is zero. Nobody would believe him. Not after my evasions. Not after my repeated failures to mention him in my interview.

I think about Russell and how Michael had manipulated me. I was the one who'd brought Michael and all the dark energy that came with him into our lives. I know that now. I am guilty of that. I allowed him to control me. The way I wore my insecurities was a pennant. It signalled to Michael everything he needed to know to predict me as well as he did. No, I wasn't carrying a debt for Russell. I loved him. *Love* him.

I pat myself down for my phone because I think about calling Mum. Then I remember I have no phone except Michael's, and that is too dangerous to use. A beat later I remember that Mum is not there any more, and my heart breaks again. I wipe away the tears but there are more behind my eyes and they come in steady, copious streams until my eyes sting.

I spend what remains of the day trying to keep myself in the living room on this sofa. I can't move if I am to survive the night. If go upstairs the weight of my life in that room will crush me. I put the TV on but there is nothing that I can hook my attention into. In the end I content myself with the warmth of the colours on the screen. My mind begins to slide suggestions into my consciousness and as soon it does, I will them away. But it's a war of attrition. It will pick minutely at me until nibble by nibble there is nothing left of me to fight with. But I have to fight.

That bath is upstairs. And a knife not far away. And a small cut would do nothing to me but do everything to bring life to my dulled senses. It would be just enough to wake me up a bit – to distract me from everything for just a few minutes.

69

Now

When the light rouses me, I see in the beam it casts that my arm is red with the scratches I made in the bath. I wasn't brave enough to slice all the way through and now that fact fills me with regret.

As soon as I've showered and dressed, the doorbell rings. I half-expect Russell but it's Peter dressed in a cornflower blue shirt. He smiles softly and then rolls his sleeves up to expose his meaty forearms. I tug the sleeves of my cardigan over my wrists.

'Not too early, am I? Only, I'm not sure what the traffic is going to be like.'

'No,' I say and return the smile. 'I'm ready.'

We take Peter's car since he feels better behind the wheel than alongside it and I am too fried to argue. In fact, sinking into the seats, I feel safe here. Peter reaches the M3 without any fuss and soon we are cruising at speed in his large Mercedes. The warmth of the car, the smell of new leather, the steady hum of the engine are seductive. I close my eyes and sleep.

The sudden slowing of the car wakes me as we pull off the motorway and take signs to Southampton. Peter turns his head fractionally. 'I didn't want to wake you. We'll be there shortly.'

I rub my eyes and check the map on his satnav. We are about fifteen minutes away.

'Peter,' I say and wait till he glances over. 'It's not good, is it?'

His face doesn't change but it's all the answer I need.

'How long before they call me in?'

'They said a week but I can get a few more days if you need them? Don't worry about all your affairs. I'll get a few general forms of authority signed and we can get most things organised from prison.' When he says that last word, he drops his voice to try to take the sting out of it.

But the sting is there – there is no way of avoiding it. 'Should I be pleading guilty?'

He doesn't flinch as I expect. 'Did you kill her?'

'No,' I say.

'Then no.'

'But I'll just end up with a longer sentence. If I can't avoid a conviction, isn't that the smart thing to do, to plead guilty?'

He pulls the car into the car park of the mortuary and turns off the ignition. 'Usually, yes. You'd get a discount for an early guilty plea. But the sentence for murder is life. You can't get a third off that. I'm sorry, Layla. If you didn't do it then you shouldn't plead guilty. I won't see you plead guilty for something you didn't do.'

I find the depth of his loyalty touching. We had a moment three years ago but he hardly knows me. Despite that he doesn't hesitate, now that he's heard everything I had to say, to believe me. I think that's all I ever wanted – to be heard and believed.

We are shown where Mum is being kept and Peter asks if I want him to stay. 'It's okay. I can do it,' I say and he waits outside.

Mum's face is the same face I have always known. It is grey and yellow in places but it is the same beautiful face I remember from my childhood. I touch the skin on her head and it is cold and hard. I kiss her cheek and then quietly leave. I'm glad I've seen her like this. It convinces me that she isn't there. She has flown.

Peter helps me with the arrangements. He finds a crematorium in London that can do it on Monday and then finally, once all the papers are signed and the death is registered at the local registry, we head back to London.

The sky is darkening as we pull into my road. Peter leaves the engine running.

'Thank you,' I say. 'For everything.'

He says nothing and I think this is characteristically Peter until I turn to face him before opening the door and I see that he is blinking back tears. I give him a moment and then reach to touch his hand.

'I can come if you need me there. I'll shift a few appointments,' he says at last, wiping his face hurriedly.

'No. You've done too much already,' I say.

Once inside, the sudden onset of hunger and exhaustion overtake me. I don't have the energy to cook so I eat slices of bread until the hunger subsides. I try calling Russell from the landline but he doesn't pick up. I call Sam's number but he doesn't answer either. I think about Mum's friends and whether there are any relatives here that need to be told. There's a cousin in Donegal who I manage to reach. She is ill herself so hasn't really followed what I am trying to tell her, according to her daughter Amber. She says that she is sorry for my loss and begins to make her apologies for the service, but I stop her. I understand. Of course I do.

I think about Mum and all that she went through with Dad. I still don't know whether I believe what she told me about Dad dying or whether she was trying to protect me from the pain of being deserted by him. But I hadn't been deserted by him, even if he wasn't telling the truth. She had been deserted – not me. But maybe that was enough. Maybe protecting me from the pain that she was feeling was a good enough reason.

I called Dad at the hotel but they told me he'd checked out. There would only be me there at the cremation. Did that say more about me than about Mum? If I could find a way of avoiding going, I would.

At home Michael's face keeps shuddering into view whenever I think of Mum and it so poisons my grief that I scream. I spend the rest of the evening organising paperwork to take him and myself out of my head. I need to make copies of all my bills for Peter so that he can manage things for me. It should be Russell helping me with this – most of it concerns him too. But since he hasn't returned my calls and we aren't officially allowed to communicate, I don't know how to speak to him about it.

It is late by the time I turn in for sleep. I have put away a quarter of a bottle of wine so that should help. But as I am about to fall into sleep, I begin to wonder about Dad again and why he left. It didn't make sense to me that he would leave like that for no reason. Mum never spoke about the reasons he left but we both surfaced from his departure with the sense that we had somehow caused it. We both felt inadequate. We both, from what I could judge from those years alone with Mum, felt that there was something intrinsic about us that made him leave us.

Sometimes I see Amy's face and when she comes she is holding the hands of her young children and I don't know what to do with any of that. I led her to her death. When I crossed a road all those weeks ago, some part of my unformed world intersected with her unformed world. And we crashed. I into her. Even when I wind it all back scene by scene, I can't imagine doing anything differently in the moment. I hate that Michael might have been right after all. There was no way of stopping the ripples once the stone had been dropped. The moment Michael had come into my life, I was on tracks herding us both to her certain death.

In the bathroom, in the early hours of the morning, I sit with the knife and begin to pick at the scabs on my arm. When one finally bursts open, the flowing blood feels like an opioid.

70
Now

After waiting four hours for them, the ashes are handed to me unceremoniously in a brown plastic tub. I was expecting a little brass urn but this thing is no better than a carrier bag. Nobody came. I am surprised though I shouldn't be. I thought Russell at least might have come but then he's been warned by the police not to talk to me. Despite that, I'd left a message on his phone and on Sam's phone, giving the details of the ceremony, but neither of them returned the call. Even now the thought comes to me that he might not be with Sam.

But as I walk out through the doorway, leaving the 'elevator' classical music behind me, I notice a waiting figure.

'Hi, Dad,' I say. I hardly trust my senses now so have to hold myself back until I can be sure.

He turns and smiles sadly. 'I got your message. The hotel called me, passed it on. I'm sorry I didn't make it on time. I tried to call your mobile but it was turned off.'

I think about the phone shrouded in plastic in a police station drawer. I dab at my eyes with my sleeve. 'At least you're here.'

He reaches over to me and wraps me in an embrace. He is holding tight but I can tell that he is weak and that hug is right at the edge of his strength. I can feel the bones of his chest beneath his shirt.

'Is that Mam?' he says, releasing me and indicating the plastic container. I nod and he takes it from me gently. 'I'm sorry, darling,' he says to her and then to me.

We walk arm in arm down the path until I reach my car parked on the grass verge. There is a bench opposite that has a dedication plaque on it. We sit and gaze up at the blue sky. Set so far back from the road, the silence here is interrupted only by the sound of a lone plane passing overhead.

The scent of him is like a memory. It feels like a missing colour turned up again by the world. I didn't know until now how deeply I missed it. We sit like that for some minutes. I want just to lean my head against his shoulder and cry.

'You seem tired, Layla. Are you okay?'

'Are you?' I say after a while, ignoring his question. 'Are you sorry?'

He turns to face me. 'Of course. She wasn't the reason I left. I don't know how your mother explained it to you but it wasn't because of that lady.'

'What do you mean?' I say.

'That lady. It wasn't to do with her.'

A cold wash of adrenaline runs down my face. 'Lady?'

He fidgets, and then flushes around his cheeks. 'The lady. The lady I was seeing.'

Something here rings bells in a distant church. 'You were having an affair.' It starts as a question but doesn't end as one.

'Yes. Well, as I say, I'm not proud of it. But it – she – was an alarm clock you can say. She woke me up.'

I'm scratching around in my head for this memory. I know this. 'What was her name?'

'Katharine.'

'Did I know?'

His brow is creased in concern. 'Yes, dear, you knew. I mean at the end. You and your mother came to her house. She knocked on the door and ran through all the rooms, shouting that she knew I was there because of the fire in the grate or some such.'

'Katharine?' I say more to myself. The memory is crystallising now. 'Were you there, Dad?'

He smiles. 'Mum didn't find me. I ran into the back garden.' He wants to laugh at this but my face and the shock I am processing seem to change his mind. 'I left her as well, you see.'

'Why, Dad? Was it so terrible?'

He nods and then looks at me. 'It was a different time. The world was different, I think. But I couldn't be here. At first, I thought it was your mum and you. I thought I was feeling trapped by you. But then after some time passed, I saw that it wasn't you. It was this place, *un*-trapping me if you like. It didn't want me.'

'But we did,' I say.

'It was changing me, Layla. I didn't want you to see me like that. It was more important to me then to be free. Now I am not so sure if it was worth the price.'

He checks his watch and stands up. 'It's time, Layla. And you know, I still would like you to come to me some time. Come and see your father's country. It's not a perfect place but it's a place you can be free.' He hands me a small ivory card with his name and address on it. It's flimsy and barely registers in my hand.

For a moment I think about telling him everything. Michael, Amy, Russell, the police – all of it. He's my Dad. It's his job to take this from me and to absorb all of this for me. It's been so long. He's missed so much but more than that, I've missed so much. Instead, I smile and nod.

A taxi is hovering nearby, rumbling as only black cabs can. He draws me in again for a hug and then climbs in. I get into my car and trail the taxi out to the main road. For a while as I am following it, I feel as if he is still with me, holding my hand.

71

Now

After the cremation I find a message Peter left to tell me about some papers that I need to bring with me to the interview in two days. At the end of the call, he hesitates.

'Pack a bag, clothes and a few toiletries. If it's logged in as your property when they charge you then it follows you to your prison.' After thirty seconds of crackle, he says, 'Sorry. I just – I'll see you Friday at the station at eleven.'

I do pack a small bag and collect whatever papers I can find for Peter. It doesn't matter anyway. The house will be looked after by Russell and when the time comes, he can deal with whatever needs to be done to sell it if that's what we want to do. I called him again this morning but he's determined to avoid a conversation. The plastic tub with Mum in it is on the coffee table. I have to do something with it before the day is out. I'm desperate to leave immediately and scatter the ashes because I'm afraid the police will smash the door down looking for me. I'm not sure what progress they've made with Michael's death. If the CCTV was working, they'd know by now that someone else was there. And they'd have seen me, or a woman at least, with a peaked cap running from the station and onto the road. I just hope that anyone watching would have seen me disappear towards Temple and not notice a different person retrieving the car.

I have resisted checking the news pages on my laptop for any details on any fatal incidents on the Tube because of the evidence it will leave. But I have to know – knowing is more important now. There is one story that talks about Temple Tube station being shut because of an incident 'involving a passenger' on the line but that is all the information there is. I keep searching and as I do I hold my breath. Finally, I navigate to the London Transport website and I see a slightly more detailed piece. This one says that the death was a 'tragic' incident and there is an appeal for witnesses.

They'd be looking for someone – me. With a jolt I realise that my laptop is now contaminated with the searches I made. If the police do make a connection to me or even if they decide to come for the Mac then this isn't going to look good. I put it into a bag with Mum's urn and pull the zip tight.

The ringing landline startles me. I reach for it and my heart beats fast. I had forgotten that this was how calls came once – anonymously.

'Layla, it's Peter.'

'Hi, Peter,' I say and my heart feels as if it has stopped.

'They want us in tomorrow. I thought I'd be able to delay it but they were insistent. New evidence.'

New evidence? My heart kicks up again and I worry now about all the extra miles I have put on the small knot of muscle in my chest. What could this be? Have they found a way of proving that I was on the roof, waiting for those fifteen extra minutes, before calling the police?

Before I put the phone down, I have already made up my mind. I have to do this now while I can. The ashes. I have to go now.

Mum always loved Seven Sisters.

It takes almost three hours but now that I am here, it feels like a different world.

The wind is intoxicating up here on the ridge, where the cold air of the sea crashes into the warmth of thermals above. We came here together once, when I was a child. Dad had gone by then and Mum and I were alone. Why do I see us like that – as alone when another way of seeing it is that we were together? Mum had been on holiday here once as a teenager and ever since then had remembered it, impossibly perfect.

'That was the one time I had pure happiness,' she said to me, as we stood here on the bluff.

I remember feeling a pang when she said that. The one time? 'Did Dad not make you happy? Not even in the beginning?' I said it about him, but meant it about myself.

'No. Well, I thought he did. But I was wrong about it, you see. My happiness with him wasn't the truth. I was happy because your father loved me – but he didn't. So, I wasn't happy. I was something else. Deluded, I think.'

But I knew what she meant about pure joy. It can't be created artificially. I think about the joy we saw and lost and how impossible it always was to keep in your hand. It was always destined to go. And knowing that didn't make it lose its beauty but it did interfere with it – with the joy of it.

'I want my ashes scattered here so I can have a view of the cliffs.'

'The cliffs are so white,' I said, taking a lungful of wind. 'You don't want to be nearer them?'

'No, here is fine. When you get closer, the whites aren't as white.'

I pick my way along the path until I get to the William Charles Campbell monument which is on a patch of wind-flattened grass at the cliff edge. It is deserted but for the odd jogger who appears out of the horizon to remind you that you are still in an inhabited world. The monument itself is a squashed cement snowman embedded with rocks. From where I am standing, it looks as if the snowman is gazing out at the cliffs.

This is the place for her.

I take the small urn and empty it at the cliff edge. The wind blows the dust back into my face and then it contrives to bury itself in every crevice and fold of my body. I'm disgusted for a second but then without warning, I am laughing so hard that I have to sit.

'Goodbye, Mam.'

I absorb as much of the view, and the air and sun as I can. I want the moment to mean something and to embed itself in my memory. The day might in fact be perfect – in the way that it has arranged itself. The sun is bright but not hot. The waves below the cliff are foamy and fresh and send spray into the air above so that I can taste the salt even from up here. And me. I am perfect for now, for these few seconds or a few seconds more.

And then another few seconds and there will be darkness. It won't come on all at once but in patches. There will be a deep sinking feeling when the despair sets it. I think again that it's the beauty that does it. Nothing lasts.

Someone once said that all things are exactly what they have to be in that moment because to change it is to change everything else and how it communicates with everything else. If that's true, I must be here exactly as I am too.

I lie down on the grass and shut my eyes. From behind the lids, the world is orange and in that orange is everything there can be.

Why did he have to ruin our family? There had to have been a way, I had said, where he could have had what he wanted but still kept us all together. I remember now I had asked him this on a visit after he had left. Until this moment I had forgotten about it, but now the memory descends like so many dropped veils.

'I'm sorry, Layla, I couldn't help it.'

I was thirteen. 'Don't be stupid, Dad. Everyone has a choice. It's called free will.'

And now I'm not so sure about free will any more. Whatever I have done in my life is because of the way I am. And I can't be responsible for how I am because I can't make myself into a different person. If I want to be more moral or less terrible, I have to be a person who wants to make myself more moral or less terrible. And if I'm not that kind of person, then what can I do about it?

I think about this as the sound of the washing waves blankets me. The ocean making only the noises it can beneath me.

When the thoughts have overwhelmed me, I think of something else to shake myself free. The laptop. I reach into my bag and take the silver slab to the edge and fling it down. It cracks as it snaps on a rock and then in seconds it is gone. And finally Michael's phone. I can't switch it on to see what is on it. The phone will ping its location as soon as I do. Whatever is there has to remain a mystery. But the threat of what he filmed is gone. I toss it into the sea and say a prayer for myself as it, too, is swallowed by sea foam.

72

Now

The sky is purple ink on wet paper. I draw back the curtains and see the street is empty of life. At times like this I can convince myself that there is only me in the world and I am confronting the vast universe by myself.

I gather all the papers I have collected in the past days and fold them into an envelope that I find in the wrong drawer. Things have been turning up in their wrong places and, at first, I thought it was me again but it's from when the police did their search. I think about the things moved and the missing objects. I thought it had been Russell but now when I think of Mum, I wonder whether it was just me. I think of Alice's bashed car and now I can see what must have happened as Mum smashed it down on the table in anger.

But I almost long for that now. I doubted Russell when all he ever did was to help Amy Blahn – and help us all.

I want to tell Russell about Michael and how he isn't a threat to him any longer. He can walk forward without ever having to look over his shoulder for him. It might be the last chance I have to talk to him on a phone that isn't being overheard. The handset is smooth and bulky and light in my hand as if a call is the most innocent and insignificant of things. But again when I dial his number and then Sam's, nobody answers. And then all there is, is Kate. And I can't bring myself to call her and bring that possibility back into my head, even though I know now that she was innocent too.

In the letter that I leave for Russell, I tell him that he can sell the house if he wants to or keep it if he can afford the payments alone. It's not anything that I need to say to him – it's just an excuse to speak to him on paper at least. I tell him which bills are in my name and which ones he needs to arrange direct debits for. I tell him the passwords for the SKY and the online grocery delivery.

I should end it there. But I don't. I find myself telling him that I love him. And that I love him beyond love. That I am sorry. That I don't think I can survive without him but that he must. And that I need him – have always needed him – and that I'm no longer ashamed by that. And can he forgive me.

When I finish I stare at the letter until there are drops on the paper. I take my debit card out of my purse and leave it next to the letter. *In case there are things I need you to buy. There's no one else*, I say on a Post-it.

I stroke the smooth new marble. The gloss is still high, but I liked the old one better, with the scratches. In time the scars would have rubbed themselves smooth, and even if they were ugly and brash when I looked at them, they'd have been familiar at least.

There is a final call that I need to make and I make it with the card in my hand. This one is answered. There is no ceremony at all. 'Hello?'

'Hi,' I say. 'You did some work in my kitchen. I haven't settled the invoice.'

'Address?' he says and I give it. Finally, when he comes back on the line, he sounds bored and overworked. 'That's three thousand five hundred pounds.' The figure is still eyewatering but then it is Italian marble. But it's only when he says the next few words that the realisation breaks like a dawn sky. 'Cash or card? I can give you a discount of two-fifty for cash. I can come round for it later if you like.'

The cash in Russell's pocket. It was that exact sum. He must have taken the cash out for him. I feel a cold river over my skin.

Peter pulls up in his Mercedes. I am in the rear car park of the police station, bag in hand. There are no angry protesters. They don't know I'm here yet. Peter parks and gets out to give me a hug. 'Okay?' he whispers. I nod and let him take my bag.

Inside we are shown into the waiting suite and left there alone. The silence is solid against my cheek like linen. Peter has a notebook open and is rereading some of what he wrote last time we were here.

'From my very brief conversation with Omer, I don't think that they've got more than a few hours of questions. Then it'll be a charging decision. If I'm honest I think they will already have the okay from the CPS. This is just topping and tailing in my opinion.'

'You think they'll charge me?'

He takes my hand in both of his. 'I think so.'

A long hour passes before the door opens. It's not one of the two detectives but an officer obviously looking for someone other than us. Peter stops him on his way out. 'Can you see where DI Omer's got to? He told us eleven. It's past twelve now.'

The officer takes our details and promises to let us know. Peter paces circles into the carpet but after a few more minutes have passed, he heads for the door. 'I'm sorry. This is ridiculous. I'm going to see what's happening. If he's off on some investigation, it might be better to draw stumps now and rebook another day.'

I nod and there is relief in the gesture. I don't want to be taken today or any day. But just as Peter is about to leave Omer walks in and my insides plummet.

'I'm sorry to be late. But in the circumstances, I'm sure you'll understand.'

Peter and I exchange looks. 'What do you mean?' Peter asks for us both.

Omer stares at us for a second before recovering. 'Oh, I'm sorry. I assumed that you knew.' He waits for one of us to supply an answer or a comment but neither of us knows what he means.

'Russell. He's confessed to the stabbing. We've been in interview with him since nine. We're releasing you under investigation for now, but with things the way they're looking, we expect to be charging him with the murder of Amy Blahn.'

Omer leaves Peter and me alone in the room. The air is electric. Peter is as shocked as I am. 'Did you know?'

All those times that I had called and tried to reach him, I'd assumed that he was avoiding me. He was – but not for the reasons I had thought. 'No,' I said faintly. 'I couldn't get through to him.'

Back in the house, the walls are echoing again. There isn't enough life in here now for this house and already the ghosts are gathering. If I had managed to tell Russell about Michael, I am certain that he wouldn't have done this. It must have been fear that had driven the decision to hand himself in. He's not the kind of man that can keep looking over his shoulder.

I stare at the reflection in the bathroom mirror. There is a cascade of blonde hair around my bare shoulders. The air is chilled now that autumn has taken hold. I wear one of the wigs downstairs into the living room and sit in front of the fireplace. I take it off slowly and place it like an offering in the grate together with the other one and the letter I had written for Russell and light a match to them. They go up immediately. There was a time when the dying embers of a fire smothered any strands of happiness that I had gathered to myself. As I watch the fire take and then quickly die, I see the sensation is as alive as it was when I was thirteen.

I can't believe that he has done this. I don't think that the weight of what he has done is something I can recover from. Not because of what it will cost him but because of what it will cost me.

EPILOGUE

We are at an early stage of the trial process. Russell has been brought to court for a preliminary hearing. There's no press, and the court-room is empty as if in the aftermath of an office party. Relics of the previous trial – old papers – are scattered over counsels' row. After some minutes of waiting in what feels like a liminal space, the judge comes in and sits as we all rise and then fall.

'Can the defendant be arraigned?' he asks seriously.

Russell's counsel, younger than I expected her to be, nods and the clerk stands and bids Russell up too. When I look at his face, I see it wrapped in a sheet of panic.

'You are charged that on the twenty-second of September you murdered Amy Blahn. To that charge how do you plead? Guilty or not guilty?'

The few of us in court turn to face Russell.

Time stretches until it feels as though it will snap. Finally, at the last possible moment, he says, 'Not guilty . . .' His voice cracks. His face too.

I breathe out.

He's not spoken to me at all since he said goodbye at the house. I tried to call but he passed a message to me through his solicitors that he couldn't talk to me. So, although I expect them, have heard them in my head, it's a relief to hear the words spoken.

And then he speaks again.

'. . . but guilty to manslaughter.'

I stand and see his face contorted with the effort of holding himself back. He wants to say something to me but there are still things being discussed by the barristers and the judge. They're choosing witnesses, and timetabling the trial date.

When the judge finally rises and slips away into the corridors that run behind him, I race over to the dock and place my palms flat against the glass and put my ear to the gap.

'I didn't have a choice, Lay. It was my knife. She was killed with my knife.'

He doesn't want me as a witness in the trial. The prosecution doesn't either. Neither side can rely on my evidence because of the evasions in my interview. There were too many equivocations to make anything I have to say reliable.

Almost a year has passed and in all that time, I haven't seen him. He won't take my calls and is refusing me a visiting order to see him in prison. So now the trial has begun, I come to court to see him every day. When it comes to the part where I would have been called as a witness, they instead read sanitised parts of my statement out to the jury, dealing with my presence at the scene and my call to the ambulance. When he addresses the jury, the prosecution silk's words run cold down my back.

'Don't be under any illusions,' he says, looking back at me. 'She's not a witness of truth, at all, the Crown say. She was protecting him. It was a scheme arranged between them. Husband and wife.'

I expect Russell's QC to get up to say that I was protecting myself but I don't think he's allowed them to do it. There is something about that statement, despite its glibness, that cuts through. The idea that I had manufactured it all to protect him. Because it is true.

Peter comes when he can – and always when it's a high publicity day. He comes to shepherd me in and out safely. I sit in the trial every day – from the minute it starts until the court is locked for the night. On some nights when I leave, I see the van with Russell in it leave the court building with all the other remand prisoners. I can't see through the windows but I know he's there and that more than anything the thought of him being carted off to prison every night breaks my heart afresh every time.

The press is interested on some days, and come in packs when there are speeches or when Russell is being cross-examined. And on other rainier, greyer days, the courtroom becomes empty and the scars and dust on the wood call attention to themselves.

Throughout the trial I listen for the name of the man who'd died on the tracks, Michael – if that had been his real name. I spend many tension-filled days wondering whether they'll be able to link him to *e-Vinc*. If they did they might link his death to me. But if he had ever worked for anyone at the company, *e-Vinc* disclaimed him. Of course they did.

As the trial nears its end and I have become as much a fixture as the lawyers. Russell's solicitor, Nimisha, brings me coffee in the morning. She speaks to me kindly and treats me as if I am a person who matters to Russell, updating me with legal applications and some of the strategy. I ask her about *e-Vinc*.

'We managed to get some disclosure about a chemical compound that they had unlawfully licensed but *e-Vinc* put out a press release about how it was an error in the application process. They've withdrawn the compound from their inventory.'

I ask her about Russell's plea. What could possibly have convinced him to plead guilty to manslaughter.

'It was the gloves. That was part of it. They had his prints and DNA on the outside. There was no other way to explain them.'

Nothing but the truth, I think.

When the verdicts come, Peter and I sit in the public gallery. I hold on to his arm, my nails digging into the heavy flesh. I know this jury. I know who makes notes and who closes their eyes when they think nobody is looking. I know who is going to be the foreman. The jurors take their seats and the courtroom becomes rigid. I look at their faces but they're skittish now and won't return my gaze. When the foreman stands up and is asked by the clerk if they have reached a verdict on which they all agree, I think I am going to collapse.

The foreman hesitates. 'All of us? No.'

There's some mumbling as the judge reminds the clerk in a low voice that they've been given a majority direction. 'Have you reached a verdict on which at least ten of you are agreed?'

The foreman looks at a slip of paper in his hand. 'Yes,' he answers.

'And on the count of murder contrary to common law, how do you find the defendant?'

The room makes a sound like a *katana* pulled from its *saya*. My heart fights everything, everyone in the room.

'Not guilty.'

I have been in agony over this verdict. If he had been convicted, he would have been given a life sentence. That's the law. And we wouldn't have survived. And even as this relief at the avoidance of the worst calamity is rushing through me, I know what is coming. Though he's been acquitted of murder, Russell still has to be sentenced for his plea to manslaughter.

His barrister stands and offers some mitigation. I hear her say that his life had been torn apart and that his marriage is all but over. I glance at Russell but he's looking at the floor. The judge seems unmoved one way or the other. He's had plenty of time to decide what the right number is.

It's five years.

He'll serve half.

Russell smiles at me from the dock in abject relief. Five years is lenient, considering everything. His face just as he is led away, carries a pure expression of release. He's exhausted but it's finally over.

Two years from the trial and nothing has changed. And everything has. I'm still here in this house. I eat in the same kitchen and lie in the same bedroom. But I don't sleep so I take myself off wherever I can in my head.

I spend a lot of my time in Pakistan, in Dad's country. Sometimes all I see is just the land. In my mind's eye it is red and deep and dry like a canyon. But when I see Dad in it, I understand that it wasn't the ground under his feet or the air around his body that he meant when he spoke about his home. It was him. In my head the country transforms him so that his body becomes fleshed and real. For example, right now, we are sitting in his garden. I close my eyes and see that the trees are ripe with huge pink grapefruits the size of melons. We are taking, as he would say, a cup of tea and enjoying the healing of the bright morning light. The sun bounces off his skin. A breeze blows the scent of jasmine into the air in front of us. When I knew him, in England, at home, I realise now as I watch him that I had known only his shadow. But here the ethereality of him has misted away. I'd loved that about him when I was a child. That he seemed hardly connected to the world. I loved how he weaved through the days barely touching the air. I thought it made him special but now I see that it made him, and all of us, ghosts.

But I can't keep hold of it for long enough. One day I will have to go there physically and see him and touch the land and try to understand whether it was worth what it cost us all.

I look at my watch. Peter is late. It's not like him and it's not like me to notice but I have come to notice things about him. Because when he is here, there is nothing but him taking up space in great slabs. He feels real. He is real. And whenever he comes in, I watch as all the ghosts from all the dark corners jump up and flee.

After he was sentenced there was still no visiting order from Russell for me to see him at HMP Pentonville. So, finally, I did the only thing left to me and wrote to him.

And he replied.

We wrote long, intricate letters to one another. When I wrote to him it was as if my heart became liquid and stained the pages red. But there was also something in the act of writing them I think that healed the wounds we had torn into our own skins. He wrote beautifully. He wrote about me and how I'd changed his life. He told me things he felt about me that I never knew.

But that was then. There are months' worth of letters from him on my bedroom wall. I keep them pinned there so that I can see his face in the tangled lines he has drawn before I sleep.

But those letters are in the past.

Today is a different day.

Today there is a visiting order.

And now Peter finally is here. And when he drives me to the prison, he will do it quietly and with care. I know what he feels about me under it all though he won't name it. I haven't myself had the chance to untangle my own feelings for Peter. I think with space and time what I feel for him might have found the room to come alive. But my life and heart are submerged by the tidal pull that Russell exerts, has always exerted over me. So that to ask about Peter is to ask about winged angels.

He is knocking at the door now.

And I am renewed. Because today, I see Russell. And today, maybe for the first time, I can give in to the cause and effect of my husband and our entwined lives. The inevitability of it is comforting, finally. And to give into it knowingly, in this way, is to fall into a warm embrace.

ACKNOWLEDGEMENTS

To Mama whose prayers scatter light liberally over my days and my nights. Thank you for your faith. Thank you for everything you have given me and keep giving me without asking. Thank you for life. And for love. And for more than I will ever know. I love you.

To Dad whose light continues to reach us all. You are my guide. I think about you every day. Thank you for the stories. And for the mischief. And for being proud when I hadn't earned it. We are coming for you, step by step, and will see you, one by one, on a day not too far away.

To Sadia, my wife, my life. Thank you for all your encouragement and for the belief that you still have in me. Thank you for sharing the dream that gave life to this book. I hope that I did it justice, but if I didn't it's probably too late now to do anything about it. Thank you for allowing me to reduce the overall standards by which you would otherwise have lived your life. I love you. I couldn't survive a day in this crazy world without you. I wouldn't want to. And thank you for the idiot kids. Also blah blah blah false economy, blah legitimate expectation, blah blah natural justice.

To my brothers and sister, Kash, Omer, Khurrum and Aiysha. I miss you all every day. To me each of you is a star that helps me find my bearings whenever I go astray. Thank you.

Now the movers and the shakers – it's like the Oscars this, isn't it – the BOOK PEOPLE!

To the indomitable Camilla Bolton, my agent, my champion, my fighting companion. I say companion, but she does the fighting while I watch at a comfortable and safe distance. Thank you for the 'Camilla magic' that the books don't stand a chance without. Thank you for listening to me, for screaming with me, and for cheering with me when it all comes good. Thank you, as the theme tune to the Golden

Girls has it, 'for being a friend'. You are literally the best agent in the world. Without you there would be no books.

To all the others at Darley Anderson Agency who pool their energies on my behalf. Thank you. And especially to Sheila David for all your work. I know I'm a pain. Sorry! But that's what happens when you launch me into a whole new career as a screenwriter. Thank you also to Mary and Kristina and Georgia and Jade. You are all amazing and enormously talented people and I could not survive without all your help.

To the peerless Sara Helen, my whip-smart, talented editor. Thank you for all the incredibly hard work that you do on my behalf. You always understand the book in ways that I can't. I said this last time and I'll say it again. There's no point in having an editor unless they're cleverer and more imaginative than you are. Thank you for taking me on for more books for making me a real, if errant, member of the Raven and Bloomsbury families. Thank you to all the brilliant minds there who do such sterling and difficult but masterful work. There are countless sales and publicity and marketing heroes who work behind the scenes and have done so much to bring this book into being and I am indebted to you all. Special mentions for Amy Donegan for all her marketing magic and Philippa Cotton my publicist for all the incredible opportunities she lined up for me to promote this book.

To Greg Heinimann who designed such an evocative and striking cover. Thank you. And to Lin Vasey my copyeditor and Taliha Quadri my proofreader for all that painstaking work on timelines and punctuation and all the stuff that makes me want to put my head into a bucket.

To Ruth Kenley-Letts and Jenny Van der Land at Snowed-In Productions who made my debut into a TV show for the BBC and Netflix. I never got to thank you all properly at the time so I hope you'll allow me to do it here. Thank you also to Sam Masud, Jules Hussey, Rienkje Attoh and the fabulous cast including Samuel Adewunmi, Sophie Wilde, Roger Jean Nsengiyumva, and Tuwaine Barrett for all your sterling work. It was an honour to see it all come together.

Endless gratitude once again to Alex Tribick. It's such a privilege to work with you. The wheels of justice don't stop turning. Thanks also to Jon Smith for the talks about free will!

Next the Chillies. The Red Hot Chilli Writers host a vibrant and funny podcast if you're ever in the market for one, but they are also my writing support group. I can't count the number of times that their wit and humour, their support and solidarity have rescued me from the pits of writing despair. So. Reluctantly. Thank you in totally random (picked out of a hat) order: Amit 'A.A.' Dhand, Ayisha Malik, Nadeem Khan, Abir Mukherjee, and absolutely least of all Vaseem Khan. Talented and brilliant writers all of them and they continue be the stars in my literary sky that give me something to shoot for. There are days, to be clear, when shooting them would be the best thing all round.

Thank you to all the readers and the reviewers and the bloggers. The ones who tweet and the ones who silently read and breathe life into the paper. I fully and readily acknowledge what a huge privilege it is to be able to write at all and be published, and it is the readers who bring the books into existence as stories and I thank you all. Special thanks are reserved for Tracy Fenton, Fiona Sharp and Colin @TheBookshopMan. Oh and Mo on Twitter – who I promised a mention. Thank you to everyone who bought this book. I would love to look every one of you in the eye and tell you how much it means to me that you have spent your hard-earned cash to buy the book and taken the time to read it. But it would be weird if I did that – so instead you have my thanks in the medium of this acknowledgement.

Finally, to Zoha and Shifa. I am so proud of you both – still. My life would be an empty hollow shell without you. It would be quieter. Much more peaceful. And cheaper. But EMPTY, I tell you! I love you more than the world and everything in it. If you keep smiling, you'll keep me and your mum smiling. This year I plan to embarrass you both in some long-lasting and enduring way. (Also, Shiffs, I hope you can say 'mama' by now. And Zoha, I hope you're working on your second book.)

Finally – a cheeky one from me. If you have enjoyed this book or indeed any book, do please leave a review. It makes all the difference in the world to writers, and helps the book reach people it otherwise might not find. If you didn't like it, when I see you next I'll apologise with a KitKat and a cup of tea.

Ooh I quite fancy a KitKat now. . .